AN ETHICAL CHIANG MAI DETECTIVE AGENCY NOVEL

THE MISSING GUESTS OF THE MAGIC GROVE HOTEL

DAVID CASARETT

REDHOOK

www.redhookbooks.com

Copyright © 2017 by David Casarett, M.D.
Excerpt from *Murder at the House of Rooster Happiness* copyright © 2016 by David Casarett, M.D.

Cover design by Lisa Marie Pompilio
Cover images by Shutterstock
Cover copyright © 2017 by Hachette Book Group, Inc.

Redhook Books/Orbit
Hachette Book Group
1290 Avenue of the Americas
New York, NY 10104
hachettebookgroup.com

First Edition: December 2017

Redhook is an imprint of Orbit, a division of Hachette Book Group.
The Redhook name and logo are trademarks of Hachette Book Group, Inc.

The publisher is not responsible for websites (or their content) that are not owned by the publisher.

The Hachette Speakers Bureau provides a wide range of authors for speaking events. To find out more, go to www.hachettespeakersbureau.com or call (866) 376-6591.

Library of Congress Cataloging-in-Publication Data:
Names: Casarett, David J., author.
Title: The missing guests of the Magic Grove hotel / David Casarett.
Description: New York : Redhook, 2017. |
Series: Ethical Chiang Mai Detective Agency ; 2
Identifiers: LCCN 2017025896| ISBN 9780316270694 (softcover) |
ISBN 9780316270663 (ebook) | ISBN 9781478977018 (audio book downloadable)
Subjects: LCSH: Missing persons—Investigation—Fiction. | Women detectives—Thailand—Fiction. | Nurses—Fiction. | BISAC: FICTION / Mystery & Detective / Police Procedural. | FICTION / Mystery & Detective / Traditional British. | FICTION / Mystery & Detective / Women Sleuths. | FICTION / Urban Life. | GSAFD: Mystery fiction.
Classification: LCC PS3603.A833 M57 2017 | DDC 813/.6—dc23
LC record available at https://lccn.loc.gov/2017025896

ISBNs: 978-0-316-27069-4 (trade paperback), 978-0-316-27066-3 (ebook)

Printed in the United States of America

LSC-C

10 9 8 7 6 5 4 3 2

"And," Wiriya added, "there is one more thing.
One more...fact."

Ladarat waited, her pen poised to record this fact, whatever it might be.

"The most recent disappearance? The one a week ago? It was an American woman. From San Francisco."

"And?"

"And she was in this very hospital for several days."

"What was she in the hospital for?"

Wiriya shook his head. "I don't know. I don't have access to those records."

"Was she very sick?"

Wiriya shook his head. "I don't know, but it seems she was only admitted for less than a day. Perhaps..."

"She ate something that disagreed with her *farang* stomach." Ladarat nodded. Of course, it happened all the time.

"But you, I suppose," Wiriya said, "in your position you could—"

"I could do nothing of the sort. Looking up medical records of a patient? What if the hospitalization was not related? That would be a breach of privacy."

Wiriya looked down, suitably chastened. "Of course, of course. I only asked because...well...I thought it might be a simple matter."

But really, he asked because her explorations of medical records was what had helped them to catch the last murderer. But not this time. At least, not yet.

"Do you know where she went?"

Wiriya reached into the chest pocket of his suit and removed a folded piece of paper. He smoothed it on the desk and slid it toward her.

On the paper in uneven letters in smudged blue ink was a name: Sharon McPhiller.

And: Nong Chom Village, San Sai District.

Then: The Magic Grove Hotel.

By David Casarett

ETHICAL CHIANG MAI DETECTIVE AGENCY

Murder at the House of Rooster Happiness

The Missing Guests of the Magic Grove Hotel

Last Acts:
Discovering Possibility and Opportunity at the End of Life

Shocked:
Adventures in Bringing Back the Recently Dead

Stoned:
A Doctor's Case for Medical Marijuana

Special thanks to all of my hospice and palliative care colleagues, who make my work exciting and challenging and meaningful. And to Claire, for reminding me that there's life outside of work.

Wan jan

MONDAY

CHAPTER 1

A WOMAN, POSSIBLY CRYING

The frail woman sitting alone below in the courtyard was sad. That much Ladarat Patalung could see. Ladarat could also see that the woman wasn't Thai. She seemed to be European, or American, or at least not Asian. She was in her fifties, perhaps. Luminous blond shoulder-length hair and a simple pale-blue cotton dress with oversize buttons down the front paired with a plain gray cardigan made her seem doll-like, especially when viewed from Ladarat's office window, two stories above. And like a doll, this woman was almost perfectly still. But every once in a while, after a surreptitious glance at the doctors and nurses and families around her, she would raise a fingertip to the corner of her eye—sometimes the right but more often the left—as if she were brushing away a tear as casually as she could.

"Khun Ladarat?" The gruff but amused voice gently interrupted Ladarat's musings.

"There is something interesting out there in the courtyard? More interesting, perhaps, than the situation we were discussing a moment ago?"

Ladarat shifted slightly in her chair so she would be less tempted to sneak glances at the sad woman. The possibly sad woman.

Her visitor was correct, of course. However important a

3

possibly sad woman might be, she could not be as important as the matter at hand. So Ladarat turned her full attention to the heavyset man who was sitting on the little wooden chair facing her desk.

As the nurse ethicist for Sriphat Hospital, the hospital of Chiang Mai University, Ladarat received many important visitors, on many important errands. Indeed, it had been almost three months ago that this very chair had been occupied by the heavyset man who occupied it now. And just as it had then, once again the little chair meekly protested the bulk that it found itself supporting.

That bulk belonged to Wiriya Mookjai, a forty-two-year-old detective in the Chiang Mai Royal Police. She knew Khun Wiriya's age to the day because they had very recently celebrated his birthday together with a meal at Paak Dang, perhaps the nicest restaurant in Chiang Mai, perched on the banks of the Ping River. Just as her late husband Somboon used to, Wiriya had an astonishingly expansive appetite. Their ability to consume vast quantities was disconcertingly similar. And at that birthday dinner, Wiriya had sampled a dozen delicacies for which Paak Dang was justifiably famous, including their *kao nap het*—succulent roast duck over rice, drizzled with intensely flavorful duck broth.

And meals like that had perhaps given him a bit too much bulk. Her little chair was right to protest. It was far more accustomed to the weight of the nurses who more typically sought her counsel. But Wiriya was handsome and...solid. That was the thought Ladarat had whenever she saw him. That he was solid. Solid and dependable.

Ladarat pulled her attention away from the window, and as she did, the old wooden office chair that supported her slight frame made the meekest of protests. Hers was not a figure that would tax even the most tired and worn article of furniture. Short, thin, and bookish, Ladarat Patalung knew she lacked a presence that was either appealing or commanding. But for the work of an ethicist—and, occasionally, as a detective—an unassuming appearance proved to be quite useful.

As it had when, three months ago, her visitor had come to ask her help when he had a suspicion—no more—that a murder might have occurred. And not just any murder, but a series of murders. Something unheard of in this quiet, sleepy city in northern Thailand.

But his suspicions had in fact been correct, which surprised them both. And they had solved the case—together—with Ladarat acting as a detective of sorts. Which surprised them even more. An "ethical detective" was what the Chiang Mai *Post* had called her.

Then she and Wiriya had become something of a couple. More a couple than not a couple, if that made any sense. And now he often made social visits to her new office, which had been given to her because of her sudden fame and, perhaps, her new unofficial job title as nurse-detective.

But today's was not a social call. Khun Wiriya was here on business. Possible business.

Ladarat looked down at the pad of yellow lined paper that lay open on the desk in front of her, still blank except for today's date written in neat script at the top of the page. It was ready to receive whatever thoughts might be worthy of writing down. But as of yet, she had no such thoughts.

It would be a shame to waste a fresh page, so she wrote "Situation?" in small letters in the upper right corner of the page, as a way of making some sort of progress in her note-taking, yet without giving undue weight to that single word. Then she added a second question mark, and then a third.

Indeed, the situation that Wirya had mentioned seemed exceptionally vague and uncertain, even more uncertain than the possibility that the doll-like woman sitting alone on a bench in the courtyard was, in fact, crying. So on the far left side of the page, she wrote "Woman, crying." Then three question marks, just for the sake of symmetry. So far, the left side of the page seemed to be drawing ahead of the right, as far as plausibility went.

"And this... situation?"

Wiriya shook his head, then shrugged. "I honestly don't know what to think. Murder? Suicide? Kidnapping...? All we know with certainty is that over the past three months there have been at least eight people, all foreigners—*farang*—who have received entrance visas through Suvarnabhumi Airport, but who haven't left the Kingdom of Thailand through official entry and exit ports."

They came, but didn't leave? It seemed a stretch—a very pessimistic stretch—to think of these people as potential victims of a crime simply because—

Phhtttt.

Ladarat looked around, startled. And even Wiriya— normally unflappable—jumped just a little, causing the little chair underneath him to register yet another futile protest.

She had forgotten that they weren't alone. A small bundle of wiry white-and-brown fur lay curled at her feet, with the approximate shape of one of those annoying piles of dust that seem to find refuge under sofas and beds and other large, immovable pieces of furniture. On occasion this ball of fur would assume the shape of what could charitably be described as a dog of an indeterminate breed. A little bit of terrier, perhaps. And beagle. And who knew what else.

Every so often, Chi—that was the ball of fur's name—would

emerge from whatever dreams were entertaining him, raise his head, look around, and utter a sound like a wet sneeze. That *phhttt* seemed to summarize his deep disappointment with his present company, which was clearly inadequate for a dog of his great intellect. Then he would go back to sleep, biding his time until he was blessed with company that was more appreciative of his considerable talents.

Chi was a therapy dog. Not an exceptionally talented therapy dog, truth be told. And he was rather fat, thanks to the doting attention and treats lavished on him by nurses and patients and especially the food stall vendors lining the sidewalk in front of the hospital. He was also quite lazy. So, as therapy dogs go, Chi was not an outstanding specimen. But he was inarguably Sriphat Hospital's *only* therapy dog. That was what earned him the dubious right to wear his bright yellow vest, which identified him to any security guard and earned him the unquestionable right of entry. And that uniqueness— compounded by the added status conferred by his bright yellow vest—had perhaps led Chi to overestimate his importance and thus to underestimate the amount of work he needed to do to continue to earn his keep.

Ladarat was caring for him this afternoon, since his owner, Sukanya, a pharmacist, wasn't allowed to take him to the hospital pharmacy, where she worked. So Chi was shuttled back and forth between them, with other hospital staff stepping in to take him for walks and on rounds to see hospitalized patients whose days might be brightened by his appearance in their doorways, although sometimes it was difficult indeed to imagine why or how he could have that effect on anyone.

Phhtttt.

It was easy for dogs to feel they were special. Being a special dog didn't necessarily come with special responsibilities.

Chi just had to wag his long, fringed tail frequently, looking cute. As position descriptions go, that would be very easy. Easier than being a nurse. Or an ethicist. Or a detective. And certainly much easier than trying to be all three.

Speaking of which, Ladarat was supposed to be at least one of those things right now. She looked down at her notes, such as they were.

"So perhaps they are still here?" she asked. "These tourists?"

It wasn't unusual, Ladarat knew, for people to fall in love with her country and to stay longer than they had planned. Perhaps that was what had happened to these people. They had just found a quiet bungalow in the mountains of the Golden Triangle, or on a beach on Koh Tao, or any one of a number of small, largely untouched towns and villages. They had found a new home, a new life, and perhaps a Thai spouse, and an embarrassingly cheap standard of living, and they had forgotten to leave.

"Ah, perhaps. But if they have made that decision to stay, they don't seem to be telling their families of their plans. Indeed, it's been the families of eight people, or"—he corrected himself—"the families of at least eight people so far, who have called various embassies to inquire about their whereabouts."

"So you suspect...foul play?"

Wiriya grinned. "A detective is never so lucky as to stumble across two such enormous cases of foul play, as you put it, in one career. That would be unheard of. And greedy. No, I've had enough fame for a lifetime."

And Wiriya was not being modest. If Ladarat had become a minor celebrity, Wiriya had become the toast of the town, as they say. He was given his own investigative division on the police force and a promotion. Now he was Captain Mookjai.

And—as he was today—Wiriya often wore suits that were neatly pressed, several steps up from the rumpled trousers and shirts that had been his previous nondescript uniform.

But the best evidence of his fame, and by far the most treasured, was a letter of commendation from King Bhumibol Adulyadej himself. Ladarat knew that Wiriya kept that letter framed in his office for everyone to see. But she also knew that he kept a miniaturized version folded up in his wallet and with him at all times.

"But," he continued, tapping a pen nervously on his knee, "I'm worried."

"Worried?"

"Yes, these people are all well-to-do foreigners, not your wandering backpackers. They're all wealthy, with homes and families and jobs. These are not the sort of people to disappear. At least, not the sort of people to disappear without a trace. And certainly not the sort of people who would disappear without any contact with their families."

Dutifully, Ladarat wrote "Disappeared. No trace" on the right side of the page. Then she added a single question mark.

"No trace? No trace at all?" She thought for a moment, also tapping her pen. "But surely they stayed...somewhere? Perhaps somewhere in Bangkok?"

"It is difficult to trace the paths of these people," he admitted, shaking his head head slowly, like a dog worrying a bone in slow motion. "Very difficult. Even finding where they might have stayed in Bangkok...well, it's a challenge. But we do know that at least three of them—two Americans and one man from Germany—flew directly to Chiang Mai from Bangkok. We were able to get passenger manifests from Thai Airways so far. But for others who flew other airlines, or those who took a train or a bus..."

"Would a *farang* really take a train or a bus? That is so slow and uncomfortable. Most tourists want to...get where they're going." Ladarat herself had thought of taking the bus to the ethics conference in Bangkok she would be attending on Friday, but she had balked at the time required. That was something better left to the young backpackers.

Wiriya smiled. "It's true, that's the case for many visitors. Tourists, as you say. But some tourists want to save money, and a bus from Bangkok to Chiang Mai costs only two hundred baht. And others consider themselves travelers. They take the most difficult routes, by the most inconvenient modes of transportation."

"And you know this because...?"

"I know this because they often get lost, or lose their money foolishly, and show up at a police station in Thma Puok or Ang Thong or Kanchanaburi, asking for a ride home to New York City, or wherever they came from."

Ladarat smiled. Yes, people traveled in Thailand with far more adventurousness than they did in many other countries. There were few dangers, and Thai people were generally very friendly and welcoming. So that led many travelers to take risks they wouldn't take in, say, India or Cambodia.

"But you don't think these missing people got lost?"

"No, we would have heard from them. Or their families would have. It's true, one person just arrived in Thailand last week. She might phone her family any day now, perhaps saying that she was sick with a stomach infection and that she's been in a hospital somewhere. But the first person on our list, he vanished three months ago. It is unlikely that he will suddenly reappear."

Ladarat thought about something else. "These are all foreigners? Western foreigners?"

Wiriya nodded.

"Eeeyy. That is bad."

And it was. Not just bad for tourism, but bad for the image of Thailand as a friendly, welcoming, and above all safe country. And Wiriya admitted as much.

"The director of the Department of Tourism asked me to look into this personally, and to help the families trace these people, if I could."

The way he said that explained much about Ladarat's feelings for this kind man. He did not boast, as many people might. He didn't say: "The director asked me personally, because I am so important." But rather: "I must do this because I've been asked. And I must do it conscientiously."

Thinking about the implications of the Department of Tourism's involvement, Ladarat wrote "Very bad for tourism" underneath "Disappeared. No trace." Unsure of where this was going, she thought perhaps the result might become one of the strangest haikus ever written.

"And," Wiriya added, "there is one more thing. One more... fact."

Ladarat waited, her pen poised to record this fact, whatever it might be.

"The most recent disappearance? The one a week ago? It was an American woman. From San Francisco."

"And?"

"And she was in this very hospital for several days."

"What was she in the hospital for?"

Wiriya shook his head. "I don't know. I don't have access to those records."

"Was she very sick?"

Wiriya shook his head. "I don't know, but it seems she was only admitted for less than a day. Perhaps..."

"She ate something that disagreed with her *farang* stomach." Ladarat nodded. Of course, it happened all the time.

"But you, I suppose," Wiriya said, "in your position you could—"

"I could do nothing of the sort. Looking up medical records of a patient? What if the hospitalization was not related? That would be a breach of privacy."

Wiriya looked down, suitably chastened. "Of course, of course. I only asked because...well...I thought it might be a simple matter."

But really, he asked because her explorations of medical records were what had helped them to catch the last murderer. But not this time. At least, not yet.

"Do you know where she went?"

Wiriya reached into the chest pocket of his suit and removed a folded piece of paper. He smoothed it on the desk and slid it toward her.

On the paper in uneven letters in smudged blue ink was a name: Sharon McPhiller.

And: Nong Chom Village, San Sai District.

Then: The Magic Grove Hotel.

CHAPTER 2

WHAT WOULD PROFESSOR DALRYMPLE DO?

Wiriya had gone, leaving behind a scrap of paper and many questions. Before he left, they'd discussed their plans for the evening. Wiriya would be "working" late, he admitted sheepishly, joining a retirement party for one of his detective colleagues. So he would spend the night, as he often did, at his own small, drab apartment in the Old City. Which was fine, because Ladarat had plans of her own, which she didn't share. She promised him only that he would find out—perhaps soon—if her plans went well.

Now Ladarat was alone with the sad woman—the possibly sad woman—who was still sitting on her bench. She was still in the same place and in the same odd pose. Her head was tilted up, and every few seconds she would look around attentively, focusing now and again on someone or something that seemed to catch her interest.

Ladarat settled in to observe the woman more carefully. If she truly was crying, then of course Ladarat should comfort her. But was she?

Only a moment's further observation reinforced Ladarat's suspicion that this woman was, indeed, very sad. She was brushing away tears. That was certain.

And she had been sitting there for quite a long time. Ladarat glanced at her delicate gold watch—a too-elegant gift from

Wiriya on her own thirty-eighth birthday two months ago. It was almost one thirty, which meant that for more than a half hour, as Ladarat had discussed these very theoretical crimes, this woman had been sitting there on a bench. At least while Ladarat had watched her, the woman had spoken to no one. She hadn't taken out a cell phone, as most people do when they find themselves with a few extra minutes. She just... sat there.

A conjecture: This woman must be proud. She didn't want anyone to see her crying.

A corollary: She was proud, too, because she was sitting in a public place. She could hide away somewhere, where no one could see her. But instead, here she was in the public courtyard of a busy hospital.

Yet there were aspects of that conjecture that didn't fit. There was, for instance, the fact that the woman would look around her with what seemed to be a healthy interest. She was gazing now at the giggling cluster of nurses in front of her and next at the young boy feeding a flock of starlings. The woman even looked up occasionally, scanning the hospital windows, as if she was curious to see what they held.

No one else in the busy lunchtime courtyard noticed the woman. Certainly no one noticed these anomalies. But Ladarat Patalung did. Noticing was a talent. A skill. A calling, perhaps?

Indeed, it was her ability to notice anomalies like this probably crying woman that had let her help Wiriya solve the infamous Peaflower mystery, and which gave her this office with its commanding view of the courtyard. This was the office previously occupied by the Sriphat Hospital's director of excellence, who had been an ever-present thorn in Ladarat's side. But she'd been sent on a secondment—a sort of long-term loan— to a hospital in Bangkok. Hopefully very, very long-term. And until she returned, assuming she did return, Ladarat had this glorious office.

Until now, Ladarat had been worthy only of a small cubby buried deep in the bowels of the hospital basement. That office, in contrast, was endowed with only a tiny mail slot of a window that revealed nothing more than the passing ankles of nurses hurrying back and forth to the nursing dormitory behind the hospital.

It was thanks to her ability to see what others didn't that she was now blessed with an office that looked down, not up. She'd enjoyed both local fame and a personal acknowledgment from the hospital's director—and, of course, a new office with a window.

That fame hadn't lasted, of course. One couldn't afford to stay famous for long, when there was so much work to do. With her newfound prestige, there was work. Lots of work. And that work meant that she was not as free as she once had been to follow her heart.

Three months ago, seeing the probably crying woman in the courtyard, Ladarat would have tried to help. She would have taken off her white coat, so as to be less medical in appearance. If she'd had Chi back then, she would have nudged him gently with a toe, urging the lazy dog to his feet, and clipped on his leash. Together they would have walked down the stairs, through the grand lobby of the hospital, and out into the courtyard. They would have sat near the woman. Not next to her—that would be presumptuous—but nearby. Ladarat would have taken out her phone and would have pretended to be checking for messages.

Then Chi would have wandered over to the woman, uttering a *pffttt* or two to catch her attention. And gradually Ladarat would have let her attention wander with Chi over to the crying woman. Then she would have asked her how she was doing, using the English that she had learned during a yearlong ethics fellowship at the University of Chicago in the United States. They would strike up a conversation, and the woman would tell Ladarat what was troubling her, and...

But that was the past. Now, Ladarat Patalung found that she had no time for the informal sort of ethics work that involved comfort and support. It was of course very important work, and even—often—more important than the medical work of a hospital.

Just as she reached that conclusion, though, a sentence appeared in her mind. Unbidden, it seemed to float somewhere in the front of her brain, in type large enough to be impossible to ignore.

"Providing comfort to a patient is a nurse's primary responsibility, because we can always comfort, even when we can't cure."

That quote—which Ladarat knew by heart—came from a diminutive book that she had carried with her since she found it by chance in a small used bookstore on the north side of Chicago during her ethics fellowship. The book itself was modest in appearance, consisting of no more than a hundred pages tucked into a weathered blue cloth cover. Yet *The Fundamentals of Ethics*, by Julia Dalrymple, R.N., Ph.D., Professor of Nursing at Yale University, U.S.A., was very, very wise. That little volume had provided a hundred times its weight in wisdom over the years, and it did so again now by prompting her with a question:

Was she really too busy to comfort that woman?

Ladarat pondered that question uneasily as the sad woman

brushed a tear away and looked up and to her left, seemingly directly at Ladarat's window.

Was she really too busy to offer comfort to this crying woman? True, there was a stack of charts on her desk—more than fifty—of patients who had died in the hospital in the past week. Ladarat was looking through them to try to determine if theirs had been good deaths. This was a task she had set for herself, and it was an important one. Yet it was also a very large task and perhaps an impossible one. So many charts, and so much detail. She'd been reading this week's charts since early this morning and hadn't struggled through more than eight.

What she'd seen had not been as bad as she'd feared, which was a pleasant surprise. Yet she'd seen very few deaths that could be even charitably called "good deaths."

There were still more than forty charts she had to review and—more pressing—there was the presentation that she had to give on Friday with her assistant, Sisithorn Wichasak, in Bangkok at the National Thailand Medical Ethics Society. That presentation also began with a case three months ago. On the very same day that Wiriya had stepped into her office, the director of the ICU had knocked on her door, asking for help with the sad case of two Americans who were injured by an elephant on their honeymoon. That case had become famous, so famous that she and her assistant would soon be describing what they learned to an audience of more than two hundred physicians and nurses from throughout Thailand. Such an important presentation, and they had made very little progress in determining what they would say.

But now there was this woman. This probably crying woman. What would Professor Dalrymple do?

Ladarat didn't need more than a moment's reflection to

realize that in the time that it had taken her, Ladarat Pata-lung, to ponder these issues, the good professor would have hurried down the stairs and out into the courtyard. She would be sitting next to that sad woman right now.

Ladarat sighed. No matter how hard she worked, or how carefully she attended to her job, she could never attain the standards that the good professor had created for the profession of nursing. Her example was inspiring, to be sure. Yet sometimes Ladarat found her perfection just a little tedious.

But at least Ladarat's mind was made up, and she knew what she had to do. Ladarat turned from the window after making sure that the crying woman wasn't showing any signs of leaving. She nudged Chi with her toe, and he bounced up with much more enthusiasm than she would have believed possible from such an inanimate creature.

When had he last been out? Probably late morning, when another nurse, who had taken him on rounds, brought him in. Chi writhed in a little squirm—a sort of wiggle and hop that was as close as his profound sense of dignity would allow him to come to an expression of base pleasure. He looked up at her with eyes that might charitably be described as soulful.

Ladarat shrugged out of her white coat and hung it on the hook on the back of the office door. She was just reaching for the doorknob when she heard a tremulous knock from the other side.

Chi's tail began to wag at a furious rate, setting up a whirl-wind of tiny dust motes in the air behind him. He caught sight of them, glinting in the sunlight that slanted in through the window, and turned to snap at one. Then another. Then another. Visitor outside the door now wholly forgotten, Chi was obsessed with catching these dust motes. Since it seemed to be his only form of exercise, Ladarat would let him chase those motes as much as he liked. Besides, he usually tired quickly.

Again, a knock. Twice, and a little more insistent this time. And also the murmur of female voices. Ladarat sidestepped the whirling dervish dog and opened the door, gently nudging his spinning form toward the battered file cabinets in the corner.

The door opened to reveal two young nurses, dressed in the hospital's regulation uniform of starched blue skirt, white blouse, and white, blue-rimmed hat. As a mark of respect for the fact that it was a Monday, the birthday of King Bhumibol Adulyadej, they all wore loosely knotted yellow scarves. Ladarat herself was no longer required to wear the official nursing uniform and could instead wear one of her yellow blouses to honor the king.

Huddled in the doorway, they introduced themselves hesitantly: Sudchada, the taller and older, with severe features, and her hair, very lightly streaked with gray, wrapped in a tight bun; and diminutive Siwinee, soft-spoken, who had to repeat her name three times before Ladarat heard it distinctly.

Chi greeted them both in turn, sniffing at hands and ankles perfunctorily, as if he knew he was duty-bound to be proper. But he discovered a new energy as his keen nose came within range of Siwinee's left foot. Wagging his fringed tail and snuffling excitedly, Chi scrunched his face with intense interest, extracting and analyzing this strange and fascinating scent.

But Chi was not blessed with an extraordinarily long attention span, and he tired of his investigation after only a moment. When neither visitor offered him more affection than a perfunctory scratch behind the ears, he soon quit his duties as a greeter and assumed his customary position on the frayed blue rug next to Ladarat's desk.

Both Sudchada and Siwinee offered the same formal greeting,

with a respectful *wai*—hands pressed together and touching their foreheads in a modest bow. As befitted her station, Ladarat returned the greeting with a little less formality. But only a little.

Politeness, Professor Dalrymple pointed out, cost nothing. And one should never be stingy about something that cost nothing.

Actually, Ladarat was certain that the good professor had not written that aphorism and that therefore she, Ladarat Patalung, had made it up. Yet it seemed to her to have more authority if it came from that august personage. What was the weight of the musings of a nurse ethicist in a modest city in northern Thailand? Very little. But the pronouncement of a learned professor...well...that was something that anyone would take seriously.

So whenever she felt strongly about an opinion or an idea, Ladarat would often attribute a saying or bit of wisdom to the professor. Now she smiled a little, thinking about how that professor would have been surprised—hopefully pleasantly so—by the existence of a whole new book of wisdom that she had inspired.

But now was not the time for wisdom or aphorism, or even for the sad woman in the courtyard. Ladarat knew that these young nurses would not have made the journey away from their duties to see the hospital's nurse ethicist if this weren't a visit of the utmost importance. She knew this with an extraordinary degree of certainty because these two women were quite young. Siwinee was perhaps in her early twenties and likely barely out of nursing school. Sudchada was just a little older—in her late thirties. They wouldn't have the status to be able to shirk their clinical responsibilities. Their absence would be noticed and commented on. So their trip came with more than a little personal risk.

And indeed they seemed nervous. Siwinee, the younger, hung back behind Sudchada, looking over her shoulder at the doctors and nurses passing in the hallway. Ladarat wasn't at all surprised when Sudchada announced the reason for their visit.

"We have come here, Khun, on a matter of grave concern."

A matter of grave concern? Well, perhaps. Certainly they would not have left their duties if they were not convinced of the importance of their mission. But in Ladarat's experience, many such matters turned out to be...not so grave.

Ladarat wished she could invite the two nurses in, but her office—while it boasted an improved view—had only one chair besides her own, and there was little room for anyone other than a nurse ethicist and a therapy dog.

She gestured at the office behind her and smiled at Sudchada, who shook her head.

"It's no matter, Khun Ladarat. We have very little time, and we don't want to keep you. We can share what needs to be shared without the benefit of sitting down."

When Sudchada smiled again, she seemed to have aged ten years. Ladarat saw lines around her eyes. She was perhaps quite a bit older than Siwinee, and perhaps even older that Ladarat herself.

"We have a concern, you see, about a physician."

"About a...physician?" This was not what she'd expected.

"But I don't know what I can do about concerns related to a physician," Ladarat said. This certainly was not her territory at all, especially if there were concerns that were—or might be—grave ones.

"Those sorts of concerns should go the physician's department chairman, of course," she pointed out. "They are not matters of ethics. Unless, of course, this does have to do with matters of..."

"Of ethics. Exactly so," Sudchada said quickly. "Ethics, and...helping a physician who is having a difficult time."

"It is Dr. Taksin," Siwinee said quickly, with a half smile and glance at Sudchada. "He is...not himself. He is behaving strangely, and making mistakes."

"Is he...endangering patients?" Ladarat asked. Now she was certain that this situation was beyond her circumscribed authority as a nurse ethicist.

"Yes," Siwinee said.

"No," Sudchada corrected her. Then: "We don't know that."

They looked at each other with a wry understanding that Ladarat didn't follow. Then Siwinee gave her colleague that most common of Thai smiles: *yim thak thaan.* It was a smile that meant, more or less, "Of course I respect your opinion, even though it's completely wrong."

In the midst of this exchange, Siwinee had also been watching the hallway carefully, her head swiveling from side to side like some strange forest bird, alert for predators. Now she put her finger to her lips as the chairman of the oncology department walked by with a troop of medical students. He was lecturing to them as he steered their little parade down the hallway, facing forward and talking as if to himself. In his wake, the students jockeyed for a position that would let them hear the great man's words. Ladarat and the three nurses could have been throwing a party in Ladarat's little office, and none of the entourage would have noticed. Yet Ladarat appreciated Siwinee's caution. Especially if this query was about a physician's performance, it would not do for it to become known that she had become involved in such discussions. No, better to stop this conversation as soon as possible.

"In matters of this type," Ladarat said, with as much authority as she could muster, "it is always best to go through the approved channels. There are risks that someone like me, who is not a doctor, may not appreciate all of the issues. You understand? Or—what is much worse—there is the possibility that what are small issues might be inflated out of proportion."

She shook her head, looking at each of the nurses in turn. "No, I'm afraid I cannot be helpful with such concerns."

Sudchada nodded emphatically, as if to say, "I told you so." Siwinee was still scanning the hallway behind them but seemed unconvinced.

"Yes, of course, Khun. We know that is the...usual approach. But this case is different."

"Different in what way?"

"In this case..." Siwinee hesitated, leaning back against the half-open door. "There are...complications."

"Complications?"

She turned to Sudchada, who shrugged.

"Do you know Dr. Taksin?" Siwinee asked.

Ladarat nodded vaguely. She knew of him: a young physician who had recently come to Sriphat Hospital to provide palliative care to oncology patients. He had started a palliative care unit that offered comfort and support to patients who were dying. It was an odd coincidence that his name should arise now— she'd meant to reach out to him for help in her project to review deaths in the hospital.

Very well thought of and highly regarded, he was quite popular, particularly among the nurses on the unit. It was said that he was always respectful of the nurses' opinions. Also that he was handsome. And single.

Yet he had detractors. There were those physicians— including the oncology department chair—who believed that there was no need for such a physician. They believed that they already provided palliative care very well and couldn't see the need for another physician to help them. These detractors would be eager to hear reports that Dr. Taksin was perhaps not performing his duties adequately. The oncology chair in particular would be delighted to learn of such concerns.

"Ah," was all that Ladarat said.

"Exactly so." Siwinee and Sudchada both nodded. "So you see, we would like to try to find out what Dr. Taksin's trouble might be. We'd like to help him, if we can."

Siwinee looked at Sudchada and smiled. "She in particular would like to help him."

"Ah," Ladarat said again. She was beginning to think that this little syllable was being put to more use than it had been designed for. Then she thought of the question she should have asked in the beginning.

"You're from the palliative care unit? You work with Dr. Taksin?"

They both nodded in unison.

"Will you help us?" Siwinee asked. "Perhaps you could… talk with him. Find out how he's doing?"

"Or inquire about whether the kind of work he does is emotionally burdensome. You could ask that, could you not, Khun, as a nurse ethicist?" Sudchada asked.

That was clever, Ladarat admitted. Very clever. And she could ask that, she supposed. But…

"But if I learn anything that is concerning, you understand, I would be obligated to mention these concerns to the department chair. I could not possibly keep such information to myself."

Siwinee nodded, but Sudchada smiled a sad smile. "Well, if that happens, it cannot be helped. But as things are going, it seems likely that the department chair will get involved sooner or later. Better, perhaps, to see if we can avoid that outcome."

Eeeyy. If the department chairman is already concerned, then things must be very bad indeed. Or at least, perhaps, too far gone to intervene. And yet, if these nurses were concerned, she ought to help, particularly since they'd taken the risk of coming here.

She could hardly turn them away, could she? Ladarat didn't need to consult the teachings of the wise Professor Dalrymple. There was no question: She could not turn these nurses away.

Ladarat thought for a moment, looking from Siwinee to Sudchada and back again. She wondered what their interest was. Why their concern? And why did Sudchada seem to have a special interest?

But perhaps it would be better not to ask such questions. Knowing what she knew was probably enough to begin, at least. She could…investigate. But gently. She could talk with Dr. Taksin and see if there were any concerns that she could discover.

Ladarat explained this to the two hopeful nurses, to be absolutely certain they understood what she could and couldn't do. Did they understand? Perhaps they did. They seemed relieved, at any rate, and thanked her warmly as they backed out through the door, offering respectful *wais* before they hurried back to the palliative care unit.

Ladarat looked down at Chi, who had woken up as the nurses left. Now the little therapy dog was busily sniffing at the spot where Siwinee had stood. At a loss, for a moment, Ladarat remembered where she had been going. But when she turned to the window to look down into the courtyard, she found herself unaccountably disappointed that the sad woman was no longer there. Now her seat was occupied by two young doctors sharing a meal of *kao niew moo yang*—grilled pork skewers—the most perfectly classic street food.

Until that moment, Ladarat hadn't realized how much she'd been looking forward to the chance to meet the sad woman. She'd thought she might do some good and offer some comfort. But there was the slightest twinge of curiosity as well. Was the woman truly sad? Or had that been nothing more than a story that Ladarat had made up for herself? And what might she be sad about?

Perhaps it was just as well that the crying woman had gone. After all, Ladarat had work to do. It was all very well for Chi to fall asleep. But for the rest of us, we have responsibilities that don't disappear when we shut our eyes.

Responsibilities...such as these stacks of medical charts that had virtually taken over Ladarat's little desk. She looked at them, squared just so, with a mix of foreboding and satisfaction. Foreboding, of course, because there were a lot of charts here. And she needed to read every single one. But satisfaction, too. She was doing this because she had decided she should. This was her decision. Her project, you could say.

Just a few weeks ago, sitting in her cousin's tea shop on a quiet Sunday morning, and apropos of exactly nothing, Ladarat had decided that it was important to know whether patients dying in her hospital were dying well. Didn't she have an obligation to ensure that their patients' deaths were good deaths? If they couldn't keep someone alive—and often, too often, they couldn't—then they had an obligation to make sure that the person's death was as peaceful and comfortable as possible.

That, Ladarat had decided, was a very clear duty. So as she finished her peaflower tea—steeped extra long to a unique and unnervingly deep blue—and set out across the Ping River for the open-air market to look for fresh papaya and perhaps some strawberries, she had decided that she would look through

THE MISSING GUESTS OF THE MAGIC GROVE HOTEL

the charts of every patient who had died at Sriphat Hospital recently. She would see if their deaths were good deaths.

She made that commitment, of course, not knowing exactly how many deaths that might be or how long it would take her to read a chart, or, truth be told, how she was going to figure out whether a death was a good death. That is, she'd made this promise to herself without the benefit of anything resembling a plan.

But feeling peaceful and contented after her cup of tea, and looking forward to a morning of shopping and perhaps an afternoon in her garden with a good book, Ladarat hadn't concerned herself with those details. If there was a responsibility to do something, then she would see that it was done. Ladarat didn't need the good professor Dalrymple to tell her that was the right course of action.

So now, here she was, facing stacks of what Panit Booniliang, the medical records clerk, told her were fifty-two charts of patients who had died in the hospital in the last two weeks. Despite the meaning of his first name—*Panit* means "beloved"—Ladarat had not been enamored of the man as he cheerfully wheeled the charts into her office this morning. Nevertheless, she would read every one, putting them into piles. Before sitting down at her desk that morning, Ladarat had made up three labels on note cards, labeling them "Good," "Bad," and "Mixed." Stacks of charts on the far left side of the desk were untouched, while those that she had reviewed were gradually being sorted into those three categories.

If only it were that easy to determine which of those three piles a person's death should fall into. Ladarat pulled the top chart off the stack to her left. It was several centimeters thick—a dimension that indicated this was someone who had been in the hospital for quite some time. A sixty-four-year-old man from Isaan—quiet, peaceful farm country to the east of Chiang Mai—whose physician diagnosed him with liver cancer. That physician couldn't offer specialized treatment so he had sent the man here, where he stayed with a nephew while he was getting treatment. But treatment didn't go well, with many complications, and he had to be hospitalized. One complication led to another, and he was transferred to the intensive care unit for treatment of a widespread infection. The infection finally resulted in his death, despite antibiotics and other very aggressive treatment.

Ladarat closed the chart, thinking about the poor man's story. Was his a good death? He was unconscious in an intensive care unit of a hospital far from home. He died alone, as near as she could tell, without any family nearby. Was that a good death? It was not.

Ladarat pushed the chart to the far right side of her desk and put the "Bad" card on top of it. She sighed. This was not going to be a pleasant task.

And indeed it was not. Eight charts later, each one of which added a couple of centimeters to the "Bad" pile, Ladarat had become dispirited. She knew she should keep reading, but found that she was relieved when Chi's needs interrupted her train of thought.

Pfftttt.

Chi was looking up at her expectantly, his tail steadily sweeping back and forth across the white tile floor. Bits of dust swirled in eddies and glinted in the sunlight streaming in the windows.

Pfftttt. With a little more urgency this time.

Ladarat looked at her watch. Three fifteen. Chi needed to go outside, no doubt.

"All right."

The tail wagging increased in frequency and intensity, to the point that Chi's rump was swinging back and forth in wide arcs as he crouched, waiting. It looked as though some humorous child with a long string was pulling his entire behind back and forth.

With some difficulty, Ladarat managed to shoehorn Chi into his yellow service dog uniform, which, she noticed once again, was brightly reflective, presumably in case he did service dog visits in the dead of night. Then a leash was clipped to a small nylon pouch containing treats and plastic bags and hand sanitizer. Chi eyed the pouch with intense interest but proved to be easily distracted. Soon he was straining at the leash as Ladarat pulled the door open.

As the surprisingly strong little dog tugged her down the hallway toward the stairs, Ladarat decided that she would take him outside to do his business, then perhaps across to the building that housed the chemotherapy unit and the palliative care ward. Some years ago, it used to house the tuberculosis unit, but now most of that treatment was done in people's homes, so the unit had been renovated and refurbished and given over to oncology and palliative care, as part of the effort to recruit Dr. Taksin.

Perhaps she would happen to meet him. She could engage him in a casual conversation, about the unit or about Chi or...well...something would come to her.

Chi led her down the stairs past the first floor and the front entrance, choosing instead the ground floor and a rear door that led directly to a patch of lawn that separated the hospital from the doctors' parking lot.

It was a beautiful winter day and a nice, comfortable temperature. Chiang Mai was the only major city in Thailand that was far enough north to have genuine seasons. And this was her favorite: cooler and dry. Sometimes a little too dry—for the past two weeks she'd needed to water her garden almost every night. But it was so nice not to have to use air-conditioning and to be able to sleep with the windows open.

Chi bounded ahead, enraptured by his freedom. He followed the path to the parking lot at first, then veered off in a hard right turn, his nose stuck to the ground.

He showed the same perseverance that he'd demonstrated in his fascination with Siwinee's left foot.

While she waited for Chi to do whatever it was he was going to do, Ladarat sent a text to Sukanya, the pharmacist, letting her know where to meet them when her shift in the dispensary ended.

But Chi wasn't in any hurry. It was as if he'd figured out that the sooner he did his business, the sooner he'd be back inside. Such a cunning dog. So he took his time, and Ladarat was happy to let him. Simply being able to take a few minutes in the middle of the day to walk a dog was reward enough.

CHAPTER 3

GREEN SNAHE (ARTIST UNHNOWN)

It wasn't until a half hour later, after a detour past the food sellers at the fringes of the hospital campus, where Chi's acute sense of smell caused a relapse of olfactory agitation, that they made their way down the circular drive to the building where the palliative care unit was housed. It had been some time since Ladarat had visited—at least a year ago, when the unit first opened. But Chi knew his way around, and he bounded up the front steps with the authority of a tour guide. Then he pointed his nose at the gap between the heavy front doors, as if he could open them through the strength of will alone.

Perhaps he could, but Ladarat decided to help him, and she opened one of the doors and followed Chi up a few more stairs into a comfortably furnished space that could have been someone's living room. There were books and games for children on bamboo shelves and a long table and a little kitchen at the far end. Although the unit couldn't escape the institutional feel of a hospital, with dusty institutional windows and a bland tile floor, someone had clearly gone to a lot of trouble to make it homelike. Flowers in vases lined the long windowsill, and children's artwork covered the walls. One watercolor caught her eye—an image of a long green snake. She was sure that this was in fact the painting's subject, because the young artist had provided a helpful label: "Green Snake."

As if guided by his own system of labels, invisible to humans, Chi pulled her to the right, into the hallway where the palliative care rooms were located. And here, too, some-one had tried very hard to make the unit's guests comfortable. There were overstuffed chairs in the hallway and pale blue carpet on the floor. Even the nurses' station was disguised to look less institutional. Charts were hidden from view, and the countertop held only a single blooming orchid.

Ladarat found herself thinking that she very much looked forward to reviewing deaths that took place in this unit. Surely those deaths would be good ones by any standard?

"Oh, Chi. We missed you!"

This from the nurse behind the counter, the older of the two: Sudchada.

"And Khun Ladarat, welcome!"

It was nice to be welcomed, of course. But Ladarat tried not to take offense that the dog apparently had precedence in the social etiquette of this unit, especially since it was Sudchada her-self who had asked her to look into the matter of Dr. Taksin's... difficulties.

"Are you... taking Chi on rounds now, too?"

Ladarat explained that she mostly just housed him in her office, but she'd recently started to take him on visits. She found it both peaceful and oddly comforting, although she hadn't yet figured out the proper protocol.

"When Sukanya brings him here, does she go to each room?"

"Ah, no. You see, some people do not like dogs. Or they have family members who are allergic. So we usually iden-tify some people who would welcome a visit." She glanced down at a piece of paper and then smoothed it on the counter between them. Running her finger down a list of patients, she stopped next to one.

"You should see Khun Melissa...Doble. Is that how you pronounce it? She is English, you see, so we do our best."

Ladarat looked over Sudchada's shoulder. The woman's name was "Double." Melissa Double.

"Yes, I think so. She lives in Thailand?"

"No, Khun. It is a sad story. She retired recently and came to Thailand on holiday. She is from...Wales. That is in England, yes?"

Ladarat wasn't sure. Perhaps a cousin of England? But she nodded helpfully.

"She was planning to explore the north of our country, then perhaps venture into Laos and then to Hanoi. But she began feeling ill. Very ill. And when her hotel doctor was called in, he sent her to the hospital in Chiang Kong, where they found that she may have cancer. Apparently she had cancer of the pancreas in the past, but she thought it was cured. Now, maybe not. And when she began having very bad symptoms—pain and nausea—and went to a rural hospital, she was transferred here. Now we are helping to make her comfortable as she decides...what to do."

"What to do?"

"Well, yes. If her cancer has returned...she is not from Thailand. She is deciding whether she should go home, while she can. As she becomes more seriously ill, perhaps with more symptoms, it will become very difficult for her to travel." Sudchada paused, glancing down the empty hall.

"Khun...?"

"Yes?"

"If you were this woman. Mrs. Double. Would you want to go home?"

Ladarat thought about that question for a moment. Well, of course, she would, to be with friends and family. Who wouldn't choose that? And yet...

"It seems obvious that she would. But…she is still here."

"Yes." Sudchada nodded.

"I mean to say, she has not gone home."

Sudchada nodded.

"I mean to say, she could have gone home, but she hasn't."

"Exactly," Sudchada said.

"So perhaps what seems like an obvious choice to us is not so obvious to her."

Sudchada nodded again. "And I don't know why that would be. She seems very outgoing and friendly. Also very intelligent. She always has books by her bed. It seems she made friends with the owner of a bookstore in the Old City, and he brings her a book every day. Why would such a person not want to go home to be with friends and family?"

Ladarat shook her head. It was something she had been wondering about this morning as she read through the medical charts of people who had died in her hospital. Did they think about it at all? Or perhaps they, and maybe this Mrs. Double, too, simply did not make a decision. They were overwhelmed by events and ended up where those events took them, like a small paper boat carried along by a stream. But all streams, no matter how peripatetic, reach the ocean eventually.

"Well, I will go to see her, certainly." She paused. "*We* will go to see her. And perhaps we will learn something."

Walking with more purpose than she felt, Ladarat followed Chi down the hall, looking for Khun Melissa's room, number fourteen.

Some of the doors were closed, but many were open, and Ladarat noticed that the unit seemed to be full. More than a few rooms held families, and in one three young children were playing with small toy cars, zooming them around the legs of a low wooden coffee table. She smiled. This, then, would be the sort of good death that she was looking for: people spending their final days with family nearby, and with children playing, nearby but unburdened.

Ladarat was still thinking of that ideal death—which she'd yet to see in her chart reviews—when she almost ran into a thin man wearing a white coat who emerged from one of the rooms to her right. A doctor. Absorbed in thought, and making notes on a clipboard he cradled in one hand, he didn't watch where he was going and tripped awkwardly over Chi's leash, which slipped between Ladarat's fingers. That probably saved him from a fall, and he managed to keep to his feet, although he lost the clipboard and most of his dignity in the process.

The doctor looked up, annoyed, with a smile that was not so much a smile as a grimace. *Yim mee lessanai*, a smile that is intended to mask wicked thoughts, but which doesn't quite succeed.

His expression changed when he saw Chi, though. Then he offered a true smile and a *wai* as his glance came to rest on Ladarat. She returned the greeting and began to apologize, but Dr. Taksin—for that's who it was—didn't let her finish.

"Ah, no, Khun Ladarat. I was lost in thought. I wasn't looking where I was going. An occupational hazard." And he reached down, picked up his clipboard and pen and then Chi's leash, which he handed to her with a mock bow.

Dr. Taksin's most arresting feature was a shock of dark hair that covered a high, intelligent-seeming forehead. That, and his eyes, which seemed to focus intently on whoever he was looking at. That intense look, if only for a few seconds, would make you feel very important, as if you were the only person who mattered in that moment. No wonder the nurses adored him; his patients, too, of course, but also the nurses. And perhaps one nurse in particular.

And yet, despite that intensity, which was still there, he seemed tired. There were bags under his eyes, suggesting that he was not sleeping well. And his tie—a bright yellow, of course—was loosened around his neck. His collar, too, was looser than was quite right. It was as if he had lost weight but hadn't had the insight to adjust his clothing accordingly. That was something a good wife would do.

He wasn't married, was he? That's what she'd heard. He wasn't wearing a wedding ring. But that didn't signify anything. Many Thai men don't wear rings.

Dr. Taksin reached down again to scratch behind Chi's ear, who responded with a dignified wag of his tail, no more. Then the doctor yawned, a barely restrained yawn of someone profoundly fatigued, and hoping only to get to sleep. They said their goodbyes, and Dr. Taksin made his way down the hall on his rounds, checking his clipboard before entering the room where the children's cars were doing laps around the coffee table.

There was, Ladarat thought, something going on there. Dr. Taksin was not himself. He was certainly not the energetic and enthusiastic doctor the hospital had recruited to run their palliative care unit. Yet he was not obviously impaired, either. He was tired, of course. Anyone could see that. But so were most physicians. They didn't seem to take care of themselves the way they should.

There would be time to figure that out. Now Chi's considerable talents of navigation had led them to the door of room number fourteen, which he seemed to have chosen from among all the other rooms. Ladarat thought that was an odd coincidence, until she knocked and entered the room and Chi made a heroic jump up onto the bed, again pulling the leash from her hand.

Startled, Ladarat reached for the leash to rein him in, but the woman on the bed laughed and tried halfheartedly to fend off Chi's affectionate kisses.

It was the sad woman. The sad woman from the courtyard. But she was no longer sad, apparently. Delighted to see Chi, she could have been his old friend.

Up close, she seemed...fairy-like. That was the best adjective Ladarat could think of. Her thin figure under the doll's dress, pale white skin, and silvery hair made her seem like someone not quite of this world. But her smile was warm and very, very human.

Ladarat offered a *wai* and an apology—something she seemed to be doing a lot lately because of this dog. But the woman on the bed waved her apologies away, smiling.

Ladarat introduced herself and Chi. Again the woman smiled. "And you should call me Melissa, please. And of course I know Chi dog. We've become good friends these last few days."

Then: "You speak English very well."

"Thank you, you're very kind," Ladarat said, dropping Chi's leash and taking a seat in a comfortable chair next to the bed. "I studied for a year at the University of Chicago, so I had the chance to learn a great deal."

The woman named Melissa Double nodded. "Of course. There is nothing like living in a place to force you to learn a language. I was hoping perhaps to settle somewhere for a few months and to do that. I thought perhaps that would help my mind to stay alert after retirement. A challenge, you know? But that wasn't meant to be."

Ladarat nodded. "Nurse Sudchada told me something about why you're here." She paused. "I'm very sorry to hear of your troubles."

Melissa shrugged. "The timing isn't great, to tell the truth. I just retired as a librarian two months ago. I was truly looking forward to this trip. I thought I was cured and was ready to celebrate with a trip. But now...perhaps it will be a very short trip. But perhaps not. Who knows?"

She shrugged again, with a bit more animation. "On the other hand, this timing also couldn't have been better. I've had a good life. I've done everything I had to do, and a little bit more." She paused as Chi reorganized himself and curled up in a ball on her stomach.

"Have you ever been reading a book and thought, 'I'll just stop when I finish this chapter'? Or when this conversation ends? Or when this character does this or that?"

Ladarat nodded. All the time. That was the only way to stop reading at night. You had to find...

"A stopping place. That's what this would be for me. If it is. That would be unfortunate, of course. I would have liked for my book to have been longer. Perhaps with a few more chapters. But this would be a good place to stop."

"Were you...?" Ladarat wasn't sure how to ask the question that she felt she had to ask.

"Yes?"

"Well," Ladarat said hesitantly, "my office, my new office..." As if that mattered. "It looks out over the hospital courtyard."

Melissa's thin eyebrows went up a fraction of a centimeter.

"And I saw, or I thought I saw you earlier today."

Melissa nodded, waiting.

"And it seemed as though...well...it seemed as though you were crying. But nobody seemed to notice, so I thought perhaps I was mistaken. And then I had a visitor, or several visitors, and by the time I could break free, you were gone."

Ladarat finished this awkward little monologue in a rush.

Melissa looked at her, furrowing eyebrows and cocking her head to one side.

Had she offended the woman? She probably shouldn't have said anything. If Khun Melissa been crying, that was her affair, wasn't it?

Besides, you ask someone whether they were crying because you want to know *why* they were crying, either because you are a kind person, or merely a curious person. But now Ladarat knew exactly why this woman was crying. So why had she asked? Stupid.

Yet Melissa didn't seem to be offended. Instead she smiled and pointed out something that Ladarat herself had been curious about.

"No one else seemed to notice. Or they did, but they were too polite to say anything. That is the Thai way, isn't it?"

Ladarat had to agree that was true.

"And yet, you, from one of those high windows…you noticed. You have impressive powers of observation."

Ladarat just shrugged. Her meager powers of observation were not really the point here, were they?

"I was crying a bit, I suppose. But that's done. I've moved on."

"You seem very…philosophical about this possibility. I meant to say, the possibility that your cancer has returned. Philosophical—is that the right word?"

Melissa nodded. "Yes, I suppose. I mean, yes, it's certainly the right word. And I think it's a good description. But it's helpful to look at things that way, I've always found. We often can't change what happens to us, but we can change how we react. Or whether we react at all."

"That is a very Buddhist thing to believe."

"Is it?" Melissa smiled, tilting her head to one side. "That's very good to know. You see, I'd hoped to learn something about Buddhism in my travels. Firsthand, you know? Not just from books. Now it looks like I won't have the chance, but perhaps I won't need to? Perhaps I'm already something of a Buddhist?"

She looked intently at Ladarat for a moment, and Ladarat recognized the same sort of single-minded focus for which Dr. Taksin was so well known. "I didn't mean any disrespect to Buddhism, you understand. I mean, I didn't mean to make light of your religion by treating it so simply."

When Ladarat didn't reply immediately, Melissa's eyes grew wide and she clapped a hand to her mouth at top speed as if she were stifling a yawn.

"I just assumed you were a Buddhist," she said hesitantly. "I read that more than ninety-eight percent of people in Thailand are Buddhist, so I just assumed..."

Ladarat smiled. "That's correct, we are. Or most of us are. And I am, too, so no offense taken. Besides, Buddhism is more of a philosophy than a religion. So many people are Buddhists, whether they know it or not. So perhaps you really are a Buddhist."

"That is certainly good to know. It's very good when one can accomplish something—especially something so weighty as becoming a philosopher—by accident."

Ladarat was having two thoughts more or less simultaneously. The first was that this was precisely why she loved taking Chi on his rounds. It wasn't, as most people would assume, because she loved dogs. Of course, dogs were fine, and often excellent company. Truth be told, Chi was often better company than her own cat, Maewfawbaahn, whose strange predilection for solitary nocturnal hunting often drew him away from human company. (The name was a play on words, literally: *Maewfawbaahn* meant "cat watch house," or watchcat.) He was at home presumably doing precisely that at this very moment.

No, it was because the presence of an animal—any animal—caused people to let down their guard, just a little. Animals make people comfortable, enough, sometimes, to say things they wouldn't otherwise say. And sometimes enough to speak truths, whether they knew it or not.

But it was the second thought that surprised her. And that was that Melissa Double was wrong. So that's what she said.

"But it's not really by accident, though, is it?" Ladarat asked. "You didn't just become a Buddhist. I'm guessing that you've always had...similar thoughts. You'd always been philosophically minded in that way?"

Melissa smiled and then winced as Chi shifted his position on her lap. "I think it's time for my pain medication again." She paused. "But yes, I suppose you're right. When I was younger, much younger, I had a cancer scare. The doctors thought I had advanced breast cancer that had spread to many lymph nodes."

Ladarat nodded. That would be very bad indeed. Advanced breast cancer was very hard to cure. It could be treated, and contained, sometimes, often for years. But a cure was difficult.

Melissa shrugged. "It turned out to be nothing. Or not nothing—just an infection or some sort of inflammation. They were never quite sure. But anyway, while all that was going on, I had a chance to think about what I would do if someone gave me a terminal diagnosis—You know the word 'terminal'? Is that the right word to use?"

Ladarat nodded.

"Well, I had a lot of time to think about that. Going back and forth to the doctors and waiting for all sorts of blood tests and scans and biopsies and whatnot. And somewhere in there I started thinking that if this diagnosis turned out to be real—which was looking pretty likely—I would just...go away."

"Away? Away where?"

Melissa smiled a sad smile. If Melissa were Thai, what would be called *yim sao*: a smile of regret.

"Honestly, I hadn't figured that out yet. And, fortunately, I never had to. But I just thought..." She trailed off, focusing her attention on the blissful ball of fur in her lap, who would have been purring contentedly if he were a cat. She seemed deep in concentration for a few moments, marshaling her thoughts before she continued.

"I just thought that by going away somewhere, I could get distracted from being sick," she said finally. "I didn't want to be sick, and I certainly didn't want to be 'dying.' And I didn't want other people to think of me that way."

Melissa shook her head sadly and made the sort of pursed-lip grimace you'd make if you bit into a particularly sour kumquat.

"I'd just be the woman who was going to die at such a young age, and isn't that such a shame. Instead, I thought I'd go somewhere that no one knew me. And where I didn't know anyone, either. It would be a new place, or hopefully many new places. And I'd keep traveling, and I'd be a tourist, seeing new things and asking questions, and probably taking lots of pictures." Melissa smiled, thinking about what that would be like.

Ladarat wasn't following. Not at all.

"And then?"

Melissa stopped smiling, and her right hand stopped in the middle of Chi's neck. Chi looked up, blinked, and put his head back down with a soft *pffttt*.

"And then...well...I hadn't gotten to that point. Would I come home as I got sicker? Maybe. Or maybe I was hoping that someday I would just . . . die suddenly. I know that doesn't make sense. But that's what I was thinking then. So even twenty years ago, I was thinking that perhaps it might be better for me not to struggle. Just to accept the inevitable. Is that what a Buddhist would have done?" She smiled. "If it is, then I've truly been a Buddhist for a very long time."

Was it? Ladarat wasn't sure. She was no Buddhist scholar, that was for certain. Besides, what this woman was saying didn't really make sense. Given a terminal diagnosis, she would just . . . what? Travel halfway around the world, leaving her friends and family behind her? Ladarat couldn't fit that into any belief system she could think of.

At a loss, unsure what to say, whether to agree or plead ignorance, Ladarat was saved when her cell phone rang. It was Sukanya, the pharmacist. She excused herself, answered, and told her where to find her dog.

"It's Chi's owner. She's the official . . . how do you say it? Dog handler?" Melissa nodded.

"She's coming to pick Chi up. I can have her meet us here, if you like? She'll be here in a few minutes."

"No; thank you, though. It's time for my pain medication, and after I take those two little blue pills I'll be asleep for the next few hours."

As she shifted her legs under the covers, Chi recognized his cue with the alacrity of a professional actor. He stood, stretched, shook himself in a wriggling happy dance, and bounded off the bed. Melissa winced again, but she was smiling.

"It's been a good day, so thank you for that."

"A good day?"

"My friend from Back Street Books in the Old City brought me two new books to read. And I saw Chi again. And I met you, and had a fascinating conversation. Like I said, it was a good day. As long as I can still have good days like this, I'm happy that I'm still here."

Ladarat didn't know what to say to that. But as Professor Dalrymple admonished, often the most important thing a nurse can say to a patient is...nothing.

Instead, she promised to ask Sudchada on her way out to bring in Melissa's two blue pills. "And perhaps I can stop by tomorrow?"

Melissa nodded. "I'd like that very much. It would be another good day."

CHAPTER 4

THE PARROT GANG

A single pale pink cloud billowed high above the hospital, lit by the sun that was just thinking about retiring for the night. In the short space of time she and Chi had visited with Melissa, the temperature outside had cooled, and Ladarat found that she was glad she had her white coat for warmth.

Most *farang* couldn't imagine that northern Thailand had a cool season. Every day in Bangkok was the same heat and humidity. But here, from December through February, days were warm and sunny—occasionally even hot—but always dry. Nights were clear and cool. Of course, Chiang Mai would get hot and humid in March. And as the farmers started burning their fields to clear them after the harvest, the sky would fill with smoke, and everyone would stay inside, wishing they lived on the beach in Krabi or Phuket or Koh Tao. But for now, this was ideal.

Sukanya hadn't arrived yet, but there was a comfortable-looking bench on the far side of the small patio in front of the building. Perfect. There was an experiment Ladarat wanted to conduct.

She'd noticed that when people brought their dogs to the Saturday market down by the Ping River, strangers who would never notice you if you were just...you would come over and begin talking. It was as if dogs had some sort of as yet undiscovered magnetic properties. Now she would see if Chi had this effect on people.

Ladarat took a seat, and Chi hopped up on the bench next to her and assumed his customary fur ball configuration, falling asleep instantly. Ladarat waited, smiling at two doctors on their way back to the hospital. Talking energetically about their respective weekends, they didn't glance at Chi. Then one young nurse, and then an older one, glanced at her, smiled politely, and kept walking. A third nurse smiled, narrowed her eyes as if to say: "What is that furry object next to you?" Then she kept walking.

So perhaps Chi was not endowed with that gift of magnetism. But certainly he had other gifts, although, truth be told, Ladarat couldn't think of what those gifts might be. Perhaps they had yet to be revealed.

As she settled back to see what gifts those might be, Ladarat's cell phone rang and the caller ID informed her that the caller was someone she hadn't expected to hear from. This would perhaps be an awkward phone call, and Ladarat thought for a moment about not answering. She looked down at Chi, who had nestled his furry bulk into the corner of the bench between Ladarat's insubstantial hip and the bench's equally thin arm. He had ignored the shrill ring of her phone, and she supposed that she could do the same.

But this could be important. Well, it might be. So she answered.

"Khun Ladarat, I have good news." A pause. "Important news."

Ahh, this is what she had been afraid of. Ladarat was curious what important news her assistant, Sisithorn Wichasak, might have for her at five p.m. on a Monday afternoon, although she could guess.

Sisithorn had traveled to Bangkok to interview for a job

as the ethicist at Sukhumvit Hospital—one of the best hospitals in that large city full of excellent hospitals. She'd been apologetic, but her boyfriend, Ukrit Wattana, a pulmonary physician, was applying for a job in the ICU there. And one must always follow one's heart, Sisithorn had said piously.

Ladarat harbored mixed emotions about the very real possibility that her assistant's heart would take her to Bangkok. It would be a shame to lose her only assistant. And Sisithorn was valuable, if a little overly ambitious. Yet this would be a grand opportunity for Sisithorn.

So it was because of those mixed emotions that perhaps Ladarat didn't respond with the full and appropriate level of enthusiasm to the promise of this important news.

"Ah," Ladarat said. She hoped that single syllable conveyed an adequate mixture of expectation and enthusiasm, perhaps disguised by uncertainty.

"Indeed, Khun Ladarat. I am at the airport."

This grave announcement was followed by a prolonged silence, punctuated by the departure from the palliative care unit of the two nurses who had come to her for assistance earlier that day, Sudchada and Siwinee. Seeing that Ladarat was on the phone, they merely smiled and hurried on. But Chi demonstrated much more enthusiasm—more enthusiasm than she would have guessed the little therapy dog possessed.

He pulled his small pink nose out from under his tail, scrambled to his feet, and began snorting enthusiastically all around him. Like a crazed compass needle that finds itself searching for true north, he spun first clockwise, then counterclockwise, sniffing at the air.

Pffttt. Now he sat, looking both intrigued and miffed, if it were possible for a dog of his stature and furriness to appear to express either of those emotions.

"At . . . the airport?" Ladarat struggled to drag her attention back to the matter at hand, which was truly not as interesting as the ballet demonstration by this therapy dog.

"Yes, Khun. You see, I gave this a great deal of thought, and I concluded that it would be wrong for me to take the bus back to Chiang Mai tonight. Doing so would leave me tired tomorrow, and I owe you my best performance. I cannot be at my best if I am tired, you see."

The passing sound of a loud bus or truck obscured Sisithorn's next words. The only word she caught was—improbably—"marriage."

"Ahh," Ladarat said. Again. "But . . . the expense. Surely it is much more expensive to travel by plane?"

In truth, Ladarat herself always flew to Bangkok when she had to go, just as she would on Friday for the annual meeting of the National Ethics Society. But Sisithorn had talked endlessly about how she needed to be frugal, about how their planned flight to Bangkok for the national ethics conference would be so expensive, although the hospital would be paying for that official trip.

"It is the price I must pay in order to be useful, Khun."

It seemed as though some expression of gratitude was in order, and Ladarat resolved to do her best. But she was spared that task.

"But that's not why I called, Khun."

"Then . . . why did you call?"

"I have discovered . . . a smuggling ring."

"A . . . smuggling ring?" Ladarat wasn't sure what a smuggling ring was, or what such an endeavor looked like. Certainly she herself would be unable to recognize such an entity if she saw it. So how was her assistant certain that she had discovered one?

"Yes, Khun Ladarat. A smuggling ring."

Ladarat found that she was speechless. But that didn't appear to present a problem, as Sisithorn was impatient to share her news.

"You know how you have always taught me to be observant?"

"Yes..."

"To observe, I mean," Sisithorn clarified.

"Yes, certainly the art of observation is important."

"Well, you see, I have been observing. Here in the passenger drop-off area of the Suwarnibunam Airport, I have been observing. Busily observing."

"And...what have you observed?"

Again the sounds of a bus passing very close intruded. But this time Sisithorn held her tongue, waiting for it to pass, which gave Ladarat an opportunity to ask the obvious question that had to be asked.

"Are you...standing in traffic, Khun Sisithorn?"

"Well, yes. Or almost. I am busily observing, but observing surreptitiously. So I am here between two buses. But do not worry, Khun. These buses, they are not moving at the moment."

Well, that was good.

"These are the large buses that pick up passengers in downtown Bangkok and take them to the airport. I am between two such buses, which allows me to observe the behavior of passengers getting off."

It would also allow you to become fatally squished, Ladarat thought.

Just then, Chi levitated again, but this time, his inner compass needle knew exactly where true north lay. He picked his head up and unerringly pointed it at a young, attractive woman with her hair tied back modestly, wearing a blue hospital uniform and a pink knapsack. Chi leapt off the bench, taking his leash with him, and bounded over to Sukanya, who expertly snatched up the end of his leash and ruffled the fur on the back of his neck as Chi wriggled with pleasure.

Sukanya saw that Ladarat was on the phone and mimed her thanks with a *wai* as she smiled and led the newly energized Chi away.

"And what have you observed?" Ladarat asked.

"There is a man. A smuggler, I believe him to be."

"And how do you know that he's a smuggler?"

"He is carrying a canvas bag, Khun. A canvas bag embellished with a picture of a parrot."

"A canvas bag?" Ladarat watched Sukanya jog down the sidewalk, encouraging the previously cataleptic Chi to trot alongside her.

"A parrot?" she added, thinking: Since when is a parrot diagnostic of a smuggling ring?

"Yes, Khun. That is why I remember him. Or before it was her, but now it is a him, if you understand me."

Ladarat admitted that she didn't. At all.

"It is a smuggling ring, you see. Many people, some men and some women, of different shapes and sizes. But all part of the same parrot smuggling ring."

"But . . . how do you know that they are part of a smuggling ring? Perhaps they all work for a tour company. Or they shop at the same souvenir stand." Or perhaps they all simply like parrots.

"Because, Khun, these people? The parrot gang?"

"Yes?"

"They are giving *packages* to the tourists."

"Packages?"

"Very small packages. In brown paper."

Well, of course. Certainly that brown paper was a sign of nefariousness.

"Perhaps they are giving the tourists gifts," Ladarat suggested mildly. "Parting gifts?"

"But no, Khun. They generally pick one person on every bus."

"Just one?"

"Just one. I have seen this because I've observed. You see, a bus pulls up, and the tourists get out. And one of them— just one, you understand?—just one will go over to the person with the parrot bag, who gives them a package. Then the tourist looks very guilty and secretive, and walks away very quickly."

"And then?" Ladarat found herself becoming interested despite herself. "And what does the...the smuggler do then?"

"Well, Khun, that's what is so interesting. That person, the smuggler, as you yourself said, will look around for another bus arriving, and will stand in front of that bus, and the same drama will be enacted."

"Hmmm," Ladarat said.

"Don't you think this sounds like a smuggling ring?" her assistant asked.

"Well...it does seem...odd."

"It is as I thought. Odd and...nefarious, too, don't you think?"

"So you think that these tourists are smuggling something out of Thailand?"

"But of course, Khun. Isn't it obvious? They're being given drugs. Heroin, probably. They are being paid to smuggle heroin out of Thailand."

Ladarat thought about that for a second as she watched a trio of nurses leave the building, talking happily.

51

But there was an obvious problem with this theory.

"Khun—it doesn't appear that they're being paid, though, does it? Or that there is any money changing hands."

Sisithorn was silent for a moment as a bus rolled past. But then she had a ready answer. "I can't say for certain—these encounters happen so quickly. Perhaps, but perhaps not. But you must remember, Khun, that these are smugglers. Evil-doers. Certainly they've found more sophisticated ways of exchanging money. Like...like bitcoins."

"Bitcoins?" Ladarat didn't recognize the English word.

"Yes, Khun. I've read about them. Bitcoins are like very small, secret bits of money that live in computers."

Money that lives in computers? Well, Ladarat would be the first to admit that she lacked sophistication when it came to matters of technology. She was almost certainly out of her depth here. But there was one thing she was certain of.

"It is difficult to smuggle drugs out of Thailand," she pointed out. "Especially out of Thailand's largest airport." Ladarat remembered the story of a young American man she knew very well who had been arrested trying to do the same thing several years ago. "You can't simply walk through customs with drugs in a paper parcel. They have...ways of detecting such things. Like dogs with a finely tuned sense of smell and...well...there are lots of dogs."

"Oh." Sisithorn seemed deflated. She had sounded so hopeful, and now Ladarat had dashed those hopes. That was unkind.

"But perhaps I have an idea."

"An idea?"

"Do you see the...smuggler now?"

"No...wait. Yes, he is walking toward another bus that pulled up a moment ago."

"Do you have much time before your flight?"

"Oh yes, Khun. I didn't want to be late, so I booked a flight at nine p.m."

That was more than three hours away. Surely her assistant was being overly cautions with regard to the chance of missing a flight?

"Well, then. Here is what you can do. You can follow this...smuggler, looking to see if he gives another package to another tourist on the bus that just pulled up."

"I see, and then what?"

"Then you must follow that tourist, but carefully. So as not to be noticed."

"I understand, Khun, but why?"

"Why, to find out what is in the package, of course."

"But these tourists are smuggling something illegal. Why would they open a package in a crowded airport terminal for all of the world to see?"

Ladarat admitted that she wasn't sure, but she pointed out that the tourists seemed very cautious. "You observed that they were eager to walk away, did you not?"

Sisithorn admitted that that was exactly what she had seen.

"So these tourists are cautious. Very cautious. If they are concerned about getting caught, then they are probably also concerned about what they are carrying, are they not? Wouldn't you wonder what you were being asked to take through security?"

"Ahh, I see your point. So they would want to unwrap the package to be sure that what they had was not more illegal than what they were told."

"Exactly so. Taking drugs through security would be very dangerous, but tempting to a smuggling ring. You could tell a tourist that they were smuggling diamonds or pearls or jade, when in fact they were smuggling—"

"Opium!"

Opium? Did anyone smuggle opium anymore? "Well, perhaps. Or something equally bad. They would want to make sure that they weren't carrying any such things into security."

"So I will follow a tourist to determine what they are smuggling. That is brilliant, Khun. You are a true mentor."

"You are too kind," Ladarat said, oddly flattered. "But you must be careful. Very careful. These tourists will not want to be seen, and they will not want you to see them. So you must be—"

"Stealthy. Oh, I will be, Khun. I will be a stealthy detective. And I will let you know what I find."

They said their goodbyes, and Sisithorn crept off to reconnoiter, as stealthily as she could. Ladarat smiled at the image of her tall, gangly, bespectacled assistant attempting such a thing. But as she stood up she stopped smiling, thinking that not too long ago, she herself had been amused at the idea that she, Ladarat Patalung, might be a detective. You never knew, did you? If she could find a mass murderer, was it inconceivable that her assistant could break up a smuggling ring? It was not.

Anyway, now was not the time to think of such things. Her wait for Sukanya had delayed her, and now it was almost six o'clock. She had only half an hour to go back to her office, exchange her white coat for her handbag, and drive to her next "appointment," if that's what she should call it.

It was less of an appointment, though, than an obligation. A duty. And not a pleasant one, but one that she needed to fulfill.

Ladarat set off across the service road that encircled the hospital, walking purposefully and quickly. Yet, truth be told, she was dragging her feet just a little and hoping for some sort of accident—some emergency—that would prevent her from keeping this appointment.

CHAPTER 5

A SAD FAILURE OF CHOPPING

Alas, no such emergency intervened. In Ladarat's experience, emergencies never seemed to arise when they would be most useful. On the whole, you couldn't count on them. Emergencies were, in general, both inconvenient and highly unreliable.

Thinking about emergencies and their usefulness, Ladarat navigated the hospital corridors and then the parking lot, seeing no one she needed to stop to talk with or—more likely—who absolutely needed to talk with her. So it was with a heavy heart and a sense of disappointment that Ladarat found herself just a few short minutes later standing next to her new car.

She looked it over with a now-familiar sense of dissatisfaction, not unlike what she felt when Wiriya had accompanied her to the dealership north of Chiang Mai to pick it out. Hers was an illogical dissatisfaction, truth be told. Illogical, because →
Ladarat had no reason to be displeased.

It was a car, inarguably a car. No one could fault its… carness. It had four wheels and four doors. It also boasted a steering wheel, that ingenious device. Even its color, an innocuous silver, now a sort of matte metallic color under a layer of dry Chiang Mai winter dust, was nothing that one could legitimately object to.

And yet, Ladarat did find her new car…disappointing, not because of anything it was, but rather because of what it wasn't.

It was a car, true enough. But it wasn't *her* car. Not yet, she corrected herself. Wiriya had said that she would become used to it, soon enough. And soon it would become hers. Like a relationship, he had said. A romantic relationship.

The problem was that this car had not yet achieved a place in her heart in the way that her previous yellow Beetle had. When she had finally sold her Beetle to a collector in California, it had certainly found a better home. Coddled and cared for, kept in a garage and waxed every week, it had achieved what was certainly the best possible retirement that a car could hope for. So she wished it well.

Perhaps eventually Ladarat would get used to this one, although—*beep*—she would never get used to using a keychain to unlock the doors remotely. What indeed was the point of that? To unlock a car's doors without approaching the car? Because surely one would need to approach the car in order to get into it, as she was doing now.

Ah well, that was not the only advance in technology that Ladarat didn't understand. Nor would it be the last, she thought as she navigated out of the rapidly emptying parking lot. Although there were features she would never, ever, get used to. Like—

"Warning in front on the right! Warning in front on the right!"

The harsh electronic voice seemed to emanate from all of the speakers in the dashboard, with a volume that rattled their plastic mountings, lending a quality of urgency to the announcement. It was as if the car were announcing an impending collision with an asteroid.

Oh, dear. The kindly salesman had recommended this car because it was Chinese ("Extreme reliability!! Extreme value!!"). Apparently this...talkativeness was a safety feature that the

Chinese had embraced with enthusiasm. Sensors around the car's corners would detect anything—or anyone—that was nearby, passing that helpful information on in its robot voice.

Ladarat could see perfectly well that a half dozen laughing nursing students in immaculate blue-and-white uniforms were passing her on their way to the dormitory on the far side of the parking lot. And yet, like a precocious student who covets the teacher's approval, this car felt the need prove how perceptive it was by noting their existence. What was worse, even Wiriya had been unable to figure out how to turn that feature off. That, certainly, was never a problem she'd had with her forty-year-old VW bug, which had lacked even the basic niceties such as air-conditioning.

Navigating out of the parking lot and onto Suthep Road, Ladarat signaled to get into the left lane and then waited. And waited. Truth be told, Wiriya was probably right—she was perhaps not as assertive as she could be. But eventually another car let her in, and she made a U-turn that would take her north and then into the Old City—the heart of Chiang Mai—then, through increasingly small streets, little more than alleys, to her destination.

All around her, drivers applied their horns liberally. In such a hurry to get home from work, they couldn't simply relax. Perhaps Ladarat was going a bit more slowly than usual. Not because she wanted to avoid her appointment, of course. It was just that one must treat a new car gently and cautiously. That's what she was doing, and those other drivers would just have to be patient.

Eventually, after a trip that was longer than necessary but not as long as Ladarat would have liked, she took the last open parking spot behind an old, traditional Lanna-style building. Made of roughhewn teak, with a wide door and generous windows, it had been modernized to fit the current taste for open spaces and roominess. But it had the traditional elevated entry to keep out evil spirits, and it had retained the aura of solidity that made it easy to imagine that this building would still be standing a hundred years from now.

That was pleasant to think about: knowing that these graceful structures would still stand, resisting weather and rain and termites. Less pleasant, by far, was contemplating what awaited her inside.

As she made her way with increasingly heavy steps up the teak stairs to the wide and welcoming front door, a pleasant young American woman met her with a cool towel in one hand and porcelain cup of chilled ginger tea in the other.

She introduced herself as Karen, but did a double take as Ladarat stepped into the brightly lit entry hall.

"You are...here for lessons?" she asked in English.

"Yes, I made a reservation online...Isn't there room?"

"Oh yes, of course. It's just that...well...I thought you were Thai. And I couldn't figure out why a Thai person would be here. That would be amusing, would it not? A Thai person here?" And the American woman laughed with a full-throated, hearty enjoyment of the humor she had just perpetrated.

Ladarat agreed that such a state of affairs would in fact be a legitimate justification for unrestrained mirth.

"We're just in here," Karen said, leading the way into a brightly lit room with tile floors and four large, metal-topped tables, each with two other people, except the one nearest the door, which was populated only by a blond girl who appeared to be perhaps eighteen at most.

"I'm Anessa," the girl said. "And you are...?"

"Melissa," Ladarat said automatically, after the host was safely out of earshot.

"So you're American Thai?"

"I grew up in Thailand, but I never learned how to cook as a little girl," Ladarat improvised.

Anessa exclaimed. "Wow! I bet now you've come back to Thailand to learn how to cook... That's awesome!"

Ladarat just nodded and smiled. She didn't feel awesome. She glanced at Karen, who was busily distributing something to the table on the far side of the room.

"My boyfriend is Thai," Ladarat added. "My boyfriend in... Chicago. So I wanted to learn how to cook for him."

Now Anessa was nodding enthusiastically. "That's so cool. I'm such a lousy cook. I'm probably hopeless. But I really wanted to learn about Thai culture, you know? And I thought every little bit helps, and—"

Karen's voice rose to a fine fairground volume as she clapped her hands for attention. Ladarat and Anessa both turned to their teacher, although Anessa did so with considerably more enthusiasm.

"Welcome, everyone. Welcome to our introduction to Thai cooking."

Oh, dear. This was as bad as Ladarat had imagined it would be. The only Thai person in the room, Ladarat/Melissa was surrounded by seven other women, plus Karen, who were all going to learn how to cook Thai food. Specifically...

"Tonight, we'll learn how to make *panang gai*, chicken smothered in red chili paste, and *yam khor moo yang*, marinated pork salad. But first, we'll start with a fresh watermelon-and-crab soup. It's the perfect introduction to the Thai science and art of balancing flavors and textures."

Ladarat found she was becoming interested despite herself, and not just because *yam khor moo yang* was one of her favorite summer dishes. Watermelon soup? Well, all right. She could see serving that to Wiriya and earning his appreciation. Certainly he would want a generous plate of chicken curry afterward. But as a demonstration of her abilities...Ladarat could even think of a white-and-green painted serving bowl in which she could present it. The bowl had sat on the top shelf of her kitchen for years, unreachable without a chair, and totally unused. She smiled.

"This is awesome, isn't it?" Anessa seemed to have caught her enthusiasm. Ladarat nodded. Perhaps it would be awesome.

But it was not, in fact, awesome. Ladarat tried to explain this to Duanphen, the friendly Isaan cook with the stall right down the street from Ladarat's small house on the outskirts of Chiang Mai. Ladarat had stopped by, as she always did after work, to pick up dinner.

"I was the only Thai person there—just me and eight *farang*. And they were all better cooks than me."

"How do you know that, Khun? How can you be sure? You didn't stay—you just walked out halfway through the first course. Maybe their *yam khor moo yang* was raw? Maybe they all got sick and needed to see a nurse! Ha!" Duanphen chuckled with a benign malevolence, halfheartedly wishing a mild case of trichinosis on those unsuspecting foreigners.

Ladarat smiled ruefully. "It was the chopping. I couldn't chop."

Duanphen looked confused. "You couldn't...*chop*? But there is nothing to chopping, it's just..." She glanced quickly at Ladarat. "Well, never mind. What was it, by the way? The first course you were making?"

"I was trying to make chilled watermelon-and-crab soup."

Duanphen made a face, her round cheek twisting into a dismissive frown, then she laughed, her fleshy arms and belly wiggling with derision. Duanphen was certainly well fed—an auspicious sign in a food stall cook.

"That? That is not Thai food—who told you that chilled watermelon soup was Thai?" She paused, grinning. "Could you imagine serving that big, strong friend of yours chilled watermelon soup?"

Actually, Ladarat could imagine that. But Duanphen had a point. Such a production might indeed be a demonstration of skills in the kitchen—skills that she obviously lacked—but it was hardly a meaningful source of sustenance for someone with as much . . . bulk as Wiriya had.

"So that's done, then. I just won't learn how to cook. I'll just come here every night . . ."

But Duanphen was shaking her head. "No, Khun. You must learn how to cook. You really must. It is important for a woman of our age, and it is truly not that hard. You just need the right teacher."

Ladarat smiled. Who would agree to teach her? A cooking school dropout?

"And that teacher would be . . . ?"

"Me, of course. I'll show you how to cook. Not that fancy stuff the Americans do—that just looks nice. I'll show you the basics. What you really need."

"But . . ."

Ladarat looked at the cook, who had turned her attention to Ladarat's meal for the evening: *tom yum goong*—spicy seafood soup. It was one of Ladarat's favorite meals, because it was so simple. Every time she had it, she could imagine making it for herself, or for Wiriya. Just a simple stir-fry of shrimp and scallops and bits of fish in oil first. Then broth and vegetables and a liberal seasoning of garlic and lime leaves and ginger with a small dose of salty fish sauce.

As Duanphen ladled a generous portion into a Styrofoam container nestling in a plastic bag, she eyed Ladarat carefully.

"You think you can't cook," she said, "but I know you can." Duanphen tied the bag and set the package down in front of Ladarat.

"You have good taste. You always tell me if what I've made is too spicy, or if it has more lime leaves that it needs, or less ginger."

Ladarat nodded uncertainly. Yes, it was true, she had a talent for eating.

"But does that make me a good cook? That's like saying that someone has a talent for getting sick, so he would be a good doctor."

Duanphen laughed and waved away her objection like someone swatting a mosquito. Then she held out another Styrofoam container.

"*Khanon krok*." Coconut dumplings. "They're from my cousin Prasert. He has a new dessert stall near the east gate. He used to be an insurance salesman, but he decided he liked baking better. And if he could learn, so could you. He does the best *kanom maprao*, but you should try these dumplings, too."

Ladarat handed over two thirty-baht notes, but Duanphen waved them away just as authoritatively as she had Ladarat's objections a moment ago.

"No, you just come back tomorrow night. Around this time, maybe seven. After the dinner crowd. I'll put some ingredients aside and I'll show you to make *gang jued*. Very simple soup, but flavorful. Clear broth, minced pork, rice noodles—so easy. You can make it, then take it home to feed your friend the detective."

Why not? She shouldn't let her one failure make up her mind for her. No, she shouldn't. So at last she nodded, and Duanphen smiled, pleased.

CHAPTER 6

THE SADNESS OF HALF A HOUSE

Ladarat carried her *tom yum goong* down the back steps of her small house, balancing the *khanon krok* on top, and a napkin and fork. Safely down the steps, she followed the path onto the small stone patio that was surrounded by dense bushes on all sides. It was a little oasis in this suburban neighborhood of Chiang Mai. Mostly young professionals and small families lived around her, so it tended to be very quiet, and the dense foliage had an insulating effect, too. When she was out here, it was easy for Ladarat to imagine that she was entirely alone.

And she loved that. It wasn't that she was antisocial. Wiriya teased her, but it wasn't true. Not really. It was just that in her daily work she got an adequate dose of people. When she came home, she was happy not to see anyone.

More than that, she liked time alone to . . . recuperate. It was as if every hour spent during the day with people demanded an equal amount of time alone, in her own head, as an antidote, of sorts.

Ladarat selected what had become, in the last month or so, "her" chair, the one closest to the house and facing the hedges that lined the rear of the small plot. The other matching chair, facing the house, had become Wiriya's. There hadn't been a formal discussion; they had simply settled into their own chairs in a way that felt comfortable and entirely natural.

Ladarat couldn't say for certain why that thought made her happy, but it did. It was nice to know that an empty chair was just temporarily empty. It wasn't really empty at all. It was simply...unoccupied.

The evening was chilly, but Ladarat had bravely decided to eat her solitary dinner on her little patio despite the cold. Her small iron table and matching chairs were calling to her. Even in northern Thailand, the weather rarely became cold enough for a winter coat.

But tonight was a reminder that her favorite little city was one of the few places in Thailand where she could put on her thick blue cardigan that she bought at Filene's Basement during her year in Chicago. And that, in turn, reminded her how far she had come since that cold and lonely winter in a strange city, learning the ethics customs of a foreign country, and suffering what was easily the worst, most tasteless food ever imagined.

Her loyal cat Maewfawbaahn had ventured out onto the patio ahead of her, flying out the back door as soon as she'd let him out. Now he'd circled back and was crouched at her feet, no doubt pondering an evening of hunting. He scanned the bushes around the patio's borders, as alert as any sentry. At the faintest rustling in the foliage—a sleepy bird, a marauding gecko—his tail twitched and he slunk silently over the still-warm stone and disappeared.

Ladarat watched him do just this, moving silently but with an unswerving sense of purpose. With no more noise than a feather falling, he glided across the stones and vanished into the shadows.

Demonstrating remarkable restraint that she wished someone besides a cat were there to witness, Ladarat set the *khanon krok* aside and instead unwrapped the still steaming *tom yum goong.* A gratifying cloud blossomed in the cool, still air, redolent of lime and ginger and cardamom.

As she inhaled the scent of spices and tangy lime, Ladarat admitted to herself that there was another reason she had wanted to eat outside tonight. Some of her fondest memories of this little garden—her little garden—were on nights like this when she could just…think. And now with Wiriya in her life, she found that she didn't have as much time to think as she used to.

She enjoyed his company, of course. And, truth be told, he could be a better thinker than she was, and so he was often very helpful in the thinking line. At the very least, he was a different sort of thinker. So in their conversations over *tom yum goong* or *gang jued* or hearty *kao niew moo yang* (grilled pork skewers on sticky rice) he would often have something to add. And he was a good question-asker.

But still, it was nice to let one's thoughts…wander where they wanted to, like Maewfawbaahn, free to sit still or wander or slink into the hedges. One's thoughts should be allowed to roam like that, once in a while, to keep them healthy.

Ladarat felt a faint flutter of air on her toes and looked down to find her cat had reappeared silently and was again crouched at her feet. In the faint light from the back door, she also noticed faint scratches on the smooth stone where the chairs had been rearranged. Those scratches made her happy, because she knew that they'd been made by two people.

Not long ago, she used to rotate her use of both chairs, ensuring that they would become equally worn, just as she tried to use all of her silverware and plates and glasses. There was nothing, she thought, that was so sad as a house that was only half inhabited. It became half a house.

But now her own house had the feel of one that was fully inhabited. It was a whole house again—or at least on its way to becoming one—for the first time since her husband, Somboon, had died thirteen years ago.

Ahh, that seems longer ago now. Longer ago than it did six months ago, if that made any sense. So much had changed.

That was perhaps inevitable. Like most Thais, Ladarat thought of life in twelve-year cycles. Each period came with changes and new expectations. So it was only right, and even predictable, that at the start of a new twelve-year cycle things would feel so very different.

Ladarat closed the Styrofoam box and set her fork balancing on top. There would be enough for a quick breakfast tomorrow, perhaps, or a late snack. She found that any leftovers vanished when Wiriya was around. He was like a good-natured dog that way. He would simply vacuum up anything edible, preferably three days old and encased in Styrofoam. He said it was because of his years as a bachelor, that it was what he was used to. But Ladarat guessed that he found some sort of satisfaction in cleaning the refrigerator out.

In his police work, too, Wiriya liked things to be neat and tidy, cases cleaned up and locked down. He was still bothered, she knew, by the last case they had solved together.

That had been the case of the woman who became known as the Peaflower murderer (because that was her name: Anchan, or peaflower). It's true, she had killed many men, many more, probably, than they would ever know. Certainly more people than was really right and proper.

She was a bad person—there was no question about that. Yet there had been mitigating circumstances, including her own history. And those men...well...they were not the finest specimens of gentlemen. That was safe to say.

So although Wiriya was convinced beyond the shadow of a doubt that Peaflower was guilty of those murders, he couldn't bring himself to be fully in favor of her prosecution. He did his duty, of course. Yet those circumstances nagged at him.

Perhaps this case of the disappearing *farang* would be another of those ethically ambiguous cases. But what could that be? These people were coming to Thailand and... disappearing. A straightforward vanishing act, was it not?

For the past few minutes, the *khanon krok* had been calling to her softly. She'd resisted well. Admirably well. So there would be no shame in having some now, would there? There wouldn't.

Inside the container, two coconut dumplings nestled together. Light and fluffy perhaps in a previous life, in this incarnation they were soaked in a delicate syrup that was tooth-achingly sweet and flavored with just a hint of ginger.

In just a few bites, one of the dumplings disappeared. Ladarat felt an overwhelming temptation to finish the second one, too. She realized that her fork was poised to attack before she had given it permission. Hurriedly, she closed the container, nestling it under the half-eaten *tom yum goong*, and placed the fork on top to dissuade her from another attack. One had to remain alert and vigilant, because desserts had a way of just... disappearing.

That was another aspect of this vanishing act that made no sense. Disappearing could be very simple. And surely there were simpler ways to do it. Why go to Thailand and travel to Chiang Mai and then vanish? Why not simply... vanish? Or find an alternative identity and then leave the country? Why so much trouble?

In fact, the more Ladarat thought about it, this method of escape was wrong. Not morally wrong, but incorrect. If someone like that woman from San Francisco went to Bangkok and then flew to Chiang Mai, she was leaving a very clear trail. Her family would know where she went. If she had wanted to disappear, that would have been a very bad way to do it.

Then did she want to be found? But that made no sense, either. Because why, then, do such a good job of disappearing?

Perhaps that woman had simply not thought through the implications of what she was doing. Perhaps it was a spur-of-the-moment decision? The trip to Chiang Mai—did the missing *farang* plan it in advance or at the last minute?

She could find out.

Scooping up the Styrofoam containers in one hand and the fork in the other, Ladarat pushed her chair back, adding four new faint white lines to the network of tiny scratches on the weathered stone. Maewfawbaahn, apparently tired of hunting, followed her into the small kitchen, where she'd left her phone, and watched expectantly as she dialed Wiriya's number.

There was a long pause until Wiriya answered. She thought it was probably him, but it was difficult to tell because there was so much noise in the background. She could barely hear his voice, but another voice, that of a male singer, was overwhelming in the background.

The sound was garbled and distorted, but she caught snatches of a song and the phrase "...still live in Texas."

"Hello? Hello?"

Then the call ended.

Perhaps he would call back. He often did when she caught him at a bad time. But tonight, he might not. He was certainly not in a place where he could talk about a case. And besides, there would be time enough for that later. She waited a minute, then two, as she put the leftover *tom yum goong* and lone *khanon krok* in the refrigerator and washed her single fork. Still her cell phone was silent.

So she whistled to Maewfawbaahn, who followed her up the narrow stairs to her bedroom, thinking about the romantic inclinations of people who live in Texas.

Wan ang kaan

TUESDAY

CHAPTER 7

AN UNACCOUNTABLE ENTHUSIASM FOR DEATH

Mornings really should not be this busy or this complicated. It was only seven o'clock and already Ladarat was exhausted. Chi, however, had discovered a secret source of energy—only accessible to lazy dogs—and was leaping around the backseat of her car as if he were possessed by an energetic *Phi Poang Khang*, a mischievous black monkey spirit that was widely believed to haunt the forests of northern Thailand—but not usually the backseats of nurse ethicists' cars.

Sukanya had woken her around five thirty, panicked and anxious. Apparently her grandmother had fallen and possibly broken her arm. Sukanya needed to take her to an emergency room and so couldn't take Chi into work.

"But he has to go to work," Sukanya had said, near tears at the thought that the deserving patients of Sriphat Hospital might have to suffer for a day without the support of this diminutive therapy dog. Personally, Ladarat thought that the patients would recover from such a loss, however devastating it might be. But Sukanya seemed to think that keeping Chi from his appointed rounds would be unprofessional, unethical, and simply wrong.

Faced with that onslaught of empathy and not yet entirely awake without having had her customary two cups of blue

71

peaflower tea, Ladarat gave in a little more easily than she might have under better circumstances.

So that was how she found herself sitting in her car in the hospital parking lot, with a black monkey spirit in the backseat, facing a conundrum.

As she had just realized a moment ago, when she'd hurriedly collected Chi from his grateful owner, Ladarat had forgotten to pick up all of the accoutrements that went with therapy dog stewardship. She had the leash, of course, but not—most urgently—Chi's bright yellow vest that identified him as a genuine service dog. And that presented a problem. Without the vest, Chi was just a dog, and therefore banned from the hospital grounds.

But what to do? She couldn't leave Chi in the car. Nor could she turn around and go back, because Sukanya had no doubt already left for her grandmother's house.

Well, then, she would just have to find another way in. And—as Sisithorn might say—she would do so surreptitiously.

Ladarat's stray thoughts about her assistant's intrepid investigation of the Parrot Gang were elbowed aside by Chi's enthusiastic efforts to escape from the backseat. She managed to clip his leash onto his collar just a second before he bolted through the partly open back door, only to be drawn up short as Ladarat reined him in.

"Whoa, little man. Such enthusiasm for work is admirable, but there will still be patients to see in five minutes."

Chi raised his snub nose and looked at her attentively for a moment, perhaps pondering the wisdom of those words, or perhaps hoping for a treat. Ladarat realized that she should take advantage of his attention, which would be short-lived once he realized that she was really not so wise, and that his treats were sitting well out of reach, on the counter of Sukanya's kitchen.

"Let's go." Maybe he knew a secret way in?

Chi looked at her intently, wagging his fringed tail once, then twice.

"Go."

Maybe not.

But then, much to her surprise, Chi spun in place and lunged against the leash, pointing his nose unerringly at a wide steel door set into the back of the hospital at a little below ground level.

"Really?"

Chi turned around just long enough to offer his most emphatic reassurance.

"*Pffftt.*"

Try as she might, Ladarat found she couldn't embrace Chi's enthusiasm for that particular door. She knew where it led, and although she didn't consider herself squeamish—at least by Thai standards—this would not have been her entrance of choice.

But it was a good strategy, she had to admit. If any entrance were unguarded, it would be this one. At least Chi seemed to think so. Perhaps Sukanya had been stuck in the same predicament before.

Pulled along by the small ball of fur that was bounding across the gravel ahead of her, Ladarat followed obediently behind. Weaving unerringly through rows of cars, Chi navigated precisely, towing her around a large Mercedes and right up to the door. She didn't have to read the sign to know where they were.

"Morgue."

Ladarat liked to think she was not particularly superstitious about death. She could afford to be dismissive of some Thai superstitions, like a fear of listing the names of people who have died, or you'll die next. That was silly. Mostly.

But walking through a morgue? That seemed to tempt fate.

Chi, however, had no such qualms. His nose was nudging the door and his fringed tail was wagging frantically.

What was that about? An enthusiasm for death? In a therapy dog?

Ladarat pulled on the heavy door, half hoping it would be locked. But it swung open easily. After only a moment's pause, Chi wriggled his way through the gap and disappeared, pulling his leash taut behind him. Ladarat followed, albeit with markedly less enthusiasm.

Once inside the cool, tiled corridor, Ladarat held her breath. There was something about the smell of this place that was wrong. It wasn't the smell of death, but more of an intensified hospital smell, as if all of the worst essence of medicine and disinfectant became concentrated tenfold down here.

Chi, on the other hand, was most certainly not holding his breath. Snuffling the air with an enthusiasm he usually reserved for those moments when Sukanya was nearby, he seemed obsessed and almost crazed: more like a *Phi Poang Khang* monkey spirit than ever.

He spun clockwise, then counterclockwise, until he pointed to an open doorway that, Ladarat knew, led to the morgue proper. Chi strained with renewed vigor in that direction. Unfortunately for him, Ladarat's sensible, rubber-soled shoes gave her a firm grip on the tile floor that Chi lacked, so the little dog succeeded only in accomplishing that running-in-place dance characteristic of a certain American cartoon coyote whose name Ladarat couldn't remember.

Perhaps his fascination with death smells was something that Sukanya wouldn't want to know about, if she didn't already. With more than a little difficulty, Ladarat succeeded in towing the enthusiastic little therapy dog backward over the tile, zigzagging around a small rug outside an office door where their battle would have become a little more even.

When would he give up?

The answer, it turned out, was when they reached the stairs leading up to the ground-floor hallway of the west wing. Momentarily confused by the change in terrain that took him by surprise—him being towed backward and all—Chi seemed to forget for a moment the goal he had been pursuing. With the abrupt and total change in priorities that is only possible in dogs, politicians, and small children, he reversed course, sped past her, and began to tow her valiantly up the stairs with just as much enthusiasm as he'd exhibited in the other direction a moment earlier.

Down a long corridor, Ladarat followed Chi up a long flight of stairs, through the back of the emergency room, and finally into the elevator hallway. Aware, presumably, that there were patients to see and support to be offered, Chi seemed to have put away childish things and was ready to get to work. He headed for the elevators with the same strength of purpose he had just displayed in the macabre search for dead people. This, Ladarat thought, was going to be an interesting day.

But that turned out not to be true. At least, so far. Busy, yes. Tiring, certainly. But after the initial excitement of Sukanya's five thirty wake-up call, her day had been almost unnaturally sedate.

She'd followed Chi on his rounds, seeing a farmer from Isaan with gallstones, a teenager from Chiang Mai with pneumonia, and a silly American backpacker who had foolishly decided that she didn't need to take her antimalaria pills on a trekking trip into the mountains.

It had been a relaxing morning, in a way—relaxing because there was very little to do on those visits. It was Chi who did all the work, making friends as efficiently as one of those Japanese geisha hostesses. Ladarat only had to smile, left to her own thoughts.

Those thoughts turned, inevitably, to her last stop, where Chi was leading her unerringly: to Melissa Double, the definitely crying woman. It's true that in a morning of thinking Ladarat had achieved no firm conclusions. Yet she'd decided that she should do...something. She'd convinced herself that despite the cheerful façade, the woman, Melissa, was suffering more than she let on. All of her brave talk of books and good days notwithstanding, there was pain there, too.

So when Chi became distracted by the food sellers arrayed in lines between the hospital and the palliative care building, Ladarat regretfully reined him in. Much as she would have liked to stop for a snack of hot *glooai tawt* (fried miniature bananas), or maybe a light lunch of *kai jiew moo ssap* (fried omelet with minced pork), her sense of duty pulled her across the pavement, dragging a bereft and hungry Chi along behind her.

The nurses' station was deserted, so Ladarat made her own way to Melissa's door, which was wide open. Trusting Chi to do the right thing, especially since there were no distractions of food nearby, Ladarat dropped his leash and Chi charged ahead and through the door.

A prolonged laugh that echoed out into the hall was evidence that Chi had found his next patient. By the time Ladarat caught up, Chi had taken up a position at Melissa's side, his nose buried under a pillow and tail wagging enthusiastically.

"Hello, Khun." Melissa was smiling, but she looked more careworn and pale than she had yesterday.

Ladarat returned the greeting and a *wai*, taking a seat next to Melissa's bed.

"And how are you feeling today?"

Melissa shrugged, then smiled. "I'm still here, if you know what I mean."

Ladarat didn't know, although she could imagine.

Melissa smiled again, but a sad smile this time, an honest approximation of the *yim soo* smile: smiling in the face of an unwinnable battle. It was the smile that officials used when they knew they were going to lose an election, or that criminals used when they knew they would be found guilty.

"Well...last night was...not a good night."

"How so?"

"Ahh, well, there was more pain than usual. Or more pain than I'm used to."

"And didn't the nurses bring you more pain medicine?"

"Oh, they wanted to, but they couldn't. You see, Dr. Taksin wasn't on call last night. He's only on call every other night. So they called this other doctor, but he wasn't willing to give me more medication because he didn't know me." She laughed halfheartedly. Ladarat didn't. "Perhaps he thought I was an addict?"

Unfortunately, that was not as silly as it sounded. Many doctors in Thailand—doctors everywhere, for that matter— were afraid to prescribe opioids, even to patients who were near the end of life. They were afraid of a patient becoming addicted, or overdosing perhaps.

Interestingly, one worry they did not have, generally speaking, was the misuse of these prescriptions by women to kill a husband. Or several. That, in fact, had been the misuse to which countless morphine prescriptions had been employed by the infamous Peaflower murderer, whom Ladarat herself had helped to catch. Perhaps someday she'd tell Melissa that story to distract her. But not now.

"Many doctors are just . . . cautious. But Dr. Taksin came in this morning, didn't he?"

"Well, yes. Not so early, though. The nurses, they told me he isn't always an early riser. So it was some time before he came to see me. Oh—"

Melissa noticed the look of surprise on Ladarat's face. "Don't worry, I'm fine now. He increased my dose, and now I feel much better. Nothing to worry about."

Why was this very sick woman trying to reassure her? That wasn't right.

As Professor Dalrymple said, we must never forget that the patient is the most important person in the room.

Nor was it right that she'd had to suffer overnight and well into the next morning, simply because no one was available to help her. That certainly did put Dr. Taksin's problems in a new light. If his inattention was hurting patients in his care like this nice woman, well, Ladarat would feel obligated to get involved. More involved, probably, than she would find comfortable. But perhaps it wouldn't come to that.

"Well, I'm glad you're feeling better, but really, you shouldn't have to wait that long for pain relief."

"But I'm all right now, aren't I?" Melissa seemed genuinely bemused. "No harm done."

Then, changing the subject as fast as Chi was fond of changing direction: "And what did you do last night? Did you have plans?"

The expression on Melissa's face seemed almost plaintive. "You see, I love hearing about everyone's lives. I won't get a chance to see much of Chiang Mai, but the nurses here, they tell me about what they do with their time off. And...well... it helps me to imagine a life outside, if that makes sense? But I know, I shouldn't have asked—"

"It's all right, really." If that would bring some comfort to this stoic woman, then of course she would do what she could.

"To tell the truth,"—Ladarat smiled—"I went to a cooking class."

"A...cooking class? That sounds like fun. Are you...a good cook?"

Ladarat laughed. "No, it turns out that I'm a horrible cook." She told Melissa about her mysterious yet stubborn inability to chop vegetables. Soon she had the woman laughing as she described the way her carved cucumbers looked like logs that had been gnawed by a rabid beaver.

"But that's a skill, isn't it? Chopping and peeling and so forth? Just because you're not...adept at those things, that hardly means you're hopeless. Isn't that why you took the class?"

"Perhaps you're right, in theory. But I was by far the worst cook in the room. And the other women—they were all women—were foreigners. How can I hope to learn how to cook Thai food when everyone else is so far ahead of me?"

Ladarat had meant that to be a rhetorical question, but Melissa didn't seem to take it that way. Instead, she became very thoughtful.

"Not all cooking requires chopping," she pointed out. "You may have other skills. Dr. Taksin, for instance. Maybe he's bad at, I don't know, surgery? But what he does, he does very well. Where would I be if he'd tried his hand at chopping... people and given up?"

Ladarat had to smile at that. To think that she might have a hidden culinary talent, perhaps lurking in her subconscious, just waiting to be discovered and nurtured.

"Perhaps I'm harboring a secret talent for... stirring soup?"

Melissa smiled, too. A *yim thak thaan* smile that meant: You're welcome to your opinion, of course. But you're wrong.

"You can laugh, but why not? Maybe the pretty dishes with elegant shapes aren't what you're meant for. And who needs them, anyway? So what if your... what was it? Watermelon crab soup?"

She made a wrinkled face when Ladarat nodded.

"So what if your watermelon crab soup isn't endowed with picturesque cucumber stars floating merrily on its surface? Would that mean the end of the world?"

Ladarat had to admit that in all likelihood the presence of misshapen vegetables in a bowl of soup would not spell the end of the world as we know it. Then she told Melissa about Duanphen's offer of a private cooking lesson.

"And maybe this Duanphen will help you find a dish that is perfect for you," she continued. "There must be, don't you think? In much the same way that becoming a nurse was perfect for you, and becoming a librarian was perfect for me."

"So why did you become a librarian?" Ladarat asked, glad to switch to any subject other than her own meager culinary talents.

"I loved browsing books. Not reading them through, you know? Just bits and pieces. I'd rather get a dozen glimpses of a dozen books than read one through cover to cover. And you can't really do that anywhere but a library, can you? That would be an expensive habit otherwise. But as a librarian it is perfect."

Their conversation meandered on, touching on travel and

work, and of course on the books they'd both read. There were more than Ladarat would have expected. But eventually Melissa grimaced once or twice when Chi moved, and her attention seemed to wander. Finally Ladarat got up to leave.

"Remember, if you have pain again, have the nurses call Dr. Taksin. Even if he's not on call, I'm sure he'll help."

As they said their goodbyes, and as Melissa coaxed Chi out of the nest that he'd created, Melissa promised that she would. Ladarat was halfway down the hall when she heard an urgent voice—or two—behind her.

"Khun Ladarat! Wait!"

It was Siwinee and Sudchada, hustling behind her as she headed for the front door. She slowed down, still towed along by Chi's enthusiasm. He'd gotten a whiff of the food stalls outside, and the smells of grilling meats had wound him up to a new and previously unprecedented level of excitement. Nevertheless, dogs and tile floors were a bad mix, and his frantically scrabbling feet were in an unwinnable battle against the combination of a leash and a smooth tile floor.

"Have you…" Sudchada looked over her shoulder. "Have you had a chance to talk to Dr. Taksin yet?"

"I have…begun to talk to him." That was a fair statement, wasn't it?

"You've *begun*?" Sudchada asked.

"And do you have any answers yet?" Siwinee asked.

"No…no answers yet. But Mrs. Double said that he came in late this morning. Is that…related?"

"Yes," Siwinee said.

"No," Sudchada said.

Well.

"It might be," Sudchada added. "Maybe. We think he has some sort of…activities at night that may impair his ability

to function. And sometimes—just sometimes, you understand?—he may arrive at work a little late."

She looked at Siwinee for confirmation, but the younger
nurse was looking over her shoulder in case Dr. Taksin was
lurking somewhere behind them.

"Well, I'll do what I can, that's all I can promise."

They said their goodbyes and Ladarat let herself be pulled
out the door by her hungry four-footed companion. She
looked at her watch: just a few minutes till one, when she was
supposed to pass Chi off to Sukanya near the man with the
fresh fruit cart. She'd take him past the food stalls, perhaps
stopping to visit Sonthi, the tiny man who made the best *kao
niew moo yang* in Chiang Mai. No doubt he and the other
vendors would take pity on Chi, who could play the poor
starving dog to perfection when it served his interests, which
was pretty much all of the time. He could muster a sorrowful
whimper that would melt the coldest heart.

And indeed that's exactly what he did. In the space of no
more than fifty meters, he'd amassed donations of two pork
dumplings, one piece of fried lamb that the stall owner said
was too small to sell, a half dozen cubes of fried eggplant, and
a generous portion of grilled chicken that Chi extracted from
its wooden skewer with the dexterity of a neurosurgeon. But
she got her *kao niew moo yang* and successfully handed Chi
off to Sukanya, who was both apologetic and grateful.

"How did you smuggle him into the hospital without his
vest?" Sukanya asked as she slipped his vest on. Chi seemed to
puff up with importance.

"Well, we found—Chi found, actually—the back door to
the morgue."

"Yes, it's strange," Sukanya admitted. "He has a very sensitive nose. Anything unusual or out of the ordinary just grabs

his attention. You know, there was a nurse on the trauma floor who lived with her parents, and her father owned a butcher shop. Just that was enough to make him crazy whenever he saw her."

Ladarat thought about Siwinee, and Chi's fascination with her. She'd have to remember to ask her whether perhaps her father was a butcher. Or a mortician.

"It's too bad," Ladarat said gently, "that we don't have any official funding for pet therapy. You have to do this...as a volunteer."

Sukanya shrugged, and a happy-sad smile flitted across her pretty face, the *yim yae-yae* smile that says, more or less: "Oh, it could be worse."

Thinking that things could almost always be worse, Ladarat watched Sukanya lead Chi away, trotting patiently at her side. Truth be told, Ladarat was sorry to see him go. She'd gotten used to his company.

Or not company, exactly. Chi really did his own thing, as they say. But now an afternoon of work loomed in front of her: stacks of charts to review, unless some emergency arose. But she couldn't count on an emergency today, so she'd spend that afternoon alone in her office with the nice view.

CHAPTER 8

THE WELL-KNOWN DANGERS OF LEECH NURSES

Well, not quite alone. Ladarat had been seated for only a few minutes before she was interrupted. She'd just sat down, in fact, in front of Sonthi's *kao niew moo yang* that she'd purchased just moments before. With his stand just at the edge of the crowd of vendors, and barely on the hospital campus, Sonthi's grilled pork nevertheless was the cause of lines of residents and nurses, and Ladarat was looking forward to enjoying the crispy, almost-burnt skin with liberal dollops of lemon and chili sauce.

The rumor was that even the dean of the school of medicine would send his secretary to pick up *kao niew moo yang*. Nothing more than richly spiced grilled pork and sticky rice, it was classic simple street food. But the dean would push the papers to the side of his desk and invite a couple of medical students in for lunch. He'd ply them with delicacies, but he'd enjoy the simplest dish himself.

And that's what Ladarat was unwrapping when there was an emphatic knock on her office door, which flew open without any assistance from the office's occupant.

Oh, dear. Only one visitor would barge in like that, the one visitor who had a talent for unerringly interrupting an otherwise perfectly good lunch.

"Have you eaten, Khun? Khun Sisithorn? What is wrong?"

Ladarat's assistant tumbled through the door and collapsed in the single rough wooden chair facing Ladarat's diminutive desk, breathing heavily. Tall and gangly, she had a tendency to slouch to the point that her big round glasses were in danger of slipping off her nose. But now she was bent almost double, her glasses in one hand as she brushed away tears with the other.

"It's Ukrit," she said between gulping sobs.

That would be Ukrit Wattana, Sisithorn's boyfriend. Ladarat remembered yesterday's hurried conversation and the word "marriage." Now perhaps he was her fiancé?

"Ukrit is...unwell?"

"Ukrit is...gone!" Sisithorn was sobbing uncontrollably now, and Ladarat could think of nothing more helpful than passing her assistant a handful of paper napkins that had been intended as the informal linens accompanying her decidedly informal lunch.

"Gone, Khun?"

Ladarat wasn't certain how a young physician could disappear. There were times, perhaps, when he was probably desirous of a little more peace and quiet than his rather opinionated girlfriend was willing to afford him. That was almost certainly true. Yet he'd always seemed to withstand her monologues with a stoic resilience. Until now.

"No, Khun." Sisithorn was shaking her head as she dabbed at her eyes.

"No?" Now Ladarat was confused.

"I mean to say, no, I haven't eaten."

Sisithorn's outlook seemed to have improved dramatically. The sight of an extra-large portion of *kao niew moo yang*, still steaming in its Styrofoam clamshell container, shut off her tear ducts most effectively. Sonthi had been especially generous, as he often was at the end of the lunchtime rush hour. Sisithorn brushed the backs of both her hands across her eyes, first the left and then the right, in something that could have been a thespian's overwrought dramatization of grief.

Ladarat deftly split the Styrofoam clamshell into its two symmetrical halves and divided the grilled pork between them. She fished a plastic fork from the bottom drawer of her desk, where it kept company with a sweater, an old white medical coat that lacked the "nurse ethicist" embroidery, a motley assortment of pens and pencils, and Chi's hedgehog-shaped dog toy that squeaked in protest whenever you picked it up. Ladarat divided the sticky rice, too, scooping it—still steaming—out of its plastic bag. She pushed the slightly larger of the two portions across the little desk toward her assistant and sat back to await developments. She didn't have to wait long.

"I just know that Ukrit met a leech nurse in Bangkok," Sisithorn said, forking up a generous bit of pork resting on a pillow of sticky rice.

"A leech nurse?" Ladarat was unfamiliar with that species of her profession, and she pondered its possible nature as she took a more modest bite of pork.

"Of course, Khun. The dangers of leech nurses are well known." Sisithorn took another bite. "Those nurses in Bangkok lie in wait for young, successful doctors and they attach themselves like tree leeches. You know tree leeches, Khun?"

Ladarat nodded. She had a passing familiarity with those most annoying of forests creatures from her childhood growing up in the rural areas of northwest Thailand.

"They sit there on tree leaves or sometimes tall grasses and ferns, waiting for unsuspecting hikers to brush up against them. And then—*thrrrrllllpppp!*—they sink their little teeth into you."

Truth be told, Ukrit Wattana would be a good catch for a nurse who was in search of such prey. Tall and gangly, with a posture that disconcertingly mirrored his girlfriend's, he put Ladarat in mind of a stork whenever she saw him. But he was a friendly, guileless, and docile stork who would earn a handsome income as soon as he finished his fellowship.

Sisithorn paused for breath. "I find tragedy whets the appetite. Don't you find that, Khun?" And she popped a morsel of pork the size of a small plum into her mouth, chewing with gusto.

"Mhhhh?"

"Excuse me?"

"This is Sonthi's, is it not?"

Ladarat admitted that it was. "But... Ukrit? Leeches?"

Aware that wasn't exactly a complete sentence, but unsure how her lunch had taken this strange turn, Ladarat was looking for answers; answers, preferably, that didn't involve leech nurses.

"Ukrit and I were in Bangkok together, of course."

"Of course..."

Sisithorn took another bite of pork and rice, thinking about what to say next. Ladarat tried to be helpful. "You were in Bangkok together, but... you left separately."

"Exactly so, Khun. You are very perceptive. Ukrit took the bus, and I took the plane, as you know. You see, I felt I could not in good conscience come to work in a fatigued state. You rely on me to be alert and perceptive, which one cannot do if one is shoehorned into an uncomfortable bus seat for twelve hours."

"Certainly not. But could Ukrit come to work in a state of less than perfect alertness? He is, after all, a pulmonary physician, caring for very sick—"

"But no, Khun. With all respect, he is still just a fellow. He is not...independent, so to speak. He has—how do you say it? A safety net? There are other, more senior physicians who protect the well-being of his patients. Whereas, although I am an assistant nurse ethicist, I like to think you rely on me for my independent judgment?"

"Of course, Khun. I rely on you implicitly."

Sisithorn beamed, grinning happily around a larger than normal piece of pork.

"Thank you, Khun. You are too kind. But as I was saying, Ukrit took the bus, mostly to save money. A young couple can't be too careful about money, can they? Anyway, Ukrit took the bus, but he seems to have disappeared."

"Disappeared?"

"Yes, Khun. He never showed up at work this morning. The technician in the pulmonary function testing laboratory called me to ask where he was. It seems that he got on the bus in Bangkok and—"

"But how could you see him get on the bus, if you took the plane?" Ladarat immediately regretted the direction this conversation was taking.

"Well, he told me that he was about to get on the bus..."

"And you heard the noise of the bus station in the background?"

"Well, he just sent me a text message..."

Ladarat's assistant was silent for a moment, even her *kao niew moo yang* temporarily forgotten.

"So do you think he perhaps didn't get on the bus at all?"

"That is one explanation, certainly. Perhaps he...missed his bus." Sisithorn frowned. Then she put her fork down pensively, leaving half her portion of Sonthi's finest grilled pork untouched.

"But if he simply missed his bus, why hasn't he replied to my texts? Certainly if he were stranded in Bangkok with nothing to do, he would be checking his text messages?"

There was a great deal that Ladarat didn't know about Bangkok, but she was reasonably certain that a young, reasonably attractive man stranded in Bangkok would have no trouble finding something—or someone—to occupy his time until the next evening bus left.

"Perhaps," she suggested gently, "you might try texting him again? Sometimes I miss one message. All the time, in fact. And it's not until the second message comes in that I see the first."

Ladarat felt she was on firmer ground now, and took a couple of bites of Sonthi's creation as Sisithorn processed this suggestion.

"But I have sent him several messages."

"Several, as in...?"

"Twenty."

Oh, dear.

"Then another message is unlikely to be revealing," Ladarat admitted.

"So what should I do?"

Ladarat thought about that question carefully, using the pause to sneak another bite of lunch, which had lost some of its flavor, thanks to Sisithorn's troubles. Truth be told, Ladarat had to admit that she would not be devastated if Ukrit had in fact taken up with a Bangkok leech nurse. She would feel bad for Sisithorn, of course. But that infidelity would mean that Ukrit would take a job in Bangkok, and that Sisithorn—the assistant whom she relied on implicitly—would stay here in Chiang Mai.

Naturally she wanted Sisithorn to be successful, but she

also appreciated her company, and, if she were being completely honest with herself, Ladarat had to admit that she also appreciated having an assistant. It was a small thing, but gratifying, in a small way. But that wasn't what Sisithorn needed to hear. No, as her mentor, Ladarat needed to be supportive.

"He will turn up soon," Ladarat said finally, with a little more conviction than she felt. "In Chiang Mai," she clarified. Sisithorn smiled bravely but looked unconvinced.

"Until he does, you should distract yourself with work. That is what you should do."

"With the ethics society presentation?"

"Exactly so. There is still much work to be done. And since you are the lead presenter, you must be familiar with all of the content."

"Me? I am the lead presenter?"

"But of course. You were there when the young American woke up, were you not? And you became a friend of the young American's wife?"

Sisithorn nodded.

"Well, then you should be the lead presenter. It is obvious."

Sisithorn's expression flowed from pensive to delighted in an instant, and she smiled the happy smile of a girl who has received exactly what she'd always wanted on her birthday.

And for the next half hour, as they both picked at their lunch until every scrap was gone, Sriphat Hospital's ethicist and assistant ethicist talked about the case of the American, who would be the subject of their presentation to the royal ethics society on Friday.

A young man from Albuquerque, very recently married, had been grievously injured by a disturbed elephant. His new wife, too, had been injured, although she was expected to recover. But the man's injuries were thought to be fatal. His family, though, didn't want to hear that. Perhaps they couldn't hear that. They insisted that everything be done to save him.

The result had been a standoff of sorts between the American's family and the Thai doctors taking care of him, a standoff that, fortunately, resolved when the American made a sudden and unexpected recovery.

It was that standoff that Ladarat had proposed presenting to the Ethics Society. How should Thai doctors and nurses handle such a case, when an American family demands much more aggressive treatment than we would give to a Thai patient? What are our obligations? What is proper, and what is fair? These were the questions that Ladarat and Sisithorn would be discussing to the best of their ability on Friday in Bangkok, before an audience of more than two hundred other doctors and nurses. *Eeehh.*

They reviewed their slides on Ladarat's computer, and Ladarat acceded to a flurry of changes that her newly confident assistant suggested. She thought of resisting many of them as either trivial or unnecessary, but the minor changes gave her assistant such pleasure, she couldn't bring herself to object. Finally, when Sisithorn had made notes of all the changes that were needed, Ladarat knew what she had to do.

"You should stay here, Khun, and work in my office. It will be quiet, and you won't be disturbed. You'll be able to make all of these changes in no time."

"But... where will you be, Khun? You will not need your office?"

Truth be told, Ladarat did very much need her office. She had several tall stacks of charts to review, as she had promised herself. But it was only right that she should give up this office to her assistant in her time of need. She, Ladarat, would find another task.

"There is … an errand I have to run. It won't take long, and you're welcome to use my office while I'm gone."

Ladarat thought of telling her assistant about the errand she had in mind. It would certainly be a distraction for her. But too much distraction wasn't a good thing. Besides, Ladarat wanted to keep this particular errand to herself until she knew more.

On her way out the door, though, Ladarat remembered something.

"Khun?"

Sisithorn was already hunched over Ladarat's computer, energetically clicking the mouse to advance through slides. She looked up.

"Yesterday, at the airport…"

"Yes, Khun?"

"The smuggling ring? Or the possible smuggling ring? What did you find when you followed the tourists?"

"Ah, Khun. I completely forgot." Just as she had apparently forgotten about her lost boyfriend. "That seems like such a long time ago. You see, I did follow someone. A young woman. I saw her passport. She was an Australian. She took a package from the Parrot Gang."

"So you followed her?"

"Yes, Khun. I followed her." And here Sisithorn's voice dropped to a whisper despite the fact that they were alone in Ladarat's office and the door was closed.

"And…?"

"And just as you said she would, Khun, she opened the package. She took one of those very slow escalators up to the second level and sat in a small coffee shop. I took a chair nearby, but behind her. And she unwrapped her package. And do you know what was in the package, Khun?"

Ladarat shook her head.

"It was jade. Jade bracelets. Perhaps ten of them. Wrapped carefully and wound around with twine."

"So perhaps you have discovered a smuggling ring," Ladarat said, impressed. Then she considered a little more. "But isn't it possible that this tourist simply bought them? Perhaps they are legal?"

"Perhaps," Sisithorn admitted. If it were drugs, of course it would be illegal. But jade, maybe or maybe not. "That would be a shame, though," she said after a thoughtful pause. "To discover a possible smuggling ring run by parrot people, only to find out that it was all legal...well, that would be a tragedy of the highest order. Perhaps..."

"Yes, Khun?"

"Perhaps you could ask your detective friend, Khun Wiriya? Perhaps he could shed some light on...the criminal possibilities?"

Ladarat agreed that she would and left her assistant tapping away at the computer, dreaming of foiling the infamous international Parrot Gang.

CHAPTER 9

FARANG DON'T KNOW HOW TO SMILE

The drive was not as long as Ladarat had expected, and it was still early afternoon—not much past three—when she pulled up in front of a pretty, well-maintained guesthouse at the end of a long, narrow gravel driveway.

The first thing she noticed about the Magic Grove Hotel was that it wasn't the usual Thai guesthouse, built quickly and grandly with the help of cheap materials and cheaper labor. Ladarat's cousin joked that any businessman could build a palace of a hotel for less than what a tiny house would cost in America. Yet the proprietor of this establishment seemed to have resisted that temptation.

The driveway of bright white gravel emerged from the trees and glowed in the late-afternoon sunlight as it circled in a broad loop around a neatly manicured lawn. Beyond it, a well-kept Lanna-style A-frame welcomed guests with a generous stone patio. Through the dense trees beyond, Ladarat could just make out the outlines of a handful of what seemed to be cottages, scattered behind the main building. This seemed to be a place that catered to those who liked their privacy. You could check in and then go to your private villa without seeing anyone, and of course without being seen.

There was no room to park, but neither were there any cars, so Ladarat wedged her car up against the shrubbery that lined the drive, ignoring its increasingly frantic warnings that there was an "obstacle to the left." There was hardly enough room for another car to squeeze by without trespassing on the manicured lawn in the center of the circle, but the likelihood of another car appearing seemed tolerably remote, so after a moment's consideration, Ladarat turned the key, forcing her car into reluctant silence.

The neatly raked gravel crunched pleasantly underfoot as Ladarat stepped out of the car, stretching a little after the drive and taking a moment to look around.

The first thing she noticed—couldn't help but notice, really—was how quiet this place was. Even the usual chirping of birds and humming of insects seemed distant, as if those sounds were filtering through the undergrowth from another hotel a kilometer away. There was the soft splash of a fountain coming from just to the left of the main house, but no sound of voices, or gardeners' tools, or anything else.

And there was, truly, no one around. The small lot was empty of cars, and indeed there seemed to be no signs of life at all. No one was waiting to take luggage or welcome guests, although, to be fair, neither were there any guests to welcome.

The gravel driveway had been freshly raked and the stone patio was newly swept of the *Pisonia* leaves—large, yellow-green leaves that carpeted the ground on either side— but there wasn't a gardener in sight. It was eerie.

Ladarat would have thought perhaps that she was in the wrong place entirely if it weren't for a small, hand-lettered sign just to the left of the main entrance: "Magic Grove Hotel" in English.

It was so quiet, in fact, that Ladarat paused before the enormous, heavy teak double doors that presumably led into the reception area. Surely they would be locked. Perhaps the hotel staff had simply packed up and left. It was as if she'd wandered into some hitherto undiscovered religious holiday that was only celebrated here, at this hotel.

She was surprised when one of the doors opened in response to her gentle push and seemed to swing open of its own accord. Like the grounds outside, this impassive door managed to be welcoming, too. The door swung shut behind her, closing with a confident thud that raised questions in Ladarat's mind about whether it would ever open again. Its closing seemed very... final.

Inside, a long, high-ceilinged room had the same air of uninhabited stillness. Not deserted, and certainly not neglected, it was as if everyone had simply stepped out just a few minutes earlier.

There was a little silver bell on the reception desk, and Ladarat had just picked it up when she had a thought. What would a detective do under these circumstance? A real detective?

Well, a real detective would...detect. She would look around. She would...snoop. Just a little. So Ladarat put the bell down as quietly as she could and resolved to snoop.

If she was discovered, she could simply claim to be looking for the hotel staff. But where should she snoop?

Behind her were the large double doors she'd come through. Ahead was an open area with small tables that seemed to be set for guests who hadn't yet shown up. Beyond that, there were sliding glass doors—now open—that led to a patio. And beyond that, two paths, left and right, seemed to wander off among the bungalows that were scattered throughout the property. The snooping opportunities outside seemed limited at best.

Back inside, to the right, a narrow corridor seemed designed for the housekeeping staff. Two carts loaded with cleaning supplies almost blocked the passage, which ended in a fire door. That didn't seem like a fruitful avenue for detection, either.

But to her left was the reception desk, and behind that a door to what could have been the manager's office. Or perhaps a closet, which would be less interesting, but Ladarat resolved to hope for the best.

Without thinking—because, when snooping, it was probably best to rely on one's intuition—Ladarat made her way around the reception desk. She paused once, just to make absolutely sure that she couldn't hear any sounds. She couldn't.

Ladarat tried the door handle, one of those European-style levers that looked a little like a stork's bill. The handle turned easily, and the door opened with a gentle tug to reveal a modestly cluttered office, not much bigger than the office she used to have at the hospital. A small window faced the rear patio, and the desk and a small wooden chair took up almost the entire space. On the desk were neat piles of unopened mail, receipts, and a diminutive bonsai pine tree.

Ladarat was thinking that such a small, graceful tree would make a welcome addition to her office when she noticed something else on the manager's desk, something more interesting than receipts or small trees.

Under the stack of letters was a weathered but neat cloth-bound book of the sort that scientists might use to record results of laboratory experiments. Perhaps it was for bookkeeping? But wouldn't a hotel use software? Even Wiriya, who was admittedly hardly a fan of technology, used a spreadsheet to keep track of his finances. He'd even offered to buy another copy of the software for her, so they could "coordinate." So romantic.

That book would not be for finances, then. That meant it must be for . . .

Ladarat nudged the letters aside, congratulating herself on her cleverness in keeping them in a neat pile. She opened the book and saw, as she'd hoped, a list of names and countries. Next to each name were a few words, or sometimes several sentences, in English, mostly. They all seemed to extoll the virtues of the Magic Grove Hotel, calling it "quiet" and "tranquil" and "peaceful."

Well, it certainly was that.

But this wasn't what she was looking for. The names and dates on the first page were from two years ago. Ladarat thumbed through the book, watching the months speed by more quickly than she'd expected. There weren't more than a page or two for every month, which meant that this place really was not so busy—as Ladarat had noticed.

It was less than a third of the way through the book that she reached a page that was full, and then another page that had only one entry. A name she didn't recognize, Demian Ober, from Berlin, had checked in the day before. Presumably Khun Demian was sleeping away the afternoon in his very private room.

Scrolling back up the list, and back to the previous page, Ladarat scanned the names and hometowns of the guests of this quiet place. Los Angeles, Amsterdam, Sidney, Chicago, another man from Berlin. It wasn't until she had flipped back and forth over the last three pages that she saw what she'd been looking for.

The handwriting was as small as the type in a newspaper or a book, each letter carefully penned. The ink, too, was different. It looked as though everyone else had used the same blue pen that presumably sat at the reception desk. But this name was lettered in black, from a very fine nib.

Ladarat had to bring her nose within a few centimeters of the page to read it, and as she did, she realized why this entry had caught the attention of her subconscious.

There, in tiny, neat lettering, was a name: Sharon McPhiller. And the hometown: San Francisco. She'd checked in, apparently about a week ago.

This woman had not been as effusive as many of the other guests had been. Whereas the cheerful Mr. Ober had proclaimed this place to be "an oasis of calm" with attentive staff, Khun Sharon had much less to say. Her only contribution was to declare the hotel "peaceful."

Not very creative, but accurate.

Ladarat heard a dull thud from out in the hallway, like the sound of luggage being set down or of a heavy book being placed on a table or...oh, dear. A door closing. The front door.

As quickly as she could, Ladarat closed the registration book, set it down on the desk, and turned toward the door.

Too late, she realized that she'd neglected to put the stack of letters on top of the register. She'd just left them on the side. But it was too late to fix now.

"So, Khun, you are the new receptionist? You are very welcome."

Ladarat heard the woman's voice as she was turning toward the door, and registered the gentle chiding in perfect Thai, with the wider, rounder accent that you'd hear from some people in the rural areas of Isaan.

So she was taken aback to realize that the woman in front of her, standing at the edge of the reception desk, was a *farang*.

She was perhaps in her forties, or a little older; it was difficult to tell with them. She had a plump face with features bunched close together in the center as if they were fleeing her ears. Her graying blond hair was tied back in a ponytail, and she was wearing a modest cotton dress with a high neck and a belt at the waist. Ladarat wondered how long she'd been standing there, and how much she'd seen.

But the woman's smile was welcoming, and she seemed to be waiting for Ladarat to answer her question.

"No, Khun, I'm not the receptionist. I..."

Ladarat thought about that for a moment. "I think I would make a poor receptionist," she said honestly.

"It's true," the woman said. "Not many of us have the patience to sit and wait behind a desk for events to unfold. And that is why"—she waved at the empty stool—"I find it impossible to keep good people."

The woman eyed Ladarat with a little more care.

"Are you...?" Her smile faded.

Ladarat found herself temporarily befuddled. What were the options? Was she...a potential guest? A potential employee? A thief?

In the space of a few silent seconds, as Ladarat wondered what this woman was thinking, and what she'd seen, she entertained a half dozen explanations—cover stories—for her appearance here and for her foray into the manager's office. Rejecting all of them as implausible, Ladarat decided to stick with the truth, or something similar.

"I'm sorry, Khun, I haven't introduced myself. My name is Ladarat Patalung and I am a nurse at Sriphat Hospital."

The woman smiled, just a little. But at least she nodded.

"And...well...I'm looking for someone."

"Someone who works here?"

"No, Khun. A guest. At least, I think she was a guest. She would have stayed here recently. Her name was Sharon McPhiller."

The woman's eyes betrayed no emotion or surprise at this rather bold admission that Ladarat was on a mission of detection. This nonchalance Ladarat found somewhat surprising. Surely that, plus the fact that Ladarat had been discovered while snooping would raise suspicions. But the woman didn't seem to notice, and indeed became almost friendly.

"Ah, of course, you're looking for a friend. A friend, did you say?"

"No, not a friend exactly. Or not at all. In fact, I've never met her. But her family is searching for her. You see, it seems that she disappeared around the time that she was in Chiang Mai. She stayed here and then...she vanished. Since she was at our hospital, the authorities contacted us. And so I thought perhaps, well, that the manager here might remember her."

At this the woman seemed to recover her sense of etiquette.

"I'm so sorry, Khun, I've forgotten my manners. I just realized that I haven't introduced myself, which is also impolite."

"Also" presumably referred to Ladarat's unauthorized exploration of the hotel's office.

"I am Delia Martin." She paused, looking around as if noticing the empty hall for the first time. "And I am the owner here."

She turned back to Ladarat.

"You speak excellent Thai, Khun."

Delia smiled modestly. "Well, I should. I've lived in Thailand for more than twenty years. I came here as a teacher, was married for a while, and then...well...I stayed. In such a beautiful country, how could I not?" She paused.

"But your friend," she continued. "She was here, I think. Recently. Then she left in a hurry."

"And you don't know where she went?"

"No, I'm sorry. She wasn't here for more than a day or two, and then...I think she may have gone to Myanmar." She smiled a smile that was impossible to interpret.

One couldn't interpret the smiles of *farang*. Thai smiles are Thai smiles. They follow a clear and almost rigid taxonomy. But *farang* didn't get them right half the time. *Farang* don't know how to smile.

Ladarat needed to take a new approach, and soon.

"This place, Khun, it's very...peaceful."

This seemed to break the tension, and the woman, Delia, smiled a genuine smile, devoid of any other meaning.

"Yes, Khun, I suppose it is. We have only one guest right now, and I've given most of the staff the week off. It can't be other than peaceful, it's so empty."

Here Ladarat smiled, too, even more broadly as Delia took a couple of steps back, allowing Ladarat to emerge from the little office where, truth be told, she'd been getting a little claustrophobic. She took a deep breath.

"But besides that, I mean. It's not just quiet, but also peaceful, if that makes any sense. It seems like..."

"Yes?"

"Well, it seems like the sort of place that's peaceful even when it's full."

Delia smiled again. "Well, if that ever happens, we'll see. But I've owned it for eight years now, and it's never been full. Especially lately, as everyone seem to be building hotels in the Old City and down by the river. Tourists don't want to come out here for peace and quiet—they want to see the sights."

"Or perhaps they would appreciate this environment if they could see it, but..."

"But they never get here. Exactly so. Still, there is a community of travelers of a certain age who value quiet and privacy. Some writers, academics, and a few celebrities who don't want to be seen." Delia smiled. "I shouldn't complain. I only wanted this hotel to make enough money to live on, so I could stay in Thailand, and it certainly does that. The hotel, and the teak we sell."

"Teak?"

"Oh, we have a small teak grove, about two hundred trees. That's where the hotel's name comes from. We grow the teak and harvest it, and the proceeds keep the hotel running. It's magic. Or close, anyway. And...many guests plant a sapling or two when they're here." She paused. "Would you like to see it?"

Would she? Not really. Yet the woman's enthusiasm was infectious. It would be rude not to.

"I'd like that, Khun."

Delia smiled and led the way out through the sliding doors and then to the right. They walked in silence, passing several low-slung bungalows, each with a front patio curtained by foliage. Ladarat found her normally quick pace slowing as they walked single file with Delia in the lead. The path of stones laid out with modest gaps between them seemed to be forcing their steps into a contemplative rhythm, and Ladarat wondered if Delia had designed this path knowing that it would impose the sort of mindfulness that was difficult to achieve in the real world.

A few moments later they emerged at a clearing from which

perhaps a dozen mature trees had recently been removed. Very recently. There were sawdust and woodchips littering the ground, and the smell of fresh, green wood. The tracks of a large truck snaked off to the left where they merged with two ruts that led back toward the road.

Delia was smiling happily as she ambled along the line of stumps. Now that they were in the midst of the trees, Ladarat could see that they were planted in circles, small circles maybe ten meters in diameter. Half of this circle and the next one over had been cut, leaving stumps alternating with mature trees.

"You can see the grove extends almost all the way to the top of that hill. It gets bigger every year, since we plant far more trees than we cut down. The trees that are removed make way for the saplings. In another twenty years, this whole hillside as far as the road will be one large teak grove, the way it used to be a hundred years ago. As I said, many of our guests plant trees." She paused, glancing back at Ladarat. "Perhaps your friend planted one when she stayed with us."

Perhaps she did. When Ladarat was silent, Delia turned and kept walking, following the tire tracks toward the crude road, then taking a path to the right that led them through dense undergrowth and out to the circular drive where Ladarat had left her car.

"Well, I hope you are successful in finding your friend."

"Thank you, Khun. Perhaps I will be. But…perhaps she doesn't want to be found."

Ladarat glanced at Delia, but the woman's expression didn't change. She just nodded.

"Indeed, perhaps not. But perhaps she will want to be found at some point in the future, if not now."

Of course that was true, but it seemed an odd thing to say. Ladarat just nodded as she opened her car door.

"And Khun?" the woman asked.

"Yes?"

"If you know of someone who might be willing to work as a receptionist in such a quiet place, perhaps you could let me know?"

In that moment, Ladarat had a very, very smart idea.

Driving slowly around the circular driveway, Ladarat thought about her very, very smart idea. She would use the drive home to plan. But she began to doubt the brilliance of her plan almost immediately, when she glanced at the rearview mirror and saw the woman, Delia, standing where she'd left her. The owner of the Magic Grove Hotel was watching Ladarat's car, as if making sure she was gone.

That stare unnerved her enough that as she turned onto the main road, she found that all she could think of was lunch. Or a snack. But a hearty snack, as a symbol and something of a reward for her detection work.

And she did deserve a reward, did she not? Because she had, in fact, performed a feat of detection.

Not a large feat, granted, but large enough. There was something just a little suspicious about Delia Martin's response.

But what was it? What was making Ladarat uneasy? That was the question. And that was a perfect question to ponder over *yam plah duk foo*—fried catfish, but not just plain fried fish like the fried catfish they have in the U.S. or England. No, *yam plah duk foo* was a delicacy of small, bite-size pieces, coated in chili and seasoning, and mixed in a sort of warm salad with mango, lime, cilantro, and peanut sauce. So tasty, and perfect for the lunch Ladarat had in mind.

CHAPTER 10

THE PLEASURES OF A SOLITARY MEAL

Ladarat thought she knew what she was looking for. She remembered a diminutive blue sign on the right side of the road—now on her left, since she was traveling in the other direction—for a small roadside restaurant, really not much more than a food stand with outdoor tables. But on her way to the Magic Grove Hotel, midmorning, there had already been a half dozen cars in a gravel parking lot just off the road. That was a good sign. Now where was it? Surely she should have passed it by now.

To either side of the road was just an impenetrable wall of forest, and above her head, a wide arch of branches and leaves gave the impression of driving down a long, narrow, deep-green tunnel, a tunnel that seemed as though it would never end, or at least that it would never lead her to a well-deserved lunch of *yam plah duk foo.*

Driving more slowly, and vaguely aware of a growing line of cars behind her, Ladarat scanned the left side of the road, waiting for that restaurant to appear. One car passed her, then another. Then a large truck loaded with teak logs rumbled past.

That truck hid the right side of the road for so long that she barely saw the restaurant in time. It was on the right, and marked by a red sign. Funny how your memory can trick your brain so effectively and so thoroughly. Musing about the tricks of the brain, and the exacerbating effects of hunger, Ladarat swerved to the right, her mind on *yam plah duk foo* rather than on the traffic.

The deafening blare of a truck's air horn rattled her little car and startled Ladarat rudely as she saw, coming up behind her, another enormous teak truck that had been passing her. Just centimeters away from her rear bumper, it seemed, all Ladarat saw in her rearview mirror was the shiny metal of a truck's grill that looked like the mouth of a metallic predator, about to swallow her little car.

"Warning, obstacle behind!" her little car warned, in the same unvaried half shriek, half whine. You'd think that a near collision with a truck the size of the reclining Buddha statue in Bangkok would warrant a little more energy or at least a somewhat greater sense of urgency. Surely a beast of a truck deserved a little more attention than that flock of giggling nursing students did.

A moment later, Ladarat had made it safely to the right side of the road, skidding to a stop at the far edge of the restaurant's little parking lot. Ladarat noticed that her hands were shaking on the car's steering wheel. And her heartbeat— surely that wasn't normal? Was she going to have a heart attack before she got to enjoy *yam plah duk foo*? That would be a tragedy indeed.

She took a deep breath. Then another. And another.

Ladarat rolled both front windows down all the way, then switched off the ignition with trembling fingers. Cool scented air wafted in, ruffling a few papers in the footwell on the passenger's side and slowly washing away the anxiety she'd felt just a moment ago. The cool forest air had the musty brown scent of compost and decay. It smelled . . . old, but fresh at the same time.

And it was quiet. Except for the intermittent roar of passing cars—and those rumbling teak trucks—the stillness was almost perfect. Just a steady and almost imperceptible drone of millions of insects, all talking abut whatever it is that insects talk about when they're not biting you or stinging you or otherwise molesting you.

There were perhaps other roadside restaurants that Ladarat could have stopped at. But if she were being completely honest, she would have to admit that this particular establishment had a feature that made it perfect. It wasn't the welcoming sign or the open tables. It wasn't even the increasingly crowded parking lot—in the time that she'd been sitting here admiring the silence, two more cars had coasted to a stop.

No, it was the presence, at the front of the building, of an informal take-out window. That's why she had risked life and limb to stop here.

Ladarat thought of herself as being generally psychologically healthy and well adjusted. But there was one thing she just couldn't do, and that was eat a meal alone, in public. She just couldn't sit down at a restaurant by herself.

The few times she'd forced herself to try—on a trip to a meeting, for instance—she'd felt as if every pair of eyes in the entire restaurant was on her, watching her, wondering why she was eating all alone.

She could hear their conversations, she was certain. *So sad. The poor middle-aged woman with no friends to eat with her. And of course no romantic interests. Certainly not, at her age. Such a pity.*

No, that would not be for her. She would pick up her *yam plah duk foo* and take it over to that rickety bench under that tree. She would enjoy her lunch in peace, away from the pitying eyes of people who didn't understand the pleasures of a solitary meal.

That's exactly what she did. Ten minutes later—the manager

was apologetic that their kitchen was short-staffed—Ladarat found herself sitting on that very bench. In the cool shade, she listened to the hum of the forest around her and she took a first bite of fried catfish, crispy on the outside and flaky and white on the inside.

Odd that this was exactly what she'd anticipated it would be. The fish was as crispy as she'd imagined, and the chili sauce was just spicy enough, with a hint of sour lime. Everything was in its place, just as it had been in her imagination.

How often did that happen, really? How often did expectations and reality overlap so neatly? Almost never, in Ladarat's experience. Some things were better than you imagined them, and others were worse, but always things were different. Yet today, right now, in this moment, the *yam plah duk foo*, the bench, the shade... were all what she'd hoped for. It was truly a moment to savor.

Which she did, for about fifteen seconds, until her phone chirped, adding its voice to those of the millions of insects all around her in the forest.

Under normal circumstances, this persistent chirping of her phone would have posed a conundrum: to answer or continue enjoying lunch? A moral conundrum.

A moment's reflection determined that she couldn't in good conscience think of a virtuous reason to ignore what was almost certainly a work-related call. It would be one thing if she were, in fact, working while she ate, back at her desk at Sriphat Hospital. But she was not. She was enjoying a peaceful, solitary lunch of some of the best *yam plah duk foo* she'd ever had. So although it might have been justifiable to escape one duty for another, it was not acceptable to privilege *yam plah duk foo* over work, particularly if that work involved a patient-related matter.

Regretfully, after a last quick bite of fish, Ladarat closed the

Styrofoam container and set it on the bench next to her, fishing her phone out of her handbag and checking the caller ID.

Well, perhaps she should have privileged the *yam plah duk foo*. But she would be virtuous. The *yam plah duk foo* would wait, for a moment.

"Khun? We have found him. That is to say, I have found him!"

Her mind still caught up with the ethics of *yam plah duk foo*, Ladarat was perhaps a little slower than she normally would have been in catching up with her assistant ethicist's train of thought

"That is good," she said slowly. Then, because more enthusiasm seemed to be called for: "Very good."

But who, exactly, had been found? Surely that mattered. And did whomever it was want to be found?

"When I saw Ukrit lying there on a bench, asleep, I was so relieved. You see, Khun, he simply fell asleep. He is still asleep now, the lazy man. Can you believe it?"

Actually, Ladarat couldn't believe it. Falling asleep on a bench in the Chiang Mai bus station? That didn't sound like Ukrit. He was hardworking and ambitious. To miss a day of work even for illness would have been unheard of. And to simply take a nap?

But he had been under a lot of stress lately, what with deciding about a future job, and, charitably, she could imagine that having her assistant as a girlfriend might be somewhat... fatiguing. Perhaps he was simply getting some rest while he could.

"And Khun? I have made another... discovery!"

Ladarat wasn't entirely sure that encountering your boyfriend asleep on a bench was enough of an event to qualify as discovery number one. But granting that, for the moment, Ladarat also wasn't at all sure she was ready for discovery number two to be revealed. Yet in all likelihood she had no choice in the matter.

"I've found another parrot smuggler!"

Ladarat's previous conversation with her assistant about smuggling did not make an immediate appearance in her confused mind. This left her, for a moment or two, contemplating the concept of a branch of organized crime that was devoted to to the illegal transportation and sale of colorful talking birds. That concept puzzled her extremely, until she remembered.

"The parrot people? From the airport?"

"Exactly so. These are not the same people, though, you understand? This is a parrot woman. A woman, not a man. But she is carrying the same parrot bag. Exactly the same, do you see? As a sort of sign. A code. And just like the smuggler at Suvarnabhumi Airport, she is handing packages wrapped in newspaper to travelers getting on buses."

Nonplussed, Ladarat searched for some expression of enthusiasm that this pronouncement seemed to call for.

"That seems...suspicious," was all she could think of to say.

"Suspicious, Khun? Of course it's suspicious! We should arrest them right now, before they escape."

"We should...arrest them?"

"Of course, Khun. It is our duty."

The duty to arrest people for passing out packages from a parrot bag seemed to stretch the core responsibilities of a nurse rather liberally. Ladarat knew the wisdom of professor Julia Dalrymple by heart, and she was certain that if nurses had any obligation whatsoever to break up a possible smuggling ring, the good professor would have made a note of it. But she had not.

"Khun? One cannot arrest these people for handing out packages. Even if those packages contain illegal jade. And besides, you personally cannot arrest anyone," Ladarat reminded her assistant. "You are a nurse."

"I am a nurse ethicist, Khun. Surely my responsibilities are broader than just nursing?"

Perhaps that was true. But however broad those responsibilities might be, Ladarat doubted that they extended to the Chiang Mai bus station and to a group of what were probably enterprising hucksters, no more.

"I will...talk to my friend Khun Wiriya. Perhaps he can suggest something. But your primary responsibility is to Khun Ukrit, is it not? Make sure he is well. I'm worried that he is sleeping during the day like this. That isn't normal. Take him home if he needs it."

"Oh, he's waking up now. I must go.

And before Ladarat could muster a murmur of something that would express the sort of relief that seemed to be called for, her assistant had ended the call.

Well, that certainly added to the parrot mystery. Should she call Wiriya? Perhaps. But did the urgency of a possible smuggling ring outweigh the not insubstantial risks of cold *yam plah duk foo*? They did not. And besides, she'd see Wiriya tonight.

Her conscience clear, at least for the time being, Ladarat opened the Styrofoam clamshell, pleased to note that the bottom of the container was still pleasantly warm. She had narrowly avoided the culinary tragedy of cold *yam plah duk foo*, which seemed not to have declined one bit in quality. It was so nice to have food that would wait patiently for you. Not all food had that valuable attribute, and Thai food is noticeably impatient, expecting people to be ready when it was.

Ladarat leaned back on her bench, picking at bits of fish, wondering what thoughts would come to keep her company.

She knew, from long experience, that this was one of the chief advantages of a solitary meal. As if they could sense when they weren't wanted, thoughts seemed to stay away from crowds. The worst place to find a thought was at a loud meal-time conversation.

But for solitary diners, there was no place that a good thought would rather be. Good thoughts seemed to seek out those situations in which a potential thinker was alone with her *yam plah duk foo*. A thought—sometimes a most excellent one—would arrive and perch on a diner's shoulder.

Sure enough, it took only the time required to eat one and a half pieces of still-steaming catfish before Ladarat realized that a thought had in fact joined her.

Two thoughts, actually, which seemed to be circling each other nervously, as thoughts often do until they come to an agreement or compromise.

One thought was about the Magic Grove Hotel and how it was the perfect place for something...nefarious to be happening. There weren't many staff around, for instance, and it was well off the trail of most tourists. It was amazing that anyone found their way there at all. If one were of a nefarious disposition, it would be the perfect place to commit a crime. That was one thought.

The other thought wasn't at all sympathetic to that view. This other thought pointed out that there was no evidence whatsoever of anything nefarious going on. Nothing more that a few people who had disappeared, one of whom had visited that guesthouse. You might as well say, this thought pointed out, that the Chiang Mai airport was nefarious, because most of those missing travelers had no doubt passed through it before vanishing.

Ladarat had to admit that both of those thoughts had a

point. It was a perfect place for a crime. But there was no evidence that any crime had been committed.

Ladarat resolved to let those two thoughts argue back and forth. She hoped they would find a resolution soon, because they were making her indescribably dizzy.

So. Although the *yam plah duk foo* was gone, Ladarat wasn't in a hurry, and she decided to wait for a moment or two to see whether another thought might make an appearance.

And one did. This one was of a more promising nature. A productive thought, or at least a pragmatic one. Into that melee of thoughts about disappearing travelers stepped a thought about the sad figure of Dr. Taksin.

She needed to talk with him. That was all. She needed to talk with him to get a sense of whether there might be personal problems or troubles that would interfere with his work. She just needed a reason for a conversation...

And as she knew it would, that reason presented itself. She would ask him to review with her the deaths that had taken place in his unit.

Who better to help her understand whether those deaths were "good deaths"? Indeed, to make that assessment without seeking his counsel would seem strange, would it not? It would. So that's what she would tell him.

They would sit down in his office, perhaps over tea. They would sit, and they would discuss cases. And she would form her own opinions about whether he was impaired.

Ladarat looked around her, noticing that the parking lot was now full of people here for lunch. You should try the *yam plah duk foo*, she wanted to tell them. Ask for extra chili sauce. And whatever you do, be sure to eat lunch by yourself, at least if you want to be able to think.

CHAPTER 11

SLEEPING IS AN INVITATION TO THIEVES

Back at Sriphat Hospital, of course there were few parking spaces available—it was in the middle of the day, after all. But Ladarat would not let that bother her. She'd had a most productive morning and could easily afford to spend a few extra minutes walking from the edge of the lot. She was so complacent, in fact, that she didn't even bother looking for those nearer spots that she knew must exist. Instead, she just drove to the very edge where there was an entire row free. She parked right in the middle.

That sense of calm lasted only for another nine minutes, until she stepped out of the elevator and walked down the hallway to find the door of her office open.

Wide open. That was strange, because Ladarat was certain she hadn't left her door in that state. Nor had she left it inhabited by her assistant and Ukrit, who seemed to have taken up residence.

The two of them seemed to be engaged in some sort of argument, although it was clear that poor Ukrit was getting the worst side of it. He had the hangdog, droopy look of a child getting scolded, which, come to think of it, was a pretty accurate description of what was going on. Ukrit was perched on the single chair in front of Ladarat's desk, and her assistant was standing over him as a schoolteacher might over a wayward student. It was Sisithorn who noticed Ladarat first, and she was the first to offer a *wai* of apology.

115

"Khun Ladarat—we're sorry to take over your office like this. But it was an emergency. A true emergency." The poor woman was breathless, but whether because of concern for this "emergency" or because she had been berating her boyfriend without pausing for breath, it was impossible to tell.

"I'd given Ukrit a ride from the bus station, as I told you, and we were going to ICU rounds, when Ukrit said he felt unsteady on his feet."

Ukrit offered a clumsy *wai* and managed to look sheepish at the same time.

"So since we were in this hallway, and your office was handy, we decided..."

"Naturally. Of course that was the right decision, Khun. You should of course feel free to use this office when an emergency of that magnitude occurs."

Hopefully such emergencies will be few and far between, lest she find her assistant getting used to having this office for her own.

It was odd, though, that the conversation Ladarat interrupted a few moments ago didn't seem to be one of a concerned girlfriend asking after her boyfriend's well-being.

"So we came in and Ukrit sat down and I called Dr. Jainukul." Suphit Jainukul was the director of the ICU, and Ukrit's supervisor, a cheerfully rotund doctor who waddled when he walked, but whose easygoing manner belied an intense devotion to his patients.

"That's when Ukrit told me he lost all his money on the bus!"

"He lost...?"

"He was robbed, Khun, do you see? He fell asleep and was robbed. That's why I was telling him that to fall asleep is an invitation to thieves. It's like leaving money on the ground, I told him. It gives thieves an opportunity they can't resist, so it's ethically wrong." She paused to catch her breath. "Don't you agree, Khun?"

"It's morally wrong to...fall asleep?" Ladarat glanced at Ukrit, who shrugged.

That seemed rather harsh. Perhaps this was yet another problem to ponder over a solitary meal sometime.

Ukrit at least knew better than to argue a point of moral philosophy with his girlfriend.

"Of course you're right, dear. You are an ethicist—you know about those things. Although it's strange, I've never done that before. I usually find it very difficult to sleep on buses and planes. But last night I had no trouble. And I suppose that was the invitation that a thief was looking for."

His apology was interrupted by the arrival of Dr. Jainukul. Comfortably dressed in a rumpled shirt and baggy white coat, he offered them all a series of informal *wais* as he entered Ladarat's now quite crowded little office. Smiling, he greeted the young couple and Ladarat, but he turned quickly to Ukrit.

"A few silly questions, you know the routine. What's your name? Where are we now? What day is it? What year is it?"

During this exchange, Dr. Jainukul's eyebrows edged closer together. Ukrit got his name right, and he knew that he was in Sriphat Hospital. But he missed the day by one and the year by two.

After a cursory exam, tapping for reflexes and asking Ukrit to follow his finger with his eyes, Dr. Jainukul perched on the edge of Ladarat's desk. He looked down thoughtfully at Ukrit, who seemed to be waking up gradually.

"Is it possible—just possible, you understand—that someone may have given you a drug...surreptitiously?"

Ukrit shook his head emphatically. "No, Khun, that would have been impossible. I ate at a market stall with a friend in Bangkok, then went to the bus station. No one gave me anything."

Dr. Jainukul didn't seem convinced. "Well, it used to happen all the time on the train. We'd go down to Bangkok for the weekend, you know? As residents? This was a long time ago, although"—he winked at Ladarat—"not so very long ago. Anyway, we'd take the bus down Friday night and spend all day Saturday and Sunday, then take the bus back Sunday night. And on the bus, well..."

The good Dr. Jainukul smiled in fond reminiscence. "You'd meet a girl, have a few drinks and then... you'd wake up with no money." But he was still smiling.

Somewhere in the middle of this story, like a storm front moving across Chiang Mai, Sisithorn's face had grown blank, then troubled, then cloudy and threatening.

"A girl, Dr. Jainukul?"

Even in his feeble state, Ukrit sensed that he needed to be very, very careful.

"But there was no girl, I swear it! None! No one."

"Ah," Dr. Jainukul said. "But perhaps you don't remember. Some of these drugs have an anterograde amnesic effect, as you know. You forget what happens. The last thing I remembered was..."

"Getting on the bus," Ukrit said sadly.

"Exactly so. So who knows what happened?" Dr. Jainukul asked him cheerfully. "Perhaps you met the love of your life,"—he laughed—"who robbed you blind and left you. Still, a small price to pay for true happiness, don't you think? Even for a few hours?"

Dr. Jainukul seemed blissfully ignorant of the domestic conflagration that his witty recollections were causing. But fortunately he was also quite busy, and soon he was gone, promising to check on Ukrit that evening, and advising him to take the rest of the day off.

"And no more liaisons on buses!"

118

Soon Sisithorn and Ukrit were gone, too, and Sisithorn offered to drive him home—somewhat reluctantly, it seemed.

Finally, Ladarat had her office to herself. The day was almost over, but it wasn't too late to get some work done. She pushed aside all thoughts of drugging and mysterious disappearances, and sleepy doctors, and pulled a pile of charts closer to her.

She thumbed through the first few charts, setting them aside. Ladarat was looking for charts from the palliative care unit. She'd look at a couple of them, just enough to have something to talk about with Dr. Taksin.

And yet, something was wrong. Ladarat put another pile of charts on top of the first. And then another. And another. That was about twenty-five charts in all, including those she'd already reviewed, about half of her little library of charts, which made a stack about thirty centimeters tall. Only then did she find a chart from a patient who died in the palliative care unit. Just one.

Curious, Ladarat leafed through the other charts on her desk and came up with only two more. So that was only three patients who died in the palliative care unit, compared with almost fifty who died elsewhere in the hospital.

Wasn't that strange? Why weren't more patients dying in the palliative care unit? Hadn't it been almost full the last time she'd visited Mrs. Double?

Not everyone on that unit would have died there, of course. Some were still receiving treatment, and many would have been discharged. But to have almost no one die there... well...that seemed statistically unlikely.

Still, at least now Ladarat had her patients for a conversation with Dr. Taksin. That's what she needed. After reading through the charts and making a few notes, she'd done everything that she could do that day.

Besides, her evening was just beginning. She had an essential errand to run, and then a cooking class that, hopefully, would not be as bad as the first. She would cook...something, and it would be edible. That was her goal. A modest goal, perhaps, but it was best to begin with goals for which one could be reasonably certain of success. And why shouldn't she be successful?

Parking spots were easy to find in this area. That fact alone should be a warning to the unwary. This was a not-so-good part of town and, admittedly, not the sort of neighborhood where the nurse ethicist at the best hospital in northern Thailand would want to be seen.

It was safe enough, of course. This was Chiang Mai, after all, not the South Side of Chicago, or even Bangkok, where people with billions lived next to people with nothing, which was a recipe for crime.

No, this was safe, Ladarat knew, but it felt creepy to her to be walking down this street alone. Alone, but for the presence of a few dozen men wandering in packs, because this was Chiang Mai's small sex district.

It was nothing like Patpong in Bangkok. All of the sex workers in Chiang Mai could fit in a tiny sliver of Patpong. Still, it seemed like every *farang* man in Chiang Mai had migrated here tonight, even though it was a slow Tuesday. Most were Americans and Australians, although she heard snatches of German or maybe Dutch, and what sounded like Spanish, and maybe Russian.

And of course Chinese. A couple of crowds of Chinese businessmen huddled together and leaned on each other for structural support. The night was young, but they'd obviously been hard at work drinking for quite some time. She gave them a wide berth.

But her favorite fruit seller was an oasis of calm, Thai normalcy.

"*Sawat dee krup, ajarn.*" He often addressed her with the honorific *ajarn* reserved for teachers, and Ladarat had never bothered to correct him.

"You are enjoying your new car? I told you—very reliable, very safe!"

"Ah, yes, Khun. It is a very...satisfactory car." That was the best that one could say about that car. But the fruit seller nodded enthusiastically.

A few minutes later, Ladarat hefted the bananas in the plastic bag he'd given her. ("Free! No charge! Special for you!") Then she made her way down the small *soi*, toward the Tea House.

Halfway down, the businesses seem to lose their focus. There was an electronic repair shop, a small crockery store, and a kitchen supply warehouse. Beyond that was another plain storefront that announced itself simply as "The Tea House." That business had the same stylized woman's figure in the lower right-hand corner of the door, but that little sign was the only indication of what went on inside. And that, Ladarat knew, was exactly the way that her cousin Siriwan Pookusuwan wanted it.

The Tea House belonged to her cousin, who, like Ladarat, had grown up in the northwestern part of Thailand near Mae Hong Son, up in the mountains near the border with Burma. They'd grown up together, played together, gone to school together. But eventually their paths diverged. Ladarat became a nurse and an ethicist. And her cousin became, well, you could most charitably say she became a businesswoman.

But at least her cousin was honest about what she did, and Ladarat should be, too. Truthfully, her cousin became a *mamasan*, the owner of one of the cleanest and most well respected brothels in Chiang Mai, and probably in all of

Thailand. She treated her girls like family, making sure that they saved most of what they earned. She kept them away from drugs and bad men, and was ruthless to any client who was less than a gentleman. In truth, she was probably more compassionate than many people Ladarat worked with every day.

She pushed through the double doors, and as her eyes adjusted to the dark, the contours of the large room emerged, stretching back into its dim corners. There were century-old teak floors and white plaster walls, with a large sunken table more than five meters long in the center. Wood carvings and silk tapestries lined the walls, and a Buddha to her right watched over the entrance.

That Buddha was the ubiquitous Thai *Hing Phra*. Many places of business had one inside, just as they had a *Saan Jao*, or spirit house, outside. It was a balance that Ladarat found comforting. Outside you'd pray for luck and good fortune or good crops—all materialist things. Inside you'd pray for harmony and enlightenment. She paused and knelt, depositing the bananas as an offering in hope of her own enlightenment regarding matters of detection.

As she rose, out of the darkness a man materialized in front of her. A blond *farang*, the biggest she had ever seen, he was easily two meters tall, with broad shoulders and a crew cut. He looked like the sort of man that a Thai director would look for if he wanted someone whose very appearance from a hundred meters away would say "Over here! Here is an American!"

The man smiled broadly. "Hello, so good to see you, Khun Ladarat." He offered a high *wai*, which she returned. "And how have you been?"

"Well, I thank you, Khun Jonah. And you? And Krista?"

"She's well, thank you. The first few months were a little rough—she had to take time off work."

Jonah's wife was a teacher at one of the schools for *farang* in town. She was pregnant—six months? Ladarat couldn't remember.

"When is she due?"

"In January." So in just a few weeks.

"Are you ready?"

Jonah shrugged. "I suppose. But nervous." He laughed. "Well, very nervous."

"I'm sure you'll be excellent parents."

"Thank you, Khun. Perhaps you're right, but I'm less nervous about being a parent than about being a son-in-law, if you follow me?"

Ladarat didn't.

"Krista's parents just came to stay with us," he explained. "We only have a small apartment and...well...there's not much room for extended family. Of course we appreciate the help, but..."

"And Krista's parents, have they ever been to Thailand?"

Jonah just shook his head.

"Have they ever been out of the United States?"

"No, I don't think they have. When Krista and I got married, we went back to Utah for the wedding because they didn't want to travel."

"So they are...learning a lot."

Jonah laughed. "Yes, I suppose you could say that. But as for shopping and dealing with the trash collection, and bribing the water delivery man to climb two flights of stairs, well, all of that is still up to us. And her father likes to be busy. Always doing things, building things, fixing and mending. I'm not sure what he's going to do with himself. That's why I'm here early; it's a way to get out of the apartment." He looked glum for a second, but only a second.

"Ah well," Jonah said, "I'm sure they'll learn to help. And it will be an adventure for them."

Ladarat agreed that was probably the truth.

"Please have a seat. I'll let Khun Siriwan know you're here. Would you like tea?"

"That would be wonderful."

Jonah nodded as he moved quickly toward the back door that led to the kitchen and offices.

Jonah had had a rough life. As a tourist just out of college, he'd gotten involved in a scam to run drugs out of Bangkok to Koh Samui to make enough money to travel on to India. But as many unsuspecting *farang* are, he'd been caught in Bangkok's airport and sentenced to prison for five years. He'd gotten hepatitis in his third year and been transferred to Sriphat Hospital, where she'd met him when his family had come over to try to get him released. She had translated for those meetings and, much to her surprise, their director had gotten involved and had intervened to get him released.

Eventually he'd found this job with a little help from Ladarat. He was sort of a bouncer and sort of a handyman. And he was so devoted to Krista and Siriwan that he was beyond the temptation of the beautiful young women all around him.

Ladarat followed the path Jonah had taken, into a very large, open room, with high-beamed ceilings from which lazy fans stirred the air. The floors were cool tile, still damp from a recent scrubbing. Small, intimate tables were scattered around the large table in the center, and comfortable rattan sofas ringed the edges of the room. There was a small bar in the back, but it seemed to have been added almost as an afterthought.

Indeed, Siriwan had told Ladarat once that the most popular drink among her "guests" was, as the establishment's name suggested, tea. Virtually all the men who came here found this place through word of mouth and referrals from friends. Siriwan kept her secrets well, even from her cousin. But she'd let it slip once that some of her best clients were high-ranking foreigners in the non-governmental organizations that worked in northern Thailand, Laos, and nearby Burma. And visiting professors at Chiang Mai University Medical School, she'd hinted.

One of the girls greeted Ladarat, seeming genuinely pleased to see her. A beautiful girl in her very early twenties, with a broad, round, open face of the Isaan farmland of eastern Thailand. Kittiya—Ya—brought a cool towel and a pot of tea, and Ladarat thanked her as she disappeared.

Months ago, Ya had asked Ladarat whether she might make a good nurse someday, and without really thinking, Ladarat had said yes. She'd even offered to write her a letter of recommendation.

Certainly that was the compassionate thing to do, and no doubt she'd earned much Buddhist merit from that offer. But she'd had cause to think about that offer many times since then.

Would Ya really be a good nurse? No doubt. But would she be able to endure nursing school? And the challenges of nursing work? Those were other questions entirely, and perhaps Ladarat didn't do well to encourage her. But only time would tell—that wouldn't be Ladarat's decision to make.

And didn't Professor Dalrymple say that the best attribute of a nurse—or a doctor—was an ability to discern a person's needs? Surely Ya had that ability to a degree that was far beyond any other aspiring nursing student.

"Ah, cousin." The woman who floated across the room surprised Ladarat every time she saw her. Below Siriwan's flowing Lanna dress, her feet seemed to glide across the floor without actually touching the tiles. Siriwan was taller than Ladarat by ten centimeters. She was taller than most Thai men, which perhaps explained why she'd never married. That and her vigorous independence.

Her cousin's long black hair, lightly streaked with gray, actually seemed to complement her complexion in a way that normal or mortal women could never manage. Even her face—long and angular, yet soft—succeeded in being graceful.

They exchanged greetings, *wais* and then hugs. In a fluid movement, Siriwan settled at the little table across from Ladarat, adding a splash of tea to Ladarat's cup before pouring her own.

Despite their differences—one was a respected nurse ethicist and the other was a brothel owner—they'd always been close. Perhaps that was because they had no other family to speak of. And neither had children. They were all of the family that each one had.

After exchanging pleasantries and news, Siriwan got to business quickly. It was early evening, and the Tea House was deserted, but it wouldn't be for long. Even on a quiet Tuesday evening there would be guests arriving shortly.

"So... you said you had a favor to ask?" Siriwan smiled and took a sip of tea. "I hope it's nothing like asking for help in finding a murderer. That was exciting, perhaps. But in my business, excitement is best avoided. So maybe something a little easier?"

"No excitement. And nothing to do with you at all. At least, not directly. You see, I need a spy."

"A... spy?"

Ladarat was about to explain, but she took a sip of tea instead, savoring the moment. It wasn't often that she was able to surprise her cousin. Given her line of work, Siriwan was an endless source of titillating gossip and intrigue: what this politician was doing, or how much that civil servant was being paid to look the other way. She had her ear to the ground of all of Chiang Mai's best gossip. It was novel to be able to offer something small and unexpected in her cousin's day.

"Well, not a spy, exactly. But an informer. You see, there have been disappearances that I have been asked to... investigate."

126

Was that a smile? Sometimes with Siriwan it was hard to tell. But...yes, almost certainly, a smile.

"No, seriously, cousin. It is a potential mystery. Maybe."

Even to Ladarat, that didn't sound very convincing.

And still Siriwan was smiling. *Yim yaw*, the teasing smile. The smile that was used, for instance, when that boy you were warned about turns out to be just as untrustworthy as gossip promised.

Ladarat explained about the missing *farang* and Wiriya's suspicions, and the possibility that the Magic Grove Hotel might be involved; also his realistic appraisal and his belief that, as with most unusual events, there was probably a logical explanation. His suspicions were most likely just that—suspicions.

"And yet," Ladarat said hurriedly, before Siriwan could interject a note of caution, "it is possible, is it not, that something...nefarious is going on?"

Siriwan was silent for a moment, taking a long sip of tea.

"Of course it's possible, cousin. Anything is possible. It wouldn't surprise me at all if these people were disappearing. Perhaps because they want to, or perhaps even if they don't. And the owner you're suspicious of...Delia?"

Ladarat nodded, trying not to show her disappointment.

"What is it exactly that you're suspicious about?"

What indeed? Nothing. And everything. "She just seemed like...she was hiding something." She paused, looking at her half-smiling cousin.

"You think this is a waste of time?" Ladarat, at least, was starting to become convinced that it was, so she was surprised by her cousin's answer.

"No, not really. Or maybe it is, but you never know. Who would have thought a nurse would catch a serial murderer?" She smiled. "Or that we'd even have a serial murderer in our midst.

It always seems to me that we don't pay nearly enough attention to things that are very unlikely. You never know, do you?"

Ladarat Patalung, the ethical nurse detective, was living proof of that. She nodded.

"But what sort of spying did you have in mind?" Siriwan continued. "You never told me."

"I thought perhaps Jonah might be persuaded to take a part-time job. Just for a week or so, during the day. He has a baby coming, and would probably appreciate some extra income, and..."

Siriwan smiled. "And it would get him out of their small apartment during the day. Very good. I'll make sure his responsibilities at night are minimal so he can get some sleep." She nodded. "Of course, I'll tell him it's fine with me. Shall I call this woman, Delia? I can give him an excellent reference."

A reference? Ladarat hadn't thought of that. Of course Delia would want a reference. She nodded. "Perhaps it would be best if you suggested this...arrangement. You could say that you heard from me that the Magic Grove Hotel was in need of a receptionist..."

Siriwan nodded quickly, but whether because this was a good idea or because she wanted to conclude this business before her first guests arrived, Ladarat wasn't sure.

Ladarat stood to leave, but Siriwan stopped her with a question.

"The woman who owns the Magic Grove Hotel—Delia. Is she married?"

Ladarat thought for a moment. She'd said something about a husband, hadn't she? That she'd been married once?

"I think not now, but perhaps in the past."

"So what happened to her husband?"

Ladarat stood very still, thinking.

"If you're suspicious of her, that might be a good place to start." She paused, smiling. "As you yourself know very well."

CHAPTER 12

ENTHUSIASM IS THE SECRET INGREDIENT

Ladarat looked down at the pieces of chicken on the plastic cutting board in front of her. She felt a sense of hopelessness mixed with a growing sense of inevitability that she would be most likely picking up her meals at a food stand for the rest of her life.

"Khun Duanphen?"

The streetside chef wiped her forehead daintily with the back of her wrist and took a customer's hundred-baht note as she turned around. She glanced at the culinary masterpiece that Ladarat was perpetrating. Then she took another, closer look.

"Ah, well, no matter. Once it cooks, you'll never know."

That wasn't exactly a ringing endorsement of Ladarat's culinary skills. But it was true. The cubes of chicken that were meant to become *gy path king*—chicken and ginger—could not even charitably be called "cubes." At best, they were amoeba-like blobs. At worst, they looked like a chicken had suddenly become fed up with its dreary chicken existence and simply exploded. That is to say, once again her chopping skills had proven to be laughable.

It was seven thirty, and Duanphen's dinnertime rush was subsiding. As agreed, Ladarat had shown up dutifully for her cooking lesson and Duanphen had started her chopping vegetables. That hadn't gone well. Now the chicken had met a similar fate.

Hopefully, Ladarat looked around for more items that she could chop into submission, but Duanphen seemed to feel that she'd done enough damage for one evening. Nevertheless, this had been Duanphen's idea, and she wasn't giving up.

"Your detective friend will never know." She winked at Ladarat. "And now..."

"We eat?"

Duanphen looked at her appraisingly, recalibrating her judgment of Ladarat's intelligence. Then she shook her head slowly, as one might in talking with someone of an inferior intellect or a three-year-old child.

"No, Khun Ladarat. Now we cook."

Ah, yes. Ladarat had perhaps forgotten a step in her haste to be done. But, in fairness, she was hungry. That fried catfish was a long, long time ago. And she'd done much to earn dinner. For instance, she'd arranged a temporary job for Jonah, and...well...wasn't that enough? It was.

"So...we cook?"

In the short pause, Duanphen seemed to be engaged in a further recalibration of Ladarat's potential culinary talents. In that moment, Ladarat felt her prospects drop from "poor" to "abysmal."

But Duanphen just nodded. She reached for a bottle next to the wok that hovered over the gas burner like some sort of ungainly spaceship.

"Sesame oil and vegetable oil mix. Special recipe. Sesame oil gives the flavor, but vegetable oil—much cheaper."

Duanphen flicked the gas on and squirted oil in curlicues around the wok's surface, starting at the edges, then working her way toward the center. She did it in a way that seemed fun, almost playful. Ladarat had noticed that before as she waited to pick up many dinners. Duanphen always did a little extra: an extra squirt of oil or a clever arrangement of green onions around the edges of a rice dish. Always creative and never the same.

"You must like to cook."

Duanphen gave her another tolerant look.

"I mean, you really … enjoy cooking. It's not just … doing a job. You love … the details. You put energy into it."

Duanphen looked at her with what could have been either amusement or utter confusion.

"Don't you?"

Then Duanphen smiled as she rotated the wok on its axis, sending a smooth flow of oil halfway up to the rim.

"You discovered my secret," she said.

"Your secret?"

"My secret ingredient."

"Which is … ?"

"It's enthusiasm. If you bring enthusiasm to cooking, you can't go wrong."

Ladarat wasn't so sure about that. She didn't think that enthusiasm would help her. And she could imagine ways in which enthusiasm might make her own lack of aptitude much, much more dangerous. Take a lack of skill, add a very sharp knife and an open flame … what could possibly go wrong?

"But enthusiasm without skill, that's…."

"Dangerous? Of course. In a doctor, probably. Or an airline pilot."

They both laughed.

"You're right, of course, Khun Ladarat. Too much enthusiasm and not enough skill is dangerous. That is true. But skill without enthusiasm won't produce results. You need both. And enthusiasm requires creativity. You can't have enthusiasm without creativity."

"You can't?" Ladarat hadn't thought about that, but she

liked the idea. It was a thought worthy of the wise Professor Dalrymple herself.

"Enthusiasm—true enthusiasm—comes from the highest emotions. Love, maybe. Or joy. And those emotions come from creating something new. That's the secret." Duanphen paused, glancing at Ladarat to see if she was paying attention. "You see, you can't have enthusiasm, real enthusiasm, if you're doing something the same way you've done it a thousand times before. It has to be unique. New. Different."

Was she really having a conversation about the secret of life with a food stall vendor? It would appear so. In that moment, Ladarat wondered how much wisdom there was lining the streets of Chiang Mai. Behind those piles of grilled pork and pots of steaming broth and piles of Thai basil, perhaps there was an entire encyclopedia of philosophies, waiting to be discovered. Who knew?

"But now, the chicken." Apparently the philosophy lesson was over and now Ladarat had to further insult the chicken that she'd already so successfully mangled.

Under Duanphan's watchful eye, Ladarat used the knife to scoop the mauled bird's remains into the sizzling oil. She stirred as directed, infrequently enough to see the chicken develop a thin golden crust. Like magic.

"Now the onions." Onions that Ladarat had chopped without mauling too badly. And then the trumpet mushrooms.

At this point, Duanphen reached under the rolling table—just a cabinet on baby carriage wheels—for two bottles, each with a mysterious dark liquid. Each had a label: "Golden Boy Sauce" and "Golden Mountain Seasoning Sauce." Duanphen handed them to Ladarat.

"The other secret ingredient. You need enthusiasm, yes. But also sauce."

"How much?"

"Three shakes of the Golden Boy and five shakes of the Golden Mountain."

Ladarat gave a tentative flick of her wrist, sending a dollop into the middle of the oil, where it sizzled. Then another. Then a third.

"Remember...enthusiasm. You need enthusiasm, especially when you're using sauce you buy. It's someone else's recipe, so you need enthusiasm to make it your own."

Ladarat made a note of that wisdom. Then she exchanged Golden Boy for Golden Mountain and flicked with abandon. In the center of the wok. Then left. Then right. And top and bottom. She snuck a glance at Duanphen, who was smiling. Then she swirled them all together in what felt like a grand gesture.

Duanphen clapped and grinned. "You see? Enthusiasm! That's the secret. Keep stirring, but gently."

"But...isn't that...cheating?"

Duanphen looked at her curiously. "Cheating?"

Then: "Don't forget to stir."

Ladarat stirred.

"You're using someone else's sauce. Someone else's recipe. Isn't that cheating?"

Duanphen pondered that for a moment, then shrugged. "Maybe a little. But you do that, too."

"I do?"

"Well, doctors, and hospitals...when a doctor writes a prescription for a medication, he doesn't go out and make that medication, does he? He doesn't grind up roots or make antibiotics in a laboratory, right? He uses someone else's... sauce."

Ladarat agreed that was true. There would be far fewer people becoming doctors if they had to search the forest for roots to make their own medications. Perhaps they would leave that up to nurses. That would be a nice break from nursing, to have the chance to wander in the forest looking for ginger root or willow bark or . . . something.

Duanphen was looking at her expectantly.

"Stir."

Ladarat stirred.

"I see your point. Where would we be if doctors had to forage in the woods to make a drug to treat high blood pressure?"

"Exactly so. And using Golden Boy sauce is no different." Duanphen said triumphantly.

Ladarat couldn't help smiling. "You argue very well, Khun. Perhaps you should have been an ethicist."

"Ah, but I'm not smart enough to be an ethicist," Duanphen said, apparently overlooking Ladarat's recent lapses in culinary intelligence. "I'll leave that to you." She reached over the steaming wok and grabbed the rubber-handled spatula deftly with quick fingers, scooping up a Styrofoam clamshell container. "Now watch—this is the hardest part."

She tilted the wok and scooped a generous serving into the container, then the rest, creating a shapeless mound.

"I think even I could probably do that."

"Watch." Duanphen exchanged the spatula for a small set of tongs that she wielded with lightning efficiency to pick out bits of chicken, mushrooms, and green onion. A second later, she had sprinkled holy basil leaves, alfalfa, peanuts, and a last curlicue drizzle of Golden Boy sauce. The result looked like an entirely different meal.

"Beautiful."

Duanphen shrugged. "It's a little thing, the presentation. But it's important. Enthusiasm, you remember? These little touches show your customer that you're enthusiastic. They're evidence—proof—of your enthusiasm. So that raises their expectations. When they take that first bite…" Duanphen's eyes widened in mock surprise. "They know that they're about to enjoy something special."

Ladarat wanted to learn more about the philosophy of culinary presentation, but Duanphen shushed her.

"This is *gy path king*! Best very fresh, and very hot. You have to go now. Tell your friend to meet you. Five minutes—no more—you should be sitting down for dinner."

It was more like fifteen minutes, but part of that delay was Duanphen's insistence on including *som tam* salad and a generous serving of Prasert's *kanom maprao*. She'd called Wiriya before her culinary class began, so he was waiting on the patio when she arrived. He'd even set the table and opened a large bottle of Singha to share. If only he could cook, too, he would be the perfect boyfriend.

Ladarat served the *som tam* on to each of their plates, and was about to dole out portions of the *gy path king*, but Wiriya stopped her as she opened the container.

"You made this?" He looked closely at the pretty mound of chicken and mushrooms and garnish. "By yourself?"

"Well, yes and no. Yes, I made it. But perhaps I had a little help."

"But all homemade, yes? Very impressive." Wiriya nodded wisely, then stifled a yawn.

"A late night?"

Wiriya nodded and yawned again. "The retirement party last night, it was… late."

"How late?"

Wiriya shrugged. "Too late. I'm too old for these sorts of…"

"Escapades?"

"Exactly. I'm too old for them."

She gave him a generous portion and herself just a little. It wasn't that she didn't trust her cooking, of course. She just couldn't afford to be getting overweight.

"Oh, very good," Wiriya said, chewing slowly and seeming to wake up a little. "This is as good as anything Duanphen would make. She's taught you well." He took another bite. "To think that you can make these flavors. Just with ingredients in a market, with no special sauces or artificial flavors." He nodded again. "Amazing."

"And what's wrong with flavors from a bottle? Do doctors make their own medicine? No, they don't. They rely on a pharmacy. Using sauces is just the same. No different."

Wiriya stopped in mid-reach for another bite, and he put his fork down, suitably chastened.

"Well, of course, I didn't mean any offense against cooks. Or sauces. Or doctors, for that matter. I just thought... Well, never mind." He laughed and took another bite. "It just shows how little I know about these things. I'll stick to being a detective."

He chewed thoughtfully for a moment, then took a sip of Singha. Ladarat saw an excellent opportunity to find out whether her boyfriend had made as much progress in investigating missing persons as she had.

"Speaking of which, how is your... investigation of the disappearances progressing?"

Wiriya shook his head. "One of the 'disappeared' people showed up at his uncle's wedding yesterday, acting as if nothing had happened. And another woman who 'disappeared' more than a month ago seems to be alive and well and living in Phuket. With a man who is not her husband." He shrugged. "So I honestly don't think there really are any disappearances. It's just a bunch of people who haven't been found yet."

Ladarat told him about her visit and her tour, and her suspicions and her confirmation that Sharon McPhiller had indeed been a guest of the Magic Grove Hotel. Then she remembered her question of the previous night.

"I don't remember offhand. Not for her. But most of the people we investigated seemed like they booked their tickets in advance. Last-minute long-haul flights trigger security alerts, and there weren't any. So these didn't seem like last-minute trips. Not like people are prompted by someone— or something—to disappear suddenly."

"But so many disappearances..."

"Most of which have an explanation."

"Except this one."

"Especially this one. Didn't the owner say Sharon McPhiller went to Burma?"

"But I'm not sure I believe her."

Wiriya shrugged. "Well, it's fine to be suspicious, but there's really not much here that's worrisome." He looked at her closely. "Trust me, if I really thought there were suspicious disappearances, I would investigate. But I really don't think there's any reason for concern."

Ladarat sighed. Was Wiriya right? Maybe. Probably.

Who was she kidding? Almost certainly he was right. He was a detective, after all. He spent his life weeding out suspicions and possibilities.

And yet... Wiriya had turned his attention to the *kanom maprao* container, as if he considered the case closed. Closed because he decided it was closed. That just wouldn't do.

Maybe he was right. Probably he was right. But she decided in that instant she wasn't going to tell him about Jonah. Perhaps he wouldn't find anything. And if not, well, at least he'd gotten out of the house.

Speaking of which...

"Something strange happened to Ukrit today."

"Your assistant's boyfriend?"

Ladarat nodded. "They were in Bangkok, interviewing for jobs. She took the plane back, of course, because her presence at Sriphat Hospital is indispensable."

Wiriya looked somewhat confused by this. When he was confused he would narrow his eyes as if under bright sunlight, as he was doing now.

"I mean that she believed she needed to be back. That perhaps she was more indispensable than she actually is."

But that was unkind. Her assistant was truly very important. Ladarat would do well to remember that—if her assistant took a job in Bangkok, that would be extra work for her, and who knew how long it would take to hire a replacement.

"Anyway, she took the plane back, and he took the bus. But he fell asleep on the bus and was robbed of all of his money."

Wiriya nodded. "There are many robberies on the buses back and forth to Bangkok. A thief can take what he wants and then disappear into the crowds. Not like the buses to Chiang Rai or even smaller towns. It's harder to disappear there." He paused. "That is certainly unfortunate, and a little unusual. Mostly the victims of those sorts of robberies are *farang*—they carry too much cash around. But it happens." He shrugged.

"Well, Dr. Jainukul, the pulmonary fellowship director—he's Ukrit's boss. He wondered whether Ukrit might have been...drugged."

Wiriya's eyes narrowed again in concentration. "Drugged? To make him fall asleep?"

"Exactly so. He thought that someone might have drugged him and then robbed him. That it was planned. He said that sort of thing used to happen a lot."

Wiriya nodded. "It did. Now, not so much. People are more suspicious of taking any food from strangers unless it's a seller they know. Especially in Bangkok. But...why did he take something from someone he didn't know?"

"But he didn't, that's what's so strange. He said he went straight from dinner with a friend to the bus station. He said he didn't buy anything, so he just got on the bus, right before it left around eight."

"And then?"

"And then he woke up in Chiang Mai."

"What does he remember?"

"He can't remember anything about the bus ride, or even about getting off the bus in the morning."

"He got off the bus?"

"It seems that he must have gotten off the bus in his sleep. At least he doesn't remember anything until Sisithorn found him a few hours later."

Wiriya shrugged. "Yes, it's likely that drugs were used somehow. That would be the preferred method. Thieves want to make sure you don't wake up to create a disturbance. A drug like chloral hydrate used to be popular."

Chloral hydrate? Ladarat had never heard of such a drug. And she was a nurse.

Wiriya smiled at Ladarat's confused expression. "I don't know much about it, except that doctors don't seem to prescribe it for anything these days. But it used to be used to help patients sleep. My father used to take it now and again when he worked the night shift and had to sleep during the day." Ladarat had learned some time ago that Wiriya's father—now deceased—had been on the police force, too.

"So...the police will do something about this?"

Wiriya smiled helplessly, then yawned and stretched. He

seemed to be fading. "But what can we do? There are a dozen buses that come from Bangkok every day. And from other towns in the north and east... who knows how many? How could we find a thief?

"Besides," he continued, "little crimes like this happen all the time. It's not a good thing, but no one is really hurt too much. They lose a few hundred baht. That's all. And they get a good night's sleep. I'm sure Ukrit woke up well rested."

That didn't seem to be the sort of thing a distinguished member of the Chiang Mai police force should say, even if he was very tired. Did Ladarat turn away requests for help in ethical matters because they were trivial? Did she tell a nurse to figure a problem out for herself if it was not a matter of life and death? No, she did not.

And Professor Dalrymple herself said: "There is no such thing as a trivial fact if it touches a patient." Even if you were out late drinking. Especially then. So there.

She looked at Wiriya, who had leaned back in his chair with his eyes closed, a satisfied smile on his face and his folded hands resting on his midriff. It was all well and good for him to be complacent about these robberies. He wasn't the one who woke up with no money on a hard wooden bench. It was true, Ukrit didn't lose much money and could easily afford it. But what if he had gotten into a car and driven to work in his confused state? Or, worse, what if he had actually gotten to work and been confused? And harmed a patient?

"It's true, this is perhaps not as prestigious a crime to solve as catching a murderer," Ladarat admitted. "And someone of your distinction should perhaps restrict his busy schedule to those more prestigious breaches of the law."

Ladarat noted with a sense of satisfaction that her boyfriend's eyes were now open. He sat up a little straighter, and his hands migrated to the chair's arms.

She smiled. "Not all crimes are worthy of a great detective's time, of course. Such a small matter—a very trivial matter, in fact—should properly be beneath the dignity of a great detective who succeeded in catching the Peaflower murderer."

Now Wiriya was sitting up straight, but he was hanging his head, appearing to be very interested in a small area of the chair's right arm where the white paint had chipped to reveal bare metal underneath.

"But perhaps there are lesser minds on the Chiang Mai police force for whom this would be an appropriately important opportunity? Such a little matter, I know, but surely someone—"

"All right, all right!" Wiriya held up both hands in surrender. "I give up. I will ask about similar incidents. I will look through reports. Is that enough?"

"And...?"

He sighed, giving up entirely.

"And...I'll make sure Somporn and Kamon are officially assigned to the case. They're young and ambitious—if there's even a chance of seeing their names in the paper, they'll do whatever they have to do to find your thief."

"Will they agree to investigate?" Even to Ladarat, this seemed like it would probably not be a very fruitful investigation.

"Ever since the Peaflower murders, all of the young detectives are eager for what they hope might become the next big case. Any assignments I dole out, from market stall license violations to petty forgeries, are deemed to be candidates for the next great bust. So no doubt these eager young detectives will imagine Ukrit's troubles as the telltale sign of a vast international conspiracy." He paused, gauging her reaction. "Is that enough?"

She smiled. "For now, yes. I knew you were a good detective."

The silence stretched out between them for a moment as Ladarat looked up at the sky, which had clouded over, portending rain later tonight. She wondered where Maewfawbaahn had disappeared to. He hadn't quite gotten used to Wiriya and didn't stick to her as closely when Wiriya was around. Usually he would be curled up at her feet now, after having made a tour of the yard and the neighbors' yards. But perhaps, with Wiriya close by, there were fewer table scraps to share. Indeed, leftovers had virtually disappeared. Very few remnants of *som tam,* or *gy path king,* or *kanom maprao* made it to her refrigerator these days.

It was getting late, and Wiriya's eyes were closed again. She'd noticed he had a remarkable ability to fall asleep anywhere. Perhaps that was one reason he'd been so nonchalant about the bus robberies. The idea of falling asleep on a bus and then a bench was hardly a foreign concept to him. In fact, he'd told her stories of having to work the night shift as a junior police officer, just as his father had. He would sneak into one of the holding cells—nothing more than a concrete platform for temporary stays—and sleep like a baby. Or so he said.

Ladarat gathered the plates, piling Duanphen's cartons on top. She'd come back for the glasses. And Maewfawbaahn. And of course Wiriya.

Ladarat looked down to push her chair back and discovered her loyal cat. He'd snuck back unnoticed, as cats were wont to do. Now he followed her inside the house.

Even if Wiriya was around more, that didn't absolve her cat of his watchcat responsibilities, which he seemed to be taking particularly seriously. Tail straight up, he padded behind her down the narrow stone walkway, then around her and up the stairs, waiting patiently for her at the door to usher her inside.

Wan put

WEDNESDAY

CHAPTER 13

PAWS TO SEE CHIANG MAI

Eeehhh, that is probably a very small apartment. This was Ladarat's first thought as she nosed her squawking car down the narrow *soi* to which Jonah had e-mailed her directions. Every few meters the little car sensed an imminent threat to its silver paint or its fenders, and it emitted a shrill warning as Ladarat squeezed by trash cans and signposts and a fruit seller's stand. The apartments in this section of the Old City seemed so crammed together that the families shared living space and balconies. Four adults plus—soon—a baby? Oh, dear. That was her first thought.

Her second thought was a fervent plea that this *soi* wasn't a dead end, because she'd never be able to back up through the twists and turns that had taken her here.

And then, in the background, an ill-defined third thought slipped into her head. Less a thought than a sense of unease, no more defined than the cool mist that would spread across the Ping River on especially cold days, it said: Is this a waste of time? Wiriya's dismissal last night of these disappearances had been easy enough to ignore in the confident afterglow of a good meal and *kanom maprao*. *Kanom maprao* was a powerful eraser of doubts and anxieties.

But now? In the harsh light of morning, without any coconut

145

dessert nearby, Ladarat had to ask herself: Was this just a silly amusement?

That possibility brought her little car abruptly to a halt.

As she sat there, hemmed in on all sides, a new worry occurred to her. As if she didn't have enough worries. What if Jonah wasn't ready? What if he didn't see her? As she woke up this morning, she'd realized that she'd neglected to get his cell phone number, so she couldn't call him.

Her car was blocking the narrow *soi* like a cork in a bottle. Only a slender person could get by on either side; perhaps a bicycle, but certainly not a motor scooter or another car.

But she needn't have worried. Jonah was waiting in a doorway just ahead, the collar of his windbreaker turned up against the cool morning air and the steady breeze that was funneled down the *soi*. He greeted her and climbed into the passenger seat as the little car settled under his not inconsiderable bulk.

Ladarat's old yellow Beetle would have found an imaginative way to protest, by squeaking or stalling. But this soulless machine lacked the necessary creativity to voice its misgivings and simply accepted its extra burden as a matter of course. As usual, it confined its communication to alarmed warnings that there was an obstacle to the left or to the right, or in this case, in all four directions, since they were surrounded by walls and trash cans that came to within half a meter of both sides of the car, which had required Jonah to execute a feat of gymnastics to shoehorn his large self into the car.

"It's lucky you were waiting—I'm afraid if I stayed here long I'd cause a traffic jam."

Jonah laughed. "No, not luck. Not so much." He paused. "To tell the truth, it's nice to be able to get out of the house. You could have come an hour earlier, Khun, and I would have been out here waiting."

Actually, she couldn't have come much earlier. She'd stayed up very late the night before, reading. Ladarat consoled herself with the thought that what she was reading was improving her mind. It was called *A Nail Through the Heart*, by Khun Timothy Hallinan. It was in English, because that's all that was available at Back Street Books.

It was a mystery—not something that Ladarat would normally pick up, but the clerk at the bookstore had recommended it heartily when Ladarat asked for a book about how to be a detective. So she thought: Why not? It would be a pleasant way to improve her detection skills, and perhaps to practice her English as well.

She'd stayed up reading about Poke, the detective, and Rose, his girlfriend, and Miaow, his daughter, long after Wiriya had fallen asleep. When Wiriya left, he turned off the alarm and let her sleep. But feeling guilty in her subconscious, she dreamed that the hospital director asked her to move her office back to the small closet in the basement that she used to inhabit.

"You are not earning your nice, new office," the dream director told her sadly. "The Director of Excellence is coming back, and in fact she's on the overnight bus from Bangkok right now. She'll arrive in the morning, and I'm afraid that you must move back to the basement."

That guilt was enough to wake Ladarat up. She was still running late, and she just had time to take a shower and dress, and drink a single cup of blue peaflower tea as she spooned some dry cat food into Maewfawbaahn's bowl, slopping half of his breakfast on the tile floor. Then she drove as fast as she could so as not to keep Jonah waiting, since he was doing her a favor, after all.

Moments later, Jonah emerged from a doorway and eased his bulk into her car, which listed under his weight. Then they were under way.

"Ah—turn left there."

That turn required a few seesaws back and forth to urge the car around, and it induced increasingly frantic warnings about impending doom on all four sides. But then this new *soi* expanded to a more welcoming width, and soon they were out on a main street and heading toward the Magic Grove Hotel.

Ladarat knew the way, so driving required little concentration. It was a little after nine o'clock—past rush hour. Besides, they were traveling out of the city, in the opposite direction of many of the harried commuters rushing in the other direction, late for work.

Once they were on the road proper, Jonah heaved a big sigh of relief. "It's not that I don't like Krista's parents, Khun Ladarat. No, not at all. It's wonderful to have them here, and of course they're very good to come. Such a long trip, and so many cultural differences that they've had to understand."

"They must love their daughter very much."

Jonah nodded, watching as they passed a woman on a bicycle balancing one child on a rack behind the seat, and another, smaller child on her lap. The car squawked its usual warning about the threat the little family posed to its paintwork.

"Khun Ladarat? That woman...do you think perhaps she is a little close to this car?"

Ladarat nodded. "Perhaps. I would think that she would be a little more careful, with two children. But I'm sure she knows what she's doing." Ladarat glanced over at Jonah. "That is why Krista's parents are here, no doubt. Because they care very much about her."

"Yes, they love her very much." Jonah turned back to look at the little family on the bicycle, although why he found them so fascinating Ladarat wasn't sure.

"And me, too, I think. But my job...well...that's not something they're fond of."

"You told them where you work?"

"Not in so many words..." He paused. "Well, not exactly." Another pause. "Well, not at all, to tell the truth. They heard from one of our neighbors that I work in a bar."

"Oh, dear."

"Exactly."

"Her parents are...Mormons?"

Jonah nodded.

"So perhaps it would be good if you found another job?"

Jonah nodded emphatically. "Of course, I wouldn't want to disappoint Khun Siriwan, but I'm sure she could find someone to take my place."

"So what would you do?"

"Well...I have an idea."

"An idea?"

"A business idea," Jonah clarified. Then: "An idea for a business."

Ladarat was wondering what that might be when she realized at the last moment that she was about to miss the turn-off from the ring road that encircles the outskirts of Chiang Mai. She swung the car resolutely across two lanes of traffic, producing frantic honks from several cars and the roar of an air horn from a rather large truck. At least its front grille was quite large—that was all she could see.

But then they were on the ramp and then the road that led through rice paddies and into the forest north of the city.

"So what kind of business? Perhaps I could offer advice?"

Jonah seemed to be having trouble catching his breath. Ladarat hoped he wasn't about to get carsick. That would be a shame, what with her new car.

"You didn't need to drive this morning, you know, Khun. I could have taken the bus."

Now Jonah was taking deep, regular breaths. Good. He would be all right. And it was nice of him to worry about her, even when he himself was feeling so poorly.

"Oh, no, that wouldn't be right. You're doing me a favor. And of course I'll give you a ride home at the end of the day."

Jonah gulped and tightened his grip on the handle above the passenger door. Perhaps her passenger wasn't well.

"You're not carsick, are you? I could pull over." She turned her attention to her passenger, who did indeed look a little green. "Khun Jonah, you're sweating." Ladarat leaned over so she could get a better look at her passenger's face, which did indeed seem unnaturally pale. "Are you sure you're not sick?"

The whoop of an air horn from a truck hurtling toward them pulled Ladarat's attention back to the road. She was surprised to note that the yellow line on the tarmac had managed to work its way under the car, from where it had been on the right, the last time she'd looked. You really did have to keep an eye on these things. She corrected the car's course, thinking that her yellow Beetle wouldn't have meandered back and forth like a drunken businessman.

"So tell me about this business idea." She snuck a quick glance at Jonah, who was still sweating and clutching the door handle like a lifeline. She should take his mind off his symptoms. She should distract him. The traffic wasn't too bad; she didn't need to devote much attention to the road ahead.

"I'm sure it's a good idea—tell me?"

"Well, it's about dogs."

"Dogs?"

"Sure." Jonah took a couple of deep breaths and focused on the road ahead. "You know how *farang* tourists come to

Chiang Mai? I see them all the time; they try to make friends with the dogs outside the shops here. And many of them say they miss their dogs back at home. But of course they can't travel with their dogs."

"So you're going to ... sell them dogs?"

That didn't seem like such an excellent idea to Ladarat, but she'd be the first to admit that her cousin Siriwan inherited all of the business acumen in their family.

"No, Khun. Not sell. Rent. We'd rent dogs to *farang*. They would feel sad because they're missing their dog at home. So they would go to our website and place a request. Then we would drop a dog off at their hotel. With a leash and supplies, of course. Then they would have that dog for a day, or perhaps longer. They could go for walks, just as they would at home. They wouldn't feel lonely. And the best part, Khun, is that they would advertise."

"Advertise?"

"Of course. That was Krista's idea. We would get them vests that identify them as one of our dogs. And those vests would have the name of our business: 'Paws to see Chiang Mai.' 'Paws' as in dog feet, you see? There would be a website and a phone number, too. So the *farang* would be walking their dog, and other *farang* would stop them and say how cute their dog is. And then they would see the advertising, and they'd think—"

"I should do that, too!"

"Exactly so. Our customers would do our advertising for us."

Ladarat had to admit that was a good plan. But there was at least one flaw that she could think of.

"And these dogs? Where would you keep them?"

"Well, that's a problem. We hardly have enough room in our flat for the two of us. And now with four ... or five ... Well, it's just not possible."

Jonah looked out the window at the passing scenery. As the rice paddies disappeared, the traffic died away and they were alone on a road that stretched out through the dense forest. That seemed to make his carsickness better. Perhaps there was something about the other cars on the road that caused people to feel ill, if they were predisposed? She would have to ask one of her doctor colleagues about that.

Now Jonah shrugged and turned to her. "Well, it is a good idea, don't you think?"

Ladarat agreed that it was a very good idea. And if the only problem was finding a place to keep a team of dogs, that wasn't such an impossible problem. But when she said as much, Jonah shrugged again.

"No, Khun. There's also the matter of getting dogs who are well trained. And vaccinations, and feeding them, and transporting them back and forth."

"You'd need a . . . what do do you call it?"

"A backer," Jonah said, shaking his head. "Exactly. We'd need a backer. But who am I kidding? Who would give me money to start a business like that?" Then he looked up, almost smiling. "Still, maybe this temporary job will turn into something permanent. I could be . . . a detective's assistant!"

Oh, dear. That was the last thing she needed. But hopefully Jonah was joking.

"So what should I be looking for?"

"Well, first, you must be careful. Very careful."

Jonah laughed, although not unkindly. "Khun Ladarat, do you really think there is any danger here? It's a hotel, after all. How perilous could it be? And what sort of danger might confront me?"

"I don't know." And, truly, she didn't. The more she thought about this, the more convinced she became that there wasn't anything nefarious going on at all, let alone any nefariousness that posed a danger to someone of Jonah's bulk.

"Well, it's possible that people who stay here then disappear."

"How many people?"

Ladarat admitted that she didn't know.

"So where do they go when they disappear?"

Ladarat admitted she had no idea.

"And the motive, Khun Ladarat? What would be the motive for a hotel to make people disappear?"

Ladarat was stumped. In all of her thinking about this, that was a question that hadn't occurred to her. What motive indeed? Why on earth would a hotel want to make paying customers disappear?

"Ah, to tell the truth, I hadn't thought of that."

"You hadn't?"

Jonah sounded genuinely surprised—as if he'd just now realized that she, Ladarat Patalung, was not in fact a detective but only a nurse. A nurse ethicist, perhaps, but not someone adept at the fine art of detection, and not someone who was skilled at thinking about motives.

"No," she admitted. "It just seemed…suspicious."

"Oh, well, it certainly is," Jonah agreed, a little too heartily, perhaps.

Whether he was trying to make her feel better or whether it was because they had slowed to turn into the hotel's gravel driveway, Ladarat wasn't sure. But as soon as the car slowed down, he began to breathe more easily and he released the door handle for the first time in the past ten minutes.

"You can let me off here," Jonah said as they turned into the circle in front of the main entrance.

"Perhaps I should wait? Perhaps if there's a problem, or if she's found someone else for the position, you'll need a ride home."

"No, no, Khun. You're very kind, but that seems unlikely. You only spoke with her yesterday, right? And Khun Siriwan called her last night while I was there, and they reached an agreement. And besides," he said, extracting his large frame and closing the door behind him, "I can always take the bus back."

Jonah leaned down through the passenger window, bending his frame like a giraffe. "I know this bus route—the bookkeeper at the Tea House lives this way, and he says the buses come very often. Very, very often."

"Well, still, be careful."

Jonah nodded, although he seemed to be suppressing a smile. "Of course, Khun. I'll be careful. And whatever happens, I'll give you a call on my way home."

"And of course call me if you need a ride," Ladarat called out after him. "I'd be happy to drive out and pick you up." But Jonah was hurrying toward the front door, and she wasn't sure that he heard her.

CHAPTER 14

THE HAZARDS OF FORTUNE-TELLING

At least the drive back to the hospital had been uneventful. Walking across the parking lot to the rear entrance, Ladarat had ample time to reflect that a lack of eventfulness was a good thing—a very good thing—when one was driving. Also cooking. And probably performing open-heart surgery. Of course, there were times when eventfulness was desirable, but not always. Not most of the time, actually.

Ladarat had to park halfway across the lot, of course. The guilty dream of the director still fresh in her mind, Ladarat concluded that this was obviously a penalty for using her morning sleeping late, and then—almost as bad—on a non-work-related matter.

Passing through the lobby, she was about to turn right to the main corridor that led to the bank of elevators that would take her up to her office, but something made her keep walking straight.

That something was *moo dad diew*. Or, rather, a craving for *moo dad diew*. Small bits of crispy fried pork, with sticky rice and chili sauce (*jim jao*). And that *moo dad diew* was calling very loudly and insistently.

She followed its call straight through the cool, tiled entrance hall that had always seemed grander than was entirely right for a hospital. Just a little farther along the access road, on

Suthep Road proper, she knew, the food stalls would be just warming up for the lunchtime rush. Now, of course, would be the best time to get lunch. Everything would be fresh, the poultry straight from the market, and the vegetables—many of them—picked that morning by stall owners from their own gardens. By noon, just an hour from now, what would be left would have declined in quality to a sad degree.

When one was shopping for *moo dad diew*, there was an obligation to procure the freshest *moo dad diew* possible. Pork that sat too long became tough and rubbery. This was well known.

Her duty suddenly clear, Ladarat stood aside to let a flock of nursing students flow up the steps and through the door, then she made her way along the access road and out to Suthep. Along the way, Ladarat thought carefully about what might tempt Melissa Double.

And that gave Ladarat pause. Khun Melissa was quite sick, was she not? Perhaps *moo dad diew* would be too heavy? Perhaps. Every vendor had their own recipe for *jim jao*, and Ladarat had learned through painful trial and error which ones were just spicy enough to be interesting, but which didn't require an iron palate.

Nevertheless, even the mildest *jim jao* might be too much for a sick patient. And a *farang* at that. So no *moo dad diew* today.

Perhaps *kao man gai*? Just simple chicken and rice, usually boiled chicken, but the stalls here grilled theirs, and rice boiled in chicken stock to make it flavorful, but not heavy. Then a light mix of garlic and chili and oil and vinegar—just enough to make it interesting. That's what a sick person would appreciate. That and *kwitiau*—just a simple noodle soup with vegetables. And *kanom maprao*, of course. She would ask the vendor to go light on the syrup.

So not fifteen minutes later—another advantage of beating the lunchtime rush—Ladarat was sitting across from Melissa Double at the small table in her room. Sharing the *kao man gai* between two paper plates and the *kwitiau* in two coffee mugs borrowed form the nurses' kitchen, Ladarat was delighted to see that Melissa seemed to be in better spirits.

"You seem better, Khun... Your appetite seems good." And indeed Melissa had devoured her *kwitiau* and—after a nod from Ladarat—poured the remainder in her mug.

"And you're more comfortable, at least?"

Melissa nodded. "Much more. Dr. Taksin is a wizard when it comes to treating pain. I was on intermittent doses of morphine, but they always made me sleepy. He put me on a long-lasting form—a pill I just take twice a day—and I feel like a whole different person." She divided the *kanom maprao* between the two of them. "A wizard," she said again.

"A wizard?"

"Do you not say that in Thai? When someone is very good at doing something complicated? Like a wizard at math?"

Ladarat shook her head and shuddered. "No, in Thailand, wizards are not good. Not good at all." She paused. "Not that everyone believes in them. It's not like they've been proven to exist. But some say there are people—wizards, as you say— who are engaged in black magic."

"But not real?" Melissa was smiling: a smile that, if she were Thai, would be called *yim thak thaan*. It was the tolerant smile one used when someone was talking nonsense, but had to be humored. "Not real black magic, certainly?"

"Well, no. Honestly, I don't know much about it. There is not such a tradition of those beliefs in Thailand. Those beliefs come sometimes from Burma, and often from Cambodia. There are stories of horrible witches and wizards from the

Khmer people. Not too unlike rituals of voodoo that people in the West talk about. But mostly the Thai belief in magic runs to harmless fortune-telling. You know—whether this girl will find love, or that man will live to a happy old age."

Melissa put down her fork and seemed solemn. "I'm not sure all fortune-telling is so harmless, as you say. Of course, it seems that way. But think what damage a prediction of the future could do to a person. Telling them that things will go poorly...it can rearrange a life."

"Ah, Khun, that is true. And a favorable prediction..."

Melissa smiled. "The same, of course, but in a different way. I had a diagnosis of pancreatic cancer a year ago. They said I could be cured. That I had a 'very good' chance of being cured, actually. So I went through horrible surgery, and chemotherapy, and they said that had gotten rid of all the cancer. That was the prophecy they gave me."

"So that prophecy was wrong?"

Melissa shrugged and pushed the remains of the *kao man gai* away from her. "Perhaps. I don't know. You see, I'd always wanted to travel in Southeast Asia. No," she corrected herself. "What I really wanted to was to have a spontaneous trip. Deciding on Monday where I would be on Tuesday. Taking one day at a time. Being spontaneous. You understand?"

Ladarat nodded. Actually, that sounded like a horrible trip. Not knowing from one day to the next where you would be, or where you would spend the night? How was that amusing? But as she'd had reason to notice many times, *farang* often subscribed to odd views of what was amusing.

Americans in particular seemed to have highly idiosyncratic opinions about how to spend their time on vacation. Crisping themselves on a beach like bits of pork, or riding elephants, or—

"So as soon as I got my strength back—or some of it, at least—I came out here."

"But..." Ladarat waved in a general way at the hospital room around them. This was hardly a spontaneous side trip.

"Ah, so I started having stomach pain. I was up in Chiang Kong, about to take a boat trip on the Mekong? You know it?"

She did. It was a perfect example of the strange travel habits of *farang*: spending several days in the open air with just a thin cushion to sit on, in a swallowtail boat navigating the Mekong's rapids at a hundred kilometers per hour. Every week or two there was an accident, and many people died every year. How was that an amusing holiday? But Ladarat simply nodded.

"Well, I told the doctor in the small hospital there what my story was. He understood enough English to be worried that my cancer had come back. He did an ultrasound test that was 'inconclusive.' He didn't speak much English, but that was a word he knew. So they arranged for an ambulance to take me here. Now they're doing tests to find out how far it's spread."

"How far...? But do you know that the cancer is back? Many travelers in this part of the world get abdominal discomfort," Ladarat said. "It could be many things..."

"You're very kind, but that ultrasound test wasn't good news. I'm not a doctor, or a nurse, but I know that 'inconclusive' is never good news. And I had a scan as soon as I got here that was worrisome, too. You see, I had such extensive surgery that my...anatomy is strange." She smiled. "Those poor radiology doctors don't know what they're seeing. Everything is so twisted around and rearranged. They're having a difficult time figuring out what's normal and what's not. But they will, and when they do, I'm pretty sure it will be bad news."

Ladarat knew better than to try to offer reassurance. Such

empty reassurances or—worse—empty optimism wasn't helpful. It either accomplished nothing or it raised false hopes.

It might make the doctor or the nurse feel better, saying,
"Oh, don't worry. Everything will work out. You'll be fine."
That might make a nurse feel as though she's doing something, and saying such things was an excellent way for a busy
doctor to make a graceful exit from a patient's room. But such
empty reassurances didn't accomplish anything.

Besides, Ladarat trusted Melissa's intuition. In the same way
that detectives—even amateur detectives—could tell whether
a case was suspicious, in her experience, patients often knew
that there was a problem long before tests discovered what was
wrong.

She'd read a study once, in fact, that found that the most
sensitive indicator for a pulmonary embolus—a blood clot in
the arteries of the lung—was not a change in X-rays or even
a drop in the patient's blood oxygen. No, the most sensitive
indicator was the fact that the patient felt an unexplained
sense of anxiety. So if Melissa felt that something was wrong,
and that her cancer had come back, well...unfortunately,
that was a very good possibility.

"If it is bad news, what will you do?"

Melissa nodded as if that was a question she'd been thinking about a lot. But she answered with another question. "Do
you think I should go home, Khun?"

"Do I think...?" Ladarat was flustered. "It's not up to me,
Khun. I couldn't answer that question."

Melissa nodded again. "Of course, you can't. And I didn't
mean to ask you an impossible question. But...it would just
help to talk through this with someone."

Ladarat was tempted to point out—again—that this was
hypothetical. Maybe Melissa's cancer hadn't returned. Maybe

this was a stomach ulcer or a gallstone. Such things happened to women of their age.

But that wouldn't do. Melissa was one of those people who needed to plan. She needed to think through her options. So Ladarat would help her.

"So . . . if you were to go home . . ."

"Yes?"

"What is home like? Tell me—where do you live? Who is there?"

"Well, I don't live anywhere, at the moment. I sublet my apartment for a year. I figured I'd be traveling, and I'd use the rent to help offset some of my expenses. It was the difference between staying in hostels and decent hotels."

"So if you were to go home, you'd have nowhere to stay?"

Melissa thought for a moment. "Well, I might be able to move back into my apartment. It wouldn't be nice, but it could be possible. Or I could stay with friends. But not if I were very sick. I wouldn't want to burden anyone."

"Do you have family?"

"I have a sister in Tenby—that's in the far western part of Wales, where I grew up. Now I live in Cardiff—that's the capital city. I have friends there, of course. But no family nearby."

"So who would help care for you . . . if you got sicker? After a long trip home, you wouldn't feel well . . ."

"Or as my cancer gets worse, you mean?" Melissa smiled.

Ladarat nodded. That was exactly what she meant. If in fact her cancer had really come back.

"I'm not sure how much I could ask my friends to do. It's just a few of us who are close." She paused, picking up a fork and toying with the remains of her *kao mok gai*.

"And besides, they have their own families, most of them. And a few are having troubles of their own. Health troubles, some of them. Or financial problems. So...I don't know. I'd rely on our hospice. They have nurses to come to the house. And they have a hospice house—although not as nice as this one." She looked down again, thinking. "Could I stay here?"

"Here? In this room?"

Melissa nodded. "It's comfortable here. People are nice. There are great restaurants nearby that deliver." She smiled and pointed to the food cartons that were scattered between them on the table. "And I know I won't be a burden to anyone."

"Well, it's true that you're not a burden. But this room—this unit—isn't designed for people to stay for a long time."

Most patients were admitted for a short period of time, until their symptoms were controlled. It wasn't a place where people stayed for weeks or months.

But why not? That wasn't the purpose, it was true. But it could be. And Melissa was well liked as a patient. If Dr. Taksin agreed, it could be possible.

So that's what she told Melissa, that it might be possible, but that she should think about it. There might be someplace more comfortable, if she really didn't want to go home.

"But the scan," Ladarat asked. "When will you learn those results?"

"Today, Dr. Taksin said. Probably today."

"Are you nervous about the results? I could come back later, perhaps with Chi?"

Melissa smiled and shook her head. "No, Khun. You are very kind. Too kind. You've brought me lunch, and company and good conversation. I already owe you a debt. How do you say it? *Bunkhun*?"

Ladarat smiled and nodded. "*Bunkhun*, yes, that's how you say it. A debt of gratitude. Something owed in return for a gift. Or sometimes for help. But, Khun, there is no debt here. I'm a nurse. This is my job."

Now it was Melissa's turn to smile. "Your job? Truly? It's your job to take your lunch hour and bring food to hungry patients and sit and talk with them? That's a most unique job description."

"So perhaps it isn't exactly my job. Not all the time, at least. But it falls within the scope of my responsibilities. And it's well within my scope of expertise—choosing the best dishes from the best vendors on Suthep Road. That is a specialty the hospital entrusts only to me. And one of those specialties is *kanom maprao*—coconut cake. It's from Chanitnai the baker."

Ladarat took the last container out of the plastic bag and cleaned up the paper plates and forks, using the bag for trash.

"She used to be in pharmacy school, but she dropped out to take care of her parents. Now she makes the best *kanom maprao* in all of Chiang Mai."

Ladarat almost took that back as soon as she said it, because now there was Duanphen's cousin Prasert, the ex-insurance salesman. His *kanom maprao* was excellent, too. Someday, she and Wiriya would have to do a taste test of the two.

"Chanitnai owns a bakery," Ladarat continued, suppressing the vision of two servings of *kanom maprao*, from two bakers, on the same table. "But she'd rather be at the stalls out in front of the hospital. Here, I'll leave this for you. It's good to have some *kanom maprao* on hand. And it's an excellent bribe for the nurses here. Everyone knows Khun Chanitnai's baking skills."

"Khun?"

Ladarat stopped partway to the door.

"I've been so busy talking about myself, I forgot to ask.

Your cooking lesson with...Duanphen?" Ladarat nodded. "How did it go?"

Ladarat thought about that for a moment. True, they were not lessons so much as it was cooking with training wheels. But she did make something edible. Not just edible, but recognizable as food.

"It went well, thank you. Amazingly well, actually."

"I'm glad to hear it. We should all try new things. New things that are a little scary. And especially new things that we don't think we'll do well at. So we can be surprised."

Ladarat agreed that was true, and she promised to visit the following day. She thought about Melissa's wisdom as she made her way back to the nurses' kitchen to dispose of the plates and wash their mugs.

It made sense, of course, but Ladarat was surprised to hear that advice from someone like Melissa, who wanted to plan her life out, someone who wanted to know what the possibilities would be, and someone who was already thinking about who would take care of her in Cardiff.

On the other hand, this was the same woman who wanted to come to Southeast Asia so she could take one day a time. That was a strange mixture, was it not? This desire to plan, on one hand, and on the other, this call to go and do surprising things. Perhaps Melissa Double was trying to turn over a new leaf.

As she was pondering that possibility, Ladarat noticed that the door next to the nurses' station was open. That was Dr. Taksin's office. She'd never seen the door open. But now it was. Ladarat should take advantage of that opportunity, shouldn't she? She should.

"Dr. Taksin?"

Oh, dear. It seemed that the doctor was not in the best condition to receive visitors. Facedown on the desk, his head rested on one forearm, while the other hand held a pen. In the space of however long the good Dr. Taksin had been asleep, the pen had traced an interesting pattern on the light wood surface of the desk, making it look like his head was smack in the middle of a map of a mysterious island.

"Dr. Taksin?"

Perhaps she had better leave. She should definitely leave.

But as she was considering whether it would be polite to close the door so as not to alarm passing patients or families, Dr. Taksin gave a start and rejoined the living.

"Ah, Khun Ladarat." The poor doctor lifted his head off the desk with a suddenness that Ladarat wouldn't have believed possible a moment before. He rubbed his eyes and blinked once, twice. Then he seemed to be perfectly awake. Perhaps that was a skill of doctors? Her late husband, Somboon, could wake up with the suddenness of a sunrise and fall asleep as abruptly.

"I... have been working, lately," Dr. Taksin said.

"Working?"

Dr. Taksin shook his head as if to clear his mind. "Late work, I mean. That is to say, working late. Often very late."

"But... the palliative care unit... it doesn't seem busy."

And indeed it didn't. Ladarat had passed several empty rooms on her way to and from Melissa. The unit had the quiet, calm feeling that nurses loved: no frantic rushing around, and no matters requiring urgent attention. Surely there was not enough work so justify a doctor staying late enough to lose sleep?

"Ah, well, it is not work here, you understand."

Ladarat didn't. She admitted as much.

"It is... Would you promise not to tell anyone, Khun Ladarat?"

Hmmm. Ladarat was intrigued. What "job" could be so incriminating that she should be sworn to secrecy? That would be interesting indeed. But no.

"Ah, no, Dr. Taksin. Much as I would like to hear about your 'job,' that would put me in a difficult position, would it not?" Ladarat smiled firmly. "I am the hospital ethicist, am I not?"

The tired doctor nodded uncertainly.

"So you see, you might tell me things that I have an obligation to divulge to others. In my role as ethicist, you understand?"

Dr. Taksin didn't. He shook his head.

"It is bad to promise not to divulge a secret, especially in my position, you see. You might tell me something bad, or dangerous, that I would have to share with your department chair...or the dean...or the police."

Ladarat watched Dr. Taksin closely for signs of anxiety to cross his tired face. Signs of anxiety that would indicate a much bigger problem. But the doctor merely smiled as if he were enjoying a good joke.

"Oh, Khun Ladarat. I assure you that this is nothing that any of those people would waste their time with. And the police?" He laughed. "Let's just say that they would approve entirely."

"Then...?"

"Then why am I being so secretive? Well, it's just not something that I would want generally known. And besides—" He waved a hand. "It doesn't really matter. Not really. I'm just tired, that's all."

He thought for a moment, then remembered his manners.

"I'm so sorry, Khun. I've been sitting here talking..." He smiled. "And sleeping. But I haven't asked you to sit, and I haven't asked you why you've come to visit me."

Dr. Taksin looked up at her curiously. He rubbed his eyes

again, as if to make sure the hospital nurse ethicist was truly standing in front of him.

"No, it was nothing." Ladarat thought quickly. What was to be gained by inventing a conversation about death? Surely she had learned what she needed to learn.

"Truly nothing. I was here to see Khun Melissa. The woman from England?" Dr. Taksin nodded.

"And I was passing by your office and...I thought perhaps you were sick."

Ladarat shrugged. She would be the first to admit that she was an awful liar. But as a nurse ethicist, she'd always figured that an inability to hide a falsehood was probably one of her most notable strengths.

As Professor Dalrymple said, "Doctors have more power than nurses, but that power lets them withhold the truth. That's why patients trust nurses more than doctors."

"Well, thank you, Khun. But as I said, I'm just tired." He thought for a moment more, then remembered Melissa Double.

"That patient—from England. You're seeing her because...?"

"Ah, well, I've seen her twice with Chi, the therapy dog." Dr. Taksin nodded.

"And we got along very well. I promised her I would come back to see her again today. She is very intelligent, I thought. And very...wise."

"Wise?" But Dr. Taksin was smiling. "I've noticed the same thing. She's very...philosophical about her situation."

Ladarat agreed that was a good way to put it. She'd never met anyone who had managed to adapt so well to what life had delivered to her. So well, in fact, that until that moment, Ladarat hadn't really thought about what it must be like to be in her position.

"To work all of your life and then retire, only to be faced

with a possible relapse like this," Ladarat said, shaking her head. "That must be terrible."

"And yet she doesn't seem...daunted," Dr. Taksin said. "She's still reading books, and making friends, and planning to travel."

"To travel?" This was news indeed.

Dr. Taksin shrugged. "I'm not sure, but I believe I heard her talking today about leaving the hospital."

"To go home?"

Dr. Taksin shook his head. "I don't think so. I think if she were going home, we would have to do much more planning. Arranging that sort of transport is time-consuming and expensive." He paused. "Very expensive. She is not well and would need medical assistance for such a long trip. But she hasn't discussed any of that with me or with the nurses. I think perhaps she may be thinking about checking out of the hospital to keep traveling."

Really? This was very different than what Ladarat had heard just a few minutes ago. And besides, there was the matter of her scan. Speaking of which...

"She will need extra support when she gets her scan results. If the results are bad, of course," she hastened to add.

Dr. Taksin looked confused. "Another scan? No, there will be no more. It's obvious that her cancer has spread throughout her liver and to her lungs. It's also around the lining of her abdomen, the peritoneum."

"Would you like me to be there when you tell her?"

Dr. Taksin's English was intelligible, but just barely. Surely for a conversation of this magnitude, it would be good to have Ladarat, or a translator, present.

The doctor looked confused. "When I tell her? But, Khun Ladarat, she knows already. Nurse Sudchada and I met with her this morning and explained everything." He reflected for a moment. "And, you know, she didn't seem very surprised. Sad, perhaps. Well, of course sad. But not as sad as I would have expected. And not surprised at all, to be honest. It was almost as if she knew the results of the scan before I told her."

Ladarat nodded uncertainly as she realized that Melissa Double was not being entirely honest.

"And not only that she knew about the results," Dr. Taksin added, "but that she'd already had a chance to get used to them, you know?"

Ladarat nodded. She'd been thinking the same thing about the woman she'd just left. That was not someone who had suddenly received unexpected news. The bad news was not a surprise, and it was news she'd been expecting. Nevertheless, she hadn't been willing to share it with Ladarat.

What did that mean?

"Well, you will tell me if you think I can be helpful, won't you?" she said. "Of course she is under a great deal of stress, even if she doesn't show it. It might be helpful for her to have someone she could talk to easily in English."

The doctor nodded, and Ladarat said goodbye, urging him to get a good night's sleep, and the doctor smiled ruefully. "That's unlikely, but I suppose it's possible."

Back out in the hallway, Ladarat made her way back down toward Melissa's room, but the door was closed. She should knock. She should ask the woman how she was doing after receiving such bad news. She should be supportive.

And yet...if Melissa had wanted that support, surely she would have mentioned her scan results. That she said nothing could only meant that she wanted to keep those results private, at least for now.

Ladarat turned back toward the nurses' station, pondering

the ethics of the situation. Walking away like this felt...wrong. But what could she do? Ladarat hesitated as she considered ruses she could use to get back in the room. A forgotten pen? A mislaid cell phone?

She considered these and a number of other options as she stood indecisively in the hallway, which was mercifully empty of people.

Perhaps it was best to let Melissa determine what she wanted to share, and when. Didn't the good Professor Dalrymple say: "Our patients tell us what we need to know if only we listen carefully."

That was not an entirely satisfying conclusion, but it would do for now. And Ladarat felt more at ease as she made her way back down the hallway toward the door. She paused just long enough at an open door to catch a glimpse of Dr. Taksin once again unconscious, with his head resting on the hard wooden desk.

CHAPTER 15

A POSSIBLY DISAPPEARED MAN

Ladarat was fumbling with the key to unlock her office door when her cell phone chirped. With one hand on the key in the door, she reached for the phone in her white coat pocket, only to realize that she wasn't wearing her white coat. It took a few extra miscoordinated seconds to fish the insistent device from her bag, unlock the door, and put her bag down inside the door. Cradling the phone against her left shoulder, she turned the key to get it out of the door.

But she stopped when she heard the voice on the other end of the phone. It was hardly more than a whisper; Ladarat had to press the phone to her ear as she closed the office door behind her.

"Khun Ladarat? There is definitely something...suspicious here."

"Khun Jonah, you are all right? You're not in any danger?"

"No, no...nothing like that. But one of the guests has... disappeared."

"Disappeared?"

"Yes, he's gone. Entirely gone."

"But isn't it possible that he..." What would be an explanation? That he stepped out for the day? Went sightseeing, and perhaps he got lost? "How do you know that he...disappeared, as you say?"

"Khun Delia, you know? The owner? She asked me to clean out this man's room. She said...she said he would not be coming back."

"She said that? She said that he wouldn't be coming back? Just like that?"

There was a moment of silence, then a loud rustling sound.

"Khun Jonah? Are you there? Are you all right?"

"Yeah, fine. All fine. I just don't want anyone to hear me, so I'm..."

"Khun Jonah? Where are you?"

"I'm in a closet. But just for a moment."

Well, that was good.

"But...why do you think this is suspicious?" Wiriya's reservations about this "case" had taken up residence in her head, and she was somewhat surprised to find that she was skeptical about the very mission that she'd sent Jonah on earlier today. "Certainly some hotel guests need to leave unexpectedly."

"Yes, Khun, but this man, he left all of his belongings. His clothes and his suitcase and..."

"Yes?"

"And his passport, Khun. He left his passport. He is a *farang*. An American, like me. And why would any *farang* leave his passport? Where can he go?"

"Eeey. That is bad. And worrisome. But how do you know this?"

"Khun Delia asked me to clean out his room, and to put his belongings in a box, and to take them to her."

Ladarat had an idea. A smart idea, in fact.

"And this box—is it nearby?"

"Of course, Khun. I have it here. With me. In this closet. I was on my way back to the manager's office when I thought to call you first."

"Don't take too long, then. Delia, she'll be suspicious if you take more than a few minutes. But, tell me, what is the man's name?"

"His name?"

"From his passport," Ladarat said patiently. "The name in his passport."

"Ah, right. Wait a moment." There were more sounds of scuffling and a soft thud. Then: "Richard April."

"April? That's an unusual last name, isn't it?"

"Maybe. But all last names are a little unusual, aren't they? Not so much as in Thailand, where family names have to be unique."

Ladarat agreed that was true.

"And—one more thing."

"Yes?"

"Another...guest. Her name was..." What was it? "McPhiller. Sharon McPhiller. Could you perhaps see if she's still a guest?"

Jonah sounded doubtful. "I really don't think so, Khun. You see, there are very few guests here. I think I know all of them by sight."

"But just make sure, yes? And if she's not a guest, perhaps you could find out when she checked out?"

"Well, I could do that. But I'm sure she's not here, Khun. Very sure."

Ladarat was about to end the call, letting Jonah get back to his task before he was missed. Yet something about the present situation bothered her. Why would Delia send a new employee on an errand to clean out Richard April's room if there were something suspicious going on? Unless...

Ladarat had a disturbing thought. Perhaps this was a test. Perhaps this was a test to see if Jonah would become curious. Or—what was more worrisome—a test that she thought necessary because Jonah was a referral from Ladarat, who was herself the focus of suspicion.

Eeyy. That would be very bad, if Jonah were being tested because she had raised Delia's suspicions.

"And Khun Jonah?"

"Yes?"

"Say nothing about this to Delia. Don't ask questions, and don't let her think that you're suspicious at all."

"Of course, Khun. We must lull her into a sense of security. She will let her guard down, and then she might make a mistake."

Well, that was true, Ladarat supposed. But she was more worried about Jonah. That was what she said before she urged him to hurry, and they hung up. As she did, she fervently hoped that no one would see Jonah emerging from a closet carrying a disappeared man's belongings. A possibly disappeared man.

Ladarat sat at her desk, still holding her phone, wondering what her next step should be. What would a detective do? A real detective?

She thought about that for moment, remembering her conversation with Wiriya the night before.

Did this change the situation? Would this make a detective— a real detective—more suspicious?

She thought of possible explanations, and she couldn't come up with any. None, at least, that would lead a *farang* to abandon his passport.

Delia had been emphatic that he would not be returning. How could she be certain of that?

Thinking about this, she dialed Wiriya's number.

Surprisingly, he answered on the first ring. Less surprising,

Wiriya was unimpressed by the suspiciousness of recent developments.

"That isn't so strange," Wiriya pointed out.

"But *farang* don't leave their passports lying around," she said. "At least, that would be a very strange thing to do."

"Well...I admit that's strange. But perhaps...just perhaps...this man Richard April had engaged the services of a sex worker. And imagine that he had left the hotel yesterday, perhaps, armed with just some money. That would make sense. If one were venturing out on such a...mission, one would want to keep one's important documents safe at one's hotel. And perhaps he was enjoying himself and simply didn't return to the hotel."

"But if that's why he came to Thailand, for such a...liaison, why would he stay in such an isolated place? *Farang* who frequent brothels and bars usually stay in a couple of the big hotels downtown or—if they're cheap—one of the hostels in the Old City. They don't usually stay way out there."

Wiriya was so quiet for a moment that Ladarat thought the connection had been lost. Just as she was about to say something, the detective spoke up.

"No...none of these theories makes sense. Not that he disappeared. This is not a man who just disappears."

"And you know this because...?"

"This man. Richard April. You should look him up. He's on two lists that Thai Airways gave us. He just arrived in Thailand two days ago and flew into Bangkok, and then a short flight to Chiang Mai. You should look him up," Wiriya said again.

"Look him up? Where?" Ladarat pondered that suggestion for a moment, confused. How could she look up flight information? "I don't have access to the database that you're looking at."

"No, but you can still look up other things. On Google. Just enter his name. Richard April."

Ladarat wiggled the mouse of her computer to wake it up, and did as Wiriya suggested, finding more than ten thousand listings. Odd, for such an unusual name.

"Click on his web page," Wiriya suggested. "It's very interesting."

Ladarat did, and found herself looking at a slick, professionally designed page for Richard April, award-winning mystery writer. There was a publicity picture prominently displayed, of an attractive man in his sixties, with angular cheekbones and closely cropped salt-and-pepper hair. Khun Richard was smiling a smile that, if he were Thai, might be called *yim yaw*: the teasing smile of someone who knows something you don't. Or, perhaps, the smile of a very successful mystery writer who has made his living by keeping his fans guessing.

He was the author of three series, one of which caught Ladarat's attention: the Josie Martin mysteries, described as a series of mysteries that were solved by a hospice nurse in the city of Philadelphia. A hospice nurse was not so different than a nurse ethicist, certainly. They must have to make the same sorts of ethical decisions. It was comforting to know that somewhere out there, in fiction, Ladarat had a kindred spirit.

"So he's a famous writer," she admitted. "But how does that change the case?"

"It means there is no case," Wiriya said simply. "A 'case' of a disappearance, as you call it, just wouldn't make sense for such a person."

Ladarat didn't think it would make sense for any person,

but certainly no less so for a man such as Richard April. "Why does his fame make a disappearance impossible?"

"It's not that it makes a disappearance impossible," Wiriya admitted. "But you have to admit that it makes the alternative much more likely." He paused. "Consider it—a very famous man who traveled to Thailand and was interested in a...liaison. He would not want to be seen in public places. He would want someplace very private."

"And he would of course leave his identification behind when he ventured out to his...activities."

"Exactly so." Ladarat envied Wiriya that satisfaction of concluding a case with finality. That was a sensation that she rarely experienced in the world of ethics. There were always...nuances. Then she had a thought.

"But what about Delia Martin's assurance that he wouldn't be coming back?"

Here, too, Wiriya had an answer ready. "No doubt they had an...understanding. If he was successful in his search, she would collect his belongings and forward them to him."

She would? But why wouldn't he come back? Ladarat wasn't convinced by that story, although she had to admit the validity of what Wiriya said next.

"And besides, could you imagine such a famous man disappearing? A man who has written dozens of books and has thousands of fans? Why would such a man want to disappear?"

Ladarat had to admit that was a good question. A very good question.

"So it is clear there is nothing nefarious going on," Wiriya concluded with a weighty finality. "No doubt he will turn up." There was a pause—a long pause—as Ladarat watched her mystery turn to smoke.

"But I suppose I should try to find him. It would be good to be sure that he does get his passport back." He sighed, as a potentially grand mystery was reduced to the pedestrian case of a missing sex tourist, albeit a famous one.

And if anyone could find him, Ladarat thought as they ended the call, it would be Wiriya. Many Thai first names had meanings—"beauty" or "brilliance" or "honesty"—that were impossible to live up to. (Somboon meant "perfect" or "complete.") But Wiriya meant "diligence" or "persistence." Ladarat wasn't sure whether that was a lucky coincidence, or whether Wiriya had worked hard to live up to the aspirational name his parents had bestowed on him forty-two years ago. She suspected the latter.

So Wiriya would look for Richard April and she would... what, exactly?

Well, she should start by telling Jonah that there was nothing to look for. She should do that. She would do that.

But it wasn't urgent, she realized. Besides, she didn't even have his cell number. She paused, gazing out her window onto the courtyard below.

Now he had a job that got him out of the house. It would be... unfair to take that from him so soon, would it not? Of course there was nothing mysterious going on at the Magic Grove Hotel. Of course. But if a "case," even an imaginary one, gave him a respite from his parents-in-law, then what was the harm? She would break the news to him eventually, but not today.

CHAPTER 16

"DO NO HARM"? DOCTORS ALWAYS DO HARM.

Ladarat looked at her watch twice, realizing with some surprise that it was past four p.m. Unsure where the day had gone, she felt very tired nonetheless.

True, she hadn't made any progress on the case of Richard April's disappearance, except to conclude that he hadn't disappeared. And she hadn't made any headway in solving his case, except to admit that there wasn't a "case." Still, that was progress, of a sort.

She'd even made progress on the strange case of Dr. Taksin. Not progress toward a solution, it was true, but a very clear recognition that there was, in fact, a problem. And that there, at least, was a "case." That was a relief, of sorts.

Ladarat had often noticed that doctors were relieved when they found an abnormal laboratory result for a patient with mysterious symptoms. Even when that lab result didn't point to a diagnosis or dictate a treatment, it was nevertheless reassuring—to the doctor, at least—proof that something was, in fact, wrong. And sometimes it reassured the patient, too.

Now Ladarat knew that there was something that Dr. Taksin wanted to hide. Wasn't that equivalent to finding that something was wrong? It was. All she had to do now was to find out what that something was.

Yet in other ways, Ladarat had to admit that her day had

been less than productive. Apart from her wasted effort at the Magic Grove Hotel, there was the matter of her ongoing review of hospital deaths, for instance. There, truth be told, she had accomplished, well, nothing. She'd promised herself a review of fifty charts this week, and here it was Wednesday, and she'd done fewer than twenty.

And, of course, there was the impending presentation to the Medical Ethics Society meeting on Friday, just two days away. True, she had the slides prepared, and Sisithorn would be responsible for the majority of it. They had practiced several times. That impending event, at least, was well in hand.

So she would use the rest of the day to review charts. She had made that promise to herself, and she would do her best to review all fifty charts before she left for Bangkok Friday morning. Ladarat picked one chart off the pile and began to read, leafing quickly through the patient demographic information in the first section, then slowing down to learn more about the patient's medical history. Finally, she read line by line about the patient's last days in the hospital. She read through thirteen charts in the next hour and a half, her eyes getting increasingly tired.

Some would be called good deaths, perhaps. Patients were given medications like morphine to treat their pain, for instance. Some were even awake and alert enough to talk with their families.

Of course there were opportunities to improve. Such opportunities were, unfortunately, very easy to find: The man with lung cancer and shortness of breath who wasn't given morphine to make him more comfortable. The woman with liver disease and nausea who had a tube placed through her nose and into her stomach for liquid feeding. Ladarat knew that would have been very uncomfortable.

Perhaps deaths were better among patients who died in the palliative care unit. Or perhaps not. That was the problem. There were hardly any of those patients. In the entire stack of fifty charts, there were only the three she'd found yesterday.

Again, Ladarat found herself wondering how that could be possible. A hospital unit dedicated to the care of dying patients that had no deaths? Or almost no deaths? How could you care for dying patients but have none of your patients die? It was a statistical anomaly, was it not? It was a mystery.

Well, not a real mystery, of course. On the scale of mysteries, this was no more than a mild one. A weak mystery.

It was not a mystery like a serial murderess was a mystery, or like disappearing tourists could be a mystery—except that it wasn't—or even like jade smuggling was a mystery.

Speaking of which, perhaps she'd been too quick to dismiss her assistant's theories about what Ladarat had come to think of as the Parrot Gang. Surely there was something suspicious going on there. Perhaps not smuggling, though. Almost certainly not smuggling. But then what?

Ladarat closed yet another chart, setting it on the pile of charts that she'd reviewed. That pile, she was pleased to note, had grown in height to be approximately equal to the pile of charts that were yet to be reviewed. It was actually a little higher, in fact, thanks to a few patients she'd just read about who had been in the hospital for a very long period of time, months, in one case. Thanks to those very thick charts, if one were assessing pages read, Ladarat was more than halfway done. That was certainly a more optimistic way to look at this process, so that's how she would look at it.

Still thinking about the mysterious jade smuggling ring that probably wasn't a jade smuggling ring at all, Ladarat packed up her bag, turned off the lights, and locked her door. It wasn't too late, not even six p.m. She had time for a detour on the way home. It was not significantly out of her way. Besides, it was a detour that would make her assistant pleased.

As she drove across town, the traffic was still heavy. Cars and tuk-tuks and taxis and *sengteos* (pickup trucks repurposed as communal taxis) were busily navigating the congested streets. Her slow progress across town gave Ladarat a chance to think. And it gave her car a chance to keep up a steady stream of warnings about dire threats to its paintwork approaching from all four quadrants.

With so much to think about—including sleepy doctors and smuggling parrots and disappearing authors—Ladarat was surprised to find herself still thinking about those charts she'd reviewed, and the others that she'd looked at. They were good deaths, as far as that went. That is, there were not many glaring errors or examples of bad care. Certainly there were some opportunities for improvement, but nothing worse, she thought, than what you'd find in any American hospital.

No... what worried her most was—

The shrill sound of a horn cut into her thoughts. Several horns, in fact.

Ladarat waved and smiled apologetically. Couldn't these cars see that she needed to turn left? Kaeo Nawarat Alley would take her straight to the bus station. If she didn't turn here, she would have to go all the way to the waterworks. And she really didn't want to go to the waterworks.

Ladarat waved again, and a kind taxi driver let her cross in front of him. Then a *sengteo* driver—with less good grace, it should be noted—let her cross as well. Then she was on Kaeo Nawarat Alley, with no further turns or drama and therefore more time to think.

Her thoughts turned from the deaths themselves to where those deaths were happening, or, more specifically, where they weren't happening. No one seemed to die in the palliative care unit. Or hardly anyone.

It wasn't because that unit was very good at saving lives, of course. That's not what that unit did. It made people comfortable. And yet no one was dying there. How could that be?

Ladarat remembered hearing a story, years ago, about hospitals in some country that had to close for some reason. Perhaps a strike? Anyway, for the period of time that those hospitals were closed, the mortality rates in that country went down. People seemed to be living longer without the benefit of hospitals.

The explanation that Ladarat remembered hearing was that hospitals cause complications and problems—infections and the like—and those problems are often fatal. But without the hospitals, and without those complications, the theory went, people were living longer.

Professor Dalrymple noted a similar phenomenon. "The admonition to do no harm doesn't make sense," she pointed out. "Do no harm? In medicine, doctors always do harm. They give medications with side effects and give treatments that make patients feel bad. We just need to try to ensure that those harms we caused are outweighed by benefits."

Perhaps something similar was happening in the palliative care unit? Without the aggressive treatment so common in the rest of the hospital, perhaps Dr. Taksin's patients were living longer?

Ah, but they were still dying eventually. People like Melissa Double didn't recover. There was no question of a different philosophy of care—even a much gentler philosophy of care—curing the cancer that had apparently spread so widely.

No, if people weren't dying in the inpatient unit—very, very sick people—then that meant that the inpatient unit was helping those people to die somewhere else. But where? And how? She would have to find out.

Now, though, she would just make a slight detour to check on the possibility—the very slight possibility—that a parrot gang was smuggling jade.

So it was without any real expectations of finding anything that Ladarat flicked the turn signal lever that would allow her to to turn into the bus station parking lot. At this time of day, the entrance was crowded with cars and taxis dropping and picking up passengers. None of those vehicles, it seemed, was willing to wait for even a moment to let her by. This was certainly not the Chiang Mai that she remembered from when she and Somboon moved here fourteen years ago. Back then, Chiang Mai was little more than a large town. People were polite and friendly. But now, no. Now, most people didn't know each other. Certainly there was an appalling lack of politeness. And the traffic, well, that was the worst. Now it was every driver for herself.

With that disturbing thought in her mind, Ladarat urged her little car out into the intersection, into the path of a *seng-teo* and, next to it, a tuk-tuk that was pondering a turn into the bus station. The tuk-tuk driver yelled something not particularly polite, and both drivers honked at her. But they did stop in the end, even before her little car could work itself up into a frenzy of shrill proximity warnings.

Then she was in the parking lot, although what she was looking for there, Ladarat couldn't really say. She just felt like she had to see the Parrot Gang with her own eyes. Even if there was a plausible, logical—and entirely innocuous— explanation for these parrot smugglers, it would help if she could at least see one of the gang in action.

She drove slowly along the loop road that circled the parking lot and led past the front doors to the station, too slowly, perhaps. The same tuk-tuk driver who had grudgingly let her pass now seemed inordinately frustrated by her pace.

Such a hurry. Why all the rush?

But then she saw the young *farang* in the back of the tuk-tuk. The man looked at his watch. Of course, they were late for a bus. That, at least, was reasonable.

Ladarat spied an opening by the curb to her left and turned into a spot that would at least give her a good view of the main entrance. If the Parrot Gang was operating here, this is where they would be. But there were no parrot bags. None at all.

Ladarat waited for a few more minutes, determined to do this correctly. It was not a stakeout, of course, not a proper example of the art of detection. Ladarat thought of Khun Timothy's Detective Poke and immediately admitted her own inadequacies of detection. She didn't have the skills for a proper stakeout, nor, honestly, did she have the time, as she'd promised to cook dinner for Wiriya—with some help from Duanphen, of course. This was presumably a problem that Detective Poke never faced.

So now Ladarat could spare only a few moments for detection. Of course that was not enough. Real detectives presumably had to be patient, and they needed lots of time.

Ah, well. It had been worth a try.

Just as she was about to pull back out into the stream of cars and tuk-tuks circulating past the main entrance, Ladarat saw the two *farang* who had been in the tuk-tuk behind her. The driver had let them off on the far side of the entrance, and now they were making their way back to the glass sliding doors.

Loaded down with luggage, they seemed ungainly. As

seemed to be the fashion among young travelers these days, they wore large backpacks on their backs and smaller day-packs in front. Why did they do that? Young travelers were otherwise reliable sources of the latest fashions. This custom made them look like pregnant camels, a strange *farang* camel epidemic that was sweeping Thailand.

Yet there was something odd about their progress. It took Ladarat a moment to realize what was wrong, though.

It was their pace, she realized eventually. They were moving much too slowly for a couple who had been in danger just a few minutes ago of missing a bus. They were walking slowly and carefully, looking around them as they walked toward the main entrance. Once there, they stood for a minute more. Waiting for something? Looking for someone?

At this point, Ladarat had forgotten entirely about her search for members of the Parrot Gang. Now she was not a detective—or even an amateur detective—but just a curious person.

She was curious, because there was something odd, too, about the way that this couple was waiting. It took a moment or two of observation for Ladarat to identify exactly what seemed odd. Then she had it.

They were looking for someone or waiting for someone. That much was clear.

But they weren't scanning the crowds around them as if for a familiar face. They weren't looking this way and that in search of one person. They weren't doing the things that we normally do when we're looking for someone in particular. They weren't turning around and studying the faces of people who passed. If they were looking for someone—and by now Ladarat was convinced that they must be—they were looking for that someone surreptitiously. It was almost as if...they didn't know precisely who it was they were looking for.

But Ladarat knew who they were looking for. She wasn't particularly surprised when a tuk-tuk pulled up in a cloud of blue exhaust smoke and a middle-aged Thai woman hopped out. Then she did something very strange.

The woman reached into an oversize handbag, which was really just a large canvas bag. She pulled out a much smaller bright blue bag. She unfolded it carefully as the tuk-tuk driver waited. Then she reached into her large bag, removing several paper parcels that she transferred to the blue bag. As she did, the sides of the blue bag flattened out, and Ladarat could make out the image of a parrot on the side that she could see.

Then, as Ladarat watched, the woman strolled along the sidewalk in front of the bus station, as if she were on a leisurely walk, accompanied by a dog rather than by a parrot. She hesitated as she passed the couple, then sped up. She stopped when the man of the couple said something to her.

Ladarat was too far away to hear what was said, but she saw quite clearly a paper package emerge from the parrot bag, which the man deposited in the daypack on his chest. Then there was a little more conversation, a pause, and the Thai woman pointed at the tuk-tuk behind her.

The *farang* woman shrugged. She reached into the bag on her chest and pulled out something that she handed to the woman.

All of this happened in less than thirty seconds. In another half minute, the couple had vanished inside the station, and the Thai woman was back in the tuk-tuk. She and the driver seemed to know each other. They were talking and laughing, as if they shared a joke.

Ladarat wished she had more time, to . . . what, exactly?

Well, she could wait to see whether the Parrot Lady gave more packages to other tourists. Her bag was certainly large enough to contain many such packages. But what would that accomplish? Her assistant had already determined that one member of the Parrot Gang—because now it almost certainly had to be a gang—would pass contraband jade to several *farang* at a time. If this was the same gang, it was only logical to assume that here, too, it was jade changing hands.

She could park her car and go ask that *farang* couple whether they had purchased those bracelets, and what the *farang* woman had given the Parrot Lady. Money? A receipt?

But what would they tell her, even if she found them? Besides, they would almost certainly be getting on a bus.

Ladarat decided to curtail her detection activities for the evening. She let her thoughts turn instead to the evening's menu, featuring *yam khor moo yang*—a salad of marinated pork, lemon, onion, and chilis. Duanphen had kindly agreed to provide her with the grilled pork and the salad ingredients; even the sticky rice and dipping sauce. All Ladarat would have to do, Duanphen had promised, was to assemble everything. Of course Ladarat would pick up dessert as well: perhaps *kanom maprao*, since she'd left the entire serving for Melissa. Yes, definitely *kanom maprao*. And maybe something more substantial from Duanphen, too. Perhaps *kai jiew moo ssap*, a deep-fried omelet. It would be a more solid accompaniment to the *yam khor moo yang*.

Having settled the evening's menu to her satisfaction, Ladarat started her little car and was about to turn back into the flow of traffic when the parrot woman again hopped out of the tuk-tuk. She didn't seem to be following any sort of signal that Ladarat could see. She just got out and strolled the width of the front of the bus station. She passed from Ladarat's view for a moment, but soon she was back. A few seconds later, she was stopped by a young *farang* man who approached her and offered a clumsy *wai*.

Again the woman reached into her parrot bag, and again

a paper parcel was passed to the man. And again, the same pause, the gesture at the tuk-tuk, and a shrug from the man, who reached into his bag and handed something to the woman. Then he was gone, and the woman resumed her stroll. Back and forth, like a palace guard, she'd walk from one end of the front walk to the other, a distance of perhaps twenty meters, then she'd turn around and come back.

As Ladarat watched, her dinner menu forgotten, the Thai woman made the same exchange with nine more *farang*. Most were couples, although a few were lone travelers. Each time there was the exchange of a newspaper-wrapped parcel that seemed to be expected and then another discussion, which wasn't. Most of the time that second discussion resulted in the *farang* handing something to the Thai woman, but not always. In fact, the last interaction Ladarat saw looked to be on the verge of turning into an argument. This was a *farang* man traveling alone. Bearded and unkempt, he shook his head violently at the point in the conversation when the other *farang* had reached into their bags for what Ladarat was becoming convinced were baht. This last *farang* wasn't having any of that, though. He just shook his head again, stowed the wrapped parcel in his backpack, slung the bag over one burly shoulder, and marched into the bus station.

That seemed to break a spell, and the tuk-tuk driver shouted something to the woman, who shrugged. Then she nodded and hopped into the tuk-tuk, which took off in a cloud of blue smoke.

Ladarat thought of following them. Surely that's what a detective would do. But truth be told, her car, however worthy and well suited to blending in unobtrusively, had no hope of catching up with a tuk-tuk that could slip between cars and sneak down narrow alleys.

A real detective would have a motorcycle, she thought. A real detective would hop on her motorcycle and track this couple—surreptitiously, of course—to their lair. But a real detective hadn't worked a long day and probably didn't have to rush home to make *yam khor moo yang* for her boyfriend.

Ah, well. Ladarat felt as though she'd just discovered a clue that would lead to a solution of the Parrot Gang case. It had been lucky that she'd stopped at the bus station when she did. Perhaps her luck would last long enough to allow preparation of dinner without disaster.

CHAPTER 17

THE PHILOSOPHY OF BREAKING EGGS

Alas, Ladarat's luck didn't last, although the evening started out well enough. Ladarat arrived at Duanphen's stall just after the dinner rush. By the time she'd driven across town and parked her car in her driveway, noting with annoyance that Wiriya hadn't yet arrived, and then walked around the corner, Duanphen had the makings of *yam khor moo yang* ready and waiting.

Duanphen vetoed Ladarat's suggestion of *kai jiew moo ssap*.

"Eeeyyy, no, Khun. That is the worst idea ever. If I make that omelet now, it will be cold by the time you get home. And cold *kai jiew moo ssap*? No good." She shook her head, thinking for a moment.

"Can you... make an omelet, Khun?"

Could she? She'd never made one before. But that's not the same thing as saying that she couldn't. Maybe she could.

Duanphen was watching her expectantly, so she nodded in a way that she hoped would inspire confidence.

Duanphen seemed satisfied. "All right, then. You will make *kai jiew moo ssap* on your own. Not deep-fried, of course. No, too messy. But a simple omelet, hot off the stove." She paused. "You do... have a stove, do you not, Khun?"

Ladarat nodded earnestly.

"And a frying pan?"

Ladarat nodded again, with a bit less confidence. There were pans in the cupboard, she knew. She'd seen them the last time she'd looked, which was...oh...well...a while ago.

Whether they were exactly the sort of equipment one might use for the operation of frying, she couldn't say. But that wasn't important, was it? What was important, certainly, were the ingredients. If she got the right ingredients from Duanphen—and, of course, if she had adequate stores of enthusiasm—what could possibly go wrong?

That seemed to be Duanphen's hope, too, more or less. She carefully doled out all of the ingredients that Ladarat would need into a towering stack of cardboard containers.

"My son made me change from Styrofoam," Duanphen explained. "He says it's bad for the environment." She shrugged. "I guess it really doesn't matter, and this cardboard is cheaper. But it's hard to get used to."

There were the grilled pork and vegetables and sticky rice, and a container for chili sauce and another for dipping sauce. And spring onions and holy basil leaves. Then, for the omelet, four eggs, minced smoked pork, and a small plastic containers of Golden Boy sauce, which Duanphen added after asking if Ladarat had any on hand and receiving a blank look in return.

"So now you're ready. You just prepare the salad, and let it sit in the refrigerator." She smiled. "I know you have a refrigerator. Then, while that's chilling, you make the omelet, and you serve them both together. And"—she reached under her makeshift counter—"Prasert's *kanom maprao*. Even if everything else is a...even if other things don't turn out perfectly, this will save any evening."

Perhaps that was true, under normal circumstances, but this evening was beginning to look like one that not even the best coconut cake in the world could salvage. Ladarat chopped the basil and cucumbers as Duanphen had shown her, then the onions and finally the pork, making a salad that looked rather pretty in a disorganized sort of way. Unsure which was the dressing and which was the dipping sauce for the pork, Ladarat poured both into the mixture in the bowl and stirred it in evenly, more or less.

She had hoped that she could at least begin the omelet before Wiriya arrived. Her heart sank as she heard his car in the driveway. Making an omelet couldn't possibly be that difficult, could it? Probably it was not. But how was someone supposed to break an egg?

That was something that people—normal people, at least—tried to avoid doing. It wasn't something a sane person would try to do. Ladarat's experience in this activity was rather limited. What was the appropriate procedure? One needed a fundamental change of philosophy in order to break an egg, she thought. Ladarat stood uncertainly at the kitchen counter, holding one egg in each hand.

That was how Wiriya found her as he let himself in through the front door and greeted her with a kiss before taking a Singha out of the refrigerator.

He looked at the *yam khor moo yang*, a little startled, perhaps. His eyebrows went up a fraction of a centimeter, just a little higher on the left than on the right, as was usual for him. Wiriya seemed surprised, but whether that was because of the appearance of this particular batch of *yam khor moo yang*, or—as Ladarat preferred to believe—the fact that it was here at all, she wasn't sure.

He looked carefully at the eggs on the counter and approvingly at the bowl and the frying pan that Ladarat had found and cleaned of dust and cobwebs. Finally he looked at the eggs she was holding gingerly in each hand.

"You are contemplating the possibility of breaking eggs?" he guessed.

Ladarat nodded and tried to explain her theory of breaking eggs, that it was something that one tried not to do, so doing it, well, seemed more complicated than perhaps it really was. It was perhaps the stupidest culinary theory that Ladarat had ever heard uttered, but Wiriya seemed to take it in stride. He even nodded.

"I've seen our new nurses in the police clinic face the same challenge. They've never drawn blood before, and they know that sticking a needle into someone is something that most normal people don't do. It's really not that difficult or complicated. But they poke gently, then a little harder. Then too hard." He paused. "But you know, breaking eggs is not so difficult."

"It isn't?"

"Not at all. You just need to use the right amount of force. And if you're not sure, then first a little bit, and then a little bit more. Here." Wiriya took one of the eggs that Ladarat had been holding.

He rapped the egg sharply on the edge of the sink, creating a substantial crack all the way around. He handed it to her, and she took it carefully in one hand.

"Two hands. Like you're peeling a rambutan."

Ladarat stuck both thumbs into the cracked egg. That analogy had made her forget for a moment that she wasn't holding a spiny, hard-skinned piece of fruit, but an egg. The shell broke into pieces, and the egg and pieces of the white shell ended up in the bowl. On the bright side, though, she had certainly broken an egg. Patiently, Wiriya helped her fish the pieces of eggshell out with a fork, and he helped her break another egg, and another and another. Then he watched approvingly as she mixed the eggs together and added the Golden Boy sauce.

"Secret ingredient," she said.

Wiriya could be a patient teacher, but he was on his second Singha, and he was hungry.

"I'll do this part." He expertly heated the pan, swirled the eggs around, and in a few minutes created a crispy brown omelet that Duanphen would have been proud of.

A few minutes later, as they were sitting outside in the garden and Ladarat had her own Singha, she thought to ask her boyfriend where he had learned to cook. He laughed.

"I'm a bachelor, remember? We have to learn to fend for ourselves. I decided a while ago that I would learn to cook some simple things. Just so I don't starve."

Such as?

"Kao mok gai."

"Kao mok gai?" That was a baked dish of rice and saffron and chicken, not complicated, but requiring vast patience. Duanphen had warned at their first lesson that it was for advanced chefs. "Too many opportunities to go wrong. Stick to dishes that are simpler at first."

Wiriya nodded, then shrugged. "Anything is easy with practice," he said, serving the pork salad and then the omelet from the pan, first to Ladarat, then to himself. He tried the pork salad first, nodding, then grimacing just a little.

"A little spicy, perhaps?"

Ladarat tried some and nodded. "Maybe that's the chili dipping sauce."

Wiriya arched an eyebrow, looking around for the dipping sauce.

"I just put it all in the salad," she explained. "I wasn't sure which one was the dipping sauce, so...."

"You added both. Makes sense. Very efficient."

After they ate for a moment or two in comfortable silence, Ladarat decided that this would be an excellent time to get some advice about the strange case of the Parrot Gang. But she also had to admit that it was nice not having a case to talk about. It was nice not having other people's problems intruding on their time together.

She sent Richard April on his way to wherever it was he was going, with whomever he'd found to go with. And she left the Parrot Gang to fend for itself. She didn't even ask what Wiriya's young, ambitious detectives had discovered in the mysterious case of the sleeping doctor.

Instead they talked about their plans for the weekend, and Ladarat's upcoming trip to Bangkok, and the value of efficiency in culinary endeavors.

Wan pareuhatsabordee

THURSDAY

CHAPTER 18

A VERY THAI SORT OF CRIME

Ladarat found herself wide awake especially early the next morning, more than an hour before her alarm went off. Even so, Wiriya was already gone. She had time for an extra cup of peaflower tea in her little kitchen; the garden was too chilly this early in the morning. With that extra time, she left the tea to steep for an extra minute, so it turned a bright, almost artificial blue.

She had time to think about how her house was empty, but not quite empty. It didn't feel empty in the same way that it was empty when she was living here all alone. There was sort of a residual presence that was oddly comforting.

She had plenty of time to think about this and other things, a rare luxury these days. Those thoughts led from one topic to another, so as she was in her car, driving leisurely toward the hospital, those thoughts had time to turn almost by accident to the misfortune that Ukrit had suffered. To fall asleep and be robbed—that sounded like something that might happen in Third World countries like India. Or perhaps London twenty years ago.

It was such an antique sort of crime. You wait for someone to fall asleep and then take their money? So sneaky, and yet gentle at the same time. A very Thai sort of crime, which avoided conflict and drama.

As Ladarat pondered this odd approach to separating people from their valuables, she found herself once again in the vicinity of the bus station. It wasn't exactly on the way to the hospital, but it wasn't exactly out of her way, either.

Deciding perhaps that fate had had a hand in her navigation this morning—and in waking her up especially early—on a whim that she couldn't have explained, once again Ladarat pulled into the long circular access road. It was still early, and the overnight buses from Bangkok were arriving and disgorging passengers, who stumbled bleary-eyed out to the front door to waiting tuk-tuks and taxis. That river of passengers parted around a *farang* couple who seemed to be arguing with a policeman.

Curious, Ladarat pulled up next to the three of them and rolled down her window. She was close enough to hear the man and the woman talking in accented English. The policeman either didn't understand them or—more likely—took them for drug addicts because they both looked confused and unsteady on their feet. Remembering Ukrit and his story, though, Ladarat got out of her car, leaving it parked conspicuously, and conspicuously illegally, and went over to offer what assistance she could.

Ladarat greeted the policeman with a respectful *wai*. He returned it perfunctorily but then, after a comic double take, considerably more enthusiastically as his eyes widened in recognition.

"Ah, Khun Ladarat." He smiled. "You are solving another murder?"

It was amazing how far her fame had spread—aided, no doubt, by her...affiliation with Wiriya. But still. Did everyone on the Chiang Mai police force know who she was?

She smiled, then shook her head. Disappointed, he shrugged and introduced himself, then explained the situation in Thai.

"These kids, they are drunk, I think. Or they've been smoking Thai sticks, or something. They seem confused. They keep saying they arrived on the day bus from Bangkok."

"You mean the overnight bus?"

The cop shook his head. "No, I'm sure they meant the day bus. The last one that gets in at two a.m.? And I guess they fell asleep on one of the benches inside. They must have slept there half of the night. And now they're saying they've lost all of their money. But that's what happens when you get drunk and fall asleep."

The couple had been watching this conversation with interest, but they were strangely silent. Neither one of them made an effort to ask Ladarat who she was. They both seemed, well, a little drunk.

"Let me talk to them," she said kindly. "I will tell them that I'm a nurse. Perhaps they'll be more honest about whatever drugs they've used."

The policeman nodded uncertainly and took a step back. Meanwhile, the man and the woman looked unperturbed by this turn of events. Perhaps they were thinking that their day couldn't get any stranger.

Looking at them more closely, Ladarat realized that they were little more than kids, as backpackers in northern Thailand all seemed to be. The boy and the girl both wore identical loose-fitting cargo shorts and T-shirts of the sort of material that promises to dry quickly. Both were blond and blue-eyed, with short, sensible hair. Ladarat pegged them immediately as pragmatic Germans.

"Where are you from?" she asked in English.

"Australia," they both said in unison.

Oh, well. She hoped her skills of detection were better than her knowledge of culture and geography.

Bit by bit, in response to repeated questions, their story emerged, as Ladarat alternately listened and translated for the bewildered policeman. Their story would have been difficult to unravel if she hadn't heard most of it already.

They'd been in Thailand for a week, the girl said. Down on the beaches, the boy added. Koh Samui, Koh Tao, Krabi, Pattaya. Here they both made a face. Too dirty, they said. Too much sex and drugs.

Then they flew back to Bangkok and took the bus here yesterday, during the day, so they could see the country. And just like Ukrit, they had fallen fast asleep. Someone had carried them off the bus and deposited them on two adjoining benches with all of their belongings stacked neatly beside them. Well, almost all. Someone had also rifled through their pockets, stealing an envelope of cash and their credit cards. The thief had also taken an expensive diving watch from the boy's bag and a necklace from the girl's. But at least the thief had left their passports.

Ladarat thought for a moment after she'd translated this story for the policeman. She turned to him and asked the logical question, the question that a detective would ask.

"So if they were robbed, do you think it happened on the bus, or while they were lying on a bench?"

The policeman shook his head emphatically. "Not on the bench. You see, there was someone very important who fell asleep on a bench yesterday. It happens a lot lately, and some people get robbed. But this man... well, he was very important. I heard he was a famous doctor visiting Chiang Mai to speak at the medical school. But he was robbed, and your friend Captain Mookjai has stepped in to help with the investigation."

Ladarat smiled as vacantly as she could.

"So the word came down that anyone who falls asleep on a

bus we should watch over like family. Even if they're drunk or stoned, like these kids. I came on at six a.m., and one of the cops working the night shift told me about them. He made sure that the bus attendant carried them very gently, and then he made sure that all of their belongings were with them, and that no one touched them."

"Does this happen... often? The falling asleep on a bus?" And waking up poor.

He didn't hesitate. "Oh, yes. All the time. One of the bus attendants explained it to me. These *farang*, she said, they travel long distances to visit our country. Sometimes they're in planes for twenty-four hours. Can you imagine? And when they get here they suffer from jet lag. You know jet lag?"

Ladarat nodded.

"So they're tired and suffer jet lag. And even though it's seven in the morning, their *farang* brains tell them that it's still late at night. Especially when they've smoked a Thai stick... You can't wake them up. So you see, it's normal for them to sleep like this. Not like that famous doctor—we still don't know what happened to him. That was a mystery."

"The bus attendant who told you this, she seems very knowledgeable... Which bus company does she work for?"

"Ah, she was from the Royal Yellow Bus Company. Very good company. Always on time. Good service. I use them whenever I go to Bangkok."

She turned to the young couple. "And which bus company did you use?"

The boy seemed confused. He shook his head. The girl thought for a moment and then said she couldn't remember. In fact, as they compared notes, it became obvious that they couldn't remember anything about the trip. They knew that they had arrived at the station in Bangkok. They remembered being rushed and not being sure whether they'd have time to eat dinner. And then...they woke up here in the middle of the night. They couldn't remember buying tickets or boarding a bus. And they couldn't remember having dinner.

There was something about this story that didn't seem right. But as Ladarat was mulling it over in her head, a flash of movement off to her right caught her attention instead. As they'd been talking, traffic had been gotten busier along the driveway that led past the bus station entrance. Cars and taxis and tuk-tuks jockeyed for position near the curb to discharge passengers. Another policeman walked up to Ladarat's car, parked in a "No Parking" zone, and had begun to write her a ticket. The cop she'd been helping shouted to him and waved him away. Ladarat had lost track of the time, but she realized that she'd gone from being exceptionally early to being quite late.

Before she left, though, she wanted to make sure the young couple would be all right. She took one of her business cards from her handbag and wrote down the name of the monastery next to the hospital. The monks there often made room for visitors to the hospital who had come long distances.

"Do you know Somporn and Kamon?" she asked the policeman.

"Ah, yes. They're assigned to the case of the famous doctor who was robbed. You think...you think these cases are related? But these kids are just on drugs."

The policeman looked both of the *farang* up and down with visible skepticism, as if he couldn't imagine any serious crimes in which these two would be on the victim roster next to a famous visiting doctor. Ladarat didn't have the time to explain that the thieves had in all probability made more off of these two backpackers than they had from a poor medical fellow who had an expensive girlfriend to support.

"Just call them, would you? And ask them to get the details, and then to take these two to the Australian consulate."

The policeman nodded, still skeptical, but intrigued despite himself.

Ladarat explained to the couple what she'd arranged, keeping one eye on her car to make sure her good efforts weren't rewarded with a ticket.

The couple seemed grateful, but distracted. The boy in particular had an odd tendency to repeat questions, as if he forgot the answers as soon as he heard them. He must have asked her four times in the space of just a few minutes how they could contact their parents.

As Ladarat thanked the policeman, he was already on the phone trying to reach Somporn and Kamon. She rescued her car and pulled into traffic, weaving carefully through the ranks of taxis and tuk-tuks. That didn't give her much attention to spare for the mystery of the sleeping travelers. Yet there were aspects of this story that were definitely strange.

The boy, for instance—so much more impaired than the girl was. Why would that be?

And the attendant who was so helpful, so confident in explaining away the fact that travelers were falling asleep mysteriously. Was that suspicious?

But no, that was being too much of a detective. People were helpful. Everyone had their theories about why *farang* did what they did. It was a national Thai pastime, trying to explain the strange behaviors of Germans and Australians and Americans.

Like pancakes. Why did backpacker hostels all serve pancakes? Banana pancakes, usually. What was the appeal of a big, tasteless slab of fried dough? That attendant was welcome to her theories. In the meantime, Ladarat would work on her own.

CHAPTER 19

THE POWER OF *JAI DEE*

Chi had been delighted to see her. At least, he seemed mildly interested. Except when he was with Sukanya or a patient, the little dog never managed to muster a great deal of enthusiasm for anything or anyone.

But when Ladarat met Chi and Sukanya outside the palliative care building, Chi good-naturedly hopped out of his owner's car as Ladarat took his leash. He even wagged his tail a little, just as much as his dignity would allow. Then he was in character, and he trotted solemnly up the steps and waited at the door as Sukanya waved and drove off to the parking lot.

Inside, the unit seemed quieter than usual. Dr. Taksin's door was closed. Perhaps he was at home, sleeping late. As Chi led her down the hall, Ladarat reflected that she had never seen anyone look as tired as Dr. Taksin had yesterday. Perhaps he needed to take a bus to Bangkok.

Ladarat stopped in her tracks at that thought, much to Chi's consternation. He knew exactly where they were going, and indeed he could see Melissa's open door just ahead. And here they were, just standing in the hallway like gawking tourists.

Pffttt.

But Ladarat wasn't paying attention. She'd just remembered Melissa's story about the scans and Dr. Taksin's revelation that those scans had already been read. Ladarat had been so

206

caught up by her other investigations that she hadn't paused to think about how this conversation would unfold.

Eeyyy. This was bad. Bad that she could be here without a plan, but worse that she hadn't even considered it. Was she so distracted by her activities of detection that she didn't have time for work? For a moment, she took stock of the previous day: the trip to the Magic Grove Hotel and to the bus station, and just a little time spent reviewing charts. She would have to be more dutiful. Starting now.

What should she do?

Should she continue to play along? As if she didn't know the truth about Khun Melissa's scans?

Chi flopped down on the linoleum, panting rapidly, as if this stately walk up the front steps and down the hallway, followed by the frustration of standing still, had taxed his cardiovascular system severely. With the philosophical wisdom for which dogs are justly known, he decided to make the best of a difficult situation.

Pffttt. Not without protest.

He was right to be impatient, of course. This was his job, and Ladarat was interfering with the exercise of his dogly duties.

Yet, this would be the best time for a pause to consider the correct course of action. Ladarat knew that Melissa had received bad news, but she knew just as certainly that Melissa had not told her what she knew. So what should she do? Should she admit that she knew of the scan results? Should she ask Melissa why she didn't share those results yesterday? Or should she pretend that she knew nothing. What should she do? Think.

She did think, but no thoughts appeared.

What would Professor Julia Dalrymple do?

Ladarat pondered that question for a good minute in the

empty hallway as Chi snuffled peacefully. She could only remember a handful of instances in which the good professor failed to offer a suggestion to a challenging conundrum. But this was, alas, one such instance. Try as she might, Ladarat found that she was unable to come up with any helpful advice from that slim 124-page volume.

A better question, then, might be what the good professor would have said—if she had anything to say about the matter, which Ladarat was pretty sure she didn't.

What would Professor Dalrymple have said if she were standing in the hallway with this nurse ethicist and her therapy dog?

Ladarat was pleased that an answer came to her almost as soon as she asked the question. That answer came in the form of a question.

Do you think Ms. Double from Wales wants to discuss the results of her CT scan with you?

Ladarat pondered that question for just a second. That was all she needed in order to arrive at a satisfactory answer. That answer, of course, was that Melissa Double most certainly did not want to discuss the results of that scan. If she had, she would have mentioned them, would she not?

Then came another question, unbidden, from the absent Professor Dalrymple.

So, Khun Ladarat, do you think its proper to force such a discussion on a patient who does not want to have such a discussion?

Ladarat barely had time feel a twinge of guilt and admit that the best answer was a firm no when she found herself facing yet another question from the very persistent professor.

Is it possible that your status as a nurse ethicist at a prestigious hospital should give you the right to override a patient's decisions about when and with whom she's ready to discuss such a weighty matter?

This time Ladarat just shook her head, waiting for the next question and wondering when the good professor had become so harsh, and so assertive. In all of their years of virtual mentorship, the professor had come to her aid more times than she could count, but always at Ladarat's bidding. This sudden appearance, armed with pointed questions, was entirely new, and a little disconcerting.

Yet at the same time Ladarat had to admit that these questions weren't without merit. Nor was the tone unjustified. The professor was right to be a little harsh; more than a little harsh.

Ladarat waited a moment more, wondering whether perhaps there was another question from the good professor on its way. Fortunately, there was not. The next question never came, and Ladarat found that she was free to proceed down the hall.

Chi woke instantly in response to a gentle tug on his leash, leaping to his feet. A little wriggling stagger was the only indication that perhaps he had assumed a vertical position before his brain had entirely roused itself. Chi circled once, then twice in a clockwise spin, as if to reorient himself and his sleepy brain to his surroundings. Then he set off down the hall, aiming unerringly for Melissa Double's room. Ladarat dropped his leash and Chi sprinted ahead, slipping through the half-open door. The sound of muffled laughter suggested that he had once again found a warm welcome.

And indeed he had. When Ladarat caught up with the intrepid therapy dog, she found him perched next to a serene-looking Melissa Double. Sitting at her side on the bed, he had assumed the pose of a benign but not-to-be-trifled-with guardian—if a ten-kilo ball of fur could be said to guard any-thing, or anyone.

"Khun Ladarat—this is a pleasant surprise. Even better than *kanom maprao*."

Personally, Ladarat didn't think that a small dog could ever be more welcome than a piece of good *kanom maprao*. But then, Melissa Double was entitled to her opinion in this as in other things.

"Better?" Ladarat smiled, sitting in the chair at the table where they'd eaten lunch yesterday. Was it just yesterday? "Well, that's probably just as well. *Kanom maprao*—really good *kanom maprao*—is a lot of work. While Chi…well, I just had to walk him in from the car and let go of his leash, and he came right in here. So easy."

"Did he really?" Melissa scratched the spot behind Chi's left ear that Ladarat had discovered after much trial and error was his favorite. She was amazed that Melissa Double had arrived at the same spot seemingly by instinct.

Ladarat nodded. "I think you have a friend." Indeed, the look that Chi gave the person who owned the hand that was scratching that hard-to-reach spot behind his left ear sug-gested undying friendship and eternal loyalty.

Melissa laughed. "I seem to be making friends at an alarm-ing rate these days."

"And you are well, Khun?" An awkward question, to be sure, but one that had to be asked. "As well as is possible?"

"As well as is possible?" Melissa asked, smiling. "Is that a Thai saying?"

Ladarat thought about that for a moment, then shook her head. "Not really. No…not at all. But we try not to bring too much attention to good fortune or good health."

"Attention? What kind of attention?"

Chi was either becoming bored with the turn this conversation was taking, or perhaps he had decided that his guard responsibilities were no longer needed. In any event, he turned around three times and planted his nose between Melissa's back and the pillows that were propping her up. Melissa winced just for a second, then smiled.

"The gods, I suppose," Ladarat said. "Or fortune. Or luck. You see, it's unwise to call attention to good fortune because someone—or something—might decide that you've had just a bit too much good fortune lately. So we find ways to downplay good health or a successful job. So someone who has just won the lottery might say that he's as well as is possible."

"So Thais are superstitious?" Melissa paused. "I didn't mean any offense. We're all superstitious, aren't we?"

Ladarat had to agree that was so. But, truth be told, Thais were perhaps a little more vulnerable to superstition than, say, Americans.

"Oh, yes. There are all sorts of superstitions we believe in...to varying degrees."

"Like what?" Melissa Double was leaning forward slightly, her head cocked to one side, and her hand strayed momentarily from Chi's left ear.

"Well..." These superstitions were everywhere, so it was odd that her mind was a blank when she was asked to think of one. "Well, we often say it's bad luck to say a baby is cute, or something bad might happen to it."

"Like saying you're very well?"

"Exactly so." That one made sense, perhaps. But the others that she was thinking of right at this moment seemed silly.

"Are there others?"

"Oh yes. Many." Very many. Lots.

Melissa waited expectantly.

"Well, you should be careful not to break anything on your wedding day, or your marriage will break apart."

Melissa smiled. "You know, I was never married, but perhaps that's a good thing. I'm quite clumsy. Any marriage to me wouldn't have stood a chance. Are there others?"

Now Ladarat's memory was returning to her, just in time. "We say you should always step out of the house with your right foot, for instance. Never with your left. And you shouldn't pluck your eyebrows at night because bad things will happen. And you shouldn't recite the names of people who have died, or you'll be next."

Just mentioning those superstitions made Ladarat feel just a little bit embarrassed. It made it sound like Thai people were little better than savages. Don't pluck your eyebrows at night? Really? This is a belief for an ancient civilization and an internationally respected culture?

But Melissa didn't see it that way.

"Everyone has superstitions. Don't walk under ladders or don't let a black cat cross your path. When you say them like that, they sound silly. But they're just a way of trying to control the world."

"They are?" Ladarat hadn't thought of them that way before.

"Well, not control, exactly. But convincing yourself that you're in control. They're a way of convincing yourself that you have some control over events that are in reality outside your control." She paused, thinking, as her hand wandered back to Chi's left ear.

"Back when I was being treated for cancer I used to invent these strange rituals. Or..."—she corrected herself—"my brain did, if that makes any sense."

Ladarat nodded. It did, sort of.

"I would find myself thinking that if I found a parking spot easily at the cancer center, then the CT scan that day would be good news." She smiled. "So of course I started leaving the house earlier, just to be sure I'd find a parking space. I knew it wasn't true, but once my brain made that connection, leaving the house earlier made me feel better, somehow. As if by just getting up thirty minutes earlier, I could improve my chances of survival."

"But you knew it wasn't true?"

"Of course, I knew. I just didn't think about it *not* being true, if you see what I mean. It was like I could believe that it was true and that it wasn't, at the same time. Then it was simply a matter of focusing on the true part. And it made me feel better."

"Then it's useful?" Ladarat hadn't thought about superstitions that way before, certainly not about how superstitions might be helpful to her patients. This was a lesson about which Professor Dalrymple, although generally a fount of useful knowledge, was strangely silent.

"It was for me," Melissa said simply. She thought for a moment. "And it still is, in a way. Not about getting up early," she said quickly. "But more about . . . not being home. Not that it makes any sense."

"What doesn't make sense?"

"You promise you won't laugh?"

Ladarat promised.

"Well, in the back of my mind, I have this idea that I couldn't get sick . . . and die . . . while I'm on a vacation. I mean, who ever heard of someone dying while on a vacation?"

Ladarat thought about the tragedy of the Americans that she had to present at the medical ethics conference tomorrow. True, they didn't actually die. But they came much closer than

213

anyone would want to. On the other hand, that was an accident, not an illness.

"One might expect to die as the result of an accident on a vacation, but a serious illness..."

"Exactly," Melissa said. "Not that it makes any sense. If you're sick when you get on the plane, you have the same chance of dying as you would if you stayed at home in Cardiff."

"My home," she said in response to Ladarat's blank look. Ah, Melissa had said that in one of their conversations. Cardiff. She would have to remember to look it up on a map later.

Ladarat nodded. "That makes sense, in a way. Or at least as much sense as believing that you shouldn't pluck your eyebrows at night."

Melissa shook her head. "Well, I still don't understand that, but I don't need to. Anyway, I got this fixed idea that as long as I'm traveling, I can't die. I know that's not logical, and I wouldn't count on it." She laughed, a little sadly. "It's not like I'm canceling my life insurance policy. But as long as I'm traveling, I can believe that just enough—just barely enough—to get along from day to day. I guess it's not much different than thinking that as long as you're plucking your eyebrows only in the morning, at least you're doing something to ward off harm. Even if you don't believe it, you're doing something, you know?"

Ladarat nodded. "But...are you sure it's not just a distraction, this traveling? That maybe when you're traveling you're thinking about other things?"

Melissa thought about that carefully and paid close attention to Chi's left ear for a moment. "Maybe," she said finally. "Well, almost certainly. There's some of that. I mean, who wants to think about the fact that they're dying? Or maybe dying?"

"So that's a good reason to travel, isn't it?"

"Well, not for everyone. Or even for most people. But there wasn't a lot keeping me at home. And there is a whole world of things to see. So yes, for me, even though I knew I had a fatal disease, traveling seemed like the best way to go. The only thing to do, really."

"For the distraction?" she asked.

"That, and a way not to be sick."

"Not to be sick?"

Melissa took a long time to answer, and in the interval her eyes started to close just a little. But then Chi grunted, and Melissa seemed to wake up, and she picked up exactly where she'd left off.

"Sure...if I stayed at home, I wouldn't have anything to do but to be sick. To be...dying. Everyone would treat me carefully. They'd send me flowers and they'd be careful about what they said when I was nearby. And that's no fun. But here, or in Laos, or Vietnam, or anywhere, I'm not sick. I might be sick, of course. I *am* sick. But not everyone needs to know that. And they don't need to treat me any differently."

"Just as...a tourist?"

Melissa laughed. "Well, it's never good to be treated as a tourist. But it's better to be treated as a tourist than as a a a dying person."

It was at that moment that Ladarat realized that Melissa was talking about her illness as something that was a fact. That her cancer was back. And that she knew about that before she left. And...maybe, that was the reason she left.

But could that be true? Would someone really leave to tour the world, knowing that she was dying? Everything she said about not wanting to be treated like a dying person made sense, as far as it went. It made sense, in theory, so to speak.

But it was impossible to imagine leaving the comforts of home and the stability of a familiar environment to go on an adventure. But then, maybe that was a *farang* thing, to travel like that when you're dying. No Thai person would do that, would they? She had never heard of such a thing.

"So, with all of this traveling…"

"Yes?" Melissa was looking at her, although her eyes began to close after just a moment. She opened them with apparent effort and did her best to focus. Chi gave a disgruntled snort as he realized his left ear wasn't getting the attention that was its due.

There was a question Ladarat remembered learning to ask during her ethics fellowship in Chicago. It was not a question that she usually asked of Thai patients—it wouldn't really make sense to them—but for Melissa…

"With all of this travel, do you feel at peace?"

Melissa could have asked what that question meant. If she had, Ladarat wouldn't have explained it well. She knew that the person who had first asked it was a professor at Duke University in the U.S., a German professor, probably, named Steinhauser. She had said it was a question a doctor could ask to find out whether a patient was suffering spiritual distress.

"You know, I really do." Melissa seemed surprised by her answer. "I never would have thought of asking that question of myself. And no one's ever asked me before." She paused for a long minute, devoting all of her attention to Chi.

"But," she resumed as if that pause hadn't happened, "I really do feel at peace when I'm traveling. Maybe that's distraction, as you say. But whatever it is, I do feel peaceful." Then she looked at Ladarat with a new appreciation and a little more alertness.

"You must be very wise, Khun Ladarat, to ask such questions. Of course, anyone can ask a good question that's revealing. But to ask a question that will make someone feel better...well... that is an amazing thing."

Ladarat thought it was good time to bring their conversation to an end. Melissa seemed to be tiring. Her forgetfulness vis-à-vis Chi's left ear was becoming more frequent, to the little dog's infinite annoyance. He let out a prolonged *pffttt* that roused Melissa from her reverie.

"Thank you, Khun," Ladarat said as she stood to go. "That is one of the kindest things someone has ever said to me." And she meant it. "Have you heard the expression *jai dee*?" Ladarat asked.

Melissa's eyes had been closing slowly, but now they fluttered half open, and she smiled and shook her head.

"I'm not sure what the exact English translation is, but in Thai I think the closest is to say that someone has a pure heart."

Melissa's eyes were open now, and she was smiling, with one eyebrow raised, in the way that you might look if you think you're being told joke. But this was no joke.

Chi used his pet therapy sixth sense to notice that they were leaving, and he stood and wriggled to stretch his weary limbs after another bout of hard labor. He accepted one last scratch behind his left ear before hopping reluctantly off the bed.

"I think, Khun, that this question about being at peace makes you feel better because you *are* at peace. And to be at peace in the face of...of everything you're going through is the sure sign of someone who is *jai dee*."

"Thank you, Khun. In a way that proves my point about the value of travel."

"How so?"

"If I had stayed in Cardiff, I never would have discovered that I'm...how do you say it?"

"*Jai dee.*"

"Exactly. I never would have learned that, and I would have gone to the grave that much poorer."

Ladarat said goodbye, promising to visit the next day, and dragging along Chi, who came somewhat unwillingly. Walking down the hallway, she was so engrossed in congratulating herself on such a productive encounter that she didn't immediately recognize the *farang* face that materialized in her path.

"Khun Ladarat?" the face said in thinly accented Thai. "Such a surprise to see you. But then, you said you are a nurse here, are you not?"

Oh, dear.

"Khun Delia. Yes, I'm here every day." More or less.

"Except when you're looking for lost... patients."

Ladarat nodded. "But you, you're visiting... a friend?"

Delia nodded. "An acquaintance, really. Someone I knew from my previous life. I thought I should stop by."

"I'm so sorry." Ladarat thought that was the right thing to say. Anyone in this unit, by definition, was not well. Very not well. So although it might seem premature, condolences were in order. "The nurses' station is up ahead on the left—you just give them your name and tell them—"

"Oh, thank you, Khun, but I know the routine. I won't keep you." And the owner of the Magic Grove Hotel strode purposefully down the hall toward the nurses' station as if, indeed, she knew her way around as well as Ladarat did.

Walking back across the hospital driveway, Ladarat found herself momentarily distracted by the concept of lunch. An early lunch. But surely not too early? It was eleven, and it had been a long and difficult morning, had it not? It had. Certainly lunch was warranted. And it was well deserved.

Chi seemed to think so, too. Given the choice between a

straight line across the hospital driveway and up the impressive stone steps or an abrupt left turn toward the food sellers on Suthep Road, Chi turned left without hesitation. It should be noted that he did cast what might charitably be called a backward glance at his minder to assess her interest in lunch. But that was truly not more than a confirmation. His nose had detected the first scents of grilling meat over charcoal braziers, and he was not about to be dissuaded, no matter whose hand was holding his leash.

Ladarat found herself following his lead, increasingly hungry, too. But she was also thoughtful, thoughtful about two things at the same time.

The first, of course, was lunch. It should be something simple, because although it had been a busy morning, it had not been a particularly productive one. True, there was the support she'd been able to offer Khun Melissa, and a question that made her feel better. But in terms of what one might call "significant advances," the morning had been very thin indeed. There was a need for sustenance, but perhaps not celebration.

So: Sonthi's *kao niew moo yang*. Grilled pork skewers and rice: very simple and best when very fresh. It was ideal to get there early, when Sonthi had just opened for business and the coals were very, very hot.

That was her first topic of thoughtfulness. The second she attended to while placing her order, juggling her purse and a hundred baht and Chi's leash.

In between handing over the money and corralling Chi, who was busily gulping scraps of roasted chicken bestowed upon him by Sonthi's neighbor, Ladarat recognized that she had a golden opportunity; but she wasn't sure how to use it.

She completed her transaction, and Chi recognized that there would be no further scraps forthcoming, leaving Ladarat free to use her phone. She paused in the middle of the sidewalk, Chi's leash and two plastic bags of *kao niew moo yang* and sticky rice in one hand, her phone in the other.

Ladarat scrolled through her past calls—of which there were not many—until she found the call that Jonah had placed from the closet. She pressed a button to redial and waited. And waited. Eventually she got Jonah's voice mail. She ended the call.

So how, exactly, should she use this opportunity that had just presented itself?

Or maybe she shouldn't use it. Hadn't she determined definitively that there was no "case" involving the Magic Grove Hotel? At least Wiriya had determined that, and she'd agreed.

On the other hand, she did have a spy in place, whose presence shouldn't be wasted. She should at least…check in, shouldn't she? After all, he was there at her request.

That was settled. But…how?

Standing still, as Chi looked up at her with his head cocked to one side, Ladarat waited for inspiration. None came.

Pffttt.

Exactly. A glorious window of opportunity, when the owner of the Magic Grove Hotel was otherwise occupied and—more important—far away. It was a perfect chance to encourage Jonah to search for evidence of maleficence. But she couldn't reach him.

Pffttt. Chi was understandably confused. He knew that the food sellers were ten meters behind them, and his little dog brain was astute enough to recognize that a comfortable place to take a nap was just ahead, inside the main hospital doors and an elevator ride away. So why were they standing here?

"We're waiting for inspiration." A passing group of nursing

students looked at her strangely, and the tallest gave her a tolerant smile.

Yim thak thaai. The distant smile you give someone you barely know, or the odd-looking boy with the big ears who fancies you, or, in this case, the crazy nurse standing in the middle of the sidewalk with a dog, talking to herself.

But there were benefits of talking to oneself, as Ladarat just discovered. Sometimes those conversations with oneself were good for producing ideas. Who better to help you think of a solution to an intractable problem than someone—you—who knows what you're up against?

Feeling suddenly better, and now very hungry, Ladarat tugged on Chi's leash, letting him know that although a return trip to Sonthi's neighbor was not in the cards, a comfortable nap was in his future. They set off, Chi in the lead, Ladarat trailing behind, her phone clamped to her ear.

By the time they had arrived at Ladarat's office, she had been helped by the operator in directory assistance and was listening to a distant phone ringing.

"Hello? Magic Grove Hotel."

Jonah's Thai was excellent, but his accent was unmistakable. Ladarat smiled as she set her lunch down on her desk and as Chi flopped onto the floor with all the grace of a beached hippo.

Ladarat introduced herself quickly, remarking that Jonah didn't seem at all surprised.

"Honestly, Khun Ladarat, I thought it might be you calling."

"How could you possibly expect that? You have developed...psychic abilities?"

Jonah laughed quietly. "No, Khun. But, you see, the front desk phone never rings here."

"Never?"

"Never. Yesterday and today, I haven't had to answer the phone at all. Not once. So you see, when it rang just now, I thought to myself: Who might be calling? And you were the logical answer."

"Ah, such powers of deduction. Truly impressive. Then you also must have guessed that I tried to call your cell."

"Ah, yes. I mean...no. I didn't think of that. Actually, my cell is in my locker here at the hotel."

"In your locker? And that is a useful place for it?"

"Well, Krista's father just got a local cell phone, and he's been using it. A lot." Ladarat could imagine Jonah's shrug. "Anyway," he continued, "I also know why you must be calling."

"You do?"

"Well, when I heard your voice, I asked myself why Khun Ladarat would be calling now, in the middle of a busy day at work. And I concluded that you must have met Khun Delia at Sriphat Hospital." He paused, no doubt savoring his deductive achievements. "And so I said to myself, if I were in Khun Ladarat's place, which is to say, if I were a detective, and if I knew that the...object of my detection efforts was out of the picture, so to speak, then..."

"Then you would take that as a sign that I should place a call to the Magic Grove Hotel to see what you've found. A brilliant work of deduction, to be sure. And so..."

"So...?"

"What have you found?"

"Ah, right. Well. So the woman you asked me about? Sharon McPhiller?"

"Yes?"

"Khun, she was here; I was wrong. She was here for about a week."

"And?"

"And now she is gone."

"Gone?"

"Gone."

"Did she check out?"

"That's what's so strange, Khun. She didn't check out. Not officially. It's my job to make sure that all bills are settled at the time of checkout. You know, for room service and such. But sometime yesterday she must have left, without doing any of that." He paused.

"And, Khun, there is something else. Her credit card is here."

"Just one credit card?"

"Just one, tucked into the folder that we use to check guests in and out. We put the credit card there temporarily, and then give it back to the guest, of course. But her credit card is still here."

"Perhaps she was in a hurry. Perhaps she forgot to take it with her?"

"I had the same thought when I found it this morning. But when I asked Khun Delia how we should send it to her, she seemed flustered. Then very quickly she said not to bother. She seemed surprised when I asked, but she recovered quickly. She said that guests make that mistake all the time. They get confused, juggling their passports and credit cards, and sometimes leave a card at the desk. It's easier for them just to cancel the card and get a new one than it is for us to send the old card to them. Besides, once most people know that the card is out of their possession, well, they want to cancel it anyway."

"So that is odd, but not . . . nefarious, wouldn't you agree?"

Jonah reluctantly agreed. It was most unsatisfying. The sudden disappearance of a guest was unusual but not unremarkable, and the loss of a credit card could be explained easily enough. Which left them . . . where, exactly?

Perhaps with a tiny bit more reason for suspicion than Wir-iya was willing to admit, but without enough to call this a "case." Not nearly enough.

Still, Ladarat felt an uneasiness tugging at her attention. It was nothing very well defined, but a sense that there were too many things that were not quite right. Richard April's strange disappearance, and Sharon McPhiller's abrupt departure without her credit card.

In that moment, she decided she would keep looking, either until various facts fit together more comfortably or until a fact shook loose.

"Perhaps...you could look for her luggage."

"Ah, but it's not here. As soon as Khun Delia left, I went to the room where Sharon McPhiller had been staying. It was cleaned out. Empty." He paused, and Ladarat let him think for a moment. "Oh. I see. You think perhaps her luggage is still here but...somewhere else?"

"Exactly so." That was what Ladarat was thinking, although she had no idea what they would do if they found her luggage. What would that mean? To find her luggage and her credit card, but not her? What sort of theory would explain that pattern of facts? Ladarat had to admit she had no idea.

"But be careful as you look around. Even if Khun Delia isn't there now, she may have..."

"Confederates?"

"Exactly so. Confederates. People she works with who are in league with her." Even as she said that, Ladarat felt the chances of a true mystery were still quite small. Immeasurably small.

Still, you can never be too careful when you are in the business of detection. And if anything happened to Jonah, Ladarat would feel entirely responsible. She urged him to be careful.

"Yes, Khun. I will be careful, of course. And if I find anything I'll send you a text."

Each hung up, Jonah to get back to the business of detection, since it didn't seem like there was much other work for him to do, and Ladarat to her lunch, because although there was a lot of work for her to do, her mind was too full to do any of it right now.

In fact, it wasn't until she'd finished the generous portion of *kao niew moo yang*, with some help from Chi, who seemed to appreciate the sticky rice as much as he did the grilled pork, that Ladarat was ready to get back to work.

And work she did, almost all afternoon, reviewing all of the rest of the deaths in her pile of charts. All afternoon she read page after page, stopping briefly to relinquish Chi to Sukanya and for a rehearsal session with Sisithorn for their presentation at the National Ethics Society meeting tomorrow.

So it was with a sense of accomplishment that by four o'clock, Ladarat felt that she had done a full day's work. Or almost a full day's work. There was just one stop she needed to make on her way home.

Panit Booniliang did not seem entirely pleased to see her. The heavyset man put both hands palm down on the counter in front of him, as if he were steadying himself to withstand a large wave.

As the director of the hospital's medical records department, the poor man assumed that anyone in any position of any authority whatsoever who came to him probably wanted something from him. And usually they wanted whatever it was as soon as possible: old charts or very old charts, or charts from a particular doctor.

To make matters worse, it was true that, historically, his

relationship with Ladarat was rather interesting. Her requests to him were often odd, but occasionally entertaining, as when she had asked for records that helped her catch the now famous Peaflower murderer. If there was wariness in the way that he looked her over, there was curiosity, too.

"Ah, Khun Ladarat. Another murderer to catch?" His eyebrows wrinkled once, then twice, then three times with a rhythm that suggested waves crashing on a wide beach.

Well, perhaps a little too much curiosity. Certainly more curiosity than was strictly warranted by the facts.

"No, Khun. Fortunately, nothing like that."

Panit took a deep breath of relief, but his shoulders sagged just a little in disappointment.

"But there's an...oddity that I wanted to ask your opinion about."

"An oddity?" The director's left eyebrow went up up a fraction of a centimeter and he stood just a little straighter. "What kind of...oddity?"

"Well, you know the palliative care unit?"

Panit frowned. "Oh, yes, I know it. That Dr. Taksin..." The big man shook his head. "A nice man, perhaps. And certainly a good doctor. But very bad with his charts."

"His...charts?"

"Yes, Khun. It takes him forever to get them signed. You remember the royal inspection we had six months ago?"

Ladarat nodded. She certainly did. Preparing for that inspection had taken years off her life.

"That was when it started. Before then, Dr. Taksin was always very prompt in signing his charts when a patient was discharged. But right about then, he started falling behind. Of course, that's not the time when you want a doctor becoming lazy with his charts."

"And since then?"

"And since then it's only gotten worse. Sometimes the oncology chairman needs to remind him, and that's bad. Very bad." Panit shook his head sadly. "Perhaps he's a good doctor—the nurses on the unit cover for him, so they must like him. They're quick to explain that there are other causes of the delays, like pharmacy records that are incomplete, or radiology results that are pending. But I know the truth," he said, tapping his forehead. "I've been in this business for thirty-two years, and they can't fool me. I know when a doctor's just getting lazy."

"Well, maybe so. But about the unit, and the . . . oddness."

Panit looked at her attentively, and he leaned forward over the counter, perhaps hoping for yet another mystery. Well, if this was a mystery, it would be a very strange one indeed.

"Do you have a sense of how many deaths there are on that unit?"

"Deaths?" Panit leaned back and tilted his head to one side in a disconcerting way that reminded her more than a little of Chi's mannerisms. "How many?" He rubbed his chin.

Ladarat nodded. "Approximately."

"Well, not more than three or four, I'd say."

"In a day?" That seemed very high. Unusually high. Suspiciously high. But not at all in line with the charts she'd been reviewing.

"No . . . no. In a week. Three or four in a week, I'd say." He paused. "Of course, I can check. It would take some time, but I could pull the deaths from that unit . . ."

Panit looked at her strangely. "But you have those charts, don't you, Khun? My nephew Chaow pulled those charts for you a week or two ago, didn't he?"

Ladarat nodded. "That's just it. I've looked through all of those charts for the hospital in the past month. Almost fifty of them. But there were only three deaths from the palliative care unit in that time."

Panit nodded. "I see what you mean. A unit devoted to the care of very sick patients near the end of life, you'd think there would be more deaths."

Ladarat nodded again. "Many more."

"But, although that's certainly odd, there's no evidence of a crime, is there?" The poor director looked crestfallen. His shoulders sagged and he leaned forward onto the counter, letting it bear his not inconsiderable weight.

"No...no. I never thought there was a crime," Ladarat insisted. Why did everyone who saw her now think that a crime was afoot and that another murderer was loose? "It was just an...oddity about which I wanted your opinion."

"My opinion?"

"Certainly. You have the best view of what goes on in this hospital. You know all that happens. What would explain this? How could it be that the unit responsible for the care of the sickest patients, the patients closest to death, could be so free of death?"

Panit smiled. He thought for a moment, but he didn't need to consider for long.

"It's obvious, isn't it?"

Ladarat shook her head. It wasn't. Not to her.

"The patients, they are going somewhere else."

"Somewhere...else?"

"Of course. There are very sick patients there, yes? Patients who are likely to die in the next month or weeks."

"Or days," Ladarat added.

"Or days. But they aren't dying in that unit. So it stands to reason that someone is arranging to have them transferred somewhere else before they die."

"But why would someone do such a thing?"

"Well, our mortality statistics. That would be the main reason. The more people die in our hospital, the higher our death rate. And that makes us look bad in terms of national statistics, because no one wants to go to a hospital where everyone dies."

"Ah." That was all Ladarat could think of to say. She'd never thought of this aspect of end-of-life care before, that some hospitals might not want to take care of dying patients because doing so would damage their image. She thought, too, about the oncology director who was so opposed to Dr. Taksin. Could he be concerned that these deaths were marring his record? It was possible.

Still thinking about the implications of that possibility, Ladarat thanked Panit, leaving him deeply disappointed at the absence of a murder. But as she took her leave, she was pleased to note that the possibility that someone, somewhere, was trying to game the system of mortality statistics had infused him with a new sense of energy. On her way out the door into the dim basement hallway, she looked back and saw the director busily arranging piles on the counter and calling enthusiastically for his nephew and second-in-command for some urgent task. And she was sure she saw him smile.

CHAPTER 20

THE TRUTH ABOUT INFIDELITY IS NEVER AS
BAD AS WHAT WE IMAGINE

No matter how productive her day had been—and it had been rather productive—Ladarat Patalung had the western disease of guilt over an early departure. It was only four thirty and she was leaving. Going home. In her heart she felt that she should be doing...something. But because she couldn't decide what that something was, Ladarat decided to leave early.

She'd spend the extra hours of daylight pulling weeds in her neglected garden, perhaps. Or maybe she'd join Duanphen as she prepared for the evening rush and watch her...technique. She could probably learn a lot just by watching.

Ladarat was thinking so diligently about the benefits of watching Duanphen chop green onions that at first she didn't register the gangly form that was preceding her down the hospital's back hallway. Without really thinking, she'd taken the side door that led past the morgue and out to the physicians' parking lot. The person up ahead was a physician. A familiar physician. In fact, Ladarat was pretty sure she'd recognize that clumsy but quick gait even if this particular physician hadn't been right in front of her.

As she watched Dr. Taksin disappear down the stairs to the rear door, she faced a conundrum. Green onions forgotten,

Ladarat hung back so she'd be invisible if her quarry turned around.

Having so elegantly avoided detection, however, Ladarat found herself at a loss. Should she follow him? Certainly that would be within her purview as someone who was asked to evaluate the doctor's performance issues. Perhaps following doctors leaving work was not generally appropriate, but when a doctor who is under suspicion leaves work at four thirty in the afternoon, well, following would be called for, would it not?

Ladarat hitched her bag more firmly onto her shoulder and hurried down the steps, confident that Dr. Taksin was far enough ahead now that she herself could continue to evade detection. But that reassurance left her unsure exactly how she was going to follow the doctor. Because if he was leaving by this door...

And in fact as soon as Ladarat emerged, blinking, into the bright late-afternoon sunlight she knew that she had a problem. Dr. Taksin had crossed the doctors' parking lot and was now at the far edge, which was interesting, because parking in that region implied that he had come late to work, after most of the closer spots had been taken.

He was getting into a tiny yellow car that wasn't even a car: a little thing with just two seats side by side. Ladarat had seen them around town recently. They were very trendy—and very, very small.

The good news was that his little car was very distinctive. She should have no trouble following it.

The bad news, of course, was that she had nothing to follow that car in. Her own car was in the staff lot on the other side of the hospital. Now she had only her feet, which were unlikely to be able to keep up with a car, no matter how diminutive.

Unless...no, that wouldn't work. Or would it? Maybe...?

Ladarat knew she had to make a decision right now. She also had to be lucky. Very lucky. And it had been a lucky day, had it not?

Again Ladarat hitched the shoulder strap of her bag up on her shoulder so far that the bag itself was wedged in place under her arm. She set off at a run around the path that led to the front of the hospital, curling her toes in hope of keeping her pumps affixed to her feet. Ladarat was halfway around the corner when she turned quickly to see how much progress the little yellow car had made, and she slowed to a trot when she saw that it hadn't moved. She might make it after all.

But no sooner had she formed that happy thought than the little car backed out of its parking space more quickly than she would have believed possible for such a small vehicle. Without waiting to see how fast the car was racing toward the exit, Ladarat put on an extra burst of speed. A few moments later she pulled up, breathing hard, at the taxi stand in front of the hospital.

She opened the back door of the first bright white taxi in the rank and collapsed into the backseat. Unable to form a complete sentence—and unsure what that sentence would have been—she simply motioned to the elderly man behind the wheel to drive.

Perhaps the driver received many such requests, or perhaps, like Panit the hopefully suspicious medical records director, he was interested in any sort of intrigue that could infuse a little excitement into his day. In any case, he shrugged and put the car in gear. They wound around the hospital drive as Ladarat's pulse returned to something more human and she found that she was breathing almost normally.

"There is a car," she said, finally, between deep breaths. "It will be coming out of the doctors' parking lot to the right—over there—you know the exit?"

The driver looked at her curiously in the rearview mirror and nodded imperceptibly. Obviously a man of few words. That would be welcome.

"It's a small car. A very small car. Bright yellow. For two people."

"For two?"

"That's what I said, a car for two."

"No, Khun, I meant that's its name. It's called a ForTwo. Because...well...it's for two people. Hard to believe someone was paid millions of baht to come up with that name. So...you want me to follow that car?"

Ladarat nodded. "Exactly so. When you see it come out, follow it. But...don't get too close. I don't want the driver to see."

The driver nodded, gunned the engine, and swung expertly out onto Suthep Road, pulling across three lanes of traffic and then over to the curb on the far left.

"We wait here until he comes out, you see?" The driver chuckled, as if this clever maneuver were a personal invention of his. "Do you know which way he'll be heading?"

Ladarat shook her head. "No idea at all." In the back of her mind, she wondered how this astute taxi driver knew that the car they were following would be driven by a man. But she had other more pressing concerns. For instance, she didn't even know how far Dr. Taksin would be going. What if he was driving up to Chiang Rai? That would be a long and very expensive bit of detection.

"There he is." The driver pointed at the little yellow car that swung out of the doctors' parking lot heading roughly west, on the same side of the road that they were on. Like a trained operative, the driver pulled out into traffic, leaving a couple of cars in between them and the ForTwo. He cracked his knuckles loudly and settled in for what he was probably thinking would be the most interesting ride of the day.

"You know, Khun, if you don't mind me saying so, you really have nothing to worry about."

Ladarat wasn't sure that was the case. She had lots to worry about, including her presentation at the ethics society tomorrow, which she'd completely forgotten about.

"I don't?"

The driver concentrated for a moment on a tricky left turn toward the Old City, then resumed his train of thought as if there hadn't been an interruption.

"Most men, their wives think they're being unfaithful. The wives think it, you see, but it's not real. It's like women are programmed to think that men are being unfaithful. You see?"

Ladarat did not see. The taxi driver's philosophizing made no sense whatsoever. Nor did it have anything to do with her worrying about a lecture that she would have to give in less than twenty-four hours. Unsure where to start or how to reply, Ladarat found herself momentarily at a loss for words.

"Ah," was all she said.

The traffic was getting thicker now. They'd entered the part of the city that was filled with *farang* and the sorts of businesses that cater to *farang*—greasy western steakhouses, bars, karaoke clubs, and of course girlie bars. They followed the little yellow ForTwo onto Loi Kroh Road and then a smaller *soi* where Dr. Taksin whipped his car into a parking space that was not much larger than the area that a baby stroller would require. Without waiting to be told, the driver pulled off to the left side of the street in front of a dumpster to let the cars behind pass and to remain unobtrusive.

"Now we watch, Khun," he said over his shoulder. "But

don't be surprised if you don't like what you see. Your husband—I agree it looks bad for him. Very bad, it's true. For a man to come to this part of town...well...there aren't many reasons that a man would be here."

He turned to look at Ladarat in the backseat. Ladarat had rather belatedly caught on to the driver's interpretation of the situation, and was wearing an expression that she thought probably resembled total and utter confusion, which the driver mistook for the face a woman wears when she has discovered her husband venturing into this part of town.

"Ah, Khun. Well, these things happen, you know? Even the best husbands stray sometimes, it is a known fact. Ah—see, there he goes."

And indeed, Dr. Taksin was extricating himself from the tiny car and straightening up as he unfolded his limbs. After carefully locking the door, he turned to cross the street and walked purposefully down the opposite sidewalk, as if he knew where he was going.

"Should we follow him, Khun? Or..." Here Ladarat could see the gleam in the driver's eye as he glanced back in the rear-view mirror. "Or maybe I could follow him...on foot. He doesn't know me, you see? I could be like a detective."

This notion seemed to make the driver's day. It also led Ladarat to wonder how many people in her quiet city were apparently willing to leave their regular jobs behind and become detectives. As she was pondering the wisdom of sending this aspiring detective out onto the sidewalk, Dr. Taksin solved their problem by pushing through the swinging saloon-style doors of a tired-looking bar. Above the door was a broad, faded sign that read "WesternGirl."

Unsure what that meant, but feeling sure she had the general drift, Ladarat sighed. The driver nodded sympathetically.

"Well, it's better to know the truth, isn't it? That's not something you want to be surprised by. The truth about infidelity is hardly ever as bad as what we imagine. And knowledge is power, as they say."

Ladarat agreed that was so. Most of the time. Although how this knowledge would be power was impossible for her to say.

Out of delicacy, perhaps, the driver left Ladarat to her thoughts on the way back to the hospital. He even refused her offer of payment. "I know it seems bad, Khun, but you will get through this. I promise."

Unsure how a taxi driver came to acquire such wisdom, but grateful nonetheless, Ladarat thanked the man and made her way slowly and thoughtfully toward her car. There was still time to visit Duanphen to watch her work. But suddenly Ladarat felt very tired. She wanted nothing more than to go home, perhaps to pull a few weeds in her garden, and to have someone bring her dinner for a change.

CHAPTER 21

THE DANGERS OF VANITY FOR THE COMMON CRIMINAL

Two hours later, after she had in fact made more than a little progress in weeding the beds close to the patio, Ladarat discovered one very crucial advantage of having your boyfriend pick up dinner.

"So much food. Did you tell Duanphen that you were having a party?"

Wiriya flashed the teasing smile: *yim yaw*.

"It is something we bachelors learn very quickly. Cooks are much more generous with men than with women, because we have bigger appetites. It is a known fact."

Ladarat thought about that fact as she opened each of the cardboard containers that Wiriya had set down on the patio table. She'd worked up an appetite gardening for the last two hours. Wiriya had been running late, so he'd offered to pick up dinner while Ladarat weeded one bed after another. Now, fresh from the shower, she sat at the little iron table, exhausted, with barely enough energy to open cardboard containers and admire her handiwork.

Duanphen had been generous. Very generous. There was *gang som pak ruam*, a sweet, sour, and spicy soup with vegetables; *gang som cha om kai*, an omelet made of eggs and

Thai acacia leaf (a variant on last night's *kai jiew moo ssap*); and *yam khor moo yang*, salad with marinated pork, lemon, onion, and chilies. It was an Isaan specialty that Duanphen did particularly well, since that's where she was from, as Ladarat had discovered recently. Eaten with sticky rice, dipped into sauce, it was a solid accompaniment to the lighter soup and omelet.

And...Prasert's *kanom maprao*.

Wiriya smiled as he served her a generous helping of *gang som cha om kai*, which she knew was not his favorite, but which he knew was one of hers.

Ladarat would have been content to admire her gardening, happy in the knowledge that Wiriya had noticed it, too. Despite the fact that it had been almost dark when he arrived, and despite the fact that the beds around the patio were lit only by anemic outdoor lights and, a moment later, by the candles he put out, Wiriya had noticed the clean beds that ringed the patio. Pristine and weed-free, they were dotted by a few hardy Siam tulips that would be blooming soon, perhaps. She would have been content to admire her work, and not to talk about detection or crimes, or...anything.

They most definitely were not going to talk about the disappearances of *farang*. For now, Ladarat wanted to keep her continued interest—not even a suspicion—to herself. So no talk about the Magic Grove Hotel, or Jonah's visit.

But there was a point about which Ladarat needed Wiriya's expert opinion.

"So..." she said cautiously, in between bites of *gang som cha om kai*. "I was asked to look into the behavior of a certain physician at the hospital."

"Behavior?"

Ladarat shrugged. "He hasn't been himself lately. Coming to work late, leaving early, falling asleep..."

Wiriya nodded.

"Well, it seems that he might be engaged in...something."

Wiriya looked at her more closely, a forkful of *yam khor moo yang* hovering midway between plate and mouth.

"Something?"

Ladarat told him about her afternoon adventure, laughing along with Wiriya as she described her mad dash to find a taxi and the driver's mistaken impression that she was a jilted wife.

When she had finished, and after they had both mused about the driver's exciting day—one that he would no doubt share with his wife—Wiriya summed up the situation in that way that only he could.

"So you think he is meeting women at this place...the WesternGirl?"

Ladarat nodded.

"And that these meetings are distracting him from work?"

Ladarat nodded again. That was pretty much the conclusion she had reached. It was, unfortunately, a clear case of a man led astray.

And so far astray! Could he not see that at least one of the nurses—Sudchada—was attracted to him? That was a conclusion Ladarat didn't share with Wiriya, but it was obvious, was it not? Why else would she approach Ladarat to find out what was wrong with Dr. Taksin before anyone else did? And if Panit was correct—and he usually was—then she was probably also covering for him when he failed to sign his charts on time. All of that devotion, and yet here he was, wandering off to some girlie bar, staying up until all hours, and then literally falling asleep on the job.

239

"There is just one problem with your theory," Wiriya said. He speared another forkful of *yam khor moo yang*, trying, and failing, to feign nonchalance.

"What could be wrong with that theory? I followed him, didn't I? I saw him leave work early and go into this girlie bar. And, what I didn't mention before but what is just as important, he parked and went into that...establishment as if he had been there many times before. It all fits, don't you see?"

. Wiriya might have been a great detective, but sometimes he just didn't know people. He could put facts together, certainly. But this wasn't a set of facts as much as it was a story, and the plot of this particular story seemed all too clear.

"Except for one thing." Now Wiriya had put down his fork and took a modest sip of the Singha that he'd brought out: one glass between the two of them, of which he drank most, which was fine with her.

"One thing? What one thing?"

"Oh, I don't doubt your skills of detection. And your taxi-hailing skills are also impressive. But the place he went? The WesternGirl?"

"Yes?"

"It's not a girlie bar."

"And you know this because...?"

"Because I've been there. Remember the retirement party I had to go to on Monday night? That's where we went, because Arthit, the officer who was retiring, is a big fan of American country-and-western music." Wirya paused to let that information sink in. "It's a country-and-western bar, with that sort of music. And saddles on the walls, and lots of pictures of cowboys and..." Wiriya paused, trying to remember. "And horses, I think."

"Horses?"

"Yes, horses. Horses are very country-and-western, I believe."

Ladarat was having trouble processing this new information. So Dr. Taksin was risking a promising career as a palliative care physician for...horses? How would horses cause him to lose his grip on reality? How would horses cause him to function so poorly at work?

A girl, well, Ladarat could imagine how that might be a distraction. Or several girls. But a horse? Or—more correctly—pictures of horses? It made no sense.

So many questions, and Ladarat had imagined that she had the case all wrapped up. How wrong she'd been. Now there were so many questions, in fact, that Ladarat had trouble putting all those questions into words. Fortunately, one benefit of having dinner with a detective was that she didn't have to.

"So you want to know what it is about the WesternGirl that is so distracting to your young doctor?"

Ladarat nodded. Her attention had just become distracted by the last unopened container, which she knew contained Prasert's *kanom maprao*. But Wiriya was smiling in a way that she imagined could only mean he had an answer to the question he'd just asked. *Kanom maprao* could wait for a moment or two.

"Well," he said finally. "I'm not entirely sure. You see, I don't know what this doctor of yours looks like, so I can't be certain I saw him there on Monday night. But..."

"But?"

"But I think I did. In fact, I'm almost sure I did."

"And?" Now Ladarat had forgotten entirely about the *kanom maprao*. For the moment, at least.

But Wiriya shook his head. "I can't be certain. And one shouldn't jump to conclusions in a case like this, wouldn't you agree?"

Ladarat nodded. She had to admit that was good advice. Just a few moments ago she had jumped to the conclusion that Dr. Taksin had a veritable harem at the WesternGirl. To be fair, he still might. Perhaps a harem that loved to ride horses?

"Good," Wiriya said, finishing the Singha and opening the *kanom maprao*. "We'll find out together tomorrow night."

"We will?"

"Of course. We'll go to the WesternGirl together, and perhaps your doctor will be there, too."

That was an intriguing idea: a date. With detection work. And horses. But it wasn't possible.

"I'll be coming back from Bangkok late," she pointed out. "And I'll be tired, probably." Conferences and meetings with lots of people always tired her out.

Wiriya seemed strangely disappointed, pausing as he served them both portions of *kanom maprao*. "But maybe you will want to go?"

That was strange. Did Wiriya fancy horses, too? You never knew about a man's preferences, Ladarat had to admit. That was a question that she would save for another time. Instead, she shook her head. "Perhaps Saturday night, after I've recovered from the presentation and travel."

Wiriya nodded. He shook off his disappointment—if that's what it was—quickly and with good grace.

"So...your lecture tomorrow..."

Ah, yes. The lecture. Ladarat had been proud that she'd been able to push that event out of her mind. She hadn't thought about it all day. Or almost all day, with the exception of a brief rehearsal with Sisithorn.

"Are you ready?"

Ladarat didn't answer immediately. She supposed she was,

but you could never be truly ready, could you? There were always unexpected events, and of course questions.

"For the presentation, yes, I suppose we're ready." She paused, taking another bite of *kanom maprao*, which, sadly and surprisingly, didn't taste as sweet as the previous bite.

"The presentation will be fine. But the questions—that's the worry. Lots of questions. The Ethics Society meetings are always full of questions. Polite questions, almost always. But thoughtful. And thought-provoking. And difficult."

"Like what sorts of questions?"

"What sorts of questions? But how would I know? If I knew what sorts of questions the audience would ask...well...we would answer those questions...preemptively in the presentation." She smiled and took another bite of *kanom maprao*, which tasted just fine again. "Preemptively," Ladarat said again, with a certain satisfaction.

"But when you review the talk, don't you imagine the questions that people might ask?"

"Imagine?" Ladarat didn't imagine much of anything. She was just trying to remember what was on the next slide, and, if she was very, very lucky, the slide after that.

"Well, criminals do that all the time. The best criminals do it very well."

"Ah, so now ethicists are criminals? This is an interesting development. Perhaps you should give this presentation? No doubt the Ethics Society will be delighted to learn that they are all in danger of imminent arrest by a captain in the Chiang Mai Royal Police."

Wiriya held up his hands in mock surrender. "No, I didn't mean to cast—"

"Aspersions?"

"Exactly so. Aspersions. I didn't mean to cast any...of

them. I meant only that when criminals are caught, they come up with an alibi. A story, you see?"

Ladarat didn't see. She shook her head, but quickly found solace in another bite of *kanom maprao.*

"They try to convince us of their innocence, so they make up a story. It's a story about why they were in another place at the time that a crime was committed, and about how they wouldn't have wanted to commit a crime even if they had been in the right place at the right time. That is to say, they tell a story, and they strive to make that story as compelling—as convincing—as they can. You see?"

Still Ladarat didn't understand. She shook her head again, contemplating another bite of *kanom maprao* but finally deciding against it. Perhaps that coconut and syrup was dulling her faculties, because she wasn't following this discussion of ethicists and criminals and stories at all.

"Well, the best criminals, or at least the ones who succeed in staying out of prison, don't just tell good stories."

"They don't?"

"Well, they do. But they also ask themselves the right questions. The questions that a detective would ask them. You see?"

Ladarat nodded uncertainly. She was beginning to.

"Like...if you weren't at the jewelry store that was robbed," she suggested, "why were your fingerprints on the glass cases where the Rolexes were displayed?"

Wiriya stopped in the middle of a gulp of cake, then swallowed.

"Well, yes. Exactly yes." He shook his head. "I'm glad you're not a criminal. But it's thinking of those sorts of questions—those sorts of holes in the story—that keep the best criminals out of prison, at least for a while."

"So I should be thinking about the...holes...in our story?"

"Exactly so."

Ladarat really wished they'd had this conversation a little earlier. There wasn't much time to plug any holes that she found and to think up answers to these questions. Besides... what questions?

"But still... what questions? I thought of all the questions we had, like why the Americans would want aggressive treatment. And why they wanted a second opinion from their doctor in the United States. You see, we thought of all of these questions."

"And...?"

"And that is the lecture. The lecture is the answers to those questions. It's our story."

"And there are no other questions left?"

"None."

But as Ladarat said it, she was certain it wasn't true. Of course there were questions left: questions they didn't think were important enough, or questions that were too far afield, like why the patient's father didn't want to be in the room for many difficult discussions, leaving that to his wife. But Ladarat was sure that they had addressed the most important questions.

Hadn't they?

"I'm certain that there's a question or two you didn't answer," Wiriya suggested gently. "There always are. If you know the nature of the criminal, you can almost always find a question that he—or she—forgot, because it's not in their nature."

"Like what?"

"Well... imagine a middle-aged man who is very vain. Not much to look at, although he believes he is."

That was easy. There were many of those in Thailand, although, fortunately, not this one.

"So if this very vain man robs a jewelry store, he might construct an alibi that he was with a young, attractive woman, right?"

Ladarat nodded.

"To him, that alibi might seem perfectly plausible. Of course, he would think, any young, attractive woman would be delighted to spend an evening with me."

"So it wouldn't occur to him that such an alibi would draw... scrutiny?"

"Exactly so. Such an alibi would raise doubts on the part of any detective, but to him—to the criminal, you see—such questions would never occur."

"So... what are the sorts of questions that I'm blind to? Perhaps I'm vain?"

Wiriya laughed—a hearty, rolling chuckle—then scooped up the remaining *kanom maprao* on his plate.

"No, no one would accuse you of being vain. Or proud, or arrogant, or overconfident..."

"Then... what is the question I'm overlooking?"

Wiriya was thoughtful for a moment as he put his spoon down neatly in the center of his plate.

"Well, I don't know the case as well as you do, of course." Although, truth be told, he had heard about it at least a hundred times, both as it was happening and in the past few months as she was preparing this lecture. "But I can imagine there might be a question about what you and your assistant did."

"But we didn't do anything... There were no difficult decisions to be made. The American woke up on his own."

Ladarat shook her head. Surely Wiriya remembered that part of the story? He'd heard it often enough: that scene in which the American woke up in the middle of the night, pulling the breathing tube out of his throat, much to the consternation of the nursing staff and the physician on call.

"So you didn't do anything?" Now Wiriya was smiling the teasing smile of someone who had won a little victory. *Yim yaw.*

Ladarat shook her head. "We gave support to the family, it's true. And Sisithorn spent a great deal of time with the man's new wife, gaining her trust. But—"

"So you haven't anticipated a question about what a nurse ethicist did to resolve this case?"

"But we did nothing... nothing more than any other nurse would have done. How can I talk about that?"

Wiriya smiled and shrugged as he gathered up their plates. It turned out that he was highly skilled at washing dishes, and it was a skill that he enjoyed practicing. Who would have guessed?

As he disappeared inside, cardboard containers balanced on plates in one hand, and spoons and forks in the empty beer glass in the other, Ladarat thought about his warning that there would be questions about what they had accomplished. The meaning of his smile was plain enough: He was telling her that the blind spot in her nature was to ignore her own accomplishments. Just as the vain man would be surprised by questions about his alibi of a beautiful young woman, she, Ladarat Patalung, was surprised by questions that hinted at a larger and more important role.

Well.

Ladarat thought about that for quite a while, as the sound or running water in the kitchen drifted out the open window. Perhaps she and Sisithorn had done... something. Perhaps doing nothing was doing something.

Did that make sense? Even if it did, she was too tired to

figure it out. When it got to the point that doing nothing was doing something—or that doing nothing was something that one could discuss in front of the Royal Ethics Society—it was time for bed.

Ladarat arranged her chair and Wiriya's neatly on either side of the metal table. As she climbed the steps to the back door, Ladarat reflected with satisfaction that the invisible people sitting at her little table would be almost nose-to-nose, perhaps sharing a piece of Prasert's *kanom maprao*.

Wan suk

FRIDAY

CHAPTER 22

SO MANY WAYS FOR A PLANE TO CRASH

Y ou saw the packages change hands, did you not, Khun? You saw it, just as I did!"

Normally, Ladarat would be appreciative of her assistant's enthusiasm and would welcome the distraction. Their plane had left the gate and was taxiing toward the short runway, in preparation for their short flight to Bangkok. This was the worst part of flying. Not that she flew very often, but that was the problem. She could imagine disasters all too easily: the plane skidding off the runway, or crashing into a flock of migrating birds, or... The list of potential disasters was quite long.

So Ladarat was happier than she might otherwise have been to entertain her assistant's suspicions. Indeed Ladarat had seen what her assistant had seen. Even if she had not, Sisithorn's near-constant replays of the events they'd witnessed would have embedded those events in Ladarat's brain just as firmly. All previous efforts to tone down the significance of those events had been unsuccessful, and still her assistant was entranced—one could say obsessed—with what she believed was a suspicious exchange.

"It's highly suspicious, wouldn't you say?" Sisithorn seemed unperturbed as the plane's engines roared to life and Ladarat was pressed back in her seat.

Actually, and despite herself, Ladarat had to admit that there was something suspicious about this whole thing. Just as Sisithorn had reported, and just as she herself had seen at the bus station, there was a woman with a parrot bag who had handed packages to no fewer than four *farang* who were taking flights out of Chiang Mai Airport.

"Indeed I saw, Khun. And indeed it seems to be the same... parrot gang." Ladarat smiled despite herself. Was she really talking of parrots and gangs, in all seriousness? Well, it was better than thinking of all the various ways that a flight could end prematurely.

Oblivious to the lurch that was presumably taking place in Sisithorn's stomach, too, as their plane took to the air, Sisithorn nattered on.

"The same parrot bag, do you see? The same bag, but different people. That's what makes it a smuggling ring. Many people in different cities united by... by a love of parrots! Perhaps it's even an international ring? Do you think there might be similar goings-on in Malaysia or Vietnam or Cambodia? Or of course in Laos. Everyone knows that there is much corruption in Laos. They say that they are a Communist country, but that only contributes to corruption, don't you think?"

As they passed through a bank of clouds, the plane lurched down and to the left, causing Sisithorn to lose her train of thought momentarily. Perhaps she might skip a groove to another topic of conversation. Anything would be better than a repeated retelling of the tale of the parrot smuggling gang.

"Did you know, Khun, that ninety percent of all plane crashes occur in the first ten minutes of a flight, and the last ten minutes? I read that somewhere. So that means after the first ten minutes, the worst is over."

Ladarat quickly looked at her watch.

"Or halfway, at least. Or a little less than halfway. So many ways that planes can crash. Have you thought of that, Khun?

There are the engines failing, for instance. Think of that—two engines, so many moving parts. And it's not like when a car breaks down, you just pull to the side of the road and call your boyfriend for help. No, Khun, not at all. When one of those millions of moving parts fails, then...."

And she mimed with one hand the rapid and unexpected descent of a plane from its flight path, beginning at the top of the seats in front of them, down past the armrest and precipitously toward the floor. Where, presumably, many tiny passengers would meet untimely ends on the cabin's scuffed carpet.

This would be an opportune time for a nap. The flight attendants were coming through the cabin serving tea and a little breakfast, but Ladarat—like her assistant—was dressed formally in a beige Lanna skirt with delicate embroidery, and a white blouse. Without a change of clothes available, she didn't want to risk the possibility that unexpected turbulence would result in an orange juice bath. Her assistant had no such concerns, apparently, and was using the hand that had not crashed to unfold her tray table.

"Khun Sisithorn?"

"Yes, Khun?" The recently crashed plane miraculously regained altitude and came to rest on her tray.

"There is much to do today, and we will be busy."

"Indeed, Khun. Bangkok—so much to see, and so much shopping to do. And of course the conference itself. That, certainly, is most important," she said piously. "It is why we're here. But do you think perhaps there might be time to visit the Central World? They have two whole floors devoted to a food court, and every store you can imagine. And there is an art gallery on the top floor, and—"

"Khun, what I meant to say was that it will be a busy day, so I think I'll try to sleep for a moment or two."

"Of course, Khun, that is wise. To sleep while you can. Meanwhile, I will have breakfast. It's included in the price of the ticket, so there is an obligation to take advantage of what is offered, isn't there? But you should sleep if you can. Although it is a short flight. Not more than an hour, I think. Remarkable, really, how one can fly a distance in an hour that takes ten hours by bus. Why anyone would take the bus when they could fly is a mystery. Perhaps for people who don't need to be functioning at the highest level at all times..."

But Ladarat didn't hear her assistant's next hypothesis. She closed her eyes resolutely and found that her mind floated free quite easily, leaving behind her assistant's voice, drowned out by the roar of the plane's two engines, which were happily still doing their jobs.

Yet her thoughts turned back to the parrot smuggling ring. The suspected parrot smuggling ring. The pattern was clear enough, now that she'd seen it twice (and heard about it a hundred times). A woman (again, a woman) holding a parrot bag would be approached by a *farang* tourist. A small newspaper-wrapped package would be exchanged, and sometimes, but not always, something else would change hands.

There was one development: Now Ladarat was certain that it was money that was changing hands. Just pieces of paper, yet those pieces of paper seemed to spark an argument occasionally when they weren't exchanged. It stood to reason that if a piece of paper could spark an argument, that piece of paper was very probably money. How much, she couldn't say. But it was so informal—almost an afterthought—that it couldn't be much.

In each case they'd witnessed that morning, four times in all, it seemed as though the *farang* was looking for the parrot lady, and although the parrot lady didn't know who she was looking for, she seemed to know that someone would be looking for her.

The pattern was clear, it was true. But they hadn't gleaned any additional insights that might shed light on the situation. Well, perhaps there was one, but it was as much of a mystery as the parrot ring itself was.

As they watched from the small airport café where Sisithorn had insisted on stopping for tea ("to observe surreptitiously," she'd said), they saw the first two packages change hands smoothly, along with money.

The same thing happened the third time, but just as the third *farang* was handing over a few baht notes, a fourth *farang* approached the two of them. This young, scruffy backpacker type was wearing—improbably—a blue tracksuit and pink flip-flops. He looked at the previous *farang* with something resembling surprise and tried to ask a question, but the previous *farang*, an older woman, hurried away. The fourth exchange of a package happened just as the previous ones had, but with one difference. Once the scruffy *farang* had stowed the wrapped package in his oversize backpack, he turned to walk toward the security gate, his flip-flops slapping playfully on the smooth tile floor. The parrot woman called out to him, holding out a palm and wiggling her fingers in what could only be a request—a demand—for payment.

The backpacker paused long enough to say something—something rude, to judge from the parrot woman's pursed-lip expression. He pointed in the direction that the previous *farang* had gone. Then he was gone, leaving the disgruntled parrot woman seething and muttering to herself.

Ladarat considered that momentary expression of surprise as the scruffy backpacker spied the older *farang* who had just completed a transaction with the parrot woman. There was something in that little drama that would shed light on the mystery of the parrot smuggling ring. Of that Ladarat was certain. But what?

CHAPTER 23

HOW NOT TO CARE FOR A GUEST'S LUGGAGE

In the course of their short flight, Ladarat didn't reach any conclusions about the meaning of that argument between the scruffy backpacker and the parrot woman. Nor, alas, did she get to sleep. No sooner had she started to drop off than the plane began to descend. That, in turn, brought to mind Sisithorn's warning about the timing of plane crashes. The prospect of imminent disaster made sleep rather difficult.

Soon they were back on solid ground and without the burden of luggage—they were planning to return the same day. It was only a matter of minutes and not yet eight a.m. before they were in a taxi hurtling toward downtown Bangkok. Their driver proved to be an enthusiastic tout for everything Bangkok had to offer, so enthusiastic, in fact, that even if their stay were a month rather than a day, they never would have been able to accomplish even half of his ambitious itinerary.

"Or the Reclining Buddha? You haven't seen the Reclining Buddha? Biggest in the world. Biggest, and covered with gold—very rich!" The old man thumped the steering wheel for enthusiastic emphasis as he executed a lane change that sent Sisithorn careening toward Ladarat and pinned Ladarat to the door.

Ladarat opened the window a few centimeters, hoping that the sound of the wind might drown out the exhortations of their unwanted tour guide, but she decided instantly that wasn't a good idea. The acrid fumes of Bangkok's highways—diesel fuel and smoke—mingled most unpleasantly with the monkey-shaped air freshener hanging from the rearview mirror.

And the heat—*eeyyy*. The hot, humid Bangkok air, visible in ripples over the tarmac ahead, was like liquid sludge that covered the industrial parks around the airport. In the distance in front of them, past the cheerfully swaying monkey, Ladarat could see the city of Bangkok, perhaps twenty kilometers away, engulfed in a halo of smog. She closed her window and resigned herself to endure the list of attractions that she had no intention of seeing.

"Or Central World mall? Biggest in the world. Two ladies, you love to shop, yes? Of course you love to shop. I've never met a lady who didn't. Best time to go—comic book convention this weekend."

No doubt the biggest comic book convention in the world.

"Or Lumpini Park? Big park! Very beautiful. With lizards in the water. They come right up to you and let you feed them. Big lizards."

And then, inevitably: "Biggest in the world."

Slipping in and out of traffic like a wily lizard himself, and maintaining a hand on his horn almost constantly, as if its blaring was as necessary as the accelerator for locomotion, their driver managed to urge their aged taxi through the thickening morning traffic. Straining for every opening, no matter how small, he was determined to get them to their destination in record time, all the while telling them about other places they should be going instead.

"A conference? A medical conference?" he asked when Sisithorn told him, somewhat haughtily, that they were nurses, here for work, not for shopping.

"And we're just here for one day."

"Ah, a conference," he said, "and only one day? Too short for such a beautiful city. The city of angels, they call it. But still, time for shopping, no?"

Then, perhaps inspired by loosening traffic that let him accelerate vigorously, he had an idea. "The weekend market? You've been to the weekend market. Acres and acres of shops. Clothes, antiques, snakes, anything you want. If you want, I take you there. Two people, a taxi is almost the same price as two train tickets. I take you there and bring you back?"

Despite both Ladarat's and Sisithorn's protestations that they were not here to shop—or perhaps because he sensed some weakening of Sisithorn's resolve—the driver resolutely continued in this vein for the next twenty minutes until he deposited them at Sukhumvit Hospital, which was hosting the conference.

As Ladarat had hoped, they'd arrived with enough time to prepare their slides, but not so early that she would have to... mingle. She was too nervous to have the sorts of conversations that one was supposed to have at such conferences. Conversations with friends and acquaintances: "networking," it was called. That was well and good, she supposed, but now her main concern was restraining her racing pulse and taking frequent deep breaths. That, and not fainting.

As they picked up their name badges from a smiling young woman who seemed vaguely familiar, and as Sisithorn kept up a steady stream of chatter about shopping opportunities, Ladarat reflected on the phenomenon of nervousness, and how she'd become suddenly anxious once she didn't have anything else to worry about. Their plane had survived the first and last ten minutes, and she and Sisithorn had survived the taxi ride from Suvarnabhumi Airport. So, her mind seemed to be telling her, it was time to find something else to worry about.

And worry she did, as they walked down the center aisle

of the large hospital auditorium, which was filling rapidly, and up onto the stage. In part as a reason not to look at the fifty faces turned toward them, Ladarat fished the flash drive with their presentation out of her handbag as her assistant's nattering was increasingly focused on the noble attractions of the weekend market. Sisithorn seemed to be trying to convince herself that there was something virtuous about visiting the weekend market. As she opened the file with their presentation and transferred it to the PC at the podium, Ladarat vaguely wondered how such an excursion might be virtuous. She made a mental note to herself to inquire later.

But now she was distracted by the presence of the title slide, projected on an enormous screen that had to be four meters across. And there, in bright yellow text on a blue background, was the title of their presentation: "Understanding American Culture in the ICU." Below that was Sisithorn's name, and then hers. No one would call her proud, she thought, or vain, certainly. Yet she did have a feeling not unlike vanity as she gazed at that slide, and her name, and especially her title: "Nurse Ethicist."

But that vanity, such as it was, didn't last long. In the time that it had taken for them to get the presentation ready, the auditorium had filled. Now, as Ladarat looked out across the sea of faces, she could see that almost every seat was taken.

No matter how many times she had envisioned this presentation, and no matter how many times she and Sisithorn had practiced, none of that had prepared her for this crowd of people all...looking at her.

Generally young, the audience was evenly divided between men and women. All were dressed formally. Many were engaged in side conversations, but quite a few were looking at her expectantly.

Oh, dear.

Fortunately, before she could dwell on the audience's expectations, and before she could begin to pick out people she knew—which would only have made her more nervous—a small, thin, genial man in his sixties joined them on the stage. Walking carefully, as if he didn't quite trust his feet, Dr. Prasert Adulet greeted them warmly.

"Welcome to Bangkok, and to our hospital." He gave a deep *wai* to Ladarat and then Sisithorn, smiling broadly as he did. "Your trip was uneventful, I hope?"

Ladarat told him that it was, omitting the excitement engendered by the parrot smuggling ring. A very well respected surgeon, Dr. Adulet had single-handedly brought the field of medical ethics to this, one of the best hospitals in Bangkok. The force of his warm personality had removed many obstacles put up by doubters and skeptics and of course other doctors who simply wanted to care for patients as they thought best.

"We are all very much looking forward to your presentation," he said, waving a thin hand at the audience, which was growing quiet, as if to try to overhear their conversation. His gesture was perhaps a little too enthusiastic, and Dr. Adulet stumbled briefly, regaining his balance as he rested a hand on the podium.

Although it was probably invisible to the audience, that little mishap made Ladarat realize how much the good doctor had changed since she'd seen him last. Not more than six months ago, she'd invited him to Chiang Mai to give a lecture about the ethics of informed consent to the Sriphat Hospital Department of Surgery. Then, he had seemed to be in robust health, but now, one could be forgiven for thinking he more closely resembled a patient than he did someone who should be teaching surgeons. Later, if they had a private moment, she would inquire about his health.

He was a wonderful man, and well respected. Indeed, it was that reputation that had led Ladarat to introduce him to Sisithorn. If Sisithorn was going to follow her new boyfriend to Bangkok, she could do no better than working for Dr. Adulet.

But now Dr. Adulet had stepped up to the podium, with Ladarat and Sisithorn standing to his left, and he welcomed the audience. He thanked them for coming, of course. And—typical of him—he thanked them, too, for their commitment to medical ethics.

"We are becoming an important voice of conscience and humanity in many, many hospitals."

At this there was a murmur of assent from the audience, also smiles and chatter that suggested a little more enthusiasm than was entirely normal. That enthusiasm reminded Ladarat that many of these people worked alone, or almost alone. She herself worked with Sisithorn, of course, but she had no one to tell her, as Dr. Adulet had just done, that what she did every day was important. No wonder the good doctor was so beloved, and no wonder that he'd been elected president of the Royal Ethics Society four years in a row. In that moment, Ladarat promised that she would try to remind Sisithorn—and herself—that what they did was important. It was not as visible as what the surgeons did, perhaps, but it was just as valuable.

"Many of the problems you help solve every day are known only to a few people," he continued, as if he were reading her thoughts. "And that's as it should be. But every once in a while there is a high-profile case. A case that makes an ethicist into a celebrity." He smiled, turning first to Sisithorn and then to Ladarat.

"I think he's talking about us, Khun," Sisithorn whispered. "He says we are famous? How can that be?"

Ladarat wasn't sure. Perhaps Dr. Adulet was just being

polite? Perhaps. But the rapt attention of the audience of two hundred people seemed out of proportion, even by the normally high standards of Thai politeness. It made no sense. Unless...

"Khun Ladarat will not be talking today about her work as a detective, of course." Dr. Adulet smiled, but more than a few people in the audience shuffled their feet as if that was exactly what they had come to hear. "But she and Khun Sisithorn will be talking about a case that, it is safe to say, expands the boundaries of how we think of ethics and the work we do. Not so much about problems to solve, but helping the right decisions to...happen." Dr. Adulet looked as if he was about to say more, but instead he simply asked the audience to welcome their guests from Chiang Mai and stepped aside, hobbling across the stage and down the steps as Sisithorn stepped behind the podium, as they'd agreed.

"We are here," Sisithorn said somewhat formally, "to talk about the case of the Americans." There was a long pause, a very long pause, as if Sisithorn had forgotten her lines—which was impossible, given how many times they had practiced. The silence stretched into what felt like minutes, and then hours.

Ladarat held her breath. She wondered for a second whether perhaps Sisithorn's rule about planes also applied to lectures. Perhaps disasters were most likely at the very beginning and—if one survived long enough—at the very end?

But just as Ladarat was about whisper a suggestion to her assistant, Sisithorn seemed to come to life and proceeded to read the notes on the bottom of each slide.

"How would you feel," Sisithorn asked the audience, "if you found yourself in a tragic situation, facing the likely death of a loved one in Chicago, or Germany, or other places? With no friends or family, and with everyone speaking in a language you couldn't understand?"

That series of questions, which Sisithorn had embellished a little, seemed to engage the audience, many of whom grew thoughtful. No matter that this question was in fact one that Ladarat had asked her assistant in an effort to help her see the importance of empathy and compassion in such a situation and to help her see that compassion was more valuable than simply making the right ethical decision.

Then, as they'd agreed, she described the sad situation of the two young Americans, newly married, who were injured by an elephant; the treatment they received at Sriphat Hospital; the woman—Kate—and her rapid recovery; and her husband—Andrew—who seemed to be in a state very close to brain death.

Next, they exchanged places at the podium, and Ladarat spoke about the challenges of a family who wanted "everything" done to save their son; about his father's request to send Andrew's records to other doctors in the U.S.; and about their refusal to believe that their son's prognosis was truly as grim as the Sriphat Hospital doctors said it was. Then Ladarat and Sisithorn took turns describing what they did.

Ladarat and her assistant wound their way through Andrew's story, describing its various twists and turns, up to the point at which Andrew suddenly woke up, disproving the dire predictions of his doctors, who were delighted, but just a little bit embarrassed.

No sooner had they concluded their lecture then, after polite but spirited applause, they had to step back to the podium to answer questions. Just as Wiriya had predicted, many of those questions hinged on what they did and how they did it.

How did one provide support? How did one provide support, in particular, in a foreign language? How could they resist the temptation, as ethicists, to recommend decisions and to give guidance?

The questions went on almost as long as their lecture had, until finally Dr. Adulet climbed back onto the stage with some difficulty, gently cutting the discussion short, and inviting the audience to ask additional questions during the break. Again there was a round of enthusiastic applause that surprised Ladarat and delighted her assistant.

Out in the atrium, the hospital kitchen staff had laid out an elaborate tea break. There was tea, of course, and an endless array of sweets and cookies and cakes. There were also strange little crustless tea sandwiches of the sort that *farang* seem to like, but which were eyed with amusement and distrust by most of the ethicists in the crowd. A small crowd formed around Ladarat and Sisithorn, asking more questions than Ladarat would have believed possible from such a straightforward case. Ladarat was pleased to see that Sisithorn seemed to be enjoying the limelight. So much, in fact, that Ladarat didn't feel guilty about stepping away for a moment to check her text messages. There was a tardy note from Wiriya wishing her luck and a note from Sukanya asking if she could take Chi this afternoon. Alas, Chi was going to have to do without her, she replied.

And finally, the first message, which had come in more than an hour ago, from Jonah. It said, simply, "Call me."

Oh, dear. Ladarat walked down a hallway away from most of the people and stepped into an open multipurpose room that looked like it would be the site of lunch in a few hours. She sat at one of the white cloth–covered tables and called Jonah's cell phone.

He answered immediately, but whispered so softly she could hardly hear him.

"Khun, I'm calling because there's been a . . . development."

"A development?"

"You remember the writer? Richard April?"

"Of course. The man who left a few days ago."

"But, Khun, that's why I'm calling you. He didn't check out."

"You mean he's still there?" That would explain a great deal and would remove a burden of suspicion, too.

"No, Khun. He is most definitely not here. But...his luggage is. Or I should say, it was."

Ladarat was two or three steps behind.

"His luggage was there? But you...removed it."

"Yes, Khun, I did. I took it to the manager's office. But about an hour ago I found it. In the gardener's shed. In between the lawnmower and the weed trimmer and the brooms. I went in there looking for a broom to sweep the front patio and I found his luggage, piled neatly as one might store luggage that you're coming back to claim."

"And perhaps he is coming back to claim it?" As she said that, Ladarat admitted it wasn't really likely. If you wanted to take care of a guest's luggage, would you put it outdoors in a gardening shed? You would not. What self-respecting hotel would treat a guest's luggage like that?

What Jonah said next didn't surprise her. "No, Khun. I'm certain this man Richard April isn't coming back. You know the Free Bird Café in the Old City?"

Ladarat had heard of it. It was a café that took in donations of clothing and other items and sent them to Burmese refugees in the north and west part of Thailand. They had fund-raising concerts, too. She and Wiriya had been to one a month or so ago.

"Well, they sent a man with a truck to collect his things. It just left a few minutes ago. I didn't try to stop him, though. Should I have stopped him, Khun? I thought of trying, but he wasn't committing a crime. I'm not even sure there has been a crime, although it seems so, doesn't it?"

Ladarat agreed that it certainly did. A man checks in and goes missing. Then a few days later his possessions are disposed of. That certainly sounded suspicious. But not a crime. Not yet.

"No, Khun. You were right. It's not a crime to pick up luggage that has been abandoned—or which someone thought was abandoned. But...how did they know that Richard April's luggage was abandoned? Who called them?"

"I don't know, Khun. But whoever it was told a lie."

"A lie?"

"The man who picked up the luggage told me it had been left for several months. And when the hotel hadn't been able to get in touch with the guest, they decided to donate his luggage and its contents to the Free Bird."

Ladarat pondered that information. Perhaps it was an innocent mistake? Perhaps, but someone had to take the initiative to call the café. Who would do that?

"And Khun? There's one more thing," Jonah said, a little louder.

"Yes?"

"This man, he said these requests are common from the Magic Grove Hotel. Several times every month, in fact, they come out to pick up luggage that's been left."

"I wonder how often that luggage has only been left for a few days?"

"Exactly," Jonah said, as his voice dropped again to a whisper. "It almost seems like someone here is using the Free Bird donations to get rid of...incriminating evidence."

"But it's only incriminating if something is happening to these people. If they're being kidnapped...or worse. But we don't know if that's happening, do we?"

Jonah admitted that they didn't. "But I'll find out, I promise."

"Just promise that you'll be careful," Ladarat said as she ended the call.

The rest of the day's conference was delightful, partly because of the notoriety of their presentation, of course, which cast a pleasant glow around them wherever they went—even in the ladies' room, Ladarat noticed the polite smiles and nods of recognition—and the notoriety of being known as a detective. But mostly it was because of the people, many of whom she knew from previous meetings, and one or two even from her days in nursing school. She was sad at the end of the day when the auditorium began to empty out.

Searching the thinning crowd, Ladarat spotted Sisithorn deep in conversation with a short, rotund man who looked somewhat familiar. Actually, they didn't seem to be deep in conversation as much as the man seemed to be talking to her assistant. Or *at* her.

Before she could get close enough to hear what they were talking about—or what he was talking about—Sisithorn saw her. She said something to the man and made her way across the nearly empty room to Ladarat.

"A good conference, wasn't it, Khun?" She seemed cheerful. Very cheerful, buoyed up, no doubt, by the praise she'd been receiving. Praise was healthful in moderation, of course, but too much was toxic.

"But . . . I've decided I should not spend the hospital's money on a plane home. I can just take the bus. That's simpler, and easier, and I will be at work early tomorrow, just as soon as you will, Khun!"

Ladarat couldn't hide her surprise at this strange and unexpected change of heart. Just a few hours ago, it seemed, her assistant felt that her time was too valuable to spend on a bus.

"Are you sure, Khun? The bus, it's long and uncomfortable. You'll be sleepy tomorrow. "

"Oh, I sleep very soundly. Falling asleep won't be a problem. I'll get home rested and ready for the weekend." Sisithorn looked around and glanced at her watch. "Perhaps a little time to see the city before the bus leaves. Have a restful weekend, Khun!" And her assistant disappeared through the hospital's front doors into the muggy Bangkok evening.

Ladarat blinked. She should catch a taxi to the airport soon, she knew. It was past five and her flight was at seven. She hated being late. As a rule, she'd prefer to sit in the airport watching people rather than storming through the plane doors at the last minute as some businessmen seemed to enjoy doing.

But as she was hoisting her bag on her shoulder and wondering where she could find a taxi, the odd-looking heavyset man that Sisithorn had been listening to materialized in front of her.

"Ah, Khun...I enjoyed your presentation very much. It's wonderful to be able to host such an excellent presentation at our humble hospital."

There was something oily in the man's voice, as if he didn't believe what he was saying, or as if he was waiting for her to correct him and to lavish praise on Sukhumvit Hospital.

"We were delighted to be asked, of course."

Who was this man? This man who assumed that she knew him? Was she becoming senile? Did she actually know him?

"Well, perhaps you'll come here more often if Khun Sisithorn takes a job here. I look forward to having her working here, and we'd be willing to give you a chance to give a lecture. It would give you a chance to get to the big city—I'm sure that would be of interest, wouldn't it?"

It most certainly wouldn't. Ladarat gave him the formal, stiff smile of someone who doesn't really want to smile: *fuen yim*.

But he didn't take the hint. Instead he began telling her about the wonders of his hospital, his oncology practice, and his expanding role in charge of ethics and quality.

That was when Ladarat finally realized whom she was talking to. Or—more correctly—whom she was listening to, because this man seemed to have much more mouth than ear.

"Dr. Adulet...he's a nice man, certainly. And he means well. But he lacks the modern sense of energy, of innovation, don't you think?"

Fortunately, this man—whatever his name was—wasn't really interested in her opinion. He didn't even pause to draw breath.

"And his health, not good at all. It's impairing his ability to work—to function—if you see what I mean. Now I'd be the last person to accuse a colleague of not being up to his job. The bond of medicine prevents such a thing, in most cases. The brotherhood of medicine, if you will. But under special circumstances, it is an ethical obligation to...transition a failing colleague into an easier role, don't you think?"

Here again, he didn't seem to want Ladarat's opinion. And Ladarat herself certainly didn't wish to share it. She looked at her watch surreptitiously, offering again a very strained *fuen yim* smile that looked more like a grimace. Five thirty. All she really wanted was to get to the airport. She was about to make her excuses and dash for the door when the oncologist's next statement brought her up short.

"That's why, just between us, I'll be making the decisions about whether your assistant Khun Sisithorn is a good fit for our institution. As an oncologist, it's natural for me to step into that role, don't you think? That is to say, it's my responsibility to determine whether she's acceptable, and of course she'll be working for me. No point in having her begin to work for Dr. Adulet only to switch bosses when he retires, is there? No," he said, more than willing to answer his own question. "No, it wouldn't. That's why I'm taking over now—that will give Dr. Adulet a chance to slow down a bit. And so," he continued after barely a pause for breath, "what do you think of Khun Sisithorn? You wrote her a glowing rec- ommendation, but of course we all write exaggerated letters, don't we?" He chuckled to himself, then paused as he realized that Ladarat wasn't laughing, or perhaps, at last, he actually wanted to hear her opinion.

Oh, dear. This would be what is known as a moral conun- drum. Should she say good things about Sisithorn, as she deserved? Or should she...shade the truth just a bit?

And, of course, she had a plane to catch. It would be easier— easier by far—if she were to say that everything in her letter was true. Easier, and more honest, because, in fact, the glowing recommendation she'd written was true. And yet...

"So, Khun?" Now this doctor—the good Dr. Adulet's rival—looked a little worried. His eyebrows furrowed like two caterpillars rubbing noses. Did caterpillars have noses? "What do you think of your assistant? Truly?"

"Ah, Khun Sisithorn is excellent..."

"And?"

Perhaps there was a middle road: tell the truth, emphasiz- ing one part of that truth.

"She is very excellent. And very...independent."

"Independent?" Now he looked genuinely concerned. He began to chew his lower lip in a way that suggested a rabbit and a carrot. Most unbecoming. She knew she was on the right track and warmed to her description.

"Oh yes, indeed. She will certainly be able to manage an ethics program on her own. You'll have very little need to do anything, in fact. You can simply hire her and have nothing more to do with the program at all. She is a very...independent ethicist. One with plenty of ideas and ambition. No doubt she will be successful, even stepping into your role someday."

The eyebrow caterpillars on the oncologist's face now butted heads vigorously, and Ladarat knew that she'd said precisely the right thing.

"You do think there's a place for a chief nurse ethicist at Sukhumvit Hospital," she asked. "Do you not?"

Ladarat smiled as the oncologist's expression went from bad to worse, and as he realized that this assistant he was planning to hire actually had a mind of her own. And that was fair, Ladarat thought virtuously. If one was hiring a person, one should know whether they're hiring a mind, too.

"And now, Khun, if you'll excuse me? I need to go to the airport to catch a plane home. I wish you all the best." She left the poor befuddled oncologist rethinking a future in which he was perhaps not as central as he'd imagined.

Alas, if Ladarat had succeeded in dashing the oncologist's hopes, her own hopes were about to take a step backward as well. By the time she found a taxi, it was five forty-five. Not much time to catch a seven o'clock flight. But possible?

"Ah, Khun. Not possible." The old man behind the wheel shook his head, as he realized his large fare—with the possibility of a generous tip from this well-dressed passenger—had just vanished. But honesty is always best.

"This time of day? You need an hour or more. And on a Friday? Eeehh. Very slow. At seven o'clock we'd still be on the motorway." He paused. "So? What now? I can still take you," he said hopefully. "Maybe you can get on a later flight?"

But Ladarat knew there were no later flights. She'd actually thought about staying a little later, perhaps to see Central World. Not to shop, of course. That would be frivolous. But perhaps just to... browse. This was the last flight to Chiang Mai that night.

"Where are you going?"

"To Chiang Mai." Ladarat smiled despite her predicament. "Too far to drive."

The taxi driver turned around, smiling too. "Don't laugh, Khun. A *farang* asked me to make that trip once. She said she was in a hurry and didn't want to wait for the bus. I would have, but my grandson's birthday was that day, and my daughter never would have forgiven me." He shrugged.

"Well, I could take you to the bus station. I'm sure you could get a bus tonight. Plenty of seats north on Friday. Lots of people coming to Bangkok for the weekend, so buses go back empty."

Ladarat nodded, but then reconsidered. "The buses, they leave late in the evening, don't they?"

The driver nodded. "Around eleven, I think. If you get there by ten you can get a ticket easily." He smiled, closing in for the kill. "So you have to see something of Bangkok while you're here. Maybe... Central World?"

CHAPTER 24

THE IMPORTANCE OF GETTING ONE'S MONEY'S WORTH

Ladarat had harbored admittedly uncharitable thoughts about whether she wanted to end up on the same bus with her assistant. Sisithorn was perhaps not the best travel companion—a little too talkative for a nine-hour bus trip.

But she needn't have worried. Although Sisithorn spotted her and assumed that they would make this journey together, she was not as talkative as she'd been that morning. Perhaps that quietude had something to do with the seven large plastic shopping bags that she was carrying as she stumbled up to the bus just as everyone was boarding. Apparently she'd also been to the weekend market and had done very well.

"The price difference between the plane and the bus, Khun! I have spent it! Spent it exactly! I will get reimbursed for the plane ticket that I canceled. Then I can use the money I saved. Isn't that remarkable?"

That exact spending had used up her reserves of energy. The combination of the day's excitement and the evening's frantic shopping had reduced her assistant to a being with the energy and muscle tone of a bowl of custard. As they settled into seats next to each other—Ladarat by the window—Sisithorn began to nod off almost immediately. She woke only as the bored bus attendant passed through the cabin, handing out prepackaged moist towels and boxes of juice.

They were sitting almost at the back, and by the time she reached them, she'd run out of straws.

"So sorry. The owners, they try to save money and they buy from this company that sometimes forgets to put straws on some boxes. Such an inconvenience to my passengers, all for a savings of just a few baht." She apologized again, as if the poor woman was embarrassed by her boss's obsession with saving money. Then she mimed the procedure for drinking without the benefit of that useful instrument.

Ladarat couldn't be bothered; she'd just had a delightful snack of *gang jued*—clear broth, minced pork, glass noodles, and vegetables—and tea at a stall after buying her ticket. But Sisithorn woke up long enough to eagerly take both boxes of juice after confirming that they were free.

"Of course," the attendant said, offended. "They're included in the price of a VIP ticket."

"Well, if you're sure you don't want yours...?" Ladarat shook her head. "Well, we must get our money's worth. Besides, shopping is hot work, Khun. Especially in Bangkok. So many people, and no air conditioning at the weekend market." She opened one juice box after the other by tearing off a corner and emptying both. Then, mercifully, she fell asleep.

Ladarat was not so fortunate. She blamed herself for missing her flight, and unlike Sisithorn, who'd had the foresight to cancel her ticket, Ladarat would have to pay for hers. So she'd just spent three thousand baht on a ticket that went unused. At least she hadn't compounded that mistake by going shopping.

Yet, despite all of that, and despite the loss of that money—which, truth be told, she could afford—Ladarat felt oddly content as she looked out the window at the bus station scene.

A flurry of movement caught her eye, and she watched two young boys, traveling with an older woman who might have been their grandmother. Dressed in identical school uniforms of blue shorts and white shirts, they'd fashioned a crude ball of crumpled newspaper about the size of a tennis ball, and they were kicking it back and forth energetically. There was no clear objective, and there were no goal posts, and yet they seemed to be taking their game as seriously as professional players might, with careers and sportswear endorsements hanging in the balance. Their grandmother looked on with rapt attention, smiling and nodding whenever either of the boys executed a particularly tricky maneuver.

The sense of peaceful contentment that stole over her as she watched the two young football stars stayed with her as the bus pulled out of the station, and through the sluggish traffic of Bangkok, heading north. Soon they were out in the sprawling suburbs that seemed to go on forever. But even the monotony of drab low-rise apartments and warehouses didn't lull her to sleep.

Sooner than she expected, even those borders of Bangkok fell away and were replaced by broad expanses of darkness as they traveled into the vast stretches of farmland that separated Thailand's two largest cities.

The darkness had a tricky way of pulling you into it and of making you forget the daylight. Seconds would pass with nothing visible—a pure black nothingness scrolling by. Then there would be a floodlit parking lot or a glowing storefront of a gas station ringed by yellow light. Ladarat couldn't close her eyes, for fear of missing the next apparition, which would vanish almost as soon as it appeared.

Once or twice, in the dark stretches of countryside, Ladarat saw the attendant's reflection patrolling the aisle. Such devotion to ensuring her passengers' safety and comfort was admirable. Perhaps she was trying to make up for the stinginess of her bosses, providing attentiveness instead of straws.

Yet there was truly not much to do for a bus full of mostly sleeping travelers. In fact, toward the end of the journey, around five a.m., and just before Ladarat finally dozed off for a moment, she turned from the window to find the attendant leaning into their row of seats, as if she were ascertaining that they were alive. The poor woman perhaps didn't realize that Ladarat was awake and stumbled backward when Ladarat greeted her.

"I'm so sorry, Khun. You...startled me. You are...not sleeping?"

Ladarat smiled and shook her head. Such an odd question—asking someone if they were sleeping. There could only be one logical answer to such a question, and that was the answer that Ladarat provided.

"No, Khun, I can't sleep on a bus. My colleague, though, seems to have no trouble at all." She pointed to Sisithorn.

The attendant smiled, too, but with less certainty. She kept looking back and forth between Ladarat and her assistant, as if she was confused by the variation in humanity that keeps one person awake all night, while another person is seemingly able to sleep through a conversation taking place right in front of her.

"Well...there is still an hour left to Chiang Mai; perhaps you can still sleep a little." Ladarat thanked her, and the attendant retreated to her seat at the back of the bus, presumably still puzzling over such different capacities for restful sleep.

Wan sao

SATURDAY

CHAPTER 25

ENOUGH SLEEP FOR TWO

Ladarat did fall asleep, for a moment, hardly long enough to count, but enough to make her feel ready to face the day, at least for a little while.

Sisithorn, however, was not yet ready to face the day.

"Khun Sisithorn? Khun?"

Ladarat nudged her assistant gently at first, and then somewhat less so. The bus had pulled into the Chiang Mai station a few minutes ago, and groggy passengers had almost all filed out. They were the only passengers left except for an elderly woman who seemed to be waiting for someone to help her down the aisle and the attendant up in the front rows, who was tidying up the bus for the next trip.

"Khun?"

Sisithorn snored slightly in response to a particularly vigorous nudge, but showed no sign of rejoining the living. For a second, Ladarat remembered the *farang* backpackers, and of course her assistant's boyfriend. She remembered those stories and thought of the possibility that her assistant had been drugged, but dismissed the possibility almost immediately. How had she been drugged? Ladarat had been with her for the past nine hours, and Sisithorn had swept into the station a few minutes before the bus boarded.

There was the juice, of course, but everyone on the bus was

given a juice box. Knowing what she'd see, Ladarat took a quick look along the floor toward the front of the bus to find more than a dozen empty juice boxes littering the floor. There were most certainly not a dozen people still asleep. Rule out the juice as a culprit.

Ladarat thought about that for a moment, and then fished out her cell phone and sent a brief text to Wiriya, hoping that he was awake. Just as she hit "send" she looked up, startled.

"Your colleague—it seems that she got sleep enough for both of you."

The attendant had worked her way down the aisle to their row and was looking from Ladarat to Sisithorn with an expression of puzzled amusement. "She is very sleepy, isn't she?"

"Yes, well...she did a lot of shopping yesterday," Ladarat explained uncertainly.

"Could you...?"

"Help her off the bus?" The attendant nodded.

They did it together, with some difficulty. Sisithorn woke up enough to follow simple instructions, and apart from a confusing moment as they eased her down the bus's stairs, they were able to get her off the bus without injuring themselves or their patient. Ladarat parked her on a bench just inside the front doors, propping her against a wall to keep her upright. She was able to collect her handbag and Sisithorn's but was halfway back before she remembered all of her assistant's purchases.

So, dutifully, Ladarat doubled back, collecting the bags from the overhead rack above their seats. When she got back to Sisithorn, her assistant was waking up just a little. Indeed, in the early morning din of the bus station, sleep would be almost impossible. Now at least her eyes were open, but she was looking around her with the dreamy expression of, well, someone who was still dreaming.

What to do?

The first call would be the easiest.

"Khun Ukrit?"

"Hmmng? Sis?" Sisithorn's nickname.

"Ah, not exactly." Ladarat didn't have Ukrit's cell phone number, so she had used Sisithorn's phone, in which her boyfriend's number was prominently displayed. In a few words, she explained what had happened, assuring him that his girlfriend was okay. Sleepy, but okay.

"Can you come to get her?"

"Of course. I can be there in...ten minutes? But...Khun?"

"Yes?" Ladarat wasn't looking for a prolonged conversation. There was still another call she needed to make.

"Do you think this might be another example of foul play?"

Of course that was exactly what Ladarat was thinking. She looked at Sisithorn, whose drooping eyelids half hid eyes that wandered around the increasingly busy station, without any signs of reaction or recognition. Then, for a moment, Sisithorn's eyes focused on her with a glint of recognition.

"Hello, husband!" She smiled.

"Well, there are drugs involved, that is for certain," Ladarat told Ukrit. "Who knows how, but they are involved."

She ended that call and smiled as she saw she'd received a text. It was just a phone number. She made the next call, which she thought would be more difficult. And indeed it was.

"But, Khun Ladarat, you're aware that it's a Saturday?" The young police officer on the other end of the phone was not terribly pleased to hear from her. Ladarat strongly suspected she'd just woken him up.

"Actually, I was aware of that, Khun Somporn, as I, too, have access to a calendar."

"And that it is only seven in the morning? On a Saturday?"

"It doesn't become more of a Saturday if you declare it to be so multiple times," Ladarat explained patiently. "And yes, I'm aware of what time it is. And in another fifteen minutes, it will be seven fifteen, and your victim will be going home to bed, and any suspects will have disappeared. Is that what you want?"

"No, Khun, of course not. But—"

"Then you should be thanking me for finding you at such an hour. Unless you'd prefer that I simply call the station and tell them that you and your partner Khun Kamon are too tired to investigate an organized plan of drugging and robbing bus passengers, well, of course I'd be happy to do that. Do you have the number for the main police station? Or perhaps you could call for me and explain the situation, and your need for rest?"

"No, Khun." The voice on the phone managed to sound both contrite and surly at the same time: a remarkable feat of Thai social engineering.

"Thank you, Khun Somporn. We'll be here waiting."

Ladarat ended the call, thinking that it had gone better than she'd feared. Somporn and his partner, Kamon, were ambitious, it was true, and hungry for a "big case." But like most Thai men of that age, they'd probably been out very late drinking the night before.

Ladarat smiled as she thought of the next phone call taking place right now, as Somporn explained why his partner needed to be dressed in five minutes and on the back of a hired motorbike—if he could find one—just a few minutes after that. The instructions were probably delivered as Somporn himself was dressing, running a comb through unruly hair, and bolting out the door.

True to his word, Somporn arrived in fifteen minutes, stumbling in the front door on the heels of Ukrit, both of them looking as though they'd had a busy evening the night before. Ukrit at least was neatly dressed in a long-sleeved shirt, sweater, and creased trousers, whereas Somporn's blue uniform shirt had two buttons forgotten, and any work done with a comb hadn't left much of a mark. Still, at least the Chiang Mai police force was represented, doubly so when Somporn's partner, Kamon, stumbled in a moment later, looking just a little green and, truth be told, not much more awake that Sisithorn.

At least now Sisithorn had roused herself enough to recognize Ukrit. Oddly, she neglected to greet him as her husband. Even if that wasn't technically true, it would have been a little closer to the truth than her last marital proclamation had been.

Perhaps Ukrit was hungover, and no doubt he was still half asleep. But he'd had the presence of mind to bring a needle, syringe, and blood drawing apparatus.

"For a toxicology screen," he said. "I keep an emergency medical bag at home for when I work at a smaller hospital," Ukrit explained, wrapping the tourniquet around Sisithorn's upper arm. She protested mildly, but seemed not to connect Ukrit's face with the liberties he was taking with her arm. Instead, when she felt the poke of the needle, she glared at Ladarat. Ladarat hoped her assistant wouldn't remember any of this tomorrow.

Ladarat helped him hold Sisithorn's arm still as Ukrit filled two tubes of blood. Then he undid the tourniquet and applied a Band-aid.

As Ukrit tried to rouse his girlfriend, Ladarat explained the events of the previous evening to the two police officers, dutifully pointing out the bus on which they'd arrived. As unobtrusively as she could, Ladarat also pointed out their attendant, who was closing up the luggage bin below the bus. Even if that nice lady had done nothing wrong, it wouldn't do to let her think that the police were interested in her. Ladarat could think of no more certain way to ensure that she would never be found to serve as a witness to help them catch the perpetrator.

Finally, when Ladarat was certain that Sisithorn was awake enough to be helped into Ukrit's car, and when Somporn and Kamon had fanned out to interview witnesses, she felt she could go home. A nap would be most welcome. Perhaps a long nap.

It was perhaps not as long a nap as she might have wished. But it was a very effective one, as naps go. In fact, Ladarat had descended into such a deep sleep that when she suddenly woke, past three o'clock, she couldn't remember where she was. It took her a few moments to recall the events of the past day and the excitement of the morning. She remembered, too, pulling the blinds closed in hope of getting an hour or two of sleep. She'd slept for more than five.

What was most remarkable, perhaps, was Maewfawbaahn's patience. True, she'd fed him and let him out when she got home. It was nevertheless amazing that he'd let her sleep this long. He wasn't even lurking on the bed as he usually did.

That was when she heard the faint mewling through a partly open window. Oh, dear. She'd fed her trusty watchcat, and she'd let him out for a little exercise. But she'd fallen asleep before she could let him in. The watchcat, lacking opposable thumbs, had probably been mewling like this for most of the day.

If it hadn't been for that plaintive whining, Ladarat could perhaps have gone back to sleep again without much difficulty and without any guilt. Instead, she got up and made amends to her cat, aided by another generous helping of canned cat food. She couldn't feel guilty forever, though, and her cat seemed to agree. It was good to know one's cat had a spirit of forgiveness.

Besides, a few minutes later, after a shower, Ladarat belatedly checked her text messages. A note from Sisithorn, thanking her. And from Wiriya, reminding her of their date at the WesternGirl.

And, oddly, a text from Sudchada. "This is Sudchada. Please call."

Her hair still wet from the shower, barefoot with a cup of cold ginger tea in one hand, Ladarat dialed what she assumed was Sudchada's cell phone. How Sudchada had managed to get Ladarat's number gave her pause for a moment, but only a moment. Since she used one phone for both work and personal calls, no doubt Sudchada had gotten the number from the hospital operator, telling her that there was an ethical emergency that required the services of the hospital's nurse ethicist.

An ethical emergency? At three thirty on a Saturday afternoon? That seemed implausible. More likely Sudchada was hoping that Ladarat could provide an update on her ongoing investigation of Dr. Taksin. As she waited for Sudchada to answer, Ladarat suppressed a momentary twinge of annoyance. Certainly it was somewhat inappropriate to be calling for such a reason, at such a time. Yet Sudchada was obviously smitten. If that was the right word. And smitten people did odd and often inexplicable things.

"Khun Ladarat? I'm so sorry to disturb you on a Saturday. It's my day off, too. I won't be back on the unit until tonight, so the nurses on the unit called me a few minutes ago. They said it couldn't wait, and I thought you'd want to know, too."

"It's no matter. Really. I understand."

"You do?" Sudchada sounded perplexed. "Then you know that Melissa Double is gone? But how did you know?"

"Gone?" Ladarat revised her tone quickly. "Gone. Yes. Gone. Of course."

So suddenly. She just left? Without saying goodbye? That seemed very strange. And of course Ladarat was as surprised as Sudchada had been. Yet to sound as flustered as she felt would not inspire confidence, would it? It would not.

"Yes, she's gone, Khun. But where?"

There was a pause and the sound of Sudchada's phone being put down, then picked up again.

"A driver came this morning, along with an older *farang* woman. Apparently it was all very sudden, and there wasn't even time to arrange the discharge paperwork and instructions. The nurses—they were very flustered, so they didn't get all of the information they might have. But they got the name of the hotel from the driver. At least, I think it's a hotel. Someplace called the Magic Grove Hotel."

After she ended the call with Sudchada, another quick call to Jonah revealed that although he'd been supposed to work today, Delia had given him the day off.

Next: Wiriya. She called the detective to try to convince him of the urgency of the situation. And to convince herself, perhaps. He was at the bus station, supervising his young acolytes Somporn and Kamon, who were busily questioning everyone they could, hot on the trail of the devious criminal they'd begun to call "the night robber." Ladarat had to admit that it had a catchy sound.

"Although not as catchy as the 'Peaflower murderer,' wouldn't you agree?" Wiriya asked. Ladarat could imagine him smiling on the other end of the phone.

Ladarat did agree. That name would be hard to beat, in the annals of great criminal titles. But a crime at the Magic Grove Hotel might come in a close second. If, of course, there was a crime, which was unlikely, in Wiriya's mind at least.

"A patient checks out of the hospital and goes to a hotel? That's hardly the stuff of nefarious criminal activity."

"Perhaps not," Ladarat admitted reluctantly. "But...it's the perfect.... what's the term? The detective term?"

Wiriya sighed, loudly enough to be audible over the background of the busy afternoon rush of the bus station. "A cover story. We call it a cover story. But going to the hotel...to look for a patient? That's not a believable cover story."

But Ladarat wasn't concerned. "No, no. It's quite natural, you see? I knew this woman, this Melissa Double at the hospital. And no doubt the owner knows this—she saw me on the unit and no doubt Melissa told her about my visit. So it would only be natural for me to visit her at the Magic Grove Hotel, would it not?"

"No...no, it would not. Most people, they would simply call, wouldn't they?"

Ladarat hadn't thought of that. She supposed that would be a logical approach.

"But visiting isn't illogical. Certainly not illogical enough to be suspicious."

"Perhaps not, but what is there to investigate?"

Ladarat realized she hadn't told Wiriya about Jonah's latest revelation about the disappearance of guests and the disposal of their luggage. In the confusion of Sisithorn's long sleep, she'd forgotten it entirely. And perhaps she hadn't mentioned Jonah's role as a spy? Perhaps not.

"But you see, Richard April? I know that his luggage—"

"I have to go," he interrupted. Ladarat could hear one of the ambitious detectives clamoring for his attention in the background, about a clue, or a key witness, no doubt, who would crack the case of the night robber wide open. "Just get some rest, and I'll see you tonight." And he disconnected.

Well. Apparently the great detective had found a mystery that was worthy of his time and attention. Fair enough. If this was a real case, then this case would be hers and hers alone.

But now, an hour later, Ladarat wasn't at all sure she wanted this case to be hers. Here she was, eyeing the front door of the

Magic Grove Hotel from a parking spot on the wide gravel circle that couldn't have been more conspicuous, which perhaps was not ideal for the process of detection.

What had seemed a few days ago to be a quiet but perhaps slightly mysterious establishment had become—in her imagination, at least—more than a little nefarious. Yet she mustn't let her suspicions show. She was simply here visiting a friend. That was all. Someone visiting a friend would not sit in a car...skulking.

Ladarat got out of her little car and made her way across the gravel drive, which crunched loudly underfoot. If anyone had missed the sound of her car driving up a few moments ago, the sound of her footsteps now would no doubt alert the world to her presence.

She wasn't surprised when the front door opened of its own accord as she stepped onto the wide front porch. That was one thing she noticed—the automatically opening door. But the other observation tugging at her attention was almost more interesting. The patio that had been so nicely swept a few days ago—and which Jonah said he had cleared just yesterday—today was littered with yellow-green leaves from the nearby *Pisonia* tree. Ladarat slowed for a moment, as she considered why the patio had grabbed her attention so forcefully. Certainly not all patios are perfectly swept all the time. Certainly her own patio wasn't as pristine as a proud homeowner might hope. Still.

Her thoughts were interrupted by an abrupt voice that issued from the newly opened door.

"Ah...Khun...Ladarat?" Delia appeared in the doorway and made a formal *wai*, which Ladarat returned politely.

"Two visits in one week; we should feel honored that a nurse ethicist comes to visit us twice in one week."

Ladarat was flummoxed for a moment. Had she told this

woman that she was a nurse? Or a nurse ethicist? She couldn't remember. That would probably make her a highly ineffective criminal, if she was so poorly able to recall what she'd told to whom. But, fortunately, she was not the criminal here. The possible criminal.

"Yes, Khun. I was here to see one of our patients who moved out here. But, first, tell me how Jonah is doing—is he what you needed?"

In that moment, Ladarat realized why the patio had been asking so insistently for her attention. If you didn't have the staff to sweep the front patio, why would you give your staff the day off? Especially if it meant that the owner herself had to man the front door?

Ladarat was so wrapped up in these thoughts of suspicious behavior that she missed the first part of Delia's answer about Jonah, but the gist was clear. Very enthusiastic, very helpful...

"And he speaks Thai very well—well enough to handle ordering of supplies, which is a big load off my mind, I can tell you. But...Khun? You mentioned a patient from Sriphat Hospital?"

Ladarat nodded. "Melissa Double? I just saw her on Thursday and the nurses tell me she came here this morning."

"Ah, but she is not here."

"Not here?"

"She was here, it's true. Just this morning. But she changed her mind and wanted to travel on. She said she wanted to see...Laos."

The owner's eyes strayed to the trees over Ladarat's left shoulder for just a fraction of a second. Hardly noticeable, but just enough to give the impression of deceit.

Perhaps it was true that Melissa Double was not here. Indeed, why would she say such a thing unless it were true?

But that statement about her going to Laos—that seemed

false. False, and illogical. Would the Melissa Double that Ladarat knew simply travel to Laos on the spur of the moment, without a plan? What would make someone as careful and thoughtful as Melissa Double walk in the front door of this place and decide—suddenly and irrevocably—that she absolutely needed to go to Laos? Why didn't she decide that before she left the hospital?

On the other hand, Melissa had been going to Laos when she was sidetracked by her symptoms. She'd been on her way to take a boat down the Mekon from Chiang Kong, hadn't she? So Delia's claim was certainly plausible. Perhaps Melissa came here, felt better, and was inspired to resume her journey. Or perhaps she knew that the hospital would have tried to stop her from going to Laos, whereas they would have supported her decision to go to a hotel nearby.

These were the conflicting thoughts that ran through Ladarat's head as Delia stood smiling in the doorway. Either Melissa was there or she wasn't. And either she'd left for Laos or she hadn't. Regardless, Ladarat wasn't going to learn any more by standing here. She said her goodbyes as politely as she could. As she made her way back to the car, she couldn't help turning around to see that Delia was watching her.

Ladarat mused about this odd turn of events as she drove through thickening traffic back toward Chiang Mai. Even the distractions of drivers who honked angrily at her perfectly legal changes of lane didn't deter her from thinking about the woman from Wales who had been so philosophical about her illness, and who was now so difficult to find.

CHAPTER 26

THE CLUE OF THE FALLEN LEAVES

Ladarat was still thinking about Melissa's sudden and strange disappearance a few hours later, as Wiriya led her into the WesternGirl bar. It was Saturday night, which apparently was the time when all closet country-and-western fans threw their inhibitions aside, dressed up in jeans and western shirts, and crowded into what had to be Chiang Mai's foremost— and perhaps only—country-and-western bar.

The large, wood-floored room didn't seem to have tables. There was just a packed dance floor, full of dancers of all nationalities, gyrating to the music coming from the stage twenty meters away. Although the entire room full of people was between Ladarat and the stage, the music was nevertheless rather too loud for her taste. They'd been there for less than a minute, and already Ladarat was ready to leave.

"Look...just look for a minute." Wiriya leaned over so close that he was talking directly into her ear to be heard.

"Look? At what?"

Wiriya smiled. Then he pointed at the stage.

Just visible above the heads of dancing Americans and Germans and Australians and Italians, there was a band of five people. A drummer, of course, was making a terrible racket. He was a blond *farang*, but the only *farang* of the bunch. The

291

keyboard player and the bass player and the guitar player were all Thai, as was the singer.

He looked very familiar. Now Wiriya was grinning broadly.

As Ladarat processed this new information, Dr. Taksin sang in a full-throated warble about his marital troubles. At least that's what it sounded like. Ladarat recognized the song she'd heard on Monday night when she'd called Wiriya. All of Dr. Taksin's exes, he sang, still lived in Texas. It seemed like an unlikely coincidence to her. But who knew?

"Why?" Ladarat asked him.

Wiriya cocked his head to one side, then brought his ear closer to Ladarat's lips.

"Why?" she asked again. Then, because that question didn't seem to capture the essence of the problem: "What?"

Again, Wiriya's faced scrunched up in concentration. Then he shrugged and pointed at the door they'd entered just a minute ago. Ladarat nodded enthusiastically.

Outside, the sidewalk was noisy with Saturday night revelers. But after that country-and-western din, Ladarat's ears felt as though someone had plugged them with cotton. Wiriya steered her down the street just two doors to an open patio of a restaurant where he commandeered an empty table with a fine view of the street.

"So..." she said, because it seemed like the only logical thing to day. "So....Dr. Taksin is...a country-and-western singer?"

Wiriya laughed as the waitress came to hand them menus. He ordered a large Singha for both of them and waited until the waitress left before replying.

"Well, I'd say he's more of an aspiring singer, wouldn't you?"

Ladarat was tempted to agree. But truth be told, she didn't feel she was well equipped to judge the merits of a country-and-western singer.

"Perhaps," she admitted. "I wouldn't know. But this explains his poor performance at work, it seems."

Wiriya nodded. "The WesternGirl usually stays open and busy until the early hours of the morning."

"And you know this because...?"

But Wiriya was saved by the return of the waitress with a twenty-ounce bottle of Singha and two glasses, beaded with moisture. He ordered for both of them—a maneuver that only six months ago Ladarat would have found presumptuous, but now she found it vaguely comforting.

Gang som pak ruam—sweet, sour, and spicy soup with vegetables. And *gang som cha om kai*, an omelet flavored acacia leaf. Also *kao niew moo yang*—grilled pork skewers. Usually just street food, some restaurants did them really well.

"Some of the best *kao niew moo yang* in the city," Wiriya said as the waitress left. "The chef here used to have a food stand in front of the main police station, but then he won the lottery and became more ambitious."

Wiriya seemed to be stalling. He poured the two glasses of beer and took a sip of his.

"And you know about the late hours of the WesternGirl because...?"

Wiriya laughed. "Remember that retirement party on Monday night?"

Ladarat nodded.

"Well, Arhit wouldn't leave. It was his retirement party, and we couldn't very well leave him. So we were there until... I don't know. Three? Four? So I had plenty of time to determine beyond any doubt that it wasn't a girlie bar."

Well, that was one mystery solved. Granted, the problem wasn't solved. If his performance was poor at work, someone would have to talk with him forcefully about his fantasies of becoming a country-and-western star. Surely that would be an easier conversation to have than the other conversations that she'd imagined.

Ladarat took a sip of the beer, thinking that it felt good to solve a mystery. Not a mystery, exactly. Not a Mystery with a capital M. But a mystery nonetheless.

On the other hand, there was the much more concerning mystery—perhaps even a true Mystery—of the Magic Grove Hotel. Ladarat filled Wiriya in, belatedly, on Delia's suspicious behavior. She told him, too, about the *Pisonia* leaves on the front patio. She'd almost finished her explanation when their *gang som pak ruam* arrived.

She'd expected Wiriya to offer advice; ideas, perhaps; an opinion of the facts.

But instead he was silent, serving them both *gang som pak ruam*. He began to eat in silence.

"Don't you think that's odd? To give the staff the day off, when the front patio is unswept, and presumably there are many other things that need to be done? Those leaves... they are certainly a clue, are they not?"

Wiriya nodded. "Just sour enough." He took another bite and thought for a moment, as Ladarat sampled her soup, too, thinking that perhaps it was a bit too sour.

Ladarat realized that she'd somehow forgotten to inform Wiriya about her clever ruse of placing Jonah as an inside observer at the Magic Grove Hotel and, therefore, he was unaware of the highly inappropriate treatment of Richard April's luggage. She would explain all that. That information would raise his... index of suspicion to a more appropriate level.

But that piece of important intelligence was unceremoniously shoved aside to make room for Wiriya's reaction to her initiative. He wasn't pleased.

"It's very fine that you've taken this initiative, certainly. But did you ever think that you might have compromised this investigation? If indeed your spy obtains any information, how can we use that information in a prosecution?" Now Wiriya's dinner sat untouched and apparently forgotten. "It's...irregular!"

Irregular? What did that mean? Answers were answers.

"Don't we know that the man Richard April disappeared and left his luggage behind? That was thanks to my 'initiative,' as you say. And don't we know that Delia arranged to have his belongings picked up by the Free Bird Café not two days after he left? And don't we know that Delia—or someone—lied to the Free Bird Café and told them that those belongings had been left for months, when in fact they'd only been sitting there for a few days? Doesn't that help at all?"

How could Wiriya say that this information—or her methods, however unorthodox—had jeopardized the investigation? Wiriya seemed stunned by this little outburst of hers, which was a good sign. But he tried to defuse her reaction with a remark about her detective skills, which wasn't.

"Ah, so now you sound very much like a detective. A real detective."

A real detective? Not exactly. Wasn't it true that she was making progress on this case? What had the "real" detective accomplished?

"Ah, no. A real detective would just sit around and let his girlfriend do all the work. I can't be a real detective, because I'm making progress on this case. And you? What have you done?"

"Well, I've been...busy."

"Ah yes, with late-night trips to country-and-western bars. Such hard work." Ladarat wasn't sure why she was making an issue of what was almost certainly a harmless retirement party. But Wiriya's casual comments about her skills at detection were uncalled for. It wasn't just what he was saying, but its tone. It was...

"You're beginning to think of yourself as a detective, aren't you?"

It was condescending. That's what it was.

"No..." Well...yes.

"Sending in a spy, and holding...stealthy phone conversations to gather information. It sounds like you're taking this a little too seriously."

"But...don't you think this is odd?" Ladarat resolved to ignore—for now—Wiriya's unkind comments about her successes in the art of detection. He felt threatened, that was all, threatened by the possibility that she might have discovered nefarious activity that he'd dismissed.

She was used to being in this position, after all. It wasn't that dissimilar from the position that nurses found themselves in when they reached a conclusion ahead of the doctors who was supposed to be in charge.

That situation was so common that Professor Dalrymple had advice to offer: "It's rarely productive to convince doctors; you must let them believe that they've arrived at the right decision on their own."

"Well," he said. "It's odd, to be sure. But not suspicious, necessarily. And certainly not criminal."

"But to say that a guest had been gone for months when he'd only been gone for a few days? To lie in order to get rid of incriminating evidence? Surely that is nefarious?"

"But you don't know that."

"Of course I know that. And you'd know it, too, if you just paid attention."

"No," Wiriya said, affecting a genial good humor as he took another bite of his neglected *gang som pak ruam*. "You've heard it from a man who works in a brothel and who has a significant criminal record."

"But—"

Wiriya held up a hand in a way that could best be described as *imperious*. "I know Jonah is a good boy. And you know that. But you must think of how any...intelligence that he provides would be perceived by a court. Would it be valued and trusted?" Wiriya shook his head and took another bite of *gang som pak ruam*. "I think we both know the answer to that."

Ladarat found herself getting annoyed in spite of Professor Dalrymple's wise advice. As she felt her blood pressure rise, she knew that what was annoying her was not their disagreement, but the fact that Wiriya wasn't taking her seriously. That might be normal—even expected—between a doctor and a nurse. But between her and Wiriya? For him to be so... condescending...Well, that was uncalled for.

"But imagine—just imagine—that she was...up to something."

"Up to something?" Wiriya was smiling, his head cocked to one side, in a way that could be construed as friendly and supportive, but which Ladarat preferred to classify—at this moment, at least—as condescending.

Their *gang som cha om kaia* and *kao niew moo yang* arrived, along with an order of spicy *som tam* (green papaya) salad that they hadn't ordered.

"Compliments of the chef," the waitress announced.

"Please thank Khun Sirichai for me, would you?"

The waitress nodded and disappeared.

He's threatened by her success. That's all it is, she thought as she helped herself to just a taste of *som tam* and *gang som cha om kaia.*

Ladarat looked down at her plate and put down her fork. Then she took a deep breath. And another. And a third. That seemed to settle her blood pressure a little.

She would be patient and logical. She would lead him to the conclusion he needed to reach.

"Then if having a spy in the Magic Grove Hotel isn't a good tactic, how should we proceed?"

Wiriya chewed a mouthful of *gang som cha om kaia* thoughtfully.

"Honestly?"

"Honestly." Of course honestly.

"I would drop the whole thing."

"You would...what?"

"I would drop it. There's nothing there."

"Of course there's something there. Maybe I can't prove it..." Yet.

"No, with respect, all you have is a bunch of facts that don't fit together as neatly as you'd like. That's not a mystery, that's...life."

"What about Delia sending the staff home when there's work to be done?"

"Poor management."

"And lying about when Richard April left?"

"A mistake." Wiriya sighed. "We could keep going like this forever. There are things that are odd, and which don't make sense. But people are human. They make mistakes. They do things that aren't logical. That doesn't make them criminals." He paused for a bit of *som tam*, grimacing as he realized that it was quite a bit more spicy than he'd expected. "So..." He said after a breath or two. "That's why you should drop it.

You're getting excited about everyday life, which is complex and messy."

Ladarat was silent, her meal untouched, as she thought about that advice. Was she getting overly suspicious about little, insignificant inconsistencies? Perhaps. Or even probably. But she had a sense that there was something wrong, a sense that those inconvenient facts were pointing her toward a much larger mystery.

They could have left it there. Wiriya could have left it there. And they could even have agreed to disagree. But then Wiriya made a grave error. A very grave error. Perhaps the worst error a man can make in an argument with a woman.

He laughed at her.

It was just a harmless chuckle, which in another context would have been genial and charming. But any doubt that he was laughing at her was erased by what he said next, after a more modest bite of *som tam*.

"Believe me, I know how exciting it is to be hot on the trail of an investigation. It's exciting. And even addictive. But you can't let that excitement control you. You can't give in to it. You have to think critically. You have to use your head."

Wiriya would have said more, perhaps. Much more. He looked as though he was just warming up for an extended lecture. But something on Ladarat's face warned him that he had made a misstep. He wasn't sure of what that misstep was, exactly, or its magnitude, but he had the good sense to shut up.

Just in time to hear Ladarat say: "If that's your opinion of my amateur efforts at detection, well, then you can solve this case yourself."

CHAPTER 27

THE DESIRE ЛOT TO LIVE

A moment later Ladarat was half running down the street, past the WesternGirl bar, and onto Loi Kroh Road, where she could easily flag a taxi. She looked quickly behind her and was surprised but not astonished that Wiriya hadn't followed her.

He should have followed her, shouldn't he? That's what Ladarat was thinking as she waved down a taxi and gave her address to the implacable driver. He should at least have called out after her, instead of just sitting there like a lazy elephant, finishing his—and her—*kao niew moo yang*.

That would only have been right. And leaving her to find her own ride home, that was not very gentlemanly. He had picked her up at home and he should have offered to drop her off.

Ladarat's thoughts bubbled along in this style for the twenty-minute trip out to her house, and by the time she'd paid the driver and let herself in, she felt several degrees more calm. Almost peaceful. Almost, but not quite. Hadn't he dismissed her abilities of detection? She found herself getting angry all over again.

In the kitchen, Ladarat took a moment to take a deep breath, and then another. As Maewfawbaahn twined himself around her legs, she rummaged in the cupboard and found a can of cat food that emitted a little gust of fish smell when she popped it open. She dumped the whole can into Maefawnbahn's bowl with a sharp *thwack* of the can that surprised both of them. Her loyal cat looked up at her in confusion.

"No, it's not you." She rubbed his head and scooted him toward his waiting dinner. She herself hadn't eaten much, but she found she wasn't hungry. That *gang som pak ruam* had been too sour and the *gang som cha om kai* had been cold. Although she hadn't tried the *kao niew moo yang*, Ladarat was certain it was not nearly as good as Sonthi's. For sure the *som tam* was too spicy—a trick to hide papaya that was a little too green. Thinking about that disappointing meal killed her appetite entirely.

Instead, she perched on one of the two old concave wooden farmer's stools that were tucked under the counter. They didn't get much use these days; she ate dinner outside whenever she could. But they were surprisingly comfortable, worn smooth by decades of sitting.

Ladarat checked her cell phone for messages as Maewfawbaahn ate, but there was nothing from Wiriya. There was, however, a message from Sisithorn, saying that she felt much better and thanking Ladarat for taking care of her. And another message from Ukrit. "Blood test positive for trichloroethanol."

Trichloroethanol? What could that be? It wasn't a drug she'd ever heard of. Ethanol was alcohol, of course. Everyone knew that. But trichloroethanol? No idea.

She could look it up, but it was past nine, and despite her prolonged nap, somehow Ladarat still felt exhausted. She could feel her eyelids starting to droop as she watched Maewfawbaahn's finicky eating, one small bite at a time. At this rate he wouldn't be done until morning. She'd fall asleep waiting for him.

It wouldn't take long to look up one chemical, would it?

Indeed it didn't. She hustled upstairs and grabbed her iPad from her nightstand and then sat on the edge of her bed, her

301

iPad balanced on her knees. A quick search for trichloroethanol led to interesting results, results that she could, perhaps, have expected. Although those results didn't point to a culprit in the night robber case, they were proof that there was, in fact, a case.

She lay back, bunching all of her pillows behind her and putting her feet up on the bed. What did these results mean?

For a second she thought of calling Wiriya with those results. But he was the detective. The real detective. He would figure it out.

Her iPad was still open in front of her, and Ladarat found herself completely and inexplicably wide awake. Before she knew what she was doing, she found her fingers navigating to Richard April's website. She was looking for...well... she couldn't really say. Something that would shed light on his disappearance? Or some evidence that he hadn't actually disappeared?

What she found, though, wasn't what she expected. It was something, she noted with intense satisfaction, that Wiriya the real detective had missed.

On the far right of the screen were short snippets of thoughts and suggestions from the great man himself, arrayed from newest to oldest. The short line at the top, posted just three days ago, was very brief. "Sad news," it said.

Ladarat clicked on the link and was taken to another page with a black banner across the top. There were a few paragraphs of text, apparently written by Richard April.

Dear fans:

I'm sad to have to write such a sad letter, so soon. But I'm happy, at least, that there are fans to whom I can write it.

About a month ago, I started feeling unwell, and when I went to my doctor, she put me through a series of tests that were, to be honest, pretty unpleasant. (Think of the torment I put Gerald through in the first chapter of The Lighthouse Murders, *and you'll have a pretty good idea of what those doctors did to me. Perhaps it's Gerald's revenge.)*

Anyway, they found liver cancer that was very advanced. That's their way of saying cancer's not curable. Not even treatable. (In the world of cancer, you really don't want to be "advanced." You really just don't.)

They gave me maybe three months to live. If I'm lucky.

Well, I thought about that for a few days, and I figured that I've already been about as lucky as any guy can be. Successful books, lots of loyal fans. And above all, I get to make a living doing what I love. I've been lucky. Very lucky. And all luck runs out eventually. It seems like mine has.

So I'm not counting on any more luck. And rather than struggling on through the next few months, or whatever time I have, I've decided I don't want to spend my last months on earth being sick. I'd like to check out while I can.

So that's what I'm going to do. Travel a bit. See the world. Or at least a little of it. And check out while I'm still awake and with it enough to have a deep conversation.

In short, I want to check out when I'm still the person that my characters would recognize. Josie, especially.

Remember Josie? My publisher thought she was a silly idea, but she turned out to be one of my favorite characters.

I don't want to get to the point where I'd be one of her patients. So thanks for being great fans. And thanks for reading.

A full minute went by as Ladarat read that message again. And then a third time.

Ladarat sat there, vaguely aware that Maewfawbaahn had followed her up the stairs and wedged himself next to her on the bed, just as a loyal watchcat would. She was aware of her cat and his contented purring, but her mind was elsewhere.

So this man... Richard April. He was dying? So he came to Chiang Mai and the Magic Grove Hotel and he... what?

Ladarat thought back to Wiriya's theory that he'd had a liaison with a sex worker. That certainly wasn't the case. Not now.

And the notion that he'd just... disappeared seemed implausible. Someone might do that if they had debts, or if they wanted to begin a new life. But there would be no new life for Richard April.

Ladarat scanned the letter one more time, looking for a phrase that had caught her attention before. Her brain hadn't known what to do with that phrase the first time.

Richard April said he didn't want to spend the time he had left "being sick." He wanted to check out.

Ladarat's grasp of colloquial English was perhaps not all that it could be, but this was a phrase she'd become familiar with during her year at the University of Chicago. She knew what it meant. And she knew that this desire to "check out" was not uncommon among Americans who wanted to control their lives and, ultimately, their deaths.

So. This Richard April had decided to end his life. That much was clear. He'd come to Chiang Mai, and to the Magic Grove Hotel, to do it. If his discarded luggage meant what she thought it meant, it would seem that Richard April had succeeded.

Everything made sense and yet . . . it didn't. Richard April's note to his fans explained so much, but it created as many mysteries as it solved. So he'd come to Chiang Mai to end his life, but why? When he had a successful life, and probably family, and—who knew?—perhaps months left to live?

He didn't want to spend the time he had left being sick. Ladarat found herself saying that out loud. In English.

And as she did, she thought of the conversation she'd had with Melissa Double. What had she said? That she didn't want to go back to Wales—Cardiff—where people would think of her as "sick." As "dying."

So Melissa Double had been thinking the same thing?

It was at that moment that Ladarat's head recognized what her heart had figured out a few minutes before. Richard April and Melissa Double had been sick and dying. But they didn't want to be. Richard April had gotten his wish, and, Ladarat realized with a sinking feeling in her stomach, Melissa Double probably had, too.

"Oh . . . no."

She said that out loud, with enough force to wake Maew-fawbaahn, who looked up at her curiously, flicking his long tail against the pillow next to her.

"Oh, no," she said again, because the next logical thought was not far away. If it was all but certain that Richard April had traveled to the Magic Grove Hotel to end his life, and if it was very likely that Melissa Double had done the same . . .

Ladarat didn't need to finish that sentence to know that

305

things were very bad indeed. These disappearances of Sharon McPhiller and Demian Ober and probably many, many more now seemed to have a solution. But it was a solution that Ladarat didn't like one bit.

Now, at least, her course of action was clear. There could be no question of her continuing this investigation on her own. She would need to call Wiriya, and soon.

Soon. Meaning: Now.

If ever there was a time to put aside their differences, now was that time. She would extend ... what was that English saying? A branch. Some variety of branch. Whatever the appropriate variety of branch was ... well ... she would extend it.

Wirya answered, as she knew he would. Their conversation was stilted at first and uncomfortably formal. No doubt Wiriya was still miffed by her clandestine spying and, worse, her clandestine spying without his knowledge. But now at least he would appreciate the results she'd obtained by her ... unorthodox methods.

And he did. He even apologized, perfunctorily, for his skepticism.

Ladarat found she was relieved that she had another reason for this call.

Ladarat read Richard April's note in its entirety and then returned to the line that had caught her attention.

"He said he didn't want to spend his final months 'being sick.'"

"That's what he wrote?" Wiriya sounded surprised. He, too, had missed that the first time.

"Exactly."

Now Wiriya was silent for a long time. "You think that this man came to Thailand to ... stop living?"

Ladarat said that was exactly what she thought. She reminded Wiriya of Demian Ober and Sharon McPhiller and Melissa Double.

"And who knows how many other people," Wiriya said slowly. Ladarat could imagine him shaking his head.

"Is it possible," he asked, "that this desire not to live is common?"

Ladarat nodded. "Certainly I've heard about it. And in some countries in Europe, and even in America, it's permissible to take your own life."

Wiriya seemed stunned by this. "For everyone? Whenever you want?"

"No, no. Just under certain circumstances. For instance, if you're very sick, with a medical condition like what Richard April had." Or, she thought, like Melissa Double's cancer.

Now Wiriya seemed more worried than she'd ever seen him.

"What's wrong?"

"Well, I don't know. Not for sure. But I have a bad feeling about this." He paused. "We have all of these people who are coming through Chiang Mai and disappearing, right?"

Ladarat nodded.

"And one person—just one, I admit—seems like he might have been intent on ending his own life."

"And...?"

"So what if all of these people are disappearing for the same reason? What if Chiang Mai has become—unbeknownst to us—the place where people come when they don't want to be sick? When they would rather be dead?"

Like a good nurse, Ladarat congratulated herself on letting Wiriya reach this conclusion on his own.

"I'm afraid you may be right," was all she said.

There was a long pause as they considered the situation.

Eventually, after what felt like minutes, it was Wiriya who broke the silence.

"I apologize for doubting you. You were suspicious, and... well...you certainly had reason to be." Another pause. "Unfortunately."

Another time, and under different circumstances, Ladarat might have extracted a more detailed apology. She might even have gloated a little. But not now. Now the only appropriate response was a humble acknowledgment and a plan.

Much to her surprise, she found that Wiriya was looking to her for that plan. That was astonishing. He was the detective in this relationship, was he not?

Far more astonishing, to her, at least, was the fact that she did, in fact, have a plan. A good one, she thought. And one they could put into motion tomorrow morning.

Wan aathit

SUNDAY

CHAPTER 28

AN INSTRUCTION MANUAL FOR THE DYING

She woke up very early—early for a quiet Sunday—even before Maewfawbaahn, who stirred grumpily as she disturbed the covers. Getting up, she glanced at the other side of the bed. The side that was Wiriya's. The side that had become Wiriya's. Ladarat let her watchcat enjoy that extra space, sleeping soundly. She padded downstairs to make peaflower tea.

She and Wiriya had not exactly "made up," as they say, but they were not still arguing. They would resolve this difference, certainly. Almost certainly. But Ladarat couldn't help thinking that her detection strategies were not the only topic about which he had strong and seemingly intransigent opinions.

There were his opinions about her driving, for instance; so many opinions, often uttered in a very rigid, barking voice that was quite unbecoming, and just a little unmanly. They were about such silly issues, such as whether to look over one's shoulder when changing lanes or how much room to allow between oneself and the next car. Such trivial things, really. Yet he held such very strong opinions that led him to insist on driving whenever possible. If they were to remain a couple, he would have to learn not to cling so tightly to these opinions of his.

An hour later, freshly showered, a second cup of peaflower tea steeped leisurely to a deep blue in hand, Ladarat opened the back door and sat on the top step of the stairs leading down to her little garden. The sun had only just risen, and the air was cool and still. It was the perfect time of day for sitting on one's steps—one's own steps—in a house that one has paid for, and thinking.

She picked up her phone, registering the time, which was only six thirty.

Ladarat wondered at that. Only six thirty, and yet she felt wide awake. She hadn't slept well, having drifted off but then snapping wide awake as the events of last night forced their way into her head.

Now her head should be drooping with fatigue. Yet she felt... well. Energized, even. And, if she were being truly honest with herself, excited.

This plan of hers to determine what had happened to the disappearing *farang* was a good plan. It was a plan to be proud of. She hadn't told Wiriya what she had in mind. There were still some... refinements she'd wanted to work out. But in his humbled state last night, he hadn't pressed her. He'd simply agreed to meet her at his apartment at nine. He'd even agreed—without much protest—to let her drive.

That left time for two leisurely cups of peaflower tea, steeped to a disconcertingly deep blue, and another task. An awkward one, perhaps, but one that was necessary.

Thirty minutes later, Ladarat was sitting at the Kanom Tea Shop across from the hospital. A popular hangout of nursing students, it was deserted at this hour on a Sunday, and Ladarat had been able to take a coveted corner table on the patio. Under a flowering frangipani tree, the table was a favorite of couples, often medical students and nursing students, who wanted a little privacy.

Privacy was of the utmost importance this morning, less for her sake than for the sake of the woman sitting across from her.

As Sudchada sipped her tea, Ladarat tried to gauge her reaction to this early-morning meeting request. After taking yesterday off, Sudchada had worked on the palliative care unit overnight and had been eager to get home when Ladarat had called her cell phone a few minutes ago. But to her credit, and to Ladarat's infinite relief, she'd been willing to stop to share a cup of tea on her way home.

Sudchada looked tired, of course, as one might after a long night shift. Her face seemed just a little weathered. Her hair was tied back in an unusally impeccable bun, but a few wisps had escaped in front of her forehead and floated on the light breeze.

"You wanted to talk, Khun?" Sudchada smiled a little uncertainly. It was a smile that didn't really have a name in the Thai language of smiles. It was the half-confused, half-sad smile of someone who is facing something unexpected and who knows—from past experience, perhaps—that unexpected events are generally not good. "This is about Dr. Taksin, is it not?"

Ladarat nodded. "Partly. I have some information about him, but also a question for you."

Sudchada took another sip of tea, then placed the cup gently on the table. Then she waited. That was a skill that perhaps one learned being a palliative care nurse: the skill of being quiet, and waiting. It was not unlike the skill of being a detective.

"On both topics, this was a conversation that I thought it would be best to have...in private. Outside the hospital and

DAVID CASARETT

away from people who might overhear and who might…
misconstrue."

Again Sudchada nodded, but her eyebrows furrowed just
a little, as if this was a line of discussion that she hadn't been
expecting.

"First, I wanted to talk," Ladarat continued, "because I
have been reviewing the deaths that have occurred at Sriphat
Hospital—our hospital—in the past month. And…I've been
noticing something strange."

"Yes, Khun?"

"These deaths…they occur in many places in the hospital.
On the medical wards, in the trauma ICU, and in the medical
ICU, mostly. And the oncology units. But they don't seem to
occur on the palliative care unit."

"Yes?" Now Sudchada's thin eyebrows went up a few milli-
meters more and she seemed genuinely surprised.

"This is a surprise to you, Khun?"

"No…no, of course not. Hardly any of our patients die on
the palliative care unit."

"But…how could that be? They are all sick, are they not?"

"Of course, Khun, they are very sick. And most are in the
last weeks of life."

"And yet no one dies in your unit. And your mortality statistics are—"

"Very good. Yes, I know, we are very proud of that." Sudchada smiled her way through her fatigue and sat up a little
straighter in her chair. Her pride was indeed evident.

"But if these patients die, then where do they go if they
don't die in the hospital?"

"Why, we send them home, of course. That's why our mortality statistics look so good."

Ah, this is what Ladarat had been afraid of: a nurse,

ambitious to succeed, gaming the system by discharging patients just to make the numbers look good.

Sudchada smiled and poured more tea for Ladarat and then herself.

"Is that all you wanted to ask me, Khun? When you called, I admit I thought it was something more...worrisome."

Ladarat was flummoxed. Here this nurse was admitting to sending patients home in order to improve her statistics. Yet she didn't have the demeanor of someone who had made such an admission. In fact, just the opposite: She seemed proud that her cleverness was being recognized. She was not unlike a criminal who wants their genius to be appreciated and remarked upon.

"But it is worrisome, Khun. To discharge patients just to improve your mortality statistics...that is very worrisome."

Sudchada paused in the middle of a sip of tea, her eyes growing large and frightened. The teacup clattered in its saucer as she put it down hurriedly.

"Oh, but, Khun, that's not why we discharge patients. Not at all. That's just a...side effect. We discharge them because they want to go home."

"But..." This took Ladarat by surprise. Now she supposed her eyes were probably as wide at this moment as Sudchada's were. The two nurses sat across from each other, each looking at the other with astonishment. Ladarat spoke first.

"They...want to go home? But the palliative care unit... it's very beautiful, and comfortable. It's set up for patients and families to be welcoming..." Ladarat paused. "So why would anyone want to go home?"

Sudchada shook her head modestly. "What you say is very kind, Khun. And it's true that we've tried to make the ward as homelike as we can. But many of our patients come from many kilometers away, as you know. That creates enormous burdens for their families, who may need to take time away from their jobs or their farms to come here."

That was true, of course. "But for the patients...don't they get better care here?"

Now Sudchada smiled. "We like to think so, of course. But much palliative care can be done by any doctor or nurse, with the right instructions. So Dr. Taksin helped us create a checklist for when each patient leaves. It has a list of that patient's symptoms and advice for physicians to manage them. For instance, if a patient has nausea, we'll describe what treatments have worked and which ones haven't. And we'll make suggestions for what to do if that symptom gets worse. That checklist goes with the patient when the patient travels home."

Ladarat was surprised. She'd never heard of such a thing: an instruction manual for the dying. It was a very clever idea.

"But...not all people have families to go home to, do they?"

Sudchada nodded. "It's true, some don't. But most do."

"And if they don't...?"

"Then most would stay here, Khun. But there are exceptions."

"Was Melissa Double such an exception?"

Sudchada shook her head. "I don't know what to make of her departure. I really don't. She seemed very happy to stay with us. She even asked about staying...permanently. But perhaps you could visit her, Khun? Perhaps you could find out why she left so suddenly?"

"Ah..., but Khun, Melissa Double is no longer at the Magic Grove Hotel."

Now it was Sudchada's turn to look surprised in what was turning into a ping-pong match of confusion.

"But of course she is, as I told you yesterday. Besides, I

called the hotel last night. You know the owner, Khun Delia? She said that Melissa Double was getting on very well. And the instructions for managing her pain were most helpful."

"Yesterday evening?" Oh dear. "Have you ever been out to the Magic Grove Hotel?" Ladarat asked.

"Well, no. But my brother-in-law is the accountant for the Free Bird Café. He speaks very highly of Khun Delia. He says she is very saintly, the way she runs that hotel and makes frequent donations to charities."

"Khun, about how many patients would you say you've sent to the Magic Grove Hotel in the past month?"

Sudchada paused for a moment. "Well, about one or two a week, probably. Mostly *farang* who were taken ill while traveling. If they're in northern Thailand or anywhere in Laos, they come here, since of course this is the best hospital anywhere north of Bangkok. Then they go to Khun Delia's hotel as they make arrangements to return home."

"That's a lot of patients," Ladarat said. A lot of patients who were going to the Magic Grove Hotel but who, it seemed, were not leaving. She explained, briefly, what she knew about the disappearances of Sharon McPhiller and Richard April and Demian Ober.

"But what will you do?" Sudchada asked, her neglected tea cooling in front of her. "Is Captain Mookjai aware? Is he... investigating?"

"He is aware," Ladarat said quietly. "And I—we—have a plan." She tried to sound more confident than she felt. It was a good plan, but not a foolproof one.

The two nurses sat in silence for a minute, or perhaps more. Unsure whether there was anything left to say on the subject of the Magic Grove Hotel, Ladarat decided to turn to a topic about which she could be more confident.

"Then," she said gently, "there is the matter of Dr. Taksin."

Sudchada looked at her from under eyelids that had begun to droop just a little, as though her brain was telling her it would be best to go to sleep before she was confronted with more disquieting news.

"At least with regard to that matter," Ladarat said, smiling, "I can offer you better news."

At this Sudchada seemed to wake up, although she also became wary, as if good news was both unexpected and somewhat suspect.

"Khun?"

"Yes?"

"Have you ever heard of something called country-and-western music?"

CHAPTER 29

KUMQUATS ARE NOT A SOCIAL FRUIT

Ladarat was still thinking about her strange conversation with Sudchada an hour later, as she found herself once again driving up the cool, shaded driveway of the Magic Grove Hotel. This trip, though, she wasn't alone. Wiriya was sitting next to her, seemingly much more relaxed now that they'd reached their destination.

Uncharacteristically, he'd been very quiet, and very polite, almost formal, during the drive out. That was a sign that he was still feeling contrite about his brusque manner last night.

Another sign was the tight grip he maintained on the armrest between them and on the door handle to his right. So funny that men thought that they were concealing their feelings, even when those feelings were so obviously on public display. From his rigid posture and tight grip, anyone could see that Wiriya was feeling guilty, yet he wouldn't admit it.

Of course he still felt a little guilty for his behavior the previous night. But she'd been able to distract him by telling him just a little about her plan.

That plan, or at least the most important part, was making his presence felt in the backseat. Chi had apparently been dreading a quiet Sunday home alone while Sukanya went to work, but now he was delighted to be liberated, and even more delighted to find himself in a car on a road trip.

He'd been bouncing back and forth in the backseat for the twenty kilometers or so from Chiang Mai's Old City, where Ladarat had stopped to collect Wiriya at his apartment. Now, sensing perhaps that there was excitement afoot, and that he had an important role to play, Chi's level of energy increased exponentially.

They pulled into the circular drive and Ladarat shut off the engine. She was about to open the car door when Wiriya laid a gentle hand on her arm.

"It's been said," he began, "that on occasion I have the social skills of a kumquat." He smiled.

"Do kumquats lack social skills?" Ladarat was nonplussed. She'd never thought about Wiriya in that light. Nor, truth be told, had she thought of kumquats in any light at all, vis-à-vis their social skills. "I was not aware."

"Well," Wiriya admitted, "I don't really know. Not really. But the point stands." He paused, looking very intently at a point on the dashboard midway between them. "So although I felt strongly about your...unusual detective activities, I didn't express those concerns well. And," he added, "I didn't show respect for your suspicions—your instincts—which turned out to be true. In fact, it's safe to say that in the social skills department, your average kumquat would have handled this situation better than I did."

"Well, I've never really thought of kumquats as a social fruit," Ladarat admitted. "So perhaps that's fair."

"That is all I meant to say," Wiriya agreed. "When you find yourself thinking that perhaps I lack social skills, I would ask that you think of a kumquat. Think of me in that light, and you may be more favorably disposed."

"Ah," Ladarat said. "Disposed?"

"Disposed toward me," Wiriya added. "Not toward kumquats, which really have no need for anyone's esteem."

"Ah," Ladarat said again.

Wiriya nodded and opened his door, which dialed up Chi's enthusiasm to a fever pitch. Now he was racing back and forth across the backseat, spinning in a little semicircle at each end as if he believed himself to be on a tiny racetrack. She'd have to put an end to this soon, before he wore an oval into the vinyl upholstery.

Ladarat had barely closed the rear door after Chi when a flicker of movement caught the corner of her eye. The heavy front door of the hotel opened as if someone had been waiting for them. A moment later, Delia herself appeared on the front porch. Shading her eyes with one hand, the owner leaned forward a bit as if to get a better view against the glare of the sun on the white gravel. She took a step backward, then held up her hand again for another look.

As Delia was surveying these new visitors, Wiriya clambered out of the car, stretched, and closed the door behind himself. The sound of the door filled the open, empty space, echoing strangely off the front of the hotel as if Khun Delia were bouncing it back at them.

When Chi emptied his bladder on the roots of an unsuspecting tree, the hotel owner put her hands on her hips in a posture that was not particularly welcoming. Nor was it particularly flattering to her stocky figure, truth be told. That stance—elbows splayed and shoulders hunched—made the already large woman look a little like an elephant about to charge.

Even Chi got that message. They hadn't even reached the steps that led up to the patio before Chi began to hang back, feigning interest in a nondescript patch of gravel under

Ladarat's left foot. Wiriya, too, seemed to delay just a little, leaving Ladarat to perform the introductions.

"Khun Delia, so good to see you."

Delia merely nodded, offering a halfhearted *wai* that missed being rude by a hairsbreadth. Worse, she wasn't smiling.

Ladarat introduced Wiriya without mentioning his role as a detective. He offered a formal *wai*, and then she introduced Chi, who didn't. Nor did Chi evince any interest in Delia. He'd moved on from his fascination with that patch of gravel, but stood uncertainly next to Ladarat, awaiting developments.

Pffttt.

Ladarat had to admit that that was a pretty fair summary of the situation. She and Wiriya (and Chi) stood in the hot sun, while Delia stood on the patio in the shade, blocking their way to the front door. Not speaking, and without a change in facial expression, she looked first at Chi, then Wiriya, and finally at Ladarat. Her eyebrows rose just a little bit. That wasn't much, but it was at least an opening.

"We were hoping to visit Ms. Double, who came here recently," Ladarat said slowly.

Delia's expression didn't change. She looked at Ladarat, then Wiriya, then Ladarat again, ignoring Chi entirely. That was just as well, given what Ladarat had in mind.

Finally, just when Ladarat was starting to wonder whether this hotel owner had become deaf—or, more likely, was feigning deafness—Delia spoke. She seemed to be addressing Wiriya, though, just a few centimeters over Ladarat's left shoulder.

"As I told you yesterday, she is no longer here," was all she said. Then Delia lapsed into silence. Yet she didn't turn away, nor did she step out of the way, nor did she invite them in out of the sun.

Ladarat could feel a small bead of sweat making its way

down the center of her back. She turned back to Wiriya, who loosened his tie. Standing out in the sun was not wise for someone of his...density. Yet they were at an impasse.

"But I believe you told nurse Sudchada yesterday that Ms. Double was doing well?"

"I'm sure she is doing well," Delia said. She nodded, then crossed her arms and stood perfectly still.

"And do you have a forwarding address, Khun?" Ladarat turned to see Wiriya take his small, battered flip notebook out of his suit pocket, followed by a pen. "We're hoping that we might be able to speak with her."

"Speak with her?" Delia uncrossed her arms and furrowed both eyebrows into a knot. "Why would you want to speak with one of my guests?"

"So she is a guest?" Wiriya asked with the practiced smoothness of a detective. "Ah, I misunderstood. I thought a moment ago you said that she had checked out."

Now Delia looked flustered. Uncrossing her arms, she wedged her fists onto her hips as if she were trying to make them stick. Then she swung her hands behind her back and clasped them briefly. Then they crossed themselves once again on her chest. Clearly, her hands were somewhat confused about their purpose in life.

"Well, of course she checked out," Delia said, once she'd regained control of her wandering hands. "I only meant... when I said she was my guest...that she had been one of my guests." She paused, as her left hand snaked behind her back before she corralled it. "That's all I meant."

"Ah," Wiriya said. But he kept his notebook open. "So if she was a guest, and if apparently you continue to think of past guests as your current guests, perhaps you have a forwarding address? Because, Khun, as we said, we would like to speak with her."

This conversation appeared to be going nowhere. They were asking the same question over and over again of the same person, yet hoping for different answers. Surely that didn't make sense. But perhaps that was what detectives did.

As Professor Dalrymple said, "Every day is an opportunity for an observant nurse to learn something new, if only we pay attention."

Ladarat resolved to pay attention. As she did, she realized why Wiriya kept asking the same question in different ways.

"But I have no forwarding address," Delia said, looking carefully back and forth between Wiriya and Ladarat. "None."

"Did she leave unexpectedly?"

Delia shook her head, looking wary.

"Did she leave suddenly?"

Again Delia shook her head, in a more limited arc, barely more than a flick of her sturdy chin.

"Did she take her luggage?"

Delia's eyes grew large, and her hands disentangled themselves, fleeing behind her back before she pinned them to her hips.

"Of course she took her luggage. She checked out, as I told you. And people who check out from hotels take their luggage. That's the way it works."

"Ah," Wiriya said. "Of course. So she checked out...today? Yesterday?"

"Yesterday." Delia nodded.

"She checked out yesterday, taking her luggage." He paused. "All of her luggage? Nothing left behind?"

Now Delia's hands were in open revolt, flitting back and forth in asynchronous arcs from her chest to back to hips, and occasionally colliding in midair like planes piloted by teenagers.

"No, of course not," Delia said quickly. "Or, I don't think

so. Or if she did leave anything behind, I'm sure I don't know about it. I'm understaffed here, and I can't be expected to go looking around for anything that my guests leave behind, can I?"

"No, of course not, Khun. That would be too much work for one person." Wiriya paused, glancing at Ladarat and loosening his collar a little more.

"That is all we were wondering, Khun. Thank you for your time." He'd obviously gleaned enough information from the reluctant hotel owner. But what information?

They couldn't leave yet. Ladarat still had a plan. It was not much of a plan, truth be told, but it was something she felt that she had to do. So, technically speaking, it was a plan.

"Would you mind, Khun, if we took a walk around the property? To give him some exercise before the drive back to Chiang Mai?" Ladarat nodded at Chi, who sat slumped in the meager shade of Ladarat's shadow, looking like a romp around the hotel grounds was the last thing he wanted right now.

Delia's eyebrows furrowed for a moment as she looked closely at Chi for anything resembling excess energy. She glanced behind her at the front door that yawned open and then shrugged.

"Of course, Khun. Please."

Wiriya smiled and took a step forward toward the welcome shade of the patio, but Delia was too quick.

"Ah, no, Khun. The hotel lobby, it's for guests only."

Wiriya pulled up short, perplexed. He tugged at his tie, loosening it a little more. Beads of sweat had broken out on his broad forehead, and something like a frown was playing across his lips. Ladarat had never seen her boyfriend truly angry, and she had a sense that she didn't want to. Certainly not now, when so much was at stake.

"Of course, Khun. And although we are many things, we are not guests. So we'll walk around this way, if that's all right?"

Ladarat didn't wait for Delia's curt nod and headed purposefully around the left side of the building, tugging a confused Chi behind her, and hoping that Wiriya would follow her.

He did, but Delia didn't. In a moment they turned the corner of the hotel onto a well-marked path, and they were alone, wandering though a grove of young teak trees. Ladarat was pretty sure that if she kept straight on this path—more of a little road, actually—they would come to the open field where Delia had shown her the teak saplings that they were planting.

There was no one around. No sign of Delia or indeed of any other human. There was nothing but the sound of birds chirping high overhead and the buzz of cicadas in the undergrowth. It was oddly peaceful. Somehow that background noise became insulation against the outside world. Although the nearby road had been audible from the gravel driveway, now they were enveloped in a mushy sort of silence and gently dappled shade.

Now that it was ten degrees cooler in the shade, Chi shed his apathy and began to strain at his leash. After a quick glance around, Ladarat reached into her handbag and took out a small margarine container that Sukanya had given her that morning. She shook it gently, producing a sharp rattle.

Chi swung around in an instant, flying back to sit at her feet as if he'd been magnetized.

Even Wiriya was impressed. "So...he does what he's supposed to on occasion?"

Ladarat nodded. "Apparently." She opened the lid, picking out a small dog biscuit shaped like a bone. Chi sat expectantly. Wiriya's eyebrows went up.

Ladarat flipped the treat in Chi's general direction, and he rose up on his hind legs and snapped it up like a lizard catching a hapless fly. He sat back on his haunches, waiting for more. Ladarat had learned what she needed to.

She shook her head and reached down to unclip Chi's leash. Still he sat, hopeful. Ladarat shook her head again.

"Go." Go be a detective dog.

After another moment during which his hopes waned and then disappeared, Chi sat at her feet. Then he seemed to realize that the situation was not going to change.

Pffttt.

A second later he was spinning through the undergrowth, nose to the ground, in widening circles around them. She and Wiriya continued to walk.

"You're not afraid he'll get lost?"

Ladarat shook her head. "If he hears those treats, he'll come back. That's how Sukanya gets him to come inside."

Wiriya pondered that for a moment as they walked farther into the grove. Ladarat thought they should have reached the open field by now. It hadn't been this far, had it? But no matter. Chi was out there doing her detective work. All she had to do was keep an eye open for Delia.

"So...this is very pleasant, but what did you have in mind?"

"In mind?" Ladarat wasn't really paying attention. Still thinking about Chi in his widening orbit, she couldn't hear him in the undergrowth anymore. Every once in a while she thought she caught a glimpse of movement, but she couldn't tell whether it was an itinerant therapy dog or just the breeze that flowed through the grove.

"Chi," Wiriya said as he tramped along beside her. "What is his...function?"

Ladarat turned to Wiriya. "His function? Well, he has a good nose."

"In what way is that part of his anatomy...good?"

"It's very acute," Ladarat said as she stepped carefully over a large root that crossed the path. "It knows, for instance, where the hospital morgue is. And it determined well before I learned it from Sudchada that Siwinee's boyfriend is a pathology resident." Turning to see Wiriya's blank look, she added an explanation. "A doctor who works in the morgue. With dead people."

"Ah," Wiriya said. "I see." But obviously he didn't. He rubbed his chin.

"I don't think these people have actually left," Ladarat explained, stepping over a particularly large tree root that had grown across the path.

"You don't?" Wiriya's pace slowed just a little, and he glanced around in confusion, as if he expected to see Richard April or Melissa Double following them or peering out from behind a tree.

"But...you agree that it looks like they're no longer alive? At least some of them?"

Ladarat nodded, scanning the woods for a rustle of leaves that might point to her intrepid detective dog.

"So you think they're here somewhere, in a state that is not alive?"

Ladarat nodded again. "Exactly. I think they have 'checked out,' as Richard April put it so eloquently, but they have not left."

"And we're looking for them...in a teak grove?" He was silent for perhaps ten meters as they continued walking. "I hope that you're wrong," was all he said.

CHAPTER 30

A CRIME THAT DOESN'T SEEM LIKE A CRIME

Ladarat hoped she was wrong, too. But the sound of shouting up ahead suggested that perhaps she wasn't.

Wiriya picked up his pace to a jog, and Ladarat struggled to keep up. He moved quite fast for someone of his density. It was a miracle of locomotion.

The advantage of being a couple of paces behind Wiriya when they finally emerged into the clearing was that she had an extra moment to take in the scene.

It was not two women shouting at each other, or a man and a woman, as Ladarat had guessed, but a woman—Delia—shouting a mix of English and Thai at a small dog of indeterminant breed. Chi was digging frantically in a mound of earth where a teak sapling had apparently recently been planted. The sapling—about half a meter tall—had been flung to the side. It was rapidly being covered by loose dirt that Chi was churning out with furiously digging front paws. Delia, meanwhile, was alternately shouting and aiming kicks at the little therapy-dog-turned-gardener.

Wiriya and Ladarat were still twenty or thirty meters away, and Delia hadn't seen them yet. Nor was she likely to, so focused was she on aiming a kick at the little dog, who seemed to avoid her feet with an effortless grace that Ladarat, for one, would never have believed possible.

Finally, as Wiriya and then Ladarat reached the scene, Delia turned and saw them. By that point she'd become so out of breath from her exertions that she could barely speak. She just pointed at Chi and bent almost double, putting both hands on her knees. In that position, she couldn't see what Wiriya saw, and what Ladarat thought she saw.

At first, she saw little more than a flash of white in the hole that Chi was digging, just a blur that was covered by shifting dirt. Then that blur solidified and became a patch of cream-colored cloth. A sheet of some kind. Chi's front feet scrabbled against the cloth, and that dry scratching sound seemed to rouse Delia, giving her a second wind. She shouted something that was neither Thai nor English—or at least not proper English—and aimed another kick at Chi.

Ladarat had seen enough. She had an obligation to return the little therapy dog unharmed, so she hurriedly fished the margarine container out of her bag and shook it vigorously. Ladarat realized that she was hardly able to control her own hands.

"Chi!" He paused digging long enough to look at her, and at the margarine container, but his resolve to dig seemed overpowering.

Ladarat gave the margarine container a few more shakes, which wasn't difficult, because she found her hands and knees were vibrating like springs.

Reluctantly, Chi backed away from the hole he'd been digging, keeping one eye on Delia. He trotted around Wiriya, who was staring, dumbfounded, at Chi's archeological efforts, and planted himself at Ladarat's feet, his efforts of the past five minutes apparently forgotten. Ladarat clipped his leash on first, then rewarded him with a treat. And then another. And another. Anything to keep from looking at the hole he'd dug.

But Wiriya wasn't so intimidated. After overcoming his initial shock, he stepped closer and knelt down, brushing some of the dirt to the edges of the hole that measured about a half meter in diameter and about as deep. Quite an excavation for such a small dog. Wiriya gently enlarged the space at the, bottom by sweeping loose dirt away to reveal what appeared to be the facial features of a person, man or woman—it was impossible to tell—under the cloth.

Meanwhile, Delia had found a seat on the ground, still breathing hard. Wiriya remained standing, but Ladarat felt lightheaded and looked around for a place to sit, too, before she passed out. An old, weathered stump behind her seemed a likely spot, which is to say it seemed preferable to landing facedown in the dirt. She pulled Chi behind her and sat.

This was all a little too much for her brain. That face peering up through the white cloth was what she had been afraid of, of course. This was why she had borrowed Chi today, and why she had dragged Wiriya out here. But she never for a moment had truly expected to find what she'd been afraid of.

Only now did she begin to notice the smell. Sweet and rotten at the same time, it wasn't overpowering where she was sitting. Perhaps it was stronger where Wiriya was kneeling by the grave, because now he was holding a handkerchief to his face as he stood up. A moment later the breeze took even the slightest scent away, and they could have been three people and a dog, sitting in the light shade at the edge of the clearing, about to enjoy a picnic together.

Wiriya walked over to Ladarat and half sat, half collapsed next to her. They both looked at the shallow grave, and then at Delia, who sat on the ground with her knees drawn up to her chest, her denim trousers stretched tight. She looked at them defiantly.

"I haven't done anything wrong," she said in Thai. Delia glared at Ladarat, then Wiriya, where her gaze was fixed. "Oh, I know who you are. The famous detective. And you." She turned to Ladarat for just a second. "The almost-famous nurse detective. I knew all about you when you first came out here."

Not for the first time, Ladarat regretted the fame she'd gained from the Peaflower murders. It was easier to be a detective, she imagined, when the world didn't *know* that you were a detective. But there wasn't much she could do about that now.

"So I know that you're here because you think there's been a crime. Maybe even crimes that will get you on the front page of the Chiang Mai *Post* again." She turned back to Wiriya. "But you're wrong. No one's done anything illegal here."

It seemed as though Delia had said all that she was going to say. The silence stretched about between the three of them, broken only by the rustling of the trees above them and the buzzing of cicadas from the field that stretched out behind Delia.

Ladarat, for her part, didn't have much to say, either. She'd brought them this far—she and Chi—and the rest should be up to Wiriya. When one found a dead body, that was a logical time for a detective to take over.

Wiriya seemed to agree. He cleared his throat, but words escaped him for the moment. Ladarat waited. And waited. Finally, she felt compelled to ask the obvious question.

"That...is Melissa Double?"

Delia shook her head. "Sharon McPhiller."

Still Wiriya was silent.

"So...why is she here?" Even to Ladarat, that seemed like an awkward and poorly phrased question. But wasn't it more than Wiriya had managed to ask? It was. Besides, it was enough to keep Delia talking.

"Perhaps we should come back the hotel," Delia said after a moment's pause. "There is a lot to explain."

And indeed there was. A few minutes later, as they sat at one of the outside tables on the deserted patio, Delia served them chilled ginger tea and poured water into a bowl for Chi, who drank his fill and then flopped onto the stone patio under Ladarat's chair. Then Delia began to explain.

"It started maybe eight years ago. A famous writer— British. Famous enough that you've probably heard of him. He was traveling in Vietnam and Laos and came here. Then he died. I thought that was unfortunate, of course. So we contacted his family and arranged to have his body shipped home to London. I didn't think much of it at the time, aside from the challenges with the police—"

Delia glanced at Wiriya, who smiled an embarrassed smile.

But Ladarat was thinking something very different. "We?" she asked.

Delia nodded. "My husband and I." She seemed to be waiting for another question, but Ladarat wasn't quite ready. After a suitable pause, Delia resumed her story.

"With the police, and the coroner, and the airlines...well, let's just say it was a great deal of work. And that was why I was surprised when I got a note of thanks from one of his friends back home. Also a writer, I think. The letter said how much he and his friends appreciated what I had done for the man who died. I reread that letter a dozen times to make sure I wasn't misunderstanding. But it was pretty clear to me that this man— the one who wrote the letter—thought that the man who died somehow planned it that way. That he planned to die here in Thailand and perhaps right here in this hotel."

Delia shook her head, although whether in delayed disbelief that anyone could do such a thing or amusement over her own naïveté, Ladarat couldn't tell.

"So I thought that was strange. Very strange. But I was mostly glad to be done with the whole thing. And for a while I was."

Delia paused to take a sip of tea, pouring more for both Ladarat and Wiriya.

"And then I started to get...inquiries. E-mails, mostly. Plus the occasional letter. They were from people who had heard—somehow—that the Magic Grove Hotel was a place where people with terminal illnesses could come to end their lives."

"How did they hear of that reputation?" Wiriya asked.

Delia shrugged. "Maybe word got out from that writer and his circle of his friends.

"But I wasn't worried. Besides, honestly, I figured this would be a temporary thing. You know? Just a few e-mails and letters from people who had heard about the writer. I figured I'd ignore those and people would...go away."

"But that didn't happen," Ladarat prompted. That seemed like a safe guess.

Delia shook her head and took another sip of tea. "No, Khun, it didn't. And that was my fault. You see, I didn't respond to those letters and e-mails, but I read them. How could I not? These were people with serious, fatal illnesses who were dying. They were asking me for help. I couldn't just ignore them."

Ladarat and Wiriya both nodded. No, she certainly couldn't—although perhaps she should have.

"Besides, their stories were...compelling."

"Like what?" Wiriya asked.

Delia thought for a moment. "One story really struck me. I still remember—it was a letter rather than an e-mail. It was on stationery from a law firm in Berlin. Very professional and well written in English. It was from a man who had suffered from a long illness. A neurological condition. He gave the name in German—I'm not sure what it translates to in English. But it sounded horrible. He described getting weaker and weaker until he was dependent on an aide for everything. And his friends. He had no family, you see. So for the past year, he said, he'd been putting his affairs in order. That's when I realized he wasn't actually a lawyer. The letter was on legal stationery because he was too weak to write, and he was dictating the letter to his lawyer. There was a note at the end from the lawyer, handwritten, saying that the man was thinking clearly and knew what he wanted."

"And what did he want, exactly?" Wiriya asked.

Delia glanced at Wiriya and frowned. It was as if she'd forgotten that she was talking to a detective, or had managed to push that inconvenient fact out of her mind for a time. But now she remembered, and she wasn't likely to forget again.

"He wanted, he said, to go someplace peaceful where he could spend the final days of his life. That was all."

"He didn't ask for...help?"

Delia shook her head. "Never. No one asked." She glanced at Wiriya. "And I'm not saying that because you're a detective. It's really true. Besides, these people didn't need my help. These were usually wealthy, always well educated, and had traveled halfway around the world to be here. They were...prepared. They brought sleeping pills or other drugs—I'm not sure. I just gave them a peaceful setting." She paused. "That's all."

In the silence Ladarat glanced around. Despite the hot sun overhead, the trees provided enough shade to cool the stones under their feet, and a pleasant breeze did the rest. Birds chirped overhead. No other sounds intruded. Even the road that ran a hundred meters on the other side of the hotel was silent from where they sat. It was pleasant, and quiet, and... peaceful.

If Wiriya was impressed by the peacefulness of their surroundings, he wasn't distracted.

"And how many...guests, would you say have died here, Khun?"

Delia shrugged. "I do keep records, and I suppose I could find out for you. But not more than three or four every month."

A sharp intake of breath was the only sign that Wiriya had registered this fact. He gaze remained fixed on Delia, his glass of tea poised just above the table.

"For how many years?" he asked.

"Initially, not many, but more about three or four years ago."

"So...?

"So perhaps sixty or seventy."

Ladarat and Wiriya paused to ponder that number for a long moment of silence. Sixty or seventy people had died here. Many of whom no doubt had sat in the very chairs that they themselves were sitting in this afternoon.

Ladarat had another thought then—one that she was unwilling to share with Wiriya. Not only was that a lot of people, it was a lot of ghosts. Not that she believed in ghosts, necessarily, but one had to admit that with so much death, there was bound to be bad energy left behind—call it what you will.

And yet—and this is the part that she would have been unwilling to share with Wiriya or anyone else—this place didn't feel as though it was inhabited by ghosts. Certainly not vengeful ghosts—*phi tai hong*. Granted, you sometimes couldn't tell that a vengeful ghost was in a space. But here she felt nothing untoward. Just a curious peacefulness, exactly as the hotel's name promised.

"And where do they go, Khun? After they die?" Leave it to Wiriya to ask the most practical question, although they knew the answer already.

Delia shrugged. "As you've seen, Khun. There's the grove on the side of hotel that you walked through. Many of those trees are six or seven years old. And more recently in the field where your dog was such a good detective. If you look closely, you'll see there are actually rings of saplings. All teak. We plant one near the head and then a circle around."

"So you could tell us where they're buried?" Wiriya asked.

Delia started, spilling a splash of tea onto the stone patio. She set her glass down on the metal table with a clatter.

"Of course, mostly. But . . . you're not thinking of digging those bodies up, are you? It would be . . . disrespectful."

Wiriya shrugged, looking distinctly uncomfortable.

"Well, if there were an inquiry, it would be necessary," he said. "These are not . . . they're not registered deaths, you understand. They're not buried in a cemetery or cremated. That's a crime, you see?"

"A crime against whom?" Ladarat asked him. She saw his point, but really, who was harmed by the absence of a piece of paper certifying that they were in fact dead? Indeed, it wasn't long ago that the Peaflower murderer had been making use of those pieces of paper to grow rich on life insurance money.

Delia looked as though she were about to say something, but she kept her mouth closed.

Wiirya just shrugged. "How do we know?"

"Know what?" Ladarat asked. "We know they're dead."

"Do we? How do we know that sixty or seventy people

are buried here? Maybe these people have started new lives elsewhere?"

"And what would be the harm in that?"

"Well, it would be wrong, for one. People can't just... disappear."

Ladarat didn't think that was really true. What did it matter whether someone disappeared to a new identity or into the afterlife? As long as they did so willingly, what was the harm?

"Besides," Wiriya continued, now on firmer ground, "we don't even know how they died. And we won't know without an autopsy."

"Even with an autopsy," Ladarat pointed out, "you still won't know. So much time has passed, identifying a cause of death will be difficult, unless it's something obvious like a gunshot wound. Maybe impossible if poison was involved."

"But their families," Wiriya pointed out. "Their families want to know that they are gone. That's what started all of this, you remember?"

Here Delia nodded. "That's what I've always been afraid of. It's one thing for a person to make this decision, but I have to trust that they'll tell their families what they're doing, and I've always suspected that some don't. They forget to tell some people, or they shade the truth, or..."

"Or they just leave without telling anyone," Ladarat finished the thought. "I think that's what Melissa Double did. She didn't tell her sister or her friends. So they're probably wondering where she is and when she'll be back."

Delia nodded. "I should have asked them to write final letters. I should have insisted."

You probably shouldn't have gotten into this business in the first place, Ladarat thought. But then again, was what she was doing really that bad? She didn't end people's lives. She didn't even help them. She just gave them a safe place to do so. What they did was up to them.

"Did anyone...change their minds?"

Delia nodded. "Oh, yes. All the time. They'd come here, and then postpone. Sometimes they leave and travel and then come back. Sometimes they'd even go home. I often don't know what they're going to decide until they tell me."

"Maybe those people—or some of them—don't have a terminal illness? Melissa Double did, of course, but the others..."

Delia shook her head. "I always ask for some sort of proof. Some...evidence. In fact, that's why many guests come from your palliative care unit. If someone comes to me and they don't have that proof, I suggest they go to your hospital, to make sure. That's what Melissa Double did. She thought she was sick before she left home. But I couldn't be certain. So she saw a doctor in Chiang Kong, and then was transferred to Sri-phat. Then, when I was certain, she came here."

Ladarat hoped her expression didn't reveal what she was thinking—that this was a very strange use for her hospital. That, and consternation and more than a little embarrass-ment that all of this was going on under her nose, and perhaps under Sudchada's nose, and Dr. Taksin's, too.

"But surely that creates a disturbance. Someone dies, and then you need to dispose of their luggage and bury them. Surely your staff or other guests see something..."

Delia smiled. *Yim sao*: the sad smile.

"What other guests? And staff? It's just me and a few peo-ple who have worked here forever. They're very well paid and never ask questions. Not until your Jonah started getting suspicious."

But she was smiling as she said his name. "He's an excellent manager, by the way. The best I've ever had. So conscientious. He's welcome to continue to work here, you know, after his... investigations are complete."

Ladarat wasn't sure what Jonah would think about that, although she said she'd pass the message on. She also wasn't at all sure Delia and her hotel would survive an investigation. Time in jail seemed to be a very real possibility.

There was one more question Ladarat had to ask. It wasn't an easy one.

"Your husband, Khun." Delia looked at her warily, eyes narrowed. "You said you and your husband bought this hotel. But now...?"

"Now?"

Wiriya was paying close attention. This was an aspect of the story that he'd missed, as she herself almost had.

"Where is he, Khun?" Ladarat asked gently. She was almost certain she knew.

Delia nodded, as if she'd expected that question eventually. "He died. Here, of course. But of natural causes. Just about a year ago."

There was a moment of silence after both Ladarat and Wiriya said the appropriate things.

"So what do we do now?" Delia asked them. Although it was addressed mostly to Wiriya, the question seemed to include Ladarat, too. The way she asked it didn't sound belligerent or defensive, or cowed. She sounded genuinely curious.

It was Wiriya who answered, slowly, thoughtfully. "I don't know," he said eventually. "I really don't know." He rubbed his chin and took a sip of ginger tea.

"We just have her word that these... guests took their own lives. What if she realy is a murderer?"

Ladarat shook her head. "You don't really believe that, do

you? There's the stories of Ms. McPhiller and others. And there's Richard April's website..."

"Then it's a crime that doesn't seem like a crime," Wiriya admitted. "Yet it also seems like I should do...something."

"Well," Delia said. "You know where to find me."

Wiriya was unusually quiet on the drive back to Chiang Mai. He only made a few suggestions regarding the mechanics of lane changes and turn signals, which Ladarat was perfectly able to manage on her own. Wiriya only looked startled once, when the vast white wall of a truck materialized just a few centimeters outside his window.

Ladarat wasn't sure how that truck had managed to get there—the lane had been empty when she'd turned onto the Wichayanon roundabout next to the Ping River. Even Chi, who was normally rather calm during car rides, seemed to find that sudden appearance worrisome, and he barked at the truck in a way that might charitably be called ferocious. Then he went back to sleep.

Apart from that episode of excitement, Wiriya was even calm enough to make a couple of phone calls, though Ladarat couldn't tell whom he was talking to. She hoped it was not the coroner. That would only spell trouble for Delia, and Ladarat wasn't convinced that she deserved any more trouble than they'd already caused.

Ladarat was still pondering that question, while Wiriya was in his own world, when they reached the East Gate of the Old City.

"I think...you should go left," Wiriya advised her. "On Kaeo Nawarat. Then east, to the bus station. There's...an idea I have."

"An idea?" But Wiriya just nodded. Well, that was fair. She

hadn't told Wiriya much about her plan this morning, had she? Just a hint. Yet he'd agreed readily enough, so she owed him the same.

Wiriya's head was down, poking blunt but delicate fingers at his phone, typing out a text message to someone. Fine. They would go to the bus station. Then, perhaps, they could stop at her cousin's tea shop or have dinner at a nice place on the Ping River. They could celebrate the solution of another crime—if indeed what was happening at the Magic Grove Hotel was truly a crime, as Wiriya seemed to think. Perhaps that dinner would go better than last night's.

Ladarat turned left on Kaeo Nawarat as instructed. The blare of a taxi's horn startled Wiriya from his communication only briefly. He looked up and glanced around as if to get his bearings. The taxi driver who had been behind them a moment ago had now somehow materialized just to their left and was gesticulating wildly. Wiriya smiled and nodded, reaching into his suit pocket and pulling out his detective's badge. He smiled again at the taxi driver, put his badge away, and checked the tension on his seat belt before he went back to whatever message he was typing.

In fact, his head stayed down the entire trip to the bus station as he typed away furiously. Ladarat wondered that he didn't get carsick. It wasn't until they pulled up in front of the bus station, just inside the ring road, that Wiriya rejoined the living and looked around.

"Ah, so here we are," he said, as if he was a little surprised that they had arrived. "I think I'll have a surprise for you."

He told her to park her car illegally in a loading zone. Flashing his badge at a security guard, he asked him to watch it. "We won't be long," he said.

Ladarat considered leaving Chi in the car. Dozing peacefully, he probably wouldn't notice their absence. But the car was sitting in the sun, which was still hammering down as relentlessly as it had when she and Wiriya had stood on that gravel driveway two hours ago, so she nudged him awake with a foot and clipped his leash on. As if this was his signal to wake, the little dog jumped up and leapt through the back door onto the sidewalk, eager for his next adventure.

"I don't think this will be an adventure, dog. At least not like the last one. At least, I hope not," she added. She'd been half talking to Wiriya, but he had disappeared inside, leaving Ladarat to follow behind with her intrepid therapy dog.

About twenty meters away, she saw Wiriya hustling through the crowd toward the area where buses take on passengers. He turned briefly, waving at Ladarat and pointing to the door.

Well, all right. She would follow, of course, although this was excessively mysterious, wasn't it? Surely everything would make sense in a moment.

But when that moment had elapsed, and she was standing next to Wiriya, the situation had not become any clearer.

Wiriya was proudly holding two juice boxes, of the sort that she remembered receiving on the bus from Bangkok on Friday night. Next to him was the bus attendant whom Ladarat remembered from that long trip. She seemed surprised to find a detective of the Chiang Mai police force standing in front of her, and even more surprised to find him holding two juice boxes. Surprised, and annoyed.

"I don't know what this is about, detective. I assure you that we run a legitimate bus service. We have for years. All of our paperwork is in order. And you're delaying these passengers—" She gestured at the long row of Thais and *farang* looking down at them.

Ladarat suspected that to the passengers they were an odd sight. There was the heavyset man in a suit holding two juice boxes, herself, the confused attendant, and a small therapy dog who had stretched out on the cool tile floor and was watching the world from the posture of a reclining Buddha.

"The bus is supposed to leave right now, and you're delaying them. For what reason, might I ask?"

Wiriya nodded and turned to Ladarat.

"I owe you an apology, you see, for not taking your concerns about the bus robberies seriously enough."

Although this was directed at Ladarat, the attendant was paying very close attention. She opened her mouth as if to ask about the word "robberies" but then she seemed to think better of it. Besides, Wiriya wasn't paying attention to her.

"I didn't truly take them seriously because I couldn't figure out how someone could arrange for certain passengers to be drugged but not others." He smiled. "But now I know." Wiriya glanced at the attendant, who smiled and nodded as if she, too, were enjoying an excellent joke.

Then, in a single fluid movement, she kicked off her flip-flops, scooped one up in each hand, and raced across the pavement toward the rear corner of the bus station.

Ladarat glanced at Wiriya, who seemed unconcerned. He simply turned his attention back to the two juice containers.

"Which one do you think would have been given to Khun Ukrit or Khun Sisithorn?"

Ladarat looked at both boxes, which seemed identical. They were the same color, with the same picture of a flamingo on the front. She took one from Wiriya and then the other. She couldn't see any difference at all. For lack of anything else to do, she gave them both a tentative squeeze.

Wiriya stepped back on one foot and wiped his face with

the back of his hand. Then he smiled and took the box that she had been holding in her left hand and, aiming it away from them both, he gave it another firm squeeze that sent a thin, almost invisible, jet of juice out onto the tarmac.

A few drops hit Chi, who bounded up and made a quick circle, reconnoitering for threats. Then he flopped down again.

That didn't do much to clarify things, did it? So one juice box had a tiny hole in it? What did that prove?

Wiriya seemed to read her mind. "No, that's not the secret. Or maybe it's one secret. It's how they put drugs in the juice cartons. A very, very thin needle. So small that the carton won't leak unless you squeeze it really hard. That attendant used such a needle to take a little juice out, replacing it with a small amount of some sort of drug."

"Chloral hydrate," Ladarat said.

Wiriya paused, looking at the juice box in his hand. "I was going to suggest we get this tested, but you already know what the drug is?"

"Just a guess." She explained that the blood that Ukrit had drawn from his girlfriend tested positive for trichloroethanol, something Ladarat had never heard of but which Wikipedia—that helpful medical reference—had told her was a metabolite of chloral hydrate.

"You should get it tested to be certain," Ladarat said. She thought for a moment. "But I still don't understand how the robbers knew which juice went to which person. They'd squeeze each one?"

Wiriya smiled. "No—look closely." He turned the box he was holding around.

"Ah."

"Exactly. The boxes that had been tampered with don't have straws. So every trip there would be a few boxes without straws that the attendant could give to *farang* passengers, who appeared to be..."

"Wealthy." Ladarat remembered the attendant's profuse apologies that their drinks lacked straws. The oldest ploy in the book: Managers who didn't understand. So clever.

"Exactly so," Wiriya said. "Very well organized." He looked up. "Ah, I didn't think she'd get far."

Two young detectives—Somporn and Kamon—were leading the attendant between them through the rear doors of the bus station. Each had one of her arms clasped firmly in one hand, while the other was clutching one of her flip-flops, as if perhaps they were planning to use her footwear as evidence in a trial.

"Thank you, Khun!" they both said to Wiriya, offering the best version of a *wai* that they could muster given how they were encumbered. They didn't stop, though, and continued to herd the chastened attendant toward a waiting police car parked at the edge of the parking lot.

CHAPTER 31

ALL DECISIONS BENEFIT FROM THE WISDOM
OF *KANOM MAPRAO*

The best part of winter in Chiang Mai was the way that a hot afternoon could give way almost magically to a cool, dry evening. A single day would be like two seasons—seasons that the always hot, always humid pressure cooker of Bangkok would never see. It was moments like this when Ladarat couldn't imagine living anywhere else.

In celebration of two crimes solved within the space of a few hours, Wiriya had insisted on taking her to Paak Dang, perhaps the best restaurant in Chiang Mai. They hadn't been here since Wiriya's forty-second birthday party a month ago, yet the waitress seemed to remember them and gave them the same table they'd shared then. Right on the edge of the patio, it was lit only by a flock of sputtering candles and had a beautiful view down to the Ping River ten meters below, and the small longtail boats plying back and forth.

Wiriya had ordered a large Singha, and, as always, Ladarat poured a little for herself. As the waitress brought their *kao nap het*—roasted duck over rice, drizzled with intensely flavorful duck broth—they clinked glasses as the *farang* do, toasting their remarkable success in detection. Team detection.

"There's one question, still, I don't understand," Ladarat said. Wiriya paused in serving her *kao nep het*. He smiled.

"Just one question you don't understand? Why, then you must be very wise indeed."

"Well, perhaps a few questions. But just one right now. The young detectives—the ones who took that attendant away to jail. Why did they thank you?"

"Ah, well. Perhaps because they think that this arrest of the juice box robber will make their careers."

"But as the detective who discovered the robber, you would get credit, would you not?"

Wiriya shook his head as he served himself, choosing his words carefully. "No, I decided in the end that I didn't want the credit. I didn't want to be known as the detective who discovered adulterated juice boxes. That would be a step down, don't you think?" He smiled again. "Now I'm known as the detective who solved the Peaflower murders. So the sort of fame and fortune that would come with this case would be something of a demotion. Better, really, to let those two youngsters have all the credit."

"Well," she said, "that is wise, of course. You must be very careful about your career and your reputation, since you are famous. But," she added, "the jade smuggling ring. That, certainly, you will take credit for?"

Because although Ladarat was delighted by their success with two mysteries, the nefarious activities of the Parrot Gang had yet to be resolved.

"Ah, but there is no smuggling ring."

"No, but that's where you're wrong. Oh, I know that Sisithorn can be excitable, and perhaps she imagines things on occasion." Ladarat thought about that as she took a bite of duck—the crispy skin was by far the best. "Or perhaps she often imagines things. But that exchange of packages, I saw it, too. Not just once, but several times, both in Bangkok and here. How could that not be a smuggling ring?"

Wiriya's mouth was full of duck, so he took a moment to chew and swallow, followed by a swig of Singha, before he answered.

"I confess, I couldn't figure that out, either. Until I had the two youngsters confiscate a sample."

He reached into the chest pocket of his suit and pulled out a round, flat object wrapped in a handkerchief. Unwrapping it, he laid the exhibit on the table between them. It was a jade bracelet. Thin and delicate, it would have fit her own wrist nicely.

"A gift for me?"

Wiriya laughed. "No...not really. Or yes, if you want it. But it's worthless."

"But a jade bracelet—even an illegal one, must be worth ten thousand baht?"

"Ah, but it's not jade. Not real jade. I went to the bus station last night after...ummm...after dinner." Wiriya coughed. "Anyway, I saw one of the exchanges that you described, and I offered to buy a bracelet from one of the *farang* who'd just received a bunch. She was reluctant, but I showed her my badge, and she became more...willing."

That, Ladarat thought, was a very thoughtful way to make amends—one that would not have occurred to your average kumquat.

"Then I took it to a jeweler I know," Wiriya continued quickly. "He took a look at it and in a matter of seconds proclaimed it to be fake. And not even a good fake. Here, look." Wiriya arranged the candles in their jars in a semicircle around the bracelet and held it up between the candles and

Ladarat. "Look at the edges between the light green and dark green. Do you see them?"

Ladarat nodded, and Wiriya moved the bracelet in and out of the light.

"When you look through it at the light, do the edges become more clear, or more blurry?"

"More clear."

"Exactly so. That is one way my friend told me you can tell the difference between real jade and fake. There are other ways, too. And jewelers often use some sort of machine that measures light." He shrugged. "I don't understand the details of how any of that works, but he was certain that this bracelet is fake."

"So... why?"

Wiriya smiled and shrugged. "Exactly what I was asking myself. Why develop what seems to be an elaborate organization to give fake jade to departing travelers, without any money changing hands. Where is the profit?"

"But some money did change hands," Ladarat pointed out. "I saw myself sometimes the *farang* handed over a few bhat." She explained about the exchange of money, and about the instances in which no money was exchanged, but rude words were.

Wiriya nodded. "That's interesting. I didn't know that." He thought for a moment, his attention divided more or less equally between the problem at hand and the crispy duck on his plate.

"But that was just a few baht," he pointed out. "So," he concluded triumphantly, "it stands to reason that any money that changed hands wasn't for the jade."

Ladarat took a sip of beer as she thought about that. "But then... what was it for?"

Wiriya shrugged. "I honestly have no idea."

But Ladarat did. Or she thought she did. She remembered the surprise on the face of the *farang* at the Bangkok airport Friday morning, surprise that there was another *farang* making the same deal. Why would he care? Unless . . .

"Taxi money," she said.

"Taxi money?"

Now Ladarat was certain she was right. "Someone approaches a *farang* who is leaving town. Maybe as they wait for the bus that's going to take them to the airport, or perhaps outside a hotel. They find out where the *farang* is going—Tokyo or San Francisco or Boston or wherever. And they offer a deal: I just happen to have a friend in that city. What a coincidence! I have a deal for you: Smuggle this jade out of the country to my friend, and you and my friend can split the profits."

Wiriya didn't seem to be keeping up, and he'd forgotten his *kao nep het* entirely. "So someone from the . . . parrot gang gives the *farang* the jade for free?"

Ladarat shook her head. "Not entirely. Look. Imagine that one member of the parrot gang approaches a *farang* at Kao San Road as he's getting on the bus to go to Suvarnabhumi Airport. He tells the *farang* to look for the woman at the airport with—"

"The parrot bag."

"Exactly so. With the parrot bag. He identifies that woman, and he approaches her. Perhaps there's some sort of password. So she gives him the jade and then—"

"She asks him for taxi money."

"Exactly. She came all the way to the airport to give him the jade, the least he could do is reimburse her for part of the fare. Maybe she says she has hungry children at home, or maybe she says she needs the money to get back. So sometimes—often—the *farang* will give her something. Maybe not the entire five-hundred-baht taxi fare, but something." Ladarat paused. "Do you see?"

It took a moment, but soon Wiriya did, in fact, see.

The more Ladarat thought about it, the more brilliant it seemed. Give a bunch of worthless bracelets to a tourist, and collect a few hundred baht. By itself, that wasn't much of a business deal. But if that happened ten times, or twenty times, in a single afternoon...two people could make nine thousand baht (about three hundred dollars) pretty quickly, taking "taxi money" from one *farang* after another all day. Even after deducting the cost of the almost worthless bracelets and of course a real taxi ride to and from the airport, that wasn't a bad scheme.

"But is that...illegal?"

Wiriya shook his head as he finished the last of the duck. "I honestly don't know. They're not actually smuggling jade. And they're not selling fake jade, either. Even if they were, that's so common it hardly qualifies as illegal. The worst thing about this is asking dozens of *farang* to pay for a single taxi ride to the airport. And that's not much worse than what most government contractors do." He smiled. "So that's not illegal, either." He shrugged. "It's fraud, perhaps. But a very little fraud."

"Maybe we just post warnings at some of the hostels in the Old City," he suggested. "And maybe do the same in Kao San Road in Bangkok, but really—of all the trouble that *farang* can get into in Thailand, this seems pretty tame. It's hard to imagine anyone making a big deal about it."

With the possible exception of her assistant nurse ethicist. But, to be fair, Sisithorn had been right. There really was something nefarious going on, and to her credit, she had noticed it. Perhaps it was not the international smuggling ring that she had imagined, and perhaps it was not even illegal. But she had noticed . . . something worth noticing.

Wiriya leaned over and blew out all of the candles on the table except for one.

"It is . . . rather dark," Ladarat observed. And indeed it was. Their waitress fumbled a bit as she cleared away their dishes, replacing them with a small dish and fresh plates.

"*Kanom maprao*," Wiriya reminded her, as if she, Ladarat Patalung, needed to be reminded that this was coconut cake their waitress was setting down between them.

"But the lack of light?"

"Ah," Wiriya said, as he pushed the *kanom maprao* a little closer to Ladarat. "I thought perhaps our presence here might make other . . . couples uncomfortable."

"Other couples?"

"Don't look, but about halfway down the edge of the patio, there's your assistant and Dr. Wattana. They are talking animatedly. Or rather, she is busy talking and he is . . . well . . . busy not talking—No, don't turn. And also your palliative care doctor. Dr. Taksin? He's with a nurse who looks like— No, don't turn."

But that was not possible. Ladarat looked around, and in the middle of the patio Dr. Taksin and Sudchada had a table for four all to themselves. Dr. Taksin looked livelier—and more awake—than she had ever seen him. He was gesturing toward something and, sitting across from him, Sudchada was smiling, her food untouched. Farther away, Ladarat glimpsed her assistant and her boyfriend, their heads close together.

Well. Apparently this was the place to come for couples as well as for birthday parties. And of course for celebrations of the art of detection. Speaking of which, there were questions left over from their conversation with Delia that morning. Somehow, for some reason, Ladarat found she was more comfortable asking them now, over *kanom maprao*, in darkness that was almost complete.

"So what have you decided to do about the Magic Grove Hotel?" she asked.

Ladarat could barely see Wiriya in the flickering of a single candle, but she imagined him pausing in the middle of a bite of *kanom maprao*, his fork hovering midway between plate and lips as it seemed to do so often these days. The chink of the fork being set back down—proof that she'd been right—made her happy, although she couldn't have said why that should be.

There was another chink of metal on china, as if Wiriya had decided that this question could only be answered after fortification with another bite or two of coconut cake— though why anyone needed to pause in order to decide such a thing was not immediately clear to her. Surely all decisions— no matter their size or gravity—would benefit from the extra wisdom conferred by a bite or two of *kanom maprao*.

"I think," he said finally, "that the people who go to the Magic Grove Hotel probably know what they're doing." The chink of a fork being laid down punctuated his statement, giving it a little more emphasis.

"That seems likely," Ladarat agreed. "But does that make what Khun Delia is doing legal?"

Ladarat's eyes were slowly adjusting to the darkness, and she saw the form across from the table shake his head slowly.

"Maybe not legal, exactly. There are certainly no laws in Thailand that permit such a thing. And as I told her, burying people—bodies—without a death certificate in a field in unmarked graves...well, that is most certainly illegal. And yet..."

"And yet?" This was where Ladarat herself was stuck, too. She was curious to see how this detective, who had so much more experience in matters of the law, might resolve this conundrum.

"And yet, she seems to be doing people an important service, doesn't she?"

Ladarat had been thinking much the same thing. "An important service for some people. But only some people."

"That's true. People who want to leave their friends and families behind and people who are willing to die in a strange place." Ladarat could see Wiriya shaking his head in confusion. "Though why anyone would want to do that is a mystery to me."

"Perhaps..." Ladarat trailed off, thinking. "Perhaps people like that Richard April who felt that he had done everything he needed to do, and everything he wanted to do. Or Melissa Double, who wasn't afraid of dying, but who was afraid— more afraid than anything—of being sick. For people like that, perhaps a stay at the Magic Grove Hotel makes a kind of sense."

"Perhaps," Wiriya agreed. "Perhaps. But that would mean dying alone."

They both thought about that for a moment.

"To spend a life creating a family and finding friends and colleagues, and then to leave them all..."

"It's mysterious," Wiriya said.

"It's sad," Ladarat agreed. "But...sad or not, what are you going to do about Delia and her hotel?"

"Well," Wiriya said slowly. "If the main problem—the

main legal problem, you understand—is the way that she's
burying people in a field..."

"Yes?"

"Then that's the problem we should solve, is it not?"

Ladarat agreed that was sound logic. Didn't Professor Dalrymple say that as nurses, there was always much we could do
in any situation? It was just a matter of figuring out what we
could do, and ignoring everything else.

"But how? How can you make her promise that she won't
bury any more people?" Surely that agreement would be difficult to enforce.

Wiriya shook his head.

But Ladarat had an idea. A most excellent idea. She speared
the last piece of *kanom maprao* by feel in the darkness, realizing a little too late that it was rather bigger than was entirely
appropriate and ladylike, but also consoling herself that under
the cover of darkness she could perhaps avoid being chastised
for the sin of gluttony. Besides, it was a just reward for such an
excellent idea.

Sudchada and Dr. Taksin soon officially became a couple. A very happy couple, it might be added. It turned out that Sudchada had no patience whatsoever for late nights at the WesternGirl, and she put an end to that habit quickly. Immediately after Ladarat had notified Sudchada that she was competing with country-and-western music—and horses—the young nurse reined the doctor in. Apparently he didn't put up much resistance. She did, however, harbor a deep and previously secret love of sixties-era American folk songs: songs in English, of course, about walking down roads and blowing in the wind, often at the same time. Or something like that. Anyway, topics much more congenial than the residences of ex-wives. So she began to take Dr. Taksin to open-microphone nights at Back Street Books. There, he was able to sing for an audience, but only until the store closed at nine o'clock.

Ladarat and Wiriya, not surprisingly, remained a couple. A solid couple, it might be said. Certainly they had occasions for disagreement, as most couples did. Wiriya's unnecessary opinions about Ladarat's driving showed no sign of abating, but Ladarat resolved to ignore those opinions in much the same way that she'd learned to ignore the shrill warnings her car would make whenever it detected any threats close by. With just a little concentration—which she could easily spare from the easy work of driving—she found that she could effectively silence both her car and her boyfriend.

Ladarat also resolved to learn more about the art and especially the science of detection. Having finished *A Nail Through the Heart* that Sunday night, she realized just how much she had to learn about detection. That detective, a *farang* named Poke, was brave and tough and smart. And he solved crimes in Thailand. Yet that character was more bold than she could ever be. She needed a more...realistic role model. Ladarat lost no time in procuring the first mystery by Richard April that featured Josie the hospice nurse, reasoning that a nurse ethicist and a hospice nurse were surely kindred spirits.

After more than a little discussion—an excessive amount of which her assistant shared with Ladarat—Sisithorn and Ukrit decided to remain in Chiang Mai. The decision seemed to be somewhat lopsided, and Ukrit continued to display a somewhat wistful enthusiasm for life in the big city. But Sukhumvit Hospital's enthusiasm for Sisithorn seemed to have cooled markedly after the ethics conference, so a job offer wasn't likely. From then on, whenever Ukrit grew overly enthusiastic about the pleasures of Bangkok—even the most benign of enjoyments, like the indoor skating rink at Central World—Sisithorn would curb him ruthlessly. Such was the degree of her control that it was no surprise to anyone when Ukrit announced without much fanfare that the two of them would be married in the spring.

The site of the wedding, incidentally, would be a small, quiet hotel just outside the city, where Jonah and Krista and little Jacob had taken up residence, along with Krista's parents. Krista's father found his niche as a handyman. In theory, his responsibilities also included gardening. However, it had been decided that the less he knew about the contents of the teak grove, the better for all concerned.

Jonah had become the the Magic Grove Hotel's full-time manager, where he was well positioned to keep an eye out for any nefarious activities such as the covert burial of bodies. That did little to stem interest from *farang* who wanted to make the Magic Grove Hotel their final destination, and they still came. But they came now with what Delia referred to as "return postage," as well as proof that they had informed their families of their plans.

Krista also set up their dog-rental business, Paws in Chiang Mai, catering to *farang* (mostly) who couldn't stand to tour a city without a dog on a leash. She was able to take many of the dogs from the Chiang Mai pet shelter, giving them a home on the property of the Magic Grove Hotel when they were in between assignments.

Krista also displayed a remarkable gift for business as she helped to create a marketing plan for the hotel that didn't rely solely on people coming to Thailand to die. Of course, those people still came, and they still died. But they did so with the benefit of involvement by the coroner and of course official death certificates.

Ladarat wasn't sure whether the new involvement of bureaucracy produced deaths that were any better than those that had unfolded for Sharon McPhiller or Richard April or Demian Ober or Melissa Double. She wasn't even sure anymore what a good death was. In fact, she took her careful notes about the deaths in charts she'd reviewed and put them in a folder marked only with a large question mark.

ACKNOWLEDGMENTS

In the last ten years, I've been very fortunate to be able to travel often to Thailand. On those trips, I've been welcomed by the Thai people, and I've had a wonderful time exploring Thailand's culture, language, and food. But my most meaningful experiences, and my fondest memories, have been in interactions with my physician and nurse colleagues there. It's struck me many times that Thai culture highlights some of the best aspects of health care and healing, and offers lessons that I've learned a great deal from in my work as a doctor. Ladarat is, alas, not an actual person. However, her skill and wisdom are very real among the colleagues in Thailand I've worked with over the years, and I'm grateful to them for helping me to become a better physician.

And of course, I'm especially grateful to colleagues back home, both at the University of Pennsylvania, where I used to work, and Duke University, my current home.

MEET THE AUTHOR

David Casarett, M.D.

DAVID CASARETT, M.D., M.A., is a palliative care physician and health services researcher whose work focuses on improving systems of care for people with serious, life-threatening illnesses. He is a professor of medicine at Duke University and the chief of palliative care services for Duke University Health Systems. Dr. Casarett's writing has appeared in print and online in *Salon, Esquire, Discover, Newsweek*, the *New York Times*, and *Wired*. Dr. Casarett is also the author of three nonfiction books, the most recent of which is *Stoned: A Doctor's Case for Medical Marijuana*, published in 2015 by Penguin Random House.

if you enjoyed
THE MISSING GUESTS AT THE MAGIC GROVE HOTEL

look out for

MURDER AT THE HOUSE OF ROOSTER HAPPINESS

An Ethical Chiang Mai Detective Agency Novel

by

David Casarett

Two nights ago, a young woman brought her husband into the emergency room of the Sriphat Hospital in Thailand, where he passed away. A guard thinks she remembers her coming in before, but with a different husband—one who also died.

Ladarat Patalung, for one, would have been happier without a serial murderer—if there is one—loose in her hospital. Then again, she never expected to be a detective in the first place.

And now, Ladarat has no choice but to investigate....

CHAPTER 1

IT IS KNOWN THAT POISON IS
OFTEN A WOMAN'S METHOD

I have come to see you, Khun Ladarat, about a matter of the utmost urgency."

The comfortably built man sitting on the other side of the desk paused, and shifted his bulk in a way that prompted the little wooden chair underneath him to register a subdued groan of protest.

"A matter of the utmost urgency," he repeated, "and more than a little delicacy."

Ladarat Patalung began to suspect that this Monday morning was going to be more interesting than most. Her conclusion was based in part, of course, on the formal designation of the matter at hand as one of the "utmost urgency." In her experience, that didn't happen often on a Monday morning. Despite the fact that she was the official nurse ethicist for Sriphat Hospital, the largest—and best—hospital in northern Thailand, it was unusual to be confronted by a matter that could be reasonably described in this way.

But Ladarat's conclusion was also based on her observation that her visitor was nervous. Very nervous. And nervousness was no doubt an unusual sensation for this broad-faced and broad-shouldered visitor. Solid and comforting, with close-cropped graying hair, a slow smile, and gentle manners that would not have been out of place in a Buddhist monk, Detective Wiriya Mookjai had been an almost silent presence in her life for the past three years. Ever since her cousin Siriwan Pookusuwan had introduced them.

Ladarat herself didn't have much cause to meet members of the Chiang Mai Royal Police Force. But Siriwan most certainly did. She ran a girlie bar—a brothel, of sorts—in the Old City. So she had more contact of that nature, perhaps, than she would like. Not all of it good.

Khun Wiriya was that rarest of beings—an honest policeman. They did exist in Thailand, all reports to the contrary. But they were rare enough to be worth celebrating when one was discovered. In fact, Wiriya was something of a hero. He never talked about it, but Ladarat had heard that he'd been injured in a shoot-out several years ago. In fact, he was a hero to many younger officers who aspired to be injured in a similar way, though of course without unnecessary pain and with no residual disability.

She'd met him before at the tea shop her cousin also owned, although he'd never before come to see her at work. Yet now he had. And now he was sitting across from her in her little basement office in Sriphat Hospital, with just her little desk between them. And he seemed to be nervous.

How did she know that the detective was nervous? The most significant clue was his tie. Khun Wiriya was wearing a green tie. He was wearing a green tie, that is, on a particular Monday, the day of the king's birth. Today almost everyone in Thailand of a mature age—a category that included both the detective and herself—would honor the occasion by wearing something yellow. For men, it would be a tie.

Ladarat herself was honoring the day with a yellow silk

blouse, along with a blue skirt that was her constant uniform. They were not particularly flattering to her thin figure, she knew. Her late husband, Somboon, had often joked—gently— that sometimes it was difficult to tell whether a suit of clothes concealed his wife, or whether perhaps they hid a coat hanger. It was true she lacked obvious feminine…landmarks. That, plus oversize glasses and hair pinned tightly in a bun, admittedly did not contribute to a figure of surpassing beauty.

But Ladarat Patalung was not the sort of person to dwell on herself. Either her strong points or any points at all. Those people existed, she knew. Particularly in Sriphat Hospital. They were very much aware of their finer points, in particular, and eagerly sought out confirmation of those points. These were people who waited hungrily for compliments, much as a hunting crocodile lurks in the reeds by the edge of a lake.

If she were that sort of person—the sort of person who dwells on her talents and wants to add yet another to her list—it might have occurred to her to think that her deduction regarding Khun Wiriya's nervousness revealed the hidden talents of a detective. She might have reached this conclusion because she noticed things like the doctor's behavior. And not everyone did.

But she was most emphatically not the sort of person to dwell on her talents. Besides, her perceptiveness wasn't even a talent, really. Not any more than being a nurse ethicist was a talent. Anyone could do it, given the right training. Ladarat herself was certainly nothing special.

Being an ethicist was all about observing. And that was more of a…habit. Anyone could do it. You just had to be quiet, and listen, and watch. That's all.

It was a habit that was a little like finding forest elephants in her home village near Mae Jo, in the far northwestern corner of Thailand. Anybody could see an elephant in front of her nose, of course. But to sense where they *might* be, back in the undergrowth, you had to be very still. And watchful.

In that moment, as the detective fidgeted and his eyes skittered across her bookshelves, Ladarat resolved that she would be very quiet. She would be watchful. She would be patient as her father taught her to be when they went looking for elephants thirty years ago. She was only a little girl then, but he taught her to pay attention to the world around her. That was what this moment called for.

She settled back to wait, sure that the reason for Khun Wiriya's nervousness would emerge just as the shape of an elephant would materialize from the overgrowth, if you were patient enough. After all, Khun Wiriya was an important detective. His was a very prestigious position, held by a very important man. This was a man who had no time for social visits, and therefore a man who could be counted on to get to the point quickly. So Ladarat looked expectantly across her desk at the detective, her pencil poised above a clean yellow notepad that she had labeled with today's date.

She hoped she wouldn't have to wait long, though. She, too, was busy. She was the nurse ethicist for the entire hospital, and she had a full docket already. And the Royal Hospital Inspection Committee would be coming to visit next Monday, exactly one short week from now. And not only did she need to impress the committee, she also needed to impress Tippawan Taksin, her supervisor. Khun Tippawan was a thin, pinched woman with a near-constant squint who held the exalted title of "Director of Excellence." A title that was due in no small part to the fact that she was a distant relation of the Thai noble family. And what did that title mean exactly?

Anyway, impressing the inspector was one thing, but

impressing the tough Khun Tippawan would be something else altogether.

She had so much to prepare. Even if she worked twenty-four hours every day for the next week, she would never please Khun Tippawan. So hopefully the trouble—whatever it was—would emerge soon. And it did.

"I mean to say..." the detective said, "we may be looking for a murderer."

Ladarat nodded but suspected that she did not entirely succeed in maintaining a calm, unruffled demeanor. It wasn't every day that she had such a conversation about murder. In fact, she had never had such a conversation.

At least the case of the detective's nervousness had been solved. This was Chiang Mai, after all. A small city. A safe city. Where the old Thai values of respect and courtesy still flourished. A murder here would be... well, not unthinkable. But very, very unusual. Of course Khun Wiriya would be nervous—and excited—thinking that he might have discovered a murderer.

At a loss for words, she wrote: "Murder?" She looked down with new respect at her humble yellow pad, which had suddenly become very, very interesting.

"We received a call last night from a young police officer—a corporal—working at the emergency room of this hospital," Wiriya said slowly. "He called about a patient whose wife had brought him there. When they arrived, the man was quite dead apparently."

Ladarat wrote: "Woman. Man. Emergency. Quite dead."

"It seems that he had been dead for a little while—long enough, in fact, that there was nothing at all they could do for him. So they called the emergency room doctor to fill out the death certificate."

Ladarat underlined "Quite."

"But this corporal thought perhaps he recognized the man's wife," Wiriya continued. "He thought ... he'd met her before at another hospital. But he wasn't certain, you understand?"

Ladarat wasn't at all sure she understood. She nodded anyway.

The detective paused, choosing his words carefully. Ladarat waited. Thus far she wasn't seeing the need for an ethicist. But she would be patient. You must never approach an elephant in the forest, her father told her. You must always allow it to approach you.

"So the corporal asked the doctor in charge, you see. To share his concerns." He flipped open a small spiral notebook and checked. "A Dr. ... Aroon?"

He looked inquisitively at her, but Ladarat shook her head. It was no one she knew. But then, doctors were always coming and going. They'd work for a year at this government hospital, then they'd move to one of the private hospitals that paid much more. It was a shame.

He paused, and they both thought about what this coincidence might mean. Nothing good.

"But here it is," Wiriya said. "This woman? Who he thought he'd met before? You see, the last time they met was in the same exact circumstances. She'd brought her husband into the emergency room after he died. In both circumstances, the men had been brought in too late to help them."

She wrote: "Two deaths. More?"

"Some women are ... unlucky in this way," Ladarat suggested. "It was a tragedy, to be sure, but this man, was he ... an older man?"

Wiriya shrugged. "He was not a young man, it is safe to say. Neither was the other man. About forty-five, perhaps. That is not too old, is it, Khun?"

She supposed it was not.

"And what was the cause of death?"

"For the first, the corporal didn't know." He shrugged. "But for this one, the woman, she said it was his heart."

"His heart? Of course it was his heart. Your heart stops and you die. That's not an explanation, any more than saying a plane crash happened... because the plane, it hit the ground."

Wiriya looked suitably chastened. "Well, that's why I came to you, you see? You have this special medical knowledge. And, of course, you think like a detective."

A detective? Her? Most certainly not. That required skills. And penetrating intelligence, and cunning. She herself had none of those attributes. She would leave detecting to others who were better suited for the job.

"But," she said, thinking out loud, "if he did have heart failure, for instance, there might have been signs that the doctor noticed. Those would be documented in the medical record."

"The corporal said that the doctor didn't write anything. He didn't want to admit the patient because that would mean more paperwork. So he just signed the death certificate."

"I see. Well, then for two marriages to end in death, it is unlucky, to be sure. Still, it doesn't sound suspicious, does it?"

Wiriya was silent. Obviously he thought this situation *was* suspicious, or a busy man like him would not have wasted his time visiting her. Unless... perhaps this was just an excuse for a social call? Highly doubtful. He was a careful, methodical man, to be sure. Most important, a good man. And not unattractive.

But what was she thinking? He was here to ask for her help in a murder investigation. Her, Ladarat Patalung, nurse ethicist. And here she was thinking crazy thoughts.

Still the detective said nothing. He leaned back slightly in his chair and studied the ceiling above his head very carefully. He seemed to be thinking.

About what?

What do detectives think about? Real detectives. They look for patterns, don't they? They look for facts that fit together.

So perhaps there was a pattern here that Wiriya thought he saw. And maybe he wanted to see whether she saw it, too. Perhaps this was a test.

She wrote: "Pattern?"

Well, then. What sorts of patterns might there be?

"From what the young policeman said," she asked, "was there anything that these two unfortunate men had in common?"

"Ahhh." Wiriya shook his head, dragging his attention back down from the ceiling as if he had come to some important decision. "Yes, but I can't make anything of it. You see, they were both Chinese."

Ah, Chinese. Ladarat glanced at the detective. His face was a blank wall, and his gaze was again fixed with intense interest on the area of ceiling just above her head.

The Chinese. Some said that the culture of Thailand could be both gentle and intensely proud because the country had never been invaded. Never colonized. But Ladarat wasn't so sure about that. There were so many Chinese here now, one could be forgiven for assuming that the Chinese had, in fact, invaded.

It would be one thing if they were polite, but they were not. So quick to be angry. So harsh. So rude. Worse, even, than the Germans.

So it was with mixed emotions that she contemplated the nationality of these men and wrote "chinese" in big block letters.

Ladarat would be the first to admit that it was bad to stereotype. One should never judge a book by its cover. Although, truth be told, that was often the way she purchased a book—by looking closely at the cover. Like the new biography of that remarkable woman Aung San Suun Kyi. She had purchased a copy last weekend at the night market down by the Ping River largely because of the photograph of the beautiful woman on the cover, who seemed to be looking right at her, about to offer advice. So there was something to be said for the usefulness of a book's cover. But for people, no, that was wrong.

Perhaps detectives of the private sort could pick and choose their cases. But she was not a detective. She was a nurse. And an ethicist.

Where would we be if nurses and ethicists could pick and choose whom they would help? Nowhere good.

In fact, the slim volume that was sitting in the very center of her little desk had one page that was more thoroughly read than any other, and that was page 18. There was a passage on that otherwise unremarkable page that she knew by heart: "A nurse must always leave her prejudices at the door when she walks into a patient's room."

The book modestly called itself *The Fundamentals of Ethics*, by Julia Dalrymple, R.N., Ph.D., Professor of Nursing at the Yale University of the U.S.A. Ladarat regretted extremely the dullness of the title. It didn't really do justice to the wisdom of this little volume, which she'd discovered in a used bookstore in the city of Chicago in the United States when she was there for a year of ethics education. Not a day went by that she didn't seek Professor Dalrymple's wisdom to answer a question, to solve a problem, or sometimes just to be reminded of a nurse's obligations.

So she would follow the good professor's advice. She would leave her prejudices at the door.

"And the man's name?" she asked.

The detective hesitated. "It was...Zhang Wei."

"Oh no."

"Exactly. Oh no."

As she jotted this name down on her increasingly crowded—but increasingly interesting—yellow pad, Ladarat reflected that Zhang Wei was a very common Chinese name. A little like John Smith in the United States. And when a name was common in China, there weren't just thousands of them—there were millions.

"And the previous man's name?"

"We don't know. The corporal can't even remember which hospital it was—apparently he's worked at many. So it's unlikely we'll ever be able to find out."

That sparked another thought that it seemed like a detective might ask.

"And this other death, when was it?"

"Ah. Well, the corporal thinks it was in July."

That was only three months ago. Two months to find another man, get married, and have him die.

"You are sure that the woman was truly married to the man who died last night?"

Wiriya smiled. "So now you're definitely thinking like a detective. No, we don't know for sure. She claimed to be, at least."

She dutifully wrote: "Married???"

"So you think this might be...murder?"

Her first thought was for that unfortunate man, of course. But her next thought, almost immediately, was for the good name of her hospital. What would it look like if they had just let a murderer walk in and walk out? That would be very, very bad.

Especially with the Royal Hospital Inspection Committee

arriving next Monday. What would the inspectors think of a hospital that aids and abets a murderer?

And think how they would look to the public. Ehhhh, this was very, very bad. Something must be done.

"Serial murder, yes," Wiriya said. "If there are two cases we know about, there may be others."

They both thought for a moment about what that might mean. A woman out there, somewhere, who was murdering her husbands. But why? Why would she do such a thing?

Then she saw. "Insurance money? She's pretending to be married and then killing them for their insurance money?"

Wiriya nodded. "At least that's a possibility. It's all I can think of," he admitted.

"But then why bring them to the emergency room?"

Neither of them could answer that question, but one piece of the corporal's story struck her. "The death certificates," she said. "It's the death certificates. She's taking them to the emergency room so she can get a death certificate."

He nodded. "She'd need one to collect the life insurance, of course." He was smiling, now. "You're quite good at this."

For a moment she suspected that the detective had reached this conclusion ahead of her. He was, after all, a detective. Perhaps this was a test? Or maybe he was giving her a chance to figure it out for herself? In any case, she was proud of herself for reaching the correct conclusion on her own.

Ladarat Patalung, ethical nurse detective. She liked the way that sounded.